GRACE IN HOLLYWOOD

A GRACE MICHELLE MYSTERY

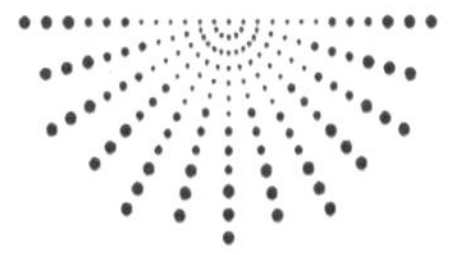

KARI BOVÉE

BOSQUE PUBLISHING

CHAPTER ONE

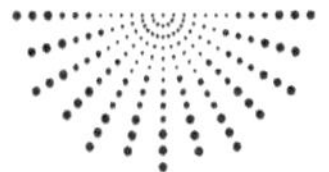

HOLLYWOOD, 1924

"Quiet on the set please!" the director shouted through his megaphone.

After a beat, a knight came onto the stage from behind a heavy velvet curtain. He held a knife above his head as he approached the king, who was seated at an elaborate table laden with food, from behind. He plunged the knife between the king's shoulder blades and then retreated behind the curtain once again.

The king stood up from the table with a roar, dropped the silver goblet he'd been holding, and arched his back in pretend pain. The queen, seated at the other end of table, rose and rushed to him, her crimson brocade skirts rustling against the floor.

As enthralled as I was by the scene, the problem with the queen's costume glared at me under the lights. The stitches between the bodice and the skirts had become frayed and were unwinding, causing a gap. It would have to be fixed as soon as possible. I just hoped no one else had noticed it. This particular scene had been shot numerous times, due to the almost perpetual intoxication of Robert Smith, the actor who played the king. I would hate for my costume to be the cause of yet another take.

As the queen reached him, he faltered, then collapsed in a heap at her feet, unconscious. The queen knelt down next to him, trying to rouse him and shouting his name. The king gave a resounding burp that vibrated across the stage.

"Cut!" the director yelled. "Damn it, Robert!"

The queen, played by Helen Clark, stood up and kicked Robert's thigh, a look of exasperation on her face. He rolled over onto his side and slowly sat up.

The director, Edward Travis, sighed loudly, his jaw visibly clenched. "Take fifteen, everyone. And I expect each of you to be back on time." He glared at his lead actor. "That goes double for you, Robert. Go drink some coffee or something."

I bit my lower lip as the actor made no attempt to disguise his sneer at the director as he struggled to his feet. Tension had been running high between the two ever since rehearsal shooting had started. We were all eager to start shooting in earnest, but things weren't really working out well enough for that to happen.

Mr. Smith had given his word that when the actual filming of *The Queen of Whitehall* started, he would be sober as a church mouse, but we all knew differently. And we also knew Mr. Travis was running short on patience with the man. Smith's last two films had been flops, and his career was teetering on the brink of disaster. The studio heads were counting on him to keep his life in order—as he *was* brilliant—but his drinking had gotten out of control.

I looked over at Lizzy, who was sitting in the chair next to me. She had her hand over her mouth, stifling a snort at the scene. Lizzy was one of the new kids who'd come to live with me and my husband at *Rancho los Niños*. Shortly after moving to California, Chet and I had purchased the ranch as a safe haven for troubled kids. Chet had been abandoned by his mother as a baby, and I lost my parents at a young age, so we both knew what it was like to feel alone in the world. We obtained the necessary licenses from the state of California two years ago and currently had four children living with us.

Sixteen-year-old Lizzy had arrived three months ago, angry and detached. Some of that anger had fallen away since she'd started working with the horses, but it had left a trail of sullenness and apathy in its wake. The girl seemed to enjoy drawing, though, and she was talented at it, so I wanted to foster that talent and offered to bring her to the studio to show her what moviemaking and costume design were all about.

"That was just the bee's knees!" The girl's face was as bright as a sunflower. In fact, it was the most animated I'd ever seen her. "Thank you so much for bringing me today. I can't believe I just saw Helen Clark at work. She's amazing!"

Delighted at her enthusiasm, I smiled at her. "I was happy to bring you along."

She looked at me with big eyes. "So did you make those costumes?"

"I've done some work on them, but we have seamstresses that actually make them. As lead designer, I work with a couple of assistant designers to create the costumes based upon the characters' personalities and the story line. It's my job to make sure they are perfect for the film in every way—and that the actors and actresses feel comfortable in them."

"Have you ever been able to use designs from your Sophia line in a film? Aren't you working on that, too?"

"Not right now." I sighed. "It's strictly an eveningwear collection. The daywear collection will have to wait until after this film."

"Didn't you name the eveningwear after your sister? The actress?"

I nodded, a pang shooting through to my heart. "Yes." I had created the line in homage to my elder sister, who had been murdered four years ago. She'd been the only family I'd had left, and now she was gone.

Lizzy leaned toward me, her eyes riveted on my face. "Did you ever want to be an actress?"

I smiled at her intense interest. "I was an actress in New York City—on Broadway—for a short period of time."

"You were?" Her eyes widened again. "Why didn't you stay one?"

I folded my hands in my lap and looked down at them. "After Sophia died, Flo—that's Florenz Ziegfeld, Jr., Sophia's and my boss—decided I needed to become an actress. He had taken us in off the streets of New York City when we were girls. He gave us a home and a family, and trained us to sing, dance, and act. He'd made Sophia a star, but I preferred the backstage life."

"Did you always want to do costume design instead?"

"Oh yes. And I had been thrilled when I got to shadow the great European designer, Lucile Duff Gordon, who'd worked with Flo for a time. I was actually the assistant to her assistant, but still, it was an amazing experience." I gave a small smile. "After Sophia died, though, Flo needed someone to fill her tap shoes, and as he put it, 'Who better than her sister?' After all he'd done for us, I couldn't refuse, even if becoming a star was the last thing on earth I wanted."

Lizzy was silent for a moment, taking it all in. "Wow. I bet you were a good actress."

I let out a chuckle. "I was passable. Not like Sophia. She lit up the stage, and she sang like an angel." My voice drifted off as I was caught in the memory.

Sophia's passing had left a hole in my life and in my heart, and I feared I wasn't getting past the loss. She'd been murdered by Joe Marciano, a New York City mob boss she'd had a brief relationship with but had ultimately rejected. It'd been years, but my dreams were still plagued with disturbing thoughts of her, especially of late, and they had robbed me of sleep.

Yes, Flo had taken us in and provided for us, but he and

Sophia also had an affair when she was nineteen, and they had kept it from me. I hadn't found out about it until just before Sophia had left the Follies. I was still having difficulty reconciling it all, as well as dealing with the loss of my family, even though I'd lost my parents some years ago. I wondered if I hadn't properly processed it all. If I was honest, most of the time I didn't want to think about it so I stuffed my feelings deep down inside.

It's exactly what Lizzy seemed to do. She still had her sister, but the two were at odds. I hadn't been able to get Lizzy to talk about it, and her sister had only come to visit Lizzy once since she'd arrived at our ranch—and Lizzy had refused to speak to her. It pained my heart to see. Before she was killed, Sophia and I hadn't been speaking, either, and now I'd give anything for one more day to try to make things right.

I was jerked out of my thoughts at the sound of the director's voice beside me. "Hello, Grace." Mr. Travis's penetrating smoky-gray eyes added to his intense demeanor when he spoke. Classically handsome with waves of dark-blond hair and an athlete's physique, he had the ability to make women weak in the knees with nary a glance, not to mention that sophisticated British accent.

"Mr. Travis," I greeted him.

"Who's this?" He appraised Lizzy. A little too closely in my opinion, but I imagine it couldn't be helped. The contrast between her dark auburn hair and her heavy-lidded, navy eyes added to her natural and striking magnetism.

"This is my friend Lizzy. She's staying with me and Chet at the ranch."

"Pleased to meet you, Lizzy." He gave her a dazzling smile.

A faint blush pinkened the girl's cheeks. "Same," she said.

"Ah yes." He returned his attention to me. "The ranch. I hear you are doing good things out there—for the kids. It's admirable. Is your husband still doing PI work?"

I shook my head. "Not anymore. He's too busy managing the ranch and the horses. He and a neighbor are rehabilitating racehorses—getting some of them back on the track and saving others from the slaughterhouses."

Chet had been an excellent private investigator but was still scarred from the tragedies of the war he'd witnessed as a former military policeman. He wanted to do something else, something that didn't require sneaking around and uncovering the sometimes horrible truths about the immorality and inhumanity of people. He found solace in saving these majestic animals, and I was starting to see his personality bloom. It was also good for the kids to help care for the horses.

"Also admirable." Mr. Travis said. "I heard Mary Pickford and Douglas Fairbanks shot some scenes for Mary's last picture there with some of the horses. Do you lease the place often?"

"Not often," I said. Really, I had done it as a favor to Mary. She had, after all, been my sister-in-law for a short time, as her brother Jack had been married to Sophia. "But we aren't opposed to the idea."

He nodded, as if giving the idea further thought. "I'll have to come out there sometime. I'd love to see it." He was speaking to me but once more was looking at Lizzy, who suddenly became flustered, probably from the concentrated scrutiny. "Your arm," he said, his gaze shifting to the inside of Lizzy's left forearm. "That's quite an unusual mark."

"Oh!" Her face flushed, and she tucked her arm behind her back. "That. Yeah. It's a birthmark." She was obviously embarrassed by it, but it truly was remarkable. About an inch in diameter, it was in the perfect shape of a heart, and deep red to boot.

"Yes, please do come visit. Anytime." I redirected the conversation away from Lizzy's birthmark and put a protective arm around her shoulders.

"Right," he said, almost under his breath, his attention still on her arm. His gaze finally shifted and met mine. "You're doing good work, Grace. The costumes look great."

"The picture is great." I deflected the compliment. It was truly a privilege to work with such a competent director. He had an uncanny knack for deepening character development through his own ideas on costuming, and I soaked up everything he did like a thirsty sponge. I'd been flattered and quite humbled that he and Alice Steinberg, one of the studio heads, had suggested to the other studio heads, Barney Steinberg, who was Alice's husband, and H.L. Combs, that I be brought on as the lead designer for this film. I had worked with Mr. Travis on his last film, but I'd been under the guidance of Michael Leishman, a genius who was supposed to be working on this film but had to take a leave of absence for health reasons. I was thrilled beyond belief, if not a little awestruck still, that they had wanted *me*. It was a dream come true.

"Mr. Travis?" A wide-eyed young woman wearing a lavender cloche hat and carrying a clipboard approached, drawing his attention away from us. "Miss Clark wants to speak with you in her dressing room."

"Of course," he said raising his eyebrows at us. "The queen beckons." His voice was tight. "Nice seeing you, Grace. And nice to meet you . . . ?" He regarded Lizzy again with a mystified air and held out his hand.

"Lizzy." She straightened her spine and took his proffered hand in a firm handshake.

I was pleased to see her step out of her initial intimidation. It hadn't been like her to wither. Strong-minded and fiercely independent, Lizzy could be a force to be reckoned with at times. She'd been our most challenging charge to date. I supposed she'd been thrown off-balance by the famous director—maybe even a little awed. And he *had* surveyed her with a good deal of keenness.

He turned to walk away from us but hesitated. "Oh, I almost

forgot. I'm having a big bash at the mansion this weekend. I'd love it if you and Chet could come. Bring Lizzy here if you want." He smiled broadly at her.

"Well, thank you," I said. "I'll check with Chet, and if we can make it, we absolutely will."

He nodded, shoving his hands in his pockets, and walked away from us.

"Wow," Lizzy said, her enthusiasm returning. "Did he just invite us to a party? Can we go?" She rattled off her questions with wide eyes.

I pressed my lips together, not at all sure I liked what had just transpired. I wished Mr. Travis hadn't mentioned the party in front of Lizzy, much less invited her.

When Lizzy's sister, Margaret Moore, had dropped her off at the ranch a few months ago, she'd told me that Lizzy had gotten in trouble with a twenty-two-year-old young man, which had ended with the two of them being arrested—him for theft, and her for aiding and abetting. The judge, having heard of our ranch, let Lizzy off easy with an assignment to *Rancho los Niños* instead of sending her to jail. It was my job to keep her out of trouble and hopefully guide her to a better way of life. I'm not sure taking her to a Hollywood party was the best course of action.

And I wasn't sure about the way the director had regarded Lizzy. Mr. Travis, though an amazing director and champion of mine, was a notorious womanizer. He might have been married to the actress Florence Thomas, but it was rumored he often had dalliances with the leading ladies of his films—currently Helen Clark. She'd been cast opposite Robert Smith in his last two films, as well, and the press blamed the pair for the failures at the box office; him for his drinking, and her for her less than stellar performance. She had been suffering from an addiction to laudanum at the time, and had been late on set often, if she'd shown up at all. When she had, she'd been either euphoric or lethargic. But she'd convinced Mr. Travis that she was off the stuff and persuaded him to ask the studio heads at Ambassador to give her another shot. I wasn't sure it was the best thing to do. Not because she wasn't talented, she was exceptional, but Mr. Travis had cast her over his wife and had given his wife a lesser, supporting role. It made for a frigid situation on set.

"I don't know," I answered honestly. "I have to think about it."

"Oh, please?" she whined.

"We'll discuss it later, Lizzy."

Luckily, Martha Mays, the lead seamstress working under me, approached us. She was a terribly efficient-looking woman, tall and straight as a stick, with round spectacles. Even though she worked as a seamstress at one of the most glamorous film studios, her own clothes were lackluster in color, and dare I say drab?

"Hello, Grace. And hello . . . ?" She pulled her glasses down to consider Lizzy.

"This is Lizzy. I brought her along today to see how we make a picture."

"Very well. Pleased to meet you, my dear." Martha looked back to me. "Grace, we have a problem in wardrobe. It's Hilda and Stella again. Can you come sort it out?" She glanced again at Lizzy. "Alone."

"Oh dear. Of course." I wondered what it was now. The two squabbled constantly.

"It's okay, Grace. I'll be fine," Lizzy said with a confident nod. "I'll just stay right here and watch when everyone gets back from the break."

"All right." I stood from my chair. "I'm sorry about this. I hope I'm not too long."

"I'll be fine," Lizzy reassured me again.

I followed Martha off the set and made my way to wardrobe, hoping that whatever she needed would be quick.

~

AMBASSADOR FILMS WAS SITUATED on a ten-acre tract of land at the base of the Hollywood hills and was comprised of three large warehouses, two of which were used for indoor sets, dressing rooms, and storage, and the third housed wardrobe and the business offices.

Given that the wardrobe room was expansive, my office, positioned in the northwest corner within it, was not. Well, it actually was bigger than it looked, there were just myriad things in there—bolts of fabric, large notebooks, bookshelves lined with fashion books and magazines, a bar cart filled with liquor and a set of six glasses, two file cabinets, and a desk as large as an airplane runway. In the corner was a raised pedestal situated in front of a three-way mirror for fittings.

Hilda and Stella were sitting in the club chairs near the three-way mirror. They sat with their backs to each other, both with their arms crossed tightly over their chests. I stifled a groan. The two were often at loggerheads over something or other. This was the worst part of the job.

"What's going on?" I asked, trepidation in my voice.

Hilda, the more senior of the two seamstresses, swung around to face me. "I can't work with her. She keeps making mistakes, and then the rest of us have to stop what we are doing and fix it. It's taking twice as long and putting us behind, and I, for one, don't want my reputation jeopardized by her shoddy work!"

I glanced over at Stella, who looked as if she was going to cry.

"I'm really sorry, Grace," Stella said with a frown. She blinked back tears. "I know it's not an excuse, but my mother has been sick. I'm up most of the night taking care of her, and I'm not getting much sleep. I know my work hasn't been up to par. I'll quit if you want."

I shook my head. Working in wardrobe was a demanding job, often with long hours. My heart went out to her. "Stella," I said, softening my voice. "We need you to do your best work. Would it help if you could do some of the work from home?"

She sniffed and wiped her nose with the back of her hand. I glanced over at Hilda, who had narrowed her eyes at the girl.

"Hilda, could I ask you to supervise Stella's work? Take her under your wing? Give her the assignments you think best, and if her work doesn't improve, we can revisit the situation. Would that be agreeable to you?"

Hilda tilted her chin upward and to the side, and pursed her lips as if considering. Finally, she gave a brief nod.

"Very well," I said with a relieved sigh. I turned to Stella. "I'm expecting improvement." And then to Hilda, "And from you, good direction."

Stella turned to Hilda. "I'm sorry, Hilda. I won't let you down."

Hilda gave her a tight smile. "I hope this works. And I'm sorry about your mother."

"Okay," I said. "Are we all right?"

They both nodded.

"Great. I have to get back on set." Thankful to have averted too much of a crisis, I left my office.

When I arrived back on set, I was alarmed to see that Robert Smith stood in front of Lizzy's chair, his hands planted on the arms and virtually trapping her there. I hadn't known Mr. Smith very long, but this behavior was strange—and inappropriate. He was usually quiet, withdrawn, broody. Such aggressiveness and outward boldness was something I had not seen in him before.

Lizzy didn't seem the least bit worried or upset about her predicament. In fact, she looked like quite the coquette, a flirtatious upturn of her lips playing up her dimples, making her look far older than sixteen. For the first time, it dawned on me that she was very aware of her natural charisma. Perhaps this was what had led to the trouble with the older boy . . .

A spasm jolted through me as an image of Sophia popped into my head. She'd had that same honey-like quality that attracted buzzing drones, their only aim in life to bask in the presence of such a captivating female. In the next second, another image waltzed its way into my mind. It was a scene from the dream I'd been having lately—Sophia, pulling a man through a doorway. Then the scene would switch to me sitting alone on the street, a basket of doll clothes in my lap. Then, me again, but this time in a room, standing over the man, a bloody knife in my hand.

I shook my head to rid myself of the images, my heart pounding.

"Lizzy?" I approached the two of them. Mr. Smith, still in costume, stood to his full six feet two inches, looking every bit like a young Henry VIII before corpulence set in. His lanky frame swayed with the effort. How much had he had to drink today?

"Hey, Grace," he said, giving me an uncharacteristic smile. I wondered what was going on with him—aside from the fact that he was drunk, but that was nothing new.

"Mr. Smith, I see you've met Lizzy." My voice was tight.

"Yeah, yeah," he said, redirecting his gaze to her again. "She's a great kid. Quite a looker. I told her she should be in pictures."

"He told me I was a real doll. Isn't that jake?" Lizzy whispered behind her hand, raising her eyebrows at me.

"Jake," I said flatly. I did not at all think this was fine, good, or satisfactory. In fact, coming from this version of Robert Smith, it made me wary. "Anyway, we need to head on over to the wardrobe room. I have some work to do. I'll give you one of my sketchbooks, and you can do some drawing."

Mr. Travis walked back on set. "All right, everyone. Places

please." He looked over at Mr. Smith, whose still stood in front of Lizzy's chair, hemming her in it.

"Leave her alone, Robert. I said *places*!" he snapped. Yes, the director was indeed growing impatient with the actor, and honestly, I couldn't blame him.

Mr. Smith gave Mr. Travis a cursory glance, and sauntered away from us.

"In your own time," Mr. Travis yelled after him, his voice dripping with sarcasm.

Mr. Smith turned around, and before I could blink, he rushed at the director, and soon had him by the lapels. Mr. Smith's eyes bulged with rage. Mr. Travis shoved him away and then delivered a blow to Mr. Smith's jaw, knocking him to the ground.

"Don't you ever, *ever*, touch me again you son of a bitch." Mr. Travis stood over Mr. Smith, who held his hand over his injured jaw. "This is your last warning. Get off the booze or I'll see that you are fired. Now get up and take your place."

Why hadn't Mr. Travis fired him on the spot? I certainly would have. Perhaps it needed to come from the studio bosses. It hadn't taken me long to learn that everyone's contract with the studio was different, though I'd heard through the rumor mill the studio bosses were considering firing Mr. Smith. I imagine this incident would expedite the event.

I grabbed Lizzy by the hand and pulled her out of the chair. I could feel Mr. Smith's eyes on us as we walked away.

"Wow! That was crazy!" Lizzy released my hand. "Are things always like that around here?"

Crazy was right. "No. Mr. Smith has been under some stress lately." I wasn't quite sure how to explain his irrational behavior.

"He sure is a hothead," Lizzy said.

"Not usually." I was still trying to figure out what had gotten into Mr. Smith.

"He asked if I was going to Mr. Travis's party. Do you think we can go?" She turned around and walked backward, facing me, her dark auburn curls bouncing up and down on her shoulders. The bright blue of her sailor-inspired dress brought out the pink in her cheeks.

"I'm still not sure yet. I need to check with Chet to see if we have anything going on at the ranch that night," I said, trying to put her off again.

"Well," she said, her cheery demeanor returning. "I hope we can go. It would be the berries."

CHAPTER TWO

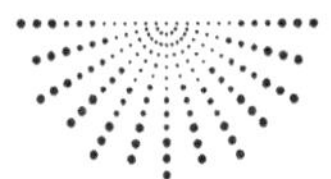

The following morning, after a quick cup of coffee, I walked out to the barn where I'd hoped to find Chet. He'd come in after I was asleep and had headed out to the barn before I was fully awake.

It was a crisp, cool, and clear Friday. Billowing white and gray thunderheads kissed the top of the Verdugo Hills. Our little ranch, situated in Burbank, was an almost perfectly rectangular, flat, hundred-acre parcel of land that sat at the base of the hills and provided us with incredible views of the Verdugo and San Gabriel Mountains. We grew alfalfa, some citrus, and cantaloupe, which provided a good little sum of money for us, and we leased some of our property to a local farmer named Mr. Lambert, who also grew cantaloupe.

Mr. Travis had told everyone on the picture to take a long weekend. I assumed it was in lieu of the imminent firing of Robert Smith. There were whispers from some of the actors that Mr. Travis and the studio bosses were currently looking for Mr. Smith's replacement. I assumed the long weekend might also have something to do with the party scheduled at Mr. Travis's house the next night.

I found Chet at the riding arena talking with our neighbor, Joseph Manetti, who was a racehorse owner and trainer. He was the one who had gotten Chet interested in rehabilitating injured racehorses.

The two were watching a beautiful bay being hand-walked by Daniel Blaine, one of our charges.

"Morning, you two," I said. I approached Chet from behind and wrapped my arms around his middle. "That one's a beauty! Is that the horse you met at the train station late last night?"

"Yep," Chet said. He stepped out of my grasp and planted a kiss on my cheek. "He's made great progress since we saw him last."

"Morning, Joe," I said.

"Hey, Grace. How you doin'?" Joe took a sip of coffee from his thermos. "You up for your lesson this morning?" Joe was small but mighty, his New York–Italian roots making him seem like a tough guy, but I didn't see him that way.

I stood back and angled my legs to show off my new jodhpurs and boots. "Ready and willing."

"She looks the part," Chet said, his gray eyes twinkling at me. His magnetic smile still made my heart stop.

"Then you better go get tacked up," Joe said.

"Meet you back here?" I asked, excited for my lesson.

Joe nodded and turned his attention back to the beautiful horse in the arena.

"I'm going to grab some more coffee and then go into town to get some supplies," Chet said. "You two have fun." He kissed me on the cheek and headed toward the house.

I made my way toward the barn where Lizzy was busy grooming my horse, Goldie, before school started. I often took a morning ride, and Lizzy had volunteered to take on the job of getting the horse ready for me. As I entered through the large double doors, I was instantly struck with the smell of hay, dust, and horse. It was a smell I had grown accustomed to and actually liked. It reminded me of fresh air, sunshine, and the wonderful feeling of freedom I always experienced when riding. Those mingling aromas took me out of my head and grounded me in a way I couldn't explain.

Goldie stood in the breezeway of the barn, tied to her stall door, and munched on some hay that had been placed in a hanging hay bag while Lizzy was absorbed in the task of making the horse's coat gleam.

"She looks happy," I said as I approached. "Thank you for doing that. I'll take over so you can get ready for school."

"It's okay," she said. "I'm ahead on my schoolwork, so Miss Meyers said I could come out to the barn this morning. When I'm finished with Goldie, I'll get one of the other horses out to ride."

I was not surprised to hear she was ahead on her coursework. The girl excelled at book learning and kept Miss Meyers busy trying to provide more advanced studies for her.

The kids usually woke at 6:00 a.m. to meet Chet outside. They'd do early-morning chores and then come in for breakfast at 8:30 a.m. After breakfast, they would go to the schoolroom for their lessons, then have lunch at 1:00 p.m. They had leisurely time after lunch to do their own thing or homework until 4:00 p.m. when they'd commence with evening chores. Lizzy was often ahead of the other children with her schoolwork so Miss Meyers was more flexible with her lessons.

Lizzy smiled as she combed out the tangles of Goldie's tail. "Chet told me you received her as a gift. From an Indian in New Mexico?"

"Yes. When I was an actress on tour with the Follies, Flo sent me on a publicity trip across the United States. One of my favorite stops was at an Indian village near Albuquerque. Our guide, Frank Deerhunter, let me ride Goldie, or Golden Ray of Light as he called her." I picked up a brush and worked on the horse's legs. "Later, when we got back to New York, we'd heard that Mr. Deerhunter had died and had bequeathed her to me. I named her Goldie after Flo's secretary. She was always so nice to me. It also just worked with the name Mr. Deerhunter had given her." I winked at Lizzy.

"I used to have a horse," she said wistfully. "When I was much younger."

"No wonder you are so good with them." I smiled at her, but she was still focused on Goldie's tail. It shined like spun gold.

"His name was Apollo. But my sister said we had to sell him. Said we couldn't afford him anymore." There was a sadness in her voice that pulled at my heart. Lizzy had been raised by her elder sister, Margaret, and from the little bit of information I had, I knew life had not been easy for them.

"I'm sorry to hear that. I'm glad you get a chance to ride here. I find it really is so good for the soul."

Lizzy stopped brushing and smoothed her hair behind her ears, revealing a pair of small, dangling gold and sapphire earrings.

I stepped closer to her to inspect the jewelry. "Those earrings are beautiful."

She absently touched one of them. "Thanks. They were my grandmother's. Or so Margaret said."

"They look lovely on you. If you want, we can put them in my jewelry box to keep them safe while we ride." I was surprised she would risk losing such a sentimental gift.

"It's okay," she said. "I have them screwed on tight."

I decided not to press further and changed the subject. "Who are you riding today?"

She ran her hands down Goldie's face. The horse stopped chewing for a moment, basking in the attention. "I think I'll ride Marley. He hasn't been out for a while."

"Good idea. You go ahead and get Marley ready. I'll finish up here and see you in the arena?" I held out my hand for the mane and tale brush.

"Okay. Thanks," she said. "But I think I'll ride him out into the hills today."

My stomach clenched a little at the thought of her riding out there by herself. She done so once before and had come back none the worse for wear, but it still concerned me. If something happened, no one would be able to get help. "I'm not sure that's such a good idea," I said. "Maybe see if Daniel or Ida will go with you?"

"They have school," she reminded me. "And even if they didn't, I wouldn't want either of them to come. Daniel is all googly-eyed around me, and Ida? I'd rather eat hay for breakfast. Besides, Daniel is helping Joe and Ida still has to feed the chickens and gather the eggs before school. She overslept, as usual. She can be such a princess sometimes."

The two girls had trouble getting along, though I had hoped they would form a bond. It would have been good for Lizzy to mentor the younger girl and good for Ida to have someone to confide in. She had a hard time expressing her feelings. But they didn't seem to mesh.

"Mrs. R had to go wake her up and wasn't very happy about it." Lizzy patted Goldie on the neck.

"I'm sure," I said with a smile.

Mrs. R—or Rose Riker—was Chet's mother, who he'd been reunited with after years of separation. For reasons I still did not know, she had been unable to care for Chet when he was little, and she had turned him over to an orphanage. Eager to reconnect with his roots, Chet had searched for her as an adult. He found her in poor health and in need of an operation. He'd helped her through it, and they'd rebuilt their relationship. She now worked for us—keeping house, cooking, and helping to look after the children. She was a tough cookie, and while not the warmest of women, she had become invaluable to the workings of the household, and I was grateful. We also employed a teacher, Miss Meyers, for the children's education. Since I was the primary breadwinner of the family, my time and resources were stretched thin as it was.

"Rose is not very forgiving about tardiness," I added.

Ned, one of our ranch workers, walked into the barn holding a cup of coffee. His gaze was focused on the ground as if he was deep in thought. He was a strapping sort of young man who was strong as a Clydesdale but who also had a sensitive side.

"Grace," he said, his face lighting up in a smile when he saw me.

"Good morning," I replied

His smile widened, showing a fine row of white teeth, enhanced by the golden color of his sun-kissed skin.

"Hi, Ned." Lizzy stepped around Goldie. Her face brightened at seeing him. It was clear she had a crush on the twenty-one-year-old. She seemed to always want the attention of older males. Perhaps it was because she hadn't had a father figure in her life. That had been the case with Sophia, too.

"Hey." Ned nodded at her, giving her a cursory glance. "Going for a ride, Grace? Can I help you saddle her?" He pointed to the horse with his coffee cup.

"No, but thank you. There is something you could do, though."

"Name it."

"Could you go out with Lizzy?" I asked. "She'd like to ride in the hills today."

Lizzy beamed, satisfied with that suggestion. She smiled at Ned, and dare I say, batted her eyelashes at him. Her eyes were large and luminous, and added to her budding sensuality. "I would enjoy that." She leaned against Goldie and flung her arm over the mare's back, that sensuality blossoming right before my eyes. I almost wished I hadn't made the suggestion. Her sister had been concerned about promiscuity in the girl after her previous relationship with the young man who had gotten them in so much trouble.

Ned gave me an apologetic look. "Chet asked me to fix the fence on the west end of the property first thing. The barbed wire is coming loose, and he's worried about the horses getting out."

Lizzy's face fell. She shrugged a shoulder. "I'll be fine, Grace. I promise." She walked away from us and headed for Marley's stall.

I supposed I was worrying over nothing. Lizzy was a proficient rider—better than me, if I was being honest—with a good seat. She was a natural in the saddle and completely confident in her skill. As Joe always reminded me, confidence went a long way with a horse.

"I'll see you later." Ned smiled warmly at me and then headed deeper into the barn.

I finished saddling Goldie and put on her bridle. She nickered at me for one of the sugar cubes I had in my pocket, and I gladly gave her a few. On my way out to the arena, I passed by Marley's stall. "You'll be careful out there?"

She nodded. "I always am." Her mood had turned sullen, likely disappointed that Ned could not ride out with her. She brushed Marley's back without looking at me.

I figured it was best to leave her alone at this point. When she'd first arrived at the ranch, she was angry, and then she'd withdrawn, suffering from melancholy. Over the last couple of weeks, she'd seemed to be coming out of it, but perhaps that had been wishful thinking on my part. Maybe riding would clear her head and improve her mood. It always did mine.

As we usually did, Goldie and I started our session with some easy walking. Today, I could see that Goldie was a bit distracted by the new horse that Daniel was still hand-walking at the other end of the arena. Instead of focusing on me, she was focused everywhere else and seemed jumpy and nervous. After trying unsuccessfully to do some minor tasks with her to get her attention, I stopped trying and looked helplessly over at Joe, who was watching us.

"You're not being provocative enough," he said, hopping down from the fence railing and coming over to us.

I couldn't imagine what he was talking about. *Provocative? Did I need to give her a come-hither glance?*

"She's upset by the new horse," I said, bringing her to a halt. With Goldie craning her neck to look at the new horse, she fidgeted, unable to keep her feet still.

"You need to keep her busy," he went on. "Be provocative. Keep her focused on what your body is telling her to do. Get her into a trot, and then do lots of circles and changing of direction. *Capisce?*"

Not entirely sure of myself, I nodded and clucked to her, letting her move out.

By some miracle, his advice worked. After about ten minutes of pretty tight figure eights at a trot, I felt her body relax under my own. I brought her to a walk, and she blew out loudly, not paying any attention to the horse.

Joe smiled with approval. "There you go."

I had been so absorbed in my task that I hadn't seen Daniel and the bay heading toward us. Both horses were now completely relaxed, and I let out a deep breath, able to enjoy the feeling of the sun on my back.

"Morning, Daniel," I said.

"Hey, Grace." He raised his chin in greeting. He and the horse stood a few feet away from us, and Goldie nickered at the bay.

"You want me to trim his feet?" Daniel asked Joe. Daniel was a gregarious yet troubled boy who liked to work with his hands. Bill March, our blacksmith, had taken him under his wing and was teaching him the craft.

Joe took off his hat and raked his fingers through his hair.

The June day was speedily warming up. "Nah," he shook his head. "Why don't you saddle Duchess for me. I want to see how she is coming along. Maybe you can work on this guy's feet after school."

Daniel nodded and led the bay toward the barn.

"He seems like a nice kid," Joe said, settling his hat back on his head. "What's his story?"

My eyes followed Daniel as he opened the arena gate. "He was caught pickpocketing. Learned the trade from his father, who is now in prison for theft. I have no idea where his mother is. The police officer who caught Daniel let him off with a warning and told him about us."

"And the boy came here of his own accord?"

I nodded. "I think he wants to be good, make something of himself."

"Good for him," Joe said. "How about we ride out today? Just for an hour or so. Are you up for it?"

"Sure," I said. Maybe we would run into Lizzy. The thought gave me some comfort. "I'm going to trot her a little more while we wait for Duchess."

"Good idea. You're doing great with her."

I smiled, pleased with his approval. I moved Goldie along, posting with her movement and enjoying the connection I felt with her. Soon, Daniel brought out Duchess. He was accompanied by Ida and Susie, our youngest charge at ten years old. She was clutching the teddy bear she always carried to her chest. She worshiped Ida and rarely left her side, even though Ida could be a bit dismissive and cruel to her.

"Are you done with your chores?" I asked the girls.

"Yes, ma'am," Susie said. "The horses ate all their oats this morning." Susie loved greeting the horses every morning with their favorite food.

"And the chickens, Ida? Were there many eggs?"

She put her hands on her hips. "A boatload. We'll be eating deviled eggs for weeks."

I laughed. The dish was one of Rose's favorite to prepare. "You'd better get ready for school, then. Miss Meyers will be waiting for you. Joe and I are going out for a bit."

Joe climbed atop Duchess, and I made my way out of the arena to meet him. We paired up and started to head into the fields. The sound of the kids laughing distracted me, and I turned to see Daniel holding Susie's teddy bear above his head and the little girl dancing around him, shouting at him to give it back. He tossed the bear to Ida, who ran toward us with it and did the same, holding it above her head and then tossing it back to Daniel.

I knew this was just playing, but Susie was a little sensitive about her bear. I was about to say something to them when Daniel lobbed the bear toward Ida, who'd come closer to us. His aim was off, however, and the stuffed toy flew in our direction.

Goldie jumped to the side, almost toppling me to the ground. Instinctively, I gripped her body with my legs, trying to regain my balance, but I only succeeded in causing her to surge forward. I was jerked backward, and Goldie took off running. The next thing I knew, I was flat on my back on the ground, gasping for breath while a kaleidoscope of stars flashed in my vision.

CHAPTER THREE

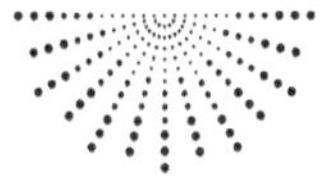

"Grace, are you okay? Don't move." I blinked to see Ned's face swimming before my eyes.

Then Joe came into view. "Catch your breath, *cara*," he said. "Does anything hurt?"

I shook my head, still unable to speak.

"Sit her up slowly," said Joe.

Ned took hold of my hand and, supporting my shoulders, gently helped me sit up. I caught his gaze, and his eyes were flooded with concern.

"Let's get her into the house," Joe said.

Before I realized what was happening, Ned swept me up into his arms as if I weighed no more than one of the feather boas I used in costuming. He hustled me through the picket fence, onto the porch, and into the house with Joe, Ida, and Susie on our heels.

"What in heaven's—" Rose met us in the living room where Ned carefully deposited me onto the sofa as if he were placing a fallen egg into a nest.

"Grace was thrown," Joe said, raising an assuring hand in the air. "She's fine—just got the wind knocked out of her." He turned to me. "You feeling better, *cara*?"

I forced a small smile. Joe often used this fatherly Italian endearment when speaking to me. "Yes," I said, finally finding my voice.

Rose scurried away toward the kitchen, and Ned released a heavy breath. "I'm so glad you're okay," he said, placing his hand on my knee. My gaze dropped to his hand, and he quickly retracted it and stood up.

Susie came around the sofa and held out her bear. "You can hold Teddy if you want," she said, her brow knit with concern. "He'll make you feel better."

I held my hand out to her and then pulled her close to me. "Why don't you sit down next to me with Teddy. *That* will make me feel better." She smiled and snuggled in next to me.

"We're awful sorry, Grace," Daniel said, his freckled face reddening with shame. "We were just playing around."

"Yeah. We're sorry," said Ida, not able to make eye contact with me.

I'd had trouble connecting with the fourteen-year-old who never could sit still long enough for me to have a conversation with her about anything. An aunt had brought her to us with very little explanation except that her father had been a drug addict since he returned from the war and had died of an overdose of morphine. She couldn't keep the girl.

"It's all right, kids. I'm fine." I was touched by their remorse and concern.

Rose bustled back into the living room, elbowing her way through to hand me a glass of lemonade. "Here you go. Some sugar to help with the shock." She was a large, stern-eyed woman, all business and no sentiment, but I didn't know what Chet and I would do without her.

I suddenly remembered Lizzy was out riding in the hills. I

had hoped to connect with her while we were out there. "Has anyone seen Lizzy? Has she come back yet?"

"I'm right here," the girl said, breezing into the room. "Marley had a stone bruise and was a little tenderfooted so I came back early. And look who I found walking up to the house . . ."

My mouth dropped open as Edward Travis stepped into the room. He'd said he wanted to come visit the ranch some time, but I hadn't expected it would be so soon—or so unannounced. Plus, I figured he'd be busy making sure all was ready for his party tomorrow night.

"What's going on?" Lizzy asked. "Why are you all in here?"

I struggled a bit to get up from the sofa, my legs still a little wobbly, but managed to stand. "Oh, I took a little spill riding is all. I'm fine." I turned to the director. "Mr. Travis, what brings you here?" I was still stunned to see him standing in my living room.

"I'd like to speak with you—about the ranch. But if it's not a good time . . ."

"No, no. It's no problem." I tried not to wince as gravity pulled down on my aching back. "What can I do for you?"

"Come on, everyone," Rose said, ushering the kids, Joe, and Ned out of the room. "Let's give Grace some privacy."

"Can I get you something to drink?" I offered. "Lemonade?"

He shook his head. "I won't be long. I was going to call but realized I didn't have your telephone number. My secretary keeps all that information for me, and, well, with the long weekend and all . . ."

"Yes. Please, sit down." I gestured to the sofa and then gingerly lowered myself into the armchair adjacent to it, my back still aching.

He leaned forward and set his elbows on his knees. "I know this is rather short notice . . ." A sheepish grin played on his lips. "But the most inconvenient thing has happened. We've had a problem with the plumbing at the mansion. Flooded part of the upstairs rooms, and we've had to turn off the water. There is quite a bit of damage, unfortunately, and it has rather put me in a bind for the party tomorrow night. I'd hate to cancel all together. We've had such a rough go with the film so far; I fear morale is taking a downturn."

He had reason to be concerned. Things had not exactly been going smoothly.

"I've contacted a few of the hotels with spaces that would be appropriate," he continued, "but they are all booked for the weekend."

"I see." I was starting to get the picture. "Are you thinking you'd like to have the party here?" I asked.

He held his hands up in a placating manner. "I would take care of all the expenses, of course, and pay whatever fee you deem suitable. I've got everything ready to go—chef, waiters, you name it. We could make use of the outdoors, as well, if you prefer. What do you say?"

I wasn't quite sure what to say and felt a little put on the spot. While it would probably be in my best interest career-wise to oblige, it was indeed short notice, and I did have the children to consider. Would it be too disruptive for them? Probably not for the older children—I imagine they would love to have the house full of movie stars. But what about Susie? She could stay with Miss Meyers in her rooms for the night, I reasoned.

Mr. Travis must have sensed my hesitancy from the awkward silence. "How about I make a donation of some kind for the kids here, as well? What do they need? Clothes, books, jobs? I'd be happy to help."

Now he was making it much more difficult to refuse. Miss Meyers had requested a newer set of textbooks and also wanted to build a small library off the schoolroom. She'd been slowly collecting books for it over the past year. We received some money from the state, but it was never enough.

"You are very generous," I said. "Can I give you a call later this afternoon? I'd like to run it by my husband first."

"Absolutely." He reached into his pocket and handed me a calling card. "This is my telephone number at the mansion."

I took the card as we stood up. "It shouldn't be too long. He just ran into town for an errand."

I showed him out, suddenly feeling very sleepy. The adrenaline from the fall had worn off and left me feeling quite tired, and I longed to rest my head on my pillow, if only for a few minutes. I climbed the stairs, my mind filled with an array of thoughts. While I wanted to help the director, and by doing so, help the kids, the idea left me feeling uncertain and I wasn't entirely sure why.

THE SUN IS SHINING bright and warm on our heads as the sheets on the double clothesline billow around us, the whiteness of them making my eyes water. Sophia's tinkling laugh fills my ears as she runs in circles around the outside of our little fort. She breaks through the gap in the sheets and places a dandelion chain on top of my head.

Our parents stand in the driveway in front of our house and then walk into the open garage set apart from the house. The car backs out a moment later as they drive away. I can see Sophia calling after them, but I can't hear her. She runs down the street after them, leaving me alone. I start to cry, and suddenly Sophia is right next to me, lying in the grass, her eyes open and staring. Blood trickles down the side of her face.

"No!" I yell. "No, Sophia!"

I woke with a start, my heart pounding and my palms sweating.

"Grace, are you all right? I heard you shouting." Chet came rushing into the bedroom and sat next to me on the bed.

"I'm, I'm—" I couldn't quite make the words come out, still reeling from the dream.

"Another nightmare?"

I nodded. Apparently they came during the day, too.

Chet pushed a stray blond wave from my eyes. "Do you want to talk about it?"

"No." I wanted to forget about it as soon as possible. I clasped my hands to hide the fact that they were trembling.

"Mother told me you took a spill. Are you all right?"

I rubbed the sleep from my eyes. "I'm fine. Guess the fall made me more tired than I thought."

"You didn't sleep well last night," he added.

I hadn't, but I didn't want to talk about that, either.

Chet took my hands in his, their warmth radiating through the iciness of my fingers. I felt myself relax at his attentiveness. He'd always been such a symbol of strength to me.

"Mr. Travis came by today." I wanted to change the subject.

"I heard that, too. What did he want?"

I studied our entwined hands and told him about Mr. Travis's party and his troubles at the mansion.

Chet let out a low whistle. "That's some hard luck."

I raised my gaze to meet Chet's light-gray eyes. "He asked if he could host the party here." I bit my lip, worried about his response. Chet wasn't crazy about big parties, especially parties filled with show business types. I wasn't crazy about them, either, preferring the quiet company of those nearest and dearest to me.

"What did you tell him?" he asked, skepticism in his voice.

I lifted a shoulder. "I told him I need to speak with you. He's offered to pay us, of course, for the use of the place, and he also said he would do something to help the kids—whatever we needed."

Chet ran a hand through his hair. "How do you feel about it?"

"To tell you the truth, conflicted. I want to help Mr. Travis, and I want to help the kids, but you know me. I don't really like these Hollywood parties any more than you do. And I just have a weird feeling . . ."

"About what?"

I shook my head. "I can't put my finger on it." The image of Sophia's dead eyes from my latest dream popped into my head, and my stomach swirled with anxiety.

Chet let out a deep breath. "We could sure use the money. There is a lot of fencing to be fixed, and we are probably going to have to do something about the roof soon. The expenses around here are never-ending. I have high hopes for this horse rehabilitation venture, but it will take some time. It would be nice to have some extra for the kids now."

"That's what I thought, too."

"Does Mother know about this?" he asked.

"No. I haven't discussed it with anyone but you and Mr. Travis."

He raised an eyebrow. "You realize it won't go over well. You know how she is about people in 'her' kitchen." He raised his fingers in quotation marks.

"That's true, but since it would help the children . . ."

Chet squeezed my hand again. "Why don't you do it, then? It sounds like it might even be fun. But there was something I wanted to discuss with you that might impact your decision."

"Oh?"

"Joe's got a line on a horse in Calabasas that has some real potential for the track in Mexico—but he's got some behavioral problems and the owners want to euthanize him. No one can handle him. But Joe thinks he can turn the horse around. I thought it would be good for Daniel and Lizzy to help him with this horse, to learn from him. They both have taken so well to the animals, but it would be really nice if they had a project. And if we can get the horse ready for the track by next season, it might be good for us financially."

"That's a wonderful idea, Chet. But how will this impact my decision about the party?"

"We have to go get him tomorrow night. I'll try to get back as soon as possible, but it may be rather late."

"I see." Although Chet didn't care for extravagant affairs, he did surprisingly well socially with his outgoing personality. I didn't like to admit it, but I depended on him to fly cover for me. The prospect of facing the partygoers without him only increased my anxiety.

"I'm sorry, darling. This is all rather last minute." He squeezed my hand again. "Joe just told me about it this morning, and it looks like we are this horse's only hope."

Well how could I argue with that? I only wished I could rid myself of this niggling feeling of doom.

CHAPTER FOUR

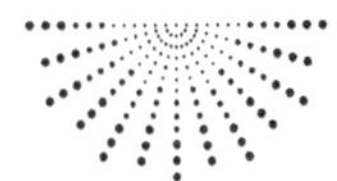

The lower floor of the house was bursting at the seams with all the people Mr. Travis invited to the party, despite the fact that we owned a rather large house. Farmhouse style with a wraparound porch, it had a bevy of bedrooms upstairs—seven, in fact—including a room I had converted into a studio. Miss Meyers and Rose resided downstairs in the generous maid's quarters. There were also spacious living areas downstairs, including a formal dining room adjacent to the kitchen and a grand formal living area, both positioned at the front of the house. At the back of the house were a sunroom and a large den. We also had a bunkhouse out near the barn where Ned and some of the other farmhands lived.

Mr. Travis was true to his word, though, and I didn't have to lift a finger for the party. As Chet had predicted, Rose was beside herself with irritation at having to share her kitchen with the caterers and the staff they employed. I did my best to ignore her grumblings.

Lizzy, Ida, and Daniel were keen to see all the movie stars so I let them attend, providing they would be on their best behavior. As I had been so aptly reminded by my incident with Goldie, the kids were prone to roughhousing and mischief. Daniel and Ida had given me their word that they wouldn't cause any trouble.

Lizzy, however, had been affronted by my entreaty, as she felt herself above the age of such nonsense. "I'm almost seventeen," she'd said.

"I know, Lizzy. You're becoming a mature young woman. I just want you to be aware that the Hollywood set is a fast crowd. Just be cautious. And no drinking. It's illegal."

She had crossed her arms over her chest defiantly. "If it's illegal to have booze here, then why are you doing it?"

"I meant it's illegal for *you* to drink. You're a minor. And it's not illegal to have alcohol in a private home if you are of age. It's illegal to make it or sell it. I'm sure Mr. Travis will have plenty on hand for the party, but it is not for you or the other kids. Understand?"

She had sighed but had given me a nod of acquiescence. We usually did not have any kind of liquor or spirits in the house, but since Prohibition had started four years ago, I had not been to a party where it wasn't served.

I scanned the living room full of beautiful people. The starlets all wore glamorous variations of the popular flapper dress, and the men wore dapper tailcoats and white ties, or the more modern tuxedo jacket with black bow tie. Among the esteemed guests were actress Clara Bow, surrounded by a bevy of young men, as well as Charlie Chaplin, Mary Pickford, and Douglas Fairbanks, who stood in a tight knot, probably talking business. The latter three were co-owners of Ambassador's rival studio, United Artists. I wondered where their fourth partner, the famed political film director D.W. Griffith, was tonight. Probably at home reading a script. I'd heard he did not often mix business with pleasure.

I spied Lizzy talking with Robert Smith, which was concerning enough, and she had a champagne glass in her hand. Why was Robert Smith here anyway? Apparently, he hadn't been fired yet. My stomach clenched at the sight of him with Lizzy, and with her drinking. I still didn't like the uncharacteristic behavior I'd witnessed from him on the set, and seeing him here was a little unsettling. Had he and Mr. Travis made up?

Lizzy was animated and vivacious, looking much older than her sixteen years. She had asked to borrow one of my dresses from the Sophia line, which I happily had complied with at the time, but now seeing her wearing it, I had second thoughts. Mr. Smith's eyes were pinned to her. The dress was one of my favorites. It was a deep-green satin that brought out the paleness of Lizzy's skin and the deep tones of her auburn hair. I had adhered a large rhinestone clip at the apex of the gathered, dropped waistline, and the chiffon skirt, cut in the popular hanky hem, graced her slender calves midway.

I hastily made my way over to them.

"Hi, Grace." Lizzy flashed a dazzling smile at me, her cheeks pink from the champagne. I wondered how much she'd had to drink.

I took the glass from her hand. "What did we talk about?" I whispered.

"Oh, you're such a killjoy," she said, her lips pressing into a pout.

"Are you having a nice time?" I asked Mr. Smith, giving him a pointed look, hoping to convey that Lizzy was my charge and he needed to take care.

A waiter approached us with a gleaming silver tray of champagne coupes. Mr. Smith deposited his empty glass and took two more.

"I hope that isn't for Lizzy," I said. I knew I was embarrassing her, but we'd had a deal.

Mr. Smith gave me a discerning look. "Oh, never fear, Miss Michelle. I don't share."

As the waiter turned to go, he bumped Mr. Smith with his shoulder, spilling the champagne. He quickly turned back around, his hand raised apologetically in the air. "I beg your pardon," he said with a hint of a British accent and then hurried off.

"That was rude," Lizzy said.

"The man is beyond the pale." Mr. Smith's words came out slow and thick. "Works for Travis. His valet or butler—some kind of indentured servant. I think his name is Johnson. Light in the loafers from what I've heard."

"Robert, darling, there you are!" An incredibly tall, willowy woman approached us. Her hair was almost the same bright silver as her gown. She was striking, probably at one time beautiful but well past her prime. The lilt in her voice gave the hint of a Scandinavian accent. Swedish or Danish, I ventured to guess.

She laid a gloved hand on Mr. Smith's shoulder, and her eyes met mine.

"This is Miss Lenora Lange. A friend of mine," Mr. Smith said. "Lenora, this is Grace Michelle, owner of this beautiful home."

She extended her hand, and I took it. "It's a pleasure to meet you, Miss Lange. Welcome." Before I could turn to Lizzy to introduce her, she scooted away from us and opened the French doors to go onto the back porch.

Miss Lange's lips turned up in a half smile, and she tilted her head, her eyes narrowing a bit. "You are an old soul," she said.

"Excuse me?" I thought it a strange greeting. No, it *was* a strange greeting. She hadn't yet released my hand.

"You haven't heard of Lenora?" Mr. Smith asked, chuckling. He swallowed down the rest of his second glass of champagne.

"No, I'm sorry. Should I have?" I wanted to pull back my hand but knew I wouldn't be able to do so without jerking it away.

"Lenora is a famous spiritualist," he went on.

"Oh." I wasn't sure what to make of that.

Miss Lange pulled me closer to her, released her other hand

from Mr. Smith's shoulder, and placed it on top of our linked palms. "She is well. She is at peace," she said, her voice almost a whisper.

A wave of dizziness slammed into me, and my hands and scalp tingled, causing an icy chill to zip down my spine. "Uh . . . Um . . . I'm sorry, I—" I looked to Mr. Smith for assistance.

"Lenora is a medium," Mr. Smith tried to explain again. "She communicates with those who've passed to the other side."

"Your sister," Miss Lange said. "She's passed?"

A pain deep in my chest nearly took my breath away. I stared up at her and actually did it—I jerked my hand away from hers as if they'd been poker hot. "Yes."

"Gracie. That is what she called you?" The woman's pale-blue eyes regarded me with tenderness.

I felt the blood drain from my face, and my knees shook with weakness. The only two people in the world who'd called me Gracie were Sophia and Flo. Suddenly, I felt the presence of all the people in the house pressing in on me. I had to get some air.

"Excuse me. I need to find Lizzy." I was just about to make my way to the double doors that led to the back porch when Miss Lange touched my shoulder.

"She's going to need you." Her gaze was so penetrating it made me want to flinch. I wasn't sure who she was talking about —Sophia or Lizzy. And what did it mean?

Flustered, I pulled myself away and stepped out into the cool night air. I took in a breath so sharp it sounded like a gasp.

Several of the guests were also on the porch chatting and laughing, probably feeling the crush inside, as well. Daniel and Ida were standing under one of the trees in the yard, talking quietly with a man and a woman. I was glad to see them interacting with the guests, and in such a mature manner.

Lizzy was talking with another one of the actors. I didn't know him but had seen him around the set. She was laughing at something he'd said. I was relieved she wasn't holding a drink this time. Standing nearby were Mr. Travis and his wife, Florence Thomas. From their body language, I could tell they were in an argument.

"Grace." I heard a familiar voice from behind me, and I turned to see my dear friend, the Southern beauty, Felicity Jones coming through the French doors. She looked lovely, as usual, in her trademark burgundy. She wore the color often, as it brought out the gold tones in her dark skin and contrasted with the blue of her eyes. Her anomalous looks were captivating, and people gravitated to her like moths to a flame, which was ironic because she really was quite shy and introverted.

I breathed a sigh of relief at seeing her. "I was hoping you'd come."

She shrugged. "Of course. I haven't seen much of you lately, and I've missed you. I hitched a ride with Edward and Florence."

"Oh right. You are still living in their guest house."

Felicity had been renting a little bungalow in Santa Monica, but a tree branch had fallen through the roof.

"Yes. It was kind of them to allow me to stay there," she said. "And convenient."

Once a reluctant Broadway star, then a reluctant screen star, Felicity had finally made her break from show business and had settled on a career in interior design. Deeply entrenched with the Hollywood set, she'd become the designer to the stars and was currently working for Mr. Travis.

"How are the renovations going?" I asked. "Aside from the plumbing problems, that is."

"Mostly well. She's quite a challenge to work with." Felicity tilted her head in Florence's direction. The woman was leaning forward, her face taut as she was delivering what looked like a hushed verbal tirade at her husband, who was nervously looking around. He took her by the elbow and ushered her out of earshot.

Felicity heaved a sigh. "Looks like trouble in paradise. Again. They are always arguing. It has to be exhausting."

"Uh-huh." I was only half paying attention. My eyes drifted to a small group of people surrounding Miss Lange in the house. Their gazes were glued to her, as if hanging on her every word. Our unsettling conversation came back to mind, and a flush of heat traveled up my torso.

"Grace, are you feeling okay? You look a little shaken." Felicity knew me so well.

I pressed the back of my hand to my forehead, then turned toward the open fields. "Just a little warm. It's pretty crowded in there." I set my hands on the railing and closed my eyes, a delicious, soft breeze giving me instant relief.

"What's the matter, sugar?" Felicity laid a hand on my shoulder.

I opened my eyes and faced her. "What do you know about Lenora Lange?"

Felicity frowned and gave a shrug of her shoulder. "She's a psychic or a medium or something. So I've heard . . . Did she come with Robert Smith?"

"As far as I know."

"He's quite the devotee. I've heard rumors they are living together." Felicity raised an eyebrow. "He claims she's been able to speak with some of the soldiers in his unit who were killed in France. Poor guy is shell-shocked from the war. That's why he drinks so much. He's really a mess."

"Yes. So I've gathered," I said absently, my mind still on Miss Lange. "Do you think she can really speak to the dead?" My voice came out weak, like a child's.

Felicity shrugged again. "Who knows? Whatever she does, she's making a good living at it. I've heard she's quite famous in Europe."

I turned fully around, leaned my backside against the railing, and crossed my arms at my waist. "She said something to me about Sophia. She wanted me to know Sophia is at peace. It really caught me off guard."

Felicity's brows pressed down over her eyes. "It does seem a strange thing to say to someone when first meeting them. But whether or not she's been in contact with your sister, the news of your sister's death was all over the papers. Maybe she was just trying to give you some comfort."

Sophia's death had only been four years ago, but it seemed like ages. I was never comfortable with the press so rarely read anything printed in the papers about me or my sister. Yes, Sophia's death had been a big story, but like everything in show business, it was literally yesterday's news the day after the headline had been printed. The public was fickle and forgetful. And it had been quite some time since anyone had brought her death up to me. I took in a deep breath and squeezed Felicity's hand.

She squeezed mine back. "She was probably just being kind. Wanting to put any fears you might have had to rest."

"You are probably right."

But what if it was something more? What if she had been in contact with Sophia? The thought sent another icy chill across my shoulders.

I guess the dreams I'd been having about Sophia and my parents lately were getting to me, not to mention causing me insufferable sleep deprivation.

Felicity was right. Miss Lange probably had read about Sophia and probably knew about me as her replacement, but how did she know Sophia's pet name for me? And who was it that needed my help?

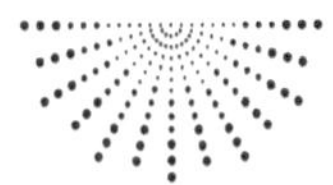

Once back in the house, my thoughts of Sophia lifted as the noise of the party distracted me more and more. The party was going full tilt. Someone had turned on the phonograph, and Eddie Cantor's "Charley My Boy" drifted on the air, competing with the loud conversations and laughter of the guests. Behind me, Florence Thomas burst in through the double doors, her mouth set in a hard line. She headed directly for the punch bowl.

Helen Clark sauntered over to me wearing a beautiful indigo beaded gown, a champagne coupe held aloft in her bejeweled hand with its perfectly manicured, vibrant red nails. "She's in a mood."

I had seen her come in earlier, noticing her gown trimmed in ostrich feathers. It was dyed the same rich blue at the sleeves and neckline, and trailed down the deep V at the back. She was stunning. "Hello, Helen," I said.

She leaned in and gave me a peck on the cheek. She smelled of booze and jasmine, and her luminous green eyes were glassy. "Nice place you have here," she said, her eyes roaming the room and the furnishings. "It's real cozy-like," she whispered and then giggled. Clearly, she had started her party much earlier. I wondered if she'd had something more than alcohol.

"Thank you," I said.

"When Edward said we were going to a farm for the party, I didn't know what to expect. But this is real sweet." She batted her eyes at me.

Helen reminded me of a fragile bird with that voice and her way of flitting about. Her gaze traveled across the room and stopped over my right shoulder. She lifted her chin and took a deep breath through flared nostrils. I turned to see what she was looking at. It was the same man who'd bumped into Robert Smith—Mr. Johnson, Mr. Smith had said—and he was talking to Lizzy.

He was nice-looking, with Romanesque features and looked to be in his early thirties. I thought he'd make a perfect Marc Antony in a film. He leaned against one of his hands, which was resting on the wall to the left of Lizzy's head. His other hand held her wrist. He turned her wrist over and then, releasing his other hand from the wall, caressed the heart-shaped birthmark on the inner part of her forearm. I supposed it was a feature of interest, so perfectly shaped, as if it had been tattooed there. Still, my stomach tightened at watching them. She was far too young for him.

Lizzy rested her back against the wall, a flirtatious smile plastered on her face. I thought I heard her say something about the horses, and then she let out an uproarious burst of laughter. I could tell she'd had more to drink, despite our agreement. It was time to intervene and get her to bed.

But before I got there, Mr. Travis stepped up to them. He pointed to the doors, saying something to Mr. Johnson. With a scowl on his face, Mr. Johnson picked up his silver tray from the side table and went out the double doors.

"Grace, I need you in the kitchen." Rose appeared at my left shoulder. Her plump face was pinched, and she glared up at me through her round-rimmed spectacles. "Now!"

"Oh." I was surprised to see she'd ventured out of the kitchen still in her apron. "Will you excuse me?" I said to Helen, who was transfixed on Lizzy and Edward. My breath quickened. I hoped this wouldn't take too long. I wanted to get back to Lizzy.

Rose abruptly made her way to the kitchen, nearly knocking into the bemused guests as she passed. I tried not to roll my eyes with embarrassment as I carefully threaded my way through with polite excuse-me's and pardon-me's. When I reached the kitchen, I was confronted by Rose, hands on plump hips and thunder in her face. Behind her, a chef in a crisp white uniform comman-deered the gas range and another stood at the wooden table in the center of the kitchen, furiously chopping vegetables. They were silent and intent on their work.

"You said they were sent to help," Rose said through clenched teeth. "But they have completely upended my kitchen. Look at this mess! I told you I could handle this party."

"I'm sorry, Rose. As I told you before, this is Mr. Travis's party and he'd already hired caterers. Why don't you go to your rooms and relax? Read a book or something."

"While these two tear apart my kitchen?" She raised her voice, and the two men looked over at us.

I gave them a sheepish smile. "I'm sure they will put every-thing back in order." I tried to inflect a soothing quality into my voice, but the look on her face told me I hadn't succeeded.

"And I think all the kids have sampled the punch, which I *know* contains alcohol. Lizzy is making a fool of herself *and* drinking champagne. Where is that teacher of theirs?"

"Miss Meyers is taking care of Susie. I will see to the others," I promised. "If you don't want to go relax on your own, why don't you grab a plate and go join Miss Meyers and Susie?"

She narrowed her eyes at me. "But what about the kitchen?"

I sighed at the reality that I'd stepped into it again with Rose.

For the most part, we got along as long as I let her "do her job," which normally wasn't a problem. And I was deeply grateful for her, as I had no idea how to cook anything aside from scrambled eggs and toast.

"I'm sorry," I relented. "But this is Mr. Travis's party, Rose, and he's paying us to have it here. I won't interfere with his staff. Look, the guests are having a marvelous time! You should join us." I tried a different tack but knew she'd never take me up on the suggestion.

She harumphed and marched out of the kitchen through the swinging door.

I sighed and set out to find Lizzy, Daniel, and Ida.

I found Ida and Ned in the family room. Ned was talking with Doug Fairbanks and Charlie Chaplin with Ida looking on. Not wanting to interrupt the conversation, I crooked my finger at Ida, summoning her to me.

"Time to go up to bed," I said.

"Aww!" She stuck out her bottom lip. "I was having so much fun."

"I know, but it's getting late. Have you seen Lizzy or Daniel?"

She shrugged. "I haven't seen Daniel, but Lizzy went out to the barn with some guy."

My heart leaped into my throat. "Oh dear. You go on up to bed now. I'll go find her."

I passed through the living room and noticed the crowd had grown thinner. People must have started to leave, which was a bit of a relief. I opened the double doors and went out onto the back porch. Only a handful of guests were out there now.

I stepped off the porch and made my way through the back-yard to the gate that opened up to the pathway by the barn. The night was cool and damp, and I shivered as I hurried down the path, the beaded, fringed hem of my dress tickling my knees. A chill went through me. In the distance, from the stall windows that opened to the horses' runs, I could see the glow of lantern light.

A noise startled me. It was coming from the outskirts of the field that backed up to the barn. It sounded like an animal of some sort crashing around, and then I heard retching. Thinking it might be Lizzy, I followed the sound. As I got closer, the figure stood up. The person was too tall to be Lizzy and looked to be male.

"Hello?" I didn't want to get too close until I could discern who it was.

The head rose, and the flash of something metal caught in the moonlight. I stepped a little closer. It was Robert Smith drinking from a flask.

"Oh, Mr. Smith. Are you all right?"

He swayed and then stumbled. Regaining his balance, he pressed his fingers against his forehead. His breathing was raspy and came sharp and shallow, and his shoulders shook. From the strangled noise coming from his throat, I could tell he was crying. I stood there for a few more moments, hoping he might say something to me, but when he didn't, I thought it best to leave the poor man alone. I continued on my way toward the barn.

The large barn doors, usually closed at night to prevent any kind of wildlife getting in and wreaking havoc, had been pulled open just wide enough for a person to fit through. I walked inside. Two lanterns hanging from nails next to the stall doors suffused the place with an eerie glow. Several of the horses were pacing in their stalls, agitated at something.

"Hello?" I called out. "Lizzy? Are you here?"

One of the horses whinnied, and several of them snorted.

I walked down the aisle, looking in each stall. The new horse, the bay with a broad wide blaze down his face, stared at me with wide, unblinking eyes, then resumed pacing so frantically I was worried for his safety. He was lathered in sweat, obviously terribly upset by something. Perhaps a racoon or coyote had found its way in through the open door.

My eye caught a flicker of light on the floor at the end of the barn—something shimmering near the area where we stored hay. As I got closer, an object started to take form. A ladies silver shoe.

I lifted one of the lanterns off its nail and walked toward the hay room. I held up the light and gasped to see Lizzy and a man lying prone in the hay. The man was facedown, the hay around him drenched in blood. Lizzy, unconscious, lay on her back, a hand over her stomach, her other arm akimbo—and both hands covered in blood.

"Lizzy!" I set the lantern down and rushed over to her. "Lizzy!" I pressed the back of my hand to her cheek. Her skin was warm to the touch. She moaned slightly. She was alive, thank God. I tried to pull her to a sitting position, but she was dead weight. I grabbed the lantern and held it over the man. I couldn't make out who it was by his clothing or his hair. Lizzy moaned again.

"Grace?" A voice called from the aisle of the barn. "Grace, are you in here?" It was Ned.

"Over here. Hurry!"

I tapped Lizzy's cheeks, trying to rouse her. My heart was pounding in my chest, my stomach ready to heave at the smell of blood. "Oh no! Please. Come on, Lizzy!"

Ned appeared, standing over us. "What's happened? What's wrong with her? Dear god, look at all this blood!"

"Lizzy, wake up," I said, trying to keep the panic out of my voice. Her eyes fluttered, and then she started to gag. Sensing what was about to happen, I turned her on her side. She vomited all over the hay, coughing and sputtering.

I looked up at Ned. "We have to get her into the house."

"But who . . . ?" He bent down, and taking the arm of the man's jacket, Ned turned him over.

My throat went dry, and I gasped. It was Edward Travis, his eyes wide and staring. A gaping wound at his neck oozed blood onto his shirt collar, and my stomach caved in on itself at the sight.

Ned pressed his fingers to the man's wrist, feeling for a pulse. He gaze slid over to mine. "He's dead. Looks like he was stabbed in the neck."

Lizzy sat up and inspected her hands. She glanced over at the body and then back at me. A sound, like something inhuman, something animal, came out of her mouth, a scream so guttural it sent a shiver down my spine.

I held my arms out to her, and she flung herself at me, sobs racking her body so violently she couldn't hold up her own weight. She sagged in my arms. The blood on her hands had an acrid, metallic smell and was now streaked across my dress. I held her for several minutes while she wailed into my shoulder.

I met Ned's gaze. "We have to get her into the house, and we have to call the police," I said. I thought about having just seen Robert Smith out near the field. Had he done this? He didn't seem capable of such a thing, even if the men didn't like each other.

Ned gently placed his hands on Lizzy's shoulders and pulled her away from me. She crumpled into his arms.

"I don't want the guests to see us bringing her in the house like this," I said. "We'll go through my studio. Then we can get her into her room." On the upper floor of the west side of the house, my studio had a private entrance via a wooden staircase. "Lizzy," I said. "Do you think you can stand up? We need to get you into the house."

Still weeping, she gave a faint nod. Together, we lifted her to her feet, but she was like a rag doll. Ned took the initiative and swept her into his arms. We hurriedly ran out of the barn and around the bunkhouse, skirting the backyard. Finally, we reached the staircase to my studio. I led the way up the stairs to open the door for Ned.

Once in my studio, I flipped on the lights. Dress forms draped with beautiful fabrics stood sentinel as we walked past. Lizzy's foot caught one of them, and it crashed to the floor. I wasn't worried about that now, though. She could knock them all over, and I wouldn't care. We hurried through the room, and I opened the door to the hallway. Lizzy's bedroom was on the opposite end of the hall. I scurried toward it to open Lizzy's door, Ned on my heels, his breathing labored with the effort of carrying Lizzy's inert body.

Once in her room, Ned deposited her onto the bed. She immediately curled into a ball and continued to sob.

"What's going on?"

I looked in the direction of the voice to find Ida was standing in the doorway. In my haste, I'd forgotten to close Lizzy's door. I didn't want Ida to see Lizzy like this.

"Ned," I whisper-shouted.

He finally tore his gaze away from Lizzy, and I jerked my head toward the door. Seeing Ida standing there with her mouth hanging open, he quickly caught my drift.

"Take her to Miss Meyers's room please. And find Daniel. Tell them that Lizzy is unwell, and I need to be with her."

"What happened?" Ida asked as Ned ushered her out. "Why are her hands bloody?" She sounded terrified. Ned took hold of her hand and closed the door, leaving Lizzy and me alone.

I heaved a sigh. What in the world had happened out there? My mind swirled with the possibilities. Who had attacked them? Could it have been Robert Smith? He was some distance away from the barn, and he could barely walk. Had Lizzy tried to help Mr. Travis? Is that why her hands were bloody? I sat down next to her on the bed and rubbed her back while she sobbed into the quilt.

There was a soft knock at the door. It opened a crack, and

Felicity peeked her head into the room. She came in, Chet on her heels.

"Chet! Thank goodness you're back." I almost cried with relief. "This is just awful, just awful! Mr. Travis—" I pressed my hand to my mouth, tears stinging the back of my eyes.

He came over and knelt down next to the bed, and gently took me by the shoulders. "Ned told me what happened. Are you all right?" His voice was calm and steady.

"Did he take Ida to Miss Meyers? Is she okay?" I asked, worried about her state of mind.

"Yes, she's fine. I told Ned to call the police." He looked over at the state of Lizzy. "Have you been able to determine what happened?"

I shook my head. *No,* I mouthed.

Chet placed a gentle hand on Lizzy's back. She flinched and grabbed me around the waist, her body trembling.

I told Chet and Felicity what I had found in the barn. Chet let out a breath through pursed lips, shaking his head. Lizzy's sobbing stopped and was followed by deep, gulping breaths. She slowly released her grip on me.

"It's okay, Lizzy. Can you sit up? We'd like to talk with you," Chet said.

She pulled away from me and raised her eyes to mine. The look of anguish and terror in them nearly broke my heart. "You're okay, Lizzy," I said, trying to calm her. "I'm here. Chet's here."

She rose and sat cross-legged, her bloody hands listless in her lap, blood smeared all over her dress. She started sobbing again.

"Lizzy," Chet said, "can you tell us what happened?"

She shook her head.

"It's important that we know," he continued, "so we can help you."

She sat there, still unresponsive. Chet and I shared a glance.

"Lizzy, what happened to Mr. Travis?" he tried again. "Was there someone with you in the barn?"

"I don't know," she squeaked.

I turned to Chet. "I saw Robert Smith out in the field. He was really drunk—vomiting, crying, just a mess."

"Do you know if he's still here?" he asked.

I shook my head and then turned my attention to Lizzy. "Was Mr. Smith in the barn?"

She hiccupped and then tried to calm her breathing. "No. I don't think so. No, he wasn't, or oh, I don't know!"

Chet met my gaze. "When you found Mr. Travis and Lizzy in the barn, did you happen to see a weapon of any kind?"

I shook my head. "No, but I didn't think to look. I was too concerned about Lizzy."

"And you didn't see anyone else out there besides Mr. Smith?"

"No. Not until Ned was there. He must have followed me out to the barn."

Lizzy sniffed, wiping her nose with the back of her hand and smearing blood on her face in the process. She crossed her arms protectively over her chest. My eyes traveled to a bruise forming on her upper left arm. She rubbed it, wincing. There surely must have been some kind of scuffle.

"What happened to your arm?" I asked her.

"I don't know," she said with more force this time. "I— I—" She rubbed her arm again.

"Did Mr. Travis hurt you?" Chet asked.

The girl shook her head. "I don't know."

The blood from her hands was getting everywhere. "I need to get her cleaned up," I said.

Chet cleared his throat. "I'll go downstairs and wait for the police. I'm also going to ask the remaining guests to stay. I'm sure the police will want to speak with them."

My gaze traveled to the door where Felicity stood silently,

her back against it. "Could you get us some water?" I asked her. "And some washcloths?"

"Of course," she said and left the room.

Chet was about to follow her, but hesitated. "If you change her clothes, don't discard them. The police will need to see them," he explained. "And did Mr. Travis give you a guest list?"

"Yes. It's in our bedroom. I studied it earlier this afternoon."

"Good. The police will need that, too." He walked out of the room just as Felicity was coming back in with a pitcher in one hand, a basin in the other, and a couple of hand towels flung over her arm. Ned had followed her. They both stepped inside, Ned shutting the door behind them.

"Are you okay, Grace?" he asked.

Lizzy looked up at him and then at me, and then her gaze dropped to her lap again. The sobs had quieted, and she sat slumped on the bed, her limbs heavy and still.

"I'm fine, Ned. Just worried about Lizzy. How are the other kids? I never found Daniel."

"Daniel's in his room. The girls are with Rose and Miss Meyers."

"Good. How is Ida?" I really wished she hadn't seen Lizzy like this. It would be traumatizing for anyone but especially Ida. She'd been no stranger to violence. She'd been the victim of her father's abuse since he'd come home from the war, and her mother had left soon after he'd returned, leaving Ida with no one to protect her.

He gave me a reassuring nod. "She seems okay. She and Miss Meyers are playing cards. Susie is asleep."

I took in a deep breath and released it, glad that the other kids were safe and being looked after. "Thank you, Ned."

"Anything else I can do for you?" he asked.

"No, we just need a little privacy. Chet might need some help downstairs, though."

"No problem." With that, he left the room.

Felicity brought the pitcher and basin over and set them on the night table next to the bed. "He's awfully attentive."

I gave a tight smile. "He is," I agreed, not wanting to engage in the obvious. I knew he'd developed a crush on me. It seemed harmless enough, so I chose to ignore it. Ned was a handsome, caring young man. Sooner or later, some young woman would catch his eye and snap him up.

Felicity poured the water into the basin. We each took a washcloth, dipped it into the warm water, and went to work gently washing the blood away from Lizzy's hands and face. She sat listless, still staring into her lap. Felicity suddenly froze and looked over at me. She raised Lizzy's hand so that I could see it. There was a gash in her palm about two inches long. The blood had almost coagulated but was still slowly oozing.

"Can you talk to us, sugar?" Felicity quietly asked Lizzy. Her Southern charm often came through when she was trying to comfort. "What happened to your hand?"

Lizzy raised her eyes and looked at her. Felicity smiled in her endearing, warm way. It was a smile that could melt even the most hardened of hearts.

"I hurt it," Lizzy said, gazing into Felicity's deep-blue eyes.

"I can see that. How did you hurt it?"

Lizzy shook her head, her brow wrinkled in confusion. "I don't remember. Everything is fuzzy. My head hurts."

I imagined the effects of the alcohol had worn off with the shock of all that blood, leaving behind a nasty headache. Felicity looked over at me and shrugged. I could tell she didn't want to put any more pressure on Lizzy at the moment. The police would ask her plenty of questions soon. For all intents and purposes, Lizzy, being the only one with the body and covered in blood, looked guilty. My stomach clenched at the thought of them shackling this poor girl and hauling her off to jail. I tried to still my shaking hands and put my worry aside, praying it wouldn't come to that.

I dipped the cloth into the basin. The water had turned bright red, and suddenly my own head was swimming and my heart racing. The vision of a bloodied hand holding a knife high in the air and then coming down to make contact with flesh pressed in on me. I put my fingers to my temples and remembered the recurring dream that had been invading my nights lately.

"Grace?" There was alarm in Felicity's voice, and it snapped me back to the present.

Both of them were staring at me, and Lizzy's eyes were tearing up again. I couldn't let her see my distress. She needed me to be strong, to be there for her, no matter what.

"Sorry." I waved a hand. "Just a twinge of a headache. Let's get you out of those clothes and into something more comfortable," I said to Lizzy, ignoring the furious staccato of my heart.

CHAPTER SIX

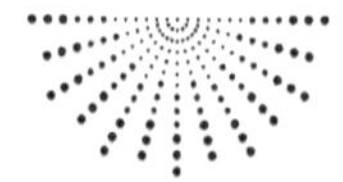

*A*fter we had gotten Lizzy into some clean clothes, she crawled back onto the bed and resumed the fetal position. She was shaking from head to toe, so Felicity grabbed another quilt from the quilt rack and wrapped her up in it. Then we both sat down in the cushioned window seat facing each other.

Felicity pulled a gold cigarette case from her dress pocket and offered me one. Wrinkling my nose, I declined. I'd tried smoking a few times—tried in earnest—but kept forgetting where I'd last put my cigarette case. I supposed I wasn't cut out for it.

We sat there in silence for a long time, the only sound in the room the crackle of Felicity's cigarette as she inhaled, the tip glowing red. I wasn't sure if we were quiet to keep from disturbing Lizzy or if we were both trying to reconcile ourselves with the horror that had happened that evening. I shuddered thinking about someone I knew, a colleague, being murdered in cold blood on my property. The place had become a refuge for me, for Chet, and for the children we were helping.

There was a soft knock at the door. I got up and opened it to find Chet. Behind him stood a portly man in an ill-fitting wool suit, holding a battered and misshapen fedora.

"This is Detective Walton," Chet whispered. "He wants to speak with Lizzy."

I opened the door. "Can I stay?"

Detective Walton made his way into the room. "We'd like to speak with Lizzy alone first."

I turned to look at Lizzy who sat up, her arms wrapped around her knees, the extra quilt discarded in a puddle around her.

Chet ushered me out the door, and Felicity followed. The detective went inside.

"Why couldn't I stay?" I asked, concerned about Lizzy's fragile state of mind.

"He doesn't want any other influences in the room. The detective has a certain way he likes to do things. We worked together on the Harper case. He's a tough customer."

"He won't be too hard on her, will he?" I imagined her crumpling under interrogation.

"I don't think so. He's just not too fond of private investigators."

"Oh no. Will your relationship with him impact Lizzy?" I asked, worry making my stomach flutter.

"It shouldn't. He's a good detective. Besides, I proved invaluable to him on the Harper case, so he got over his animosity toward me."

I breathed a sigh of relief. The last thing Lizzy needed was a personal bias against her guardian.

We headed downstairs to see the few remaining party guests standing in small groups, clustered on the sofas, or sitting in chairs that had been pulled together, quietly talking. The appearance of the police at the party infused a degree of anxiety and nervousness into the air. Cigarette smoke filled the room, and I stifled a cough. A police officer stood near the front door, guarding it, and another one stood at the double doors to the back porch.

Seeing us reach the foot of the stairs, Timothy O'Malley, another film director and a dear friend, got up from where he sat with Clara Bow and came over to us. He and Chet shook hands. He raised his chin in the direction of the stairs. "What's going on up there, lass? Why are the police here?" he asked in his thick Irish brogue.

"There's been an incident," Chet said vaguely before I could answer. More familiar with crime scenarios, he probably didn't want to give too many details to avoid causing further alarm.

Felicity pulled Timothy close and whispered in his ear.

His eyes widened in surprise. "Jesus, Mary, and Joseph."

"Keep it under your hat," Chet warned. "We don't want anyone to panic."

"And how are you, lass?" Timothy addressed me. "You look a wee bit pale."

I smiled at his concern. "I'm a little shaken, but I'm fine."

"Bit of bad luck, I'd say," he said. "I didn't care for the bloke, but I wouldn't wish this on him."

I'd heard a rumor that Timothy had met with the studio heads at Ambassador around the same time they'd started hiring the cast and crew for *The Queen of Whitehall*. According to the rumor, Timothy had been the favored contender to direct the film, but they'd decided to hire Mr. Travis. Felicity had told me Timothy had been crushed by the news.

"I could use another smoke," Felicity said with a sigh. "Need anything?" she asked me. I shook my head.

Timothy took her elbow, and they walked to the other side of the room. As they passed the sofa, my eyes were drawn to Helen Clark, who was sitting at the far end of the couch, crying into a handkerchief. Her hands shook as she dabbed at her eyes. Her husband, Charles Wilson, a tall, elegant man with a Rhett Butler–esque quality about him, stood on the other side of the room, staring at his wife with contempt in his eyes. Or was it disgust?

"What's going on?" Clara Bow stood up, stealing my attention.

"Yeah." Charles Wilson came over to us, Helen Clark behind him, still sniffling into her handkerchief. She looked positively distraught. "That policeman—" he pointed to the officer at the front door "—says we can't leave. You can't keep us here."

All eyes were on me and Chet as another officer came in the room.

"And we don't intend to," the officer said, raising a placating hand. "But please leave your name, address, and telephone number with the officer at the door, and be prepared to be contacted for questioning. And no one is to leave town until we've spoken with you, understood?"

"But what's happened?" Miss Bow said. "Was that man who went upstairs a detective? Why would a detective be here?"

Astonished murmurings filled the room.

"Please," Chet said. "You'll know in due time. Please just do as the officer says."

"Let's go, Helen." Charles Wilson took his wife by the arm. Staring daggers at him, she shook him off. He grabbed her arm again and yanked her toward the door.

"Hey!" Chet stepped up to Mr. Wilson. "Take it easy, will ya?"

"Back off, pal," Mr. Wilson warned.

Chet held his hands up in surrender. "Just give your information to the police officer and go on home." He started ushering people toward the officer taking names at the door. I breathed another sigh of relief that Chet had returned home when he had.

The officer directed his gaze at me. "Hello, Mrs. Riker. I'm Officer Clayton. Your husband told me you found the body?" His youthful countenance made me think he was far too young for the job, but he had an efficient manner about him. He was tall and broad shouldered, with reddish hair and a freckled face.

"Yes. Yes, I did." My voice hitched with emotion, and I pressed my fingers to my lips.

"Did you see anything suspicious? Anyone running away, anyone else in the barn?"

My eyes darted over to Robert Smith, who was sitting in one of the wingback chairs in the corner, his head resting in his palm, his eyes closed—passed out. "I saw him," I said, directing my gaze at Mr. Smith. "He was out in the field vomiting."

"His name?" the officer asked.

"Robert Smith."

Officer Clayton caught the attention of the other officer and motioned him over. "That man there—" he pointed to Mr. Smith "—make sure he doesn't leave before I talk to him."

The officer nodded and returned to his post at the door.

Officer Clayton turned his attention back to me. "Did the deceased have someone here with him? A girlfriend? Spouse?" he asked, his voice hushed.

I refrained from saying *both*, just tilted my head toward Florence Thomas. "That's his wife," I said. "She doesn't know what's happened."

The officer glanced at Florence. "Is there somewhere private I can speak with her?"

"Of course. Yes."

Florence, unaware that we were talking about her, stood up from her chair and was about to walk past us when I stopped her, my heart in my throat. "Florence, this is Officer Clayton. He would like to speak to you." I whispered.

"Me? Why does he want to speak to me?" she asked, not whispering back. "Where's Edward?"

"Please come with me," the officer said.

I ushered them to the sunroom on the west side of the house and turned on the lights. They cast a yellow glow in the room, darkening the floor-to-ceiling windows to an inky black. The smell of fresh greenery and dampened soil from the potted plants wafted in the air. I decided to stay with Florence for moral support, granted she didn't ask me to leave. Officer Clayton didn't seem to mind at least.

"Miss Thomas, I'm afraid your husband is dead." He didn't beat around the bush.

She blinked at him. "Excuse me?"

"It looks like murder."

I closed my eyes, the word *murder* echoing in my mind. It still didn't seem possible.

Florence faltered, her knees giving way. I slipped my arm around her waist and led her to my favorite wicker chair, plush with floral cushions. She sat down and brought her hands to her face. I glanced up at Officer Clayton, whose face was pinched with discomfort. It must be terrible to have to give people this kind of news all the time.

She lowered her hands and looked up at us. "But who . . . ?"

"He was found with a young woman in the barn." Again, the officer didn't mince words.

She closed her eyes, biting her lip. Then her eyes flashed open. "Of course he was. Who is she? Did she do it? Did she kill him?"

I cringed at the accusation. "No! Lizzy wouldn't do that." My voice came out clipped and defensive.

The officer raised his hands in the air. "Ladies, please." He turned to Florence again. "We aren't sure of anything yet, ma'am."

She stood up, wringing her hands. "Can I see him?"

"No." The officer's voice was flat. "We need to secure the scene. Ma'am, I need to ask you, is there anyone you can think of who might want to kill your husband?"

She stared at him blankly for a moment, and then her jaw clenched and her face hardened. "How much time do you have?"

I blinked in astonishment.

The officer raised his notepad and got his pencil poised and ready. "Why do you say that? Who are these people?"

A tremble started at Florence's chin and moved to her mouth. She tensed the bottom part of her face, as if trying to collect herself. "I can't name them all. Jealous husbands. Disgruntled actors. Discarded starlets. The list goes on."

"I see," he said, writing on the pad. "Is there anyone *here* who might want your husband dead?"

She harumphed. "Well, you can start with Charles Wilson, but he just left. His wife, Helen Clark, has been carrying on with my husband. And then there is Robert Smith. He despised Edward. Showed up at the mansion yesterday, demanding to see him, yelling and screaming in the yard. I'm not sure why. It was terrible."

I bit my lip. So perhaps he *had* been fired.

"Thank you." Officer Clayton wrote something on his pad. "You ladies have been most helpful. We may have more questions for you at a later time." He slipped the notepad and pencil in his breast pocket and then turned to Florence.

"Miss Thomas, my condolences. Is there someone who can take you home?"

She stared at him, almost as if she didn't hear the question.

"Miss Thomas?" he pressed.

She blinked. "Um. Yes. Yes, James can take me home."

The officer tilted his head. "James?"

"James Johnson. He works for us at the house. He's here working the party, too."

I was surprised there were yet no tears from Florence. Although, on second thought, when I'd received the news of Sophia's death, I had sat in a dry-eyed stupor for what seemed like hours. Perhaps the reality that her husband was dead— murdered—hadn't quite sunk in yet.

"I'd like to go home now," she said.

The officer glanced at me and gave me a nod. I led them both back out to the living room. Mr. Johnson was in conversation with Mr. Chaplin when we entered the room, but when he looked over and saw us, he hurried over, concern written across his face.

"What's going on, Florence? Is it Edward?" he asked.

Her face crumpled and then came the tears. She went to him, and he folded her in his arms. I blinked in surprise at the familiar manner in which they interacted.

"Take me home. Please, James," she cried.

"Florence," I touched her arm. "I'm so sorry for your loss. Please let me know if there is anything I can do to help."

She wiped her eyes and gave me a brief nod.

Officer Clayton ushered them to the door and out they went. He then approached Robert Smith and roused him from his drunken sleep. As soon as Mr. Smith started grumbling as he woke, Lenora Lange drifted over to them. I couldn't hear what they were talking about, but I assumed he was questioning Robert, who got to his feet a bit unsteadily. The officer patted him down and pulled a flask from his pocket. He then led him to the front door.

I walked over to Miss Lange, who had pulled a handkerchief from her bag and was blotting her eyes. "Miss Lange?"

She turned her luminous eyes to me and gave me a slight smile. "I'm fine, dear. Just concerned about Robert. He's very ill."

"Did the officer arrest him for something?"

She shook her head. "No, just taking him in for questioning. He also said Robert needed time to dry out. Poor man."

I gave her a moment before asking my next question. "Miss Lange, was Mr. Smith upset with Mr. Travis? Did something happen between them?" I didn't want her to know I was privy to his imminent firing.

She sniffed and placed her handkerchief back into her bag. "As you probably know, Robert was having difficulty on set—

and yes, he and Mr. Travis were at odds. But Robert would never harm him. He had too much respect for the man. I know his behavior of late did not show it, but he did so admire Mr. Travis."

No word about being fired, I mused. Perhaps Mr. Travis had wanted to wait until after the party to do the deed. Or perhaps he had fired him and Mr. Smith hadn't told Miss Lange about it and had come to the party to save face. I couldn't figure it out.

"I am sorry for his wife," Miss Lange said, her composure completely returned. "She's a terribly unhappy woman."

"Do you know Miss Thomas?" I asked.

"Yes. I met her recently." She reached into her handbag again. "The policeman said I could go."

I was about to ask if she needed someone to take her home, but before I could open my mouth, she said, "My driver is waiting for me. I'll be fine." She pulled a card from her bag and handed it to me. It had her name and telephone number printed across it. "You'll be needing this, my dear. Believe me. And she'll need you."

I was just about to ask what she meant when Detective Walton came downstairs. He had Lizzy by the elbow and escorted her to the officer at the front door.

"Wait! Lizzy!" I called out and rushed after them. Before I could reach them, the officer ushered her outside. Lizzy turned and gave me a look so pathetic and scared, I felt my heart break.

Detective Walton stepped in front of me. "She's going to be all right, ma'am. We are just taking her in for questioning."

"But I want to go with her," I said, my heart hammering in my chest. Chet came over to us and put his arm around me.

"I still need to ask you some questions," the detective said. He held his hand out, gesturing for me and Chet to go back to the living room. Chet started to steer me forward, but I didn't move my feet. They were rooted to the floor. I wanted to turn and dash out of the house and jump into the police car with Lizzy.

"I want to go with her," I told Chet.

"She'll come to no harm," Chet assured me.

My mouth had gone dry, and my hands tingled with cold. I let Chet lead me back to the living room. The detective pulled a notepad and pencil from his trench coat pocket. Chet gave my shoulders an assuring squeeze.

"You're her guardians?" the detective asked.

"Yes," I said.

"She ever been in trouble before?"

I looked up at Chet, wishing we didn't have to tell him the truth.

Chet cleared his throat before answering. "She has. Aiding and abetting a robbery. But the judge let her go, with the condition that we take care of her here until she becomes of age."

"Why you?" The detective pushed his coat open to place his hands on his hips, revealing a gun in a side holster. His belly pressed through his suspenders, protruding over his belt.

"I know the judge. He trusts me," Chet said. "We were soldiers in the war together. Grace and I have made it our mission to help wayward kids and kids in need. We're licensed by the state of California to provide foster care."

Detective Walton pursed his lips, nodding. "Admirable. Does the girl have any kin?"

"She has a sister," I said. "But they are estranged. They haven't spoken since she dropped Lizzy off here three months ago."

He nodded again. "We'll need to speak with her. And we'll need to ask you two a few more questions, but we can do that tomorrow. I'm sure you'd like to get these people out of your house. We'll need everyone to stay clear of the barn, though, as it's a crime scene."

"How long will you have Lizzy?" I asked.

"That depends. We're taking her to the Burbank station for questioning."

"But can't you do that tomorrow, too?" I implored. "She's traumatized. Let her get some rest."

He shook his head. "It's best if we take her in tonight when her memory is freshest."

I looked up at Chet, my heart squeezing with anxiety for Lizzy. I could see in his eyes he was worried, too, but he clearly wasn't going to interfere with the investigation.

He turned to the detective. "I realize the barn is a crime scene and you don't want it disturbed, but the horses will need tending to in the morning."

"I'll have my guys work through the night if we have to so we can release the scene. The coroner should be here any minute to take the body."

"Can I go to the station and wait for Lizzy?" I asked.

The detective gave me a dubious look. "I don't know how long we're going to keep her. You might as well stay here. Get some rest. We can give you a call in the morning."

"The morning!" I cried. I looked at my watch. It was nearly 1:00 a.m. It was already morning. I shook my head vehemently. I didn't care. "I want to be there when you are done questioning her."

Chet took me by the shoulders and turned me to face him. "I'll go, Grace. We're going to need to notify her sister first thing in the morning, and I think it's best if that comes from you. You go be with her. That's a conversation best had in person. And the kids might need you tonight."

"But—" I started to protest but stopped myself, taking in the wisdom of his words. What if Susie needed me? Or Ida? She'd looked so shaken when she'd seen Lizzy. I realized with aching disappointment that I couldn't be everywhere, as much as I wanted to be.

CHAPTER SEVEN

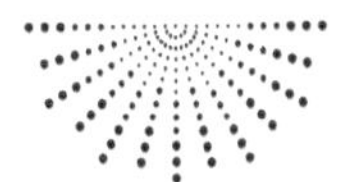

I woke early and immediately jumped out of bed and got dressed. My eyes stung from lack of sleep. I don't think I got more than three hours at the most, and those three hours were filled with more of the nightmares that were coming all too frequently. All versions of the same scene. Sometimes I was holding the knife over my head, ready to sink it into the back of a man who was attacking Sophia, and sometimes it was her holding the knife. Sometimes it was my mother holding the knife, which was the most chilling scenario of all.

My parents had been gone for twelve years. They had walked out of the house, suitcases in hand, to take what my father had claimed was a weekend trip, leaving me, twelve years old, and Sophia, thirteen years old, alone. I remember my mother crying as my father ushered her out the door. We never saw them again. We'd been told they were in a train accident.

Thinking about family, I mentally prepared myself to break the news to Lizzy's sister, Margaret. It didn't help that Chet and Lizzy had not yet returned home. How long would the police keep her? I worried about her, cold and alone in a cell, and was grateful Chet would be there when they finally released her—if they did release her. Hopefully, they wouldn't charge her for a crime she didn't commit.

I took a deep breath. I had to put my anxieties aside and get to Margaret as soon as possible. She had left us with an address in Inglewood and telephone number. I thought about calling but then thought again. As Chet had said, this was the kind of news that needed to be imparted in person, and I wanted to tell her before she found out any other way. The murder of a Hollywood director, especially one as famous as Mr. Travis, would be front-page news in no time. I simply had to drive out to Inglewood to see her toot suite. Since it was a Sunday, I assumed she'd be home. At least that is what I hoped.

I arrived at her address at around 9:00 a.m. It was a charming little pitched-roof cottage—with emphasis on the word *little*. I walked up the three steps to the covered porch and rang the bell.

Margaret answered, her hair in a headscarf. She was wearing an artist's smock speckled with paint. She was a striking woman with high cheekbones, broad forehead, and sensuous mouth. The resemblance between her and Lizzy was remarkable. I remembered thinking the same thing when I'd first laid eyes on both of them only three short months ago.

Her eyes registered surprise at seeing me there. She leaned her hand against the doorframe as if bracing herself for the worst. "Miss Michelle? Is Lizzy all right?"

I smiled at her in an attempt to hide the dread I felt at what I was about to tell her. "May I come in?"

"Of course, please," she said, her voice wavering.

She opened the door wider, and I stepped inside. The entry opened to a small living area. There were few but fine furnishings. I spied an easel in a screened porch at the back of the house. "Can I offer you some coffee?" she asked unsteadily.

"Yes. That sounds wonderful." I followed her into a tiny kitchen. It was a sunny room with white-painted cabinets, a small gas range, and a wooden icebox. Lace curtains adorned a window that looked out onto the backyard, which was well tended with rose bushes lining the fence.

She took two cups from a cupboard and set them down at the table in the middle of the room. I took a seat while she poured the coffee from a silver pot. There was sugar and cream on the table, and I stirred both into my cup, trying to find the words to say what I'd come here to say.

Margaret joined me at the table and stirred cream and sugar into her coffee, as well. "How's Lizzy? Is everything okay? She hasn't been any trouble, has she?"

"Miss Moore—"

"Margaret. Please."

"Okay. Margaret, Lizzy has been involved in an incident at the house."

She looked at me with raised eyebrows. "Oh no. She hasn't run away, has she?"

"No." I shook my head. That news would have been so much easier to deliver. "She's been taken downtown to the police station for questioning."

"Oh god. She didn't steal from you, did she? I'm so sorry. You'd think she'd learn her lesson! I told that silly girl—"

I put my hand on hers. "She was taken in for questioning regarding a murder that occurred last night at the ranch. I'm afraid she is a suspect."

Margaret blinked at me, her mouth agape. I told her how I'd found Lizzy and what had transpired afterward. Her face went white, and she placed a hand over her mouth. She slumped against the back of her chair.

After a few moments, she lowered her hand. "This man. Who was he? Why was he alone with her? If she did it, it was obviously self-defense. What did Lizzy say?"

"She claims she doesn't remember. But that's what I think, too. If she did kill him, she did it in self-defense." Although, to stab someone in the neck was extreme, especially for someone so young. That kind of killing seemed so . . . well, so expressly violent. I didn't think Lizzy capable of that kind of rage. I continued. "Either someone attacked them both or . . . The man, Edward Travis, has—well *had*—a reputation for his philandering ways."

Her eyes popped open wide, and her mouth twitched. "You mean . . . Edward Travis, the director?"

I nodded. "Yes."

She stood up from the table and went to the kitchen sink, her back to me. I got up and joined her, placing my hands on her shoulders. "I know, Margaret. It's a terrible shock. But I won't give up on Lizzy. I promise you."

She shook her head. "This can't be happening. I should never have let her go. I should have—"

"Margaret, what choice did you have? The judge mandated she come live with us or go to jail. It was out of your control."

She tilted her head back, and the next thing I knew, her knees buckled. I caught her arms and led her back to the chair. She collapsed into it, laying her head on her forearms. Her shoulders heaved with sobs, and my heart shattered into a thousand pieces. I gently stroked her hair.

She sat like that for a long time, crying into her folded arms. Poor woman. From what she'd told us, Lizzy had been difficult ever since Margaret had made the decision that the two would move to Los Angeles from Lake Tahoe.

The lingering taste of coffee on my tongue soured as I sat there helplessly watching her.

"Margaret," I said. "I promise to help Lizzy, and you, in any way that I can."

She lifted her head, wiped her eyes, and sniffed loudly. I reached into my handbag, pulled out a handkerchief, and handed it to her.

"I never should have uprooted her like that." She unfolded the handkerchief and dabbed at her cheeks with it. "It's just, the boarding house was getting so expensive to run. The woman who'd owned it previously left it to me and Lizzy in her will. I'd thought it so strange at the time. We were just boarders there, but she treated us like family. I don't think she had anyone else." She blew her nose. When she was finished, she picked up her coffee cup but didn't drink anything. She just stared into the dark-brown liquid, reliving her memories.

A sympathetic lump formed in my throat. I swallowed and did my best not to add to her discomfort by letting my own emotions get in the way.

She took a deep breath and continued. "I was able to keep painting and do my art for a while, but I needed to spend more and more time running the boarding house. It was old and needed more upkeep than I could give it. One of the boarders, who was there on an extended vacation, offered me a job here in Los Angeles—at the Art Students League. It was a wonderful opportunity, and I could continue to pursue my painting career. When I told Lizzy about it and that I needed to sell the boarding house, that's when she began to act out. Right after we moved here, she started seeing that older boy, the one who robbed that store, and now this? How could I have failed her so badly?"

I leaned in closer to her, trying to keep my tears at bay. "This isn't your fault, Margaret." Somehow, it was so much easier to say it to someone else than believe it yourself. When Sophia was murdered, I too had felt responsible. If only I had done this or said that or hadn't gotten mad at her or . . . Looking back at it now, it was so irrational. I had no control over Sophia's life. But that's what grief did.

Margaret shook her head. "But I haven't even been to see her. I haven't been there for her. She was so mad at me, I thought I would give her some space. If only I had insisted on spending time with her . . . Oh!" She wailed, lifting her hands to her face. She covered her eyes as if to block out what she'd just been told. "This is horrible. Just horrible! She didn't know . . ."

"Didn't know what?" I asked.

After a few seconds, she lowered her hands and sniffed. She righted her face, the anguish in her expression vanishing. "She didn't know any better. She was only doing what she had to, to protect herself." She wiped her tears and gave me a weak smile. "Do you think I can see her?"

"I don't know. I don't know how long they will keep her. Chet is down at the station, waiting for her."

The doorbell sounded in the other room. Margaret rose to answer it, and I followed her. She opened the door to reveal Detective Walton standing there with Officer Clayton standing behind him.

"Miss Moore? I'm Detective Walton, and this is Officer Clayton. May we come in?"

She nodded and let the officers in. When Detective Walton saw me, his face registered surprise.

"Mrs. Riker," he greeted me and removed his beat-up fedora. "I'm glad you're here."

I nodded. "Detective."

"I gather Mrs. Riker has told you about the incident involving your sister?" he asked Margaret.

"Yes," she said, closing the door. "How is Lizzy?"

"I'd like to ask you a few questions," he said, ignoring hers.

"Of course. Please, come sit down."

"Do you mind if Officer Clayton has a look around?" The detective asked.

Margaret shook her head. "No, not at all."

She showed him into the living room as the other officer wandered into a smaller room off the living room. From where it was positioned, I assumed it was supposed to be a dining room, but Margaret had two more easels set up in there. Paints, brushes, and jars of murky water graced a sideboard covered with a checkered tablecloth.

"Can I get you anything?" she asked the detective, her voice unsteady and her complexion growing pale. "Coffee?"

"No, thank you." He took off his hat and smoothed his hair. His weary eyes met mine and he gave me a brief nod. His skin had the pallor of grayness, of someone who rarely ate, or slept—and if he did eat, it was on the run, and sleep only came in short shifts.

We went into the living room as the uniformed officer made his way into the kitchen. We all sat down—Detective Walton in a low-backed burgundy armchair, and Margaret and I on her rose-and-burgundy chintz sofa. Margaret nervously fingered the handkerchief I'd given her.

The detective, still in his khaki trench coat, leaned forward, placing one elbow on his knee. "You are Lizzy's sister?"

"Yes," Margaret said, picking paint off the nail of her index finger.

"And your parents?"

She looked up at the detective then. "Both dead."

"I see. And how did they die?"

Margaret sniffed and looked up at the ceiling, as if trying to ward off more tears. "My mother died . . . giving birth to Lizzy. Lizzy was a change-of-life baby."

"I see," he said. "And how old were you?"

She covered her eyes with her hands. I scooted closer and placed an arm around her shoulder.

"Miss Moore?" the detective pressed. I shot him a look. I knew all Margaret could think about was Lizzy at the moment.

"You were how old?" he pressed.

Unable to keep silent, I spoke up. "Detective Walton, she's only just heard the news of her sister. She's in a state of shock."

The detective heaved an impatient sigh. "The sooner I can finish my investigation, the sooner we get to the truth. I need to establish background on the girl, determine her character. Now, how old were you when your mother died?"

Margaret dropped her hands to her lap. "How does this have any bearing on what's happened to Lizzy?"

"You've raised the girl, correct?" he soldiered on.

"Yes." Her eyes welled with tears, and she blinked them rapidly, taking in a deep breath.

"She's been in trouble with the law before, correct?"

"Yes, but—" She shook her head, and a tear escaped down her cheek.

Detective Walton pressed on, his expression hard. "She took up with an older boy, a young man, a criminal. Is that correct?"

"Yes, but I—"

"They robbed a grocery and severely injured the owner of the store—almost killed him and then left him for dead. Is that correct, Miss Moore?"

"No! Not Lizzy. She was driving the car. That's all! She didn't touch that man."

The detective appraised her with softened eyes. "But she has a history of violence, does she not?" he asked quietly.

Margaret squeezed her eyes shut. Her shoulders trembled beneath my arm, and I pulled her closer to me.

"Detective, is this really necessary?" I asked, the thudding of my heart pounding in my ears. I, of course, knew about Lizzy driving the getaway car, but I had no idea they'd left a man for dead.

I shuddered, memories of my own troubled youth flooding in. It was as if, all of a sudden, I was reliving it—reliving the time when Sophia and I were in living on the streets of New York. The images pushed their way into my mind. The alleyway and the man standing over her, shouting at her, beating her, and then I—

"According to her file," Detective Walton said, snapping me out of my waking nightmare. I took a sharp breath. I needed to stay focused, in the present. I blinked the images away. "Lizzy was responsible for injuring a Mrs. Hillson, the owner of the boarding house you used to live in, the same boarding house she left you in her will. Is that correct, Miss Moore?"

Margaret's whole body tensed. "It was an accident!"

"In a fit of rage, Lizzy pushed her down the stairs. Is that correct?"

I somehow managed to hold back my gasp. I had not known of this, but I couldn't reconcile Lizzy doing something so horrible. Yes, she was troubled and moody, but I had seen no violence in her.

"She tripped!" Margaret shrieked, her body shaking from head to toe. She was now beyond upset. I knew Detective Walton had a job to do, but I didn't see the need to interrogate Margaret like this. My god, how had he treated Lizzy, then? My heart broke for her once more.

I shot to my feet. "I think you need to leave, Detective."

He pressed his lips together, looking up at me like a recalcitrant child defying his teacher. Slowly, he stood up, still staring down at Margaret who was now sobbing in earnest.

"I beg your pardon," he said to her and then gave me a sideways glance.

"What about Lizzy?" I asked.

He secured the stained fedora on his head. "We're holding her for the time being, until we have more information. I sent your husband home. He was dead on his feet."

My heart leaped to my throat, and Margaret's shoulders tensed under my arm. "But can we go see her?" I asked. "Have you charged her?"

Detective Walton raised his hands. "We haven't charged her. She is still being questioned, so I can't let you see her. We will give you a call later today. Your husband gave me your number. Officer Clayton!" He hollered for the other officer who had disappeared somewhere in the house, or perhaps he'd gone outside? Suddenly, he appeared in the living room, an expectant look on his face.

"Let's go," the detective said to him. The officer obediently went to the door.

Before Detective Walton stepped outside, he turned and said over his shoulder, "We'll be in touch."

I sat down next to Margaret as she wept into the handkerchief, my stomach feeling as if it was going to heave.

CHAPTER EIGHT

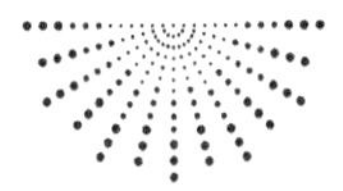

Not wanting her to be alone, I had offered to take Margaret back to the ranch with me to wait for the news about Lizzy. She claimed she would be more anxious away from the comfort of her home. I then offered to stay, but she insisted she would prefer to be alone and that I go home to the other kids. The detective had taken down her number, and we agreed we would call each other as soon as either one of us had news.

As I drove home, a headache started at the back of my neck. Must have been from lack of sleep. Suddenly, it dawned on me that Lenora Lange had visited my dreams last night. She was trying to show me something in that dreaded alleyway where Sophia and I had barely escaped with our lives. She was only there for a second, then morphed into my mother, and then vanished into the air like a wisp of a cloud. I blinked the memory away and focused on the road.

I arrived back at the ranch just as Rose was serving lunch. Only Susie and Miss Meyers were there. She was a slip of a woman with long features—long nose, long neck, long arms and legs. Not attractive in the conventional way, she had a kindness in her eyes that gave one instant comfort. I liked her from the moment I'd met her.

"Miss Grace, why can't I go to the barn to see the horses?" Susie asked as I walked into the kitchen. "Mr. Chet needs me to help him feed the oats." She held a forkful of chicken pot pie in front of her face. From her cheery demeanor, I gathered she'd not been privy to last night's horror, and I was glad of it. She didn't need any more trauma in her life. Although, we were going to have to tell her something. I just needed a little time to figure out how.

I met Miss Meyers's gaze, and I could instantly tell she knew what had happened. When Ned had taken Ida downstairs to Miss Meyers's rooms, Ida had probably mentioned something about Lizzy's bloody hands. I assumed Ned told Miss Meyers, either last night or this morning, what we'd found in the barn.

I turned my gaze to Susie. "There is some work being done in the barn today, and we mustn't get in the way," I said, stalling, trying to come up with some kind of excuse for why she hadn't been able to do her favorite daily chore. Susie had a great need for ritual. She liked to do things in a methodical, sequential way.

She had come to us from an appalling "privately run" orphanage up north. The owner of the place, a Mrs. Barstow, had been an alcoholic and the children barely had been tended to. Chaos reigned in the place. When Mrs. Barstow had died from the drink, the children were dispersed throughout California. Susie had ended up at an orphanage run by the Catholic nuns at the Notre Dame Institute in Santa Clara but had not been thriving. Sister Antoinette, whom I'd met at an orphanage in New Mexico, had been transferred to the Institute. She and I had kept up correspondence since my visit to New Mexico, and she knew about our ranch. She was the one who had sent Susie to us.

I smiled at her. "I saw the horses in the pasture. Ned must have put them there. Maybe you can help him with the grain this evening."

"But the horses count on it in the morning," she said, her eyebrows pressed together. Susie was small for ten years old. Probably due to malnourishment, according to the doctor. She reminded me of a little pixie with her round, freckled face and poker straight hair cut in a banged bob.

"I know. But I don't think they minded getting out into the pasture early. There was still dew on the grass, and they like that."

"You can help me print the lessons on the chalkboard for tomorrow," Miss Meyers said, patting her hand.

Susie grinned at Miss Meyers, satisfied with the turn of events, and recommenced eating her serving of pot pie. Ida came into the kitchen, bleary-eyed and yawning. Obviously, she'd just woken up. She probably had not slept well so I assumed Rose had let her sleep in.

Ida went directly to the coffeepot and poured herself a cup. Not much of an early riser anyway, Ida rarely spoke until she'd had a cup of Joe. I thought fourteen years old was a little young for drinking coffee, but according to her, she'd been partaking of it since she was ten. She joined Susie and Miss Meyers at the table, and I did the same.

Rose brought over another freshly baked chicken pot pie, just as Chet came into the kitchen through the side porch door. He looked exhausted. Our eyes met. I was dying to talk to him about Lizzy but knew I needed to wait until the children were out of earshot.

"Did you just get home?" I asked. "You must be starving."

He shook his head and placed his hat on the counter, the expression around his eyes tight. "No. Got home a bit ago, but I've been in the barn, had to get some things done out there."

"Did the horses get their oats this morning?" Susie asked.

He gave her a smile. "Ned took care of them, Susie. But they will be anxious to see you this evening."

"Well, wash up and I'll get you a plate," Rose told Chet.

They were the first words she'd spoken since I'd returned from Margaret's.

As Chet went over to the sink, Daniel came into the kitchen via the living room, hands in his pockets and head hanging low. I remembered Rose saying *all* the kids, except Susie of course, had been drinking last night. I wondered if Daniel had a hangover. I thought about chiding him, but he was almost seventeen —nearly a man—and the subject was moot now. Besides, I usually left any disciplining of him to Chet.

The boy walked to the cupboard, got a glass, poured himself some lemonade, and then proceeded to leave—without lunch. Such a thing was unheard of, as he was a human food bin.

"Daniel, stick around," Chet said from the sink. "We need to have a meeting."

I glanced at Miss Meyers, and taking my cue, she tapped Susie on the shoulder. "Okay, my girl. Ready to help me in the classroom?"

Susie put down her fork, swiped the napkin across her face, and then bounced out of the kitchen. I smiled at Miss Meyers. "I'll fill you in later," I said. With a tight-lipped smile, she left the kitchen, too.

"This about what happened to Lizzy?" Ida asked, getting up to pour herself more coffee.

Chet nodded. "Yes."

Daniel walked over to the kitchen window, lemonade glass in hand. He'd listened to Chet and stayed, but he seemed a million miles away.

"I don't know how much you've gathered," Chet started, "but last night, Lizzy had some kind of altercation in the barn. She was found unconscious in the hay room. Lying next to her was Mr. Edward Travis. He was dead."

"Oh my god." Ida's eyes filled with tears. She rested her forehead on her palm. I reached across the table and laid a hand on her shoulder.

Rose came over and gave Chet a plate. "Daniel?" She tilted her head toward the pot pie on the table. "Are you going to eat?"

"No," he said, still staring out the window.

"Grace?" she asked.

I shook my head, the pain in it reverberating like an echo. "Not now. Maybe later."

Her mouth turned down in a frown. "You all need to eat. You won't be much help to anyone on an empty stomach." Rose always felt that food was the answer to everything. From what Chet had told me, she'd been raised in poverty and couldn't abide anyone turning down a good meal. Still, I didn't think I could make the food go down, as good as it smelled.

Chet cleared his throat. "Detective Walton's men have been in the barn all morning. They are just finishing up. The detective has just arrived and is coming in to speak with us. He has some questions."

"Did Lizzy kill him?" Ida asked in a small voice.

"We don't know what happened," I said in what I hoped was a soothing tone.

"Is she okay? Where is she?" The note of concern in her voice was heartwarming given Lizzy and Ida were not the best of friends. I didn't entirely know what the problem between them was, but I think it had something to do with Daniel.

"She's at the police station," I said.

There was a knock at the kitchen door. Rose opened it, and Detective Walton stepped through. He took off his hat and smoothed his thinning gray hair. "Afternoon," he said.

"Detective," Chet said as they shook hands.

"Would you like some lemonade?" I got up to pour myself some, and when he heartily agreed, I got him a glass, too. We all sat down at the table, and Chet introduced him to the kids and Rose.

"Daniel," the detective said. "Mind if I start with you?"

Daniel shrugged and crossed his arms. He seemed melancholy, despondent.

"Did you attend the party?" the detective asked.

Daniel looked him in the eye. "Yeah. Only long enough to talk to some folks and get some food. Then I went up to my room."

The detective paused, taking a sip of his lemonade. "Did you see Lizzy during that time?"

Daniel gave a snort and then scowled. "Yeah. Chatting up every guy in the room."

"Did you see her talking with Mr. Travis?"

Daniel looked away from him. "I wouldn't know who that is."

"You were up in your room the rest of the night? Until yesterday morning?"

He turned back to the detective. "That's what I said." He raised his lip in defiance.

Startled at his disdain for Detective Walton, I bit back a rebuke and took a sip of my lemonade. An explosion of tartness pinched the back of my throat.

"Hey," Chet piped in, "show some respect."

"You're sure?" Detective Walton seemed nonplussed by Daniel's surly behavior. I'm sure he'd seen much worse, but Daniel's attitude made me want to squirm in my chair.

Daniel sighed. "Well, I went out on the staircase off Grace's studio to have a smoke for about five minutes."

Detective Walton jotted something down in his notepad. "What time was this?"

Daniel shrugged again. "Ten?"

"Anyone with you?"

"No."

The detective turned to me. "Your studio is where?"

I pointed westward. "The other end of the house, upstairs."

"So you wouldn't be able to see the barn from there," he stated.

"No," I answered.

He turned back to Daniel. "So you went out on the stairs for a smoke. Did you see anything unusual?"

Daniel sniffed. "No."

The detective then turned to Ida. "What about you, sweetheart? Were you at the party?"

She nodded, sitting up tall, her eyes as big as saucers. "Just for a little while. I wanted to see the movie stars." I couldn't help but smile at her eagerness to answer his questions. She really wanted to cooperate.

"And did you see any?" he asked indulgently.

"I got to talk to Mr. Chaplin. You know, Charlie Chaplin?"

The detective nodded. "Yeah, I've heard of him. Were you alone with Mr. Chaplin ?"

"No. Ned was with me. But, then Grace came to get me."

"Where'd you go?"

She cocked her head, and her eyes drifted to the ceiling, as if trying to recall. "To my room. I heard a loud crash and went to the hall to see what was happening. Grace and Ned were taking Lizzy to her room. I followed them and saw that her hands were all bloody."

I winced at the memory.

"Then what did you do?" the detective asked.

She frowned. "I was kind of upset so Ned took me down to Miss Meyers's. I stayed with her and Mrs. R for a while, and then I went to bed."

The detective nodded. "All right. Thank you."

"Can we go now?" Daniel asked.

"We're done for now," the detective said.

Ida and Daniel quickly got up and left the kitchen. Detective Walton turned his attention to Rose, asking her about what she had seen last night. She claimed she was in the kitchen most of the night, except to come out to refill the food table. She mentioned she'd seen Ida, Daniel, and Lizzy all partaking of the punch and champagne. She'd been especially concerned about Lizzy who, as Daniel had said, was talking to many of the male guests. When she mentioned that bit of information, she shot me a look. My stomach curdled at my utter failure to protect Lizzy.

After a few more questions directed to the three of us, the detective stood. "Well, I'll need one of you to come to the station with me."

"You're releasing her?" I asked, hopeful.

"Yes, into your custody. We don't have enough evidence to hold her, and we haven't been able to find a murder weapon. Just some broken glass, the shards of which aren't big enough to cause the kind of damage Mr. Travis suffered to his neck. My guess is that Travis was killed with a knife or another sharp object. We'll find out for sure from the coroner. Lizzy does have a cut on her hand that she claims she doesn't know how she got, and I am assuming that was from the broken glass. Could be she fell on it."

"That glass had to come from somewhere, Detective. We certainly would not have broken glass in the horses' feed," Chet said.

"True that. She's still our prime suspect, and I'm trusting you will keep an eye on her." He uttered the last sentence while looking at Chet.

"You have our word," he said.

AFTER CHET LEFT to go pick up Lizzy, I called Margaret. She wanted to come over so that she could be there when Lizzy arrived.

She showed up twenty minutes after we'd hung up. She was neatly dressed in a pair of cuffed palazzo pants, a sleeveless shawl collar top, and a summer tam o' shanter reined in her mass of chocolate tresses. Her eyes were puffy and red, her normally dewy, porcelain complexion splotched. My heart went out to her. I knew what it was like to be worried for a sister, especially when she was the only family you had.

"Please come in," I said as I took hold of her elbow and guided her into the house. The afternoon was warm, and her skin was hot to the touch. "Can I offer you some lemonade?"

She shook her head. "No. Not right now." Her voice had a tremor in it.

"Let's go into the living room where it's cool," I said.

She followed me through the entryway into the living room. She took a seat on the sofa, and I sat on the love seat adjacent to it.

"How are you doing?" I asked.

She gave me a weak smile. "Not very well. I'm so worried about Lizzy's state of mind. She's been through so much."

"I know. But she is being released so that is good news."

Margaret nodded. "She wouldn't kill anyone. She's not capable of it. The reason she acts out is because she really is just so sensitive and she keeps everything bottled up. I know in my heart of hearts she did not kill that man."

I took a deep breath. "If it was Lizzy, I'm sure it was self-defense. If he was trying to—"

"No!" She nearly shouted the word.

I blinked in surprise, and I decided not to offer anymore opinions. The woman was clearly distraught.

I heard the front door open, and Margaret shot to her feet. She waited until Chet and Lizzy entered the room, and then she rushed to the girl and threw her arms around her. Lizzy's arms remained at her sides.

"Oh, my darling," Margaret said, releasing her. She placed both her hands on Lizzy's cheeks. "Are you all right? I've been so worried about you."

Lizzy did not make eye contact with her. Instead, her gaze traveled to me.

"Come sit down, Lizzy." I hoped to break the tension. "I'll get you some lemonade. Are you hungry?"

She shook her head. Margaret took Lizzy's hand and led her to the sofa. They both sat down, Margaret clinging to the girl's hands.

With a tilt of my head, I motioned for Chet to come with me to the kitchen, to leave the sisters alone.

"Lizzy didn't look too happy to see her sister," Chet whispered once we were out of earshot.

"Poor thing." My heart ached at the thought of Lizzy being interrogated and spending all night in that cold jail cell. "She's probably traumatized. Did she say anything on the ride home?"

"Not a word. Just stared out the window."

"Oh dear." I bit my lip. We'd have to be careful how we handled her. I wasn't sure if we needed to give her space or if she could use the comfort of company. We'd just have to be as sensitive to her emotional state as we could.

I pulled the pitcher of lemonade out of the icebox. "Do you want a glass?" I asked Chet.

"Sure. But I need to get back out to the barn soon. The police are all done out there. Joe is coming over to exercise the new horse."

I handed him a glass of lemonade. He kissed me on the cheek and then went out the kitchen door to the barn.

I poured two more glasses, one for Lizzy and one for Margaret. She'd said no before, but just in case. If she didn't want it, I'd drink it.

As I was about to push open the swinging door separating the kitchen and the living room, Lizzy shouted, "Stop with the third degree! I'm sick of answering questions."

I stepped into the room. Lizzy's face was contorted in anger, and the tension between the two of them was thick and electric.

Margaret flinched. "I just want to know what he said to you, Lizzy."

Lizzy stood up and crossed her arms over her chest. "He didn't say anything out of the ordinary, okay? We were talking about the horses, and he wanted to go see them."

Margaret stood up, too. "Are you sure he didn't say anything more? Anything of a personal nature?" Her voice had softened.

"I don't know!" Lizzy shouted, slapping her hands against her thighs.

It was time to create a diversion. Holding the two glasses of lemonade, I walked briskly toward the sisters and tried to make my voice sound upbeat. "Here we are. Margaret, I poured you a glass. Did you change your mind?"

"Yes. Thank you." She accepted the lemonade with a shaking hand. Her brow was furrowed, and there was a tightness in the muscles around her eyes.

I held out a glass for Lizzy, but she just scowled at me. Her face was flushed, and her eyes hard with anger. "I'm going to my room. I just want to be left alone."

"Lizzy—" Margaret reached out to her, but Lizzy ignored her and walked to the staircase. She clomped all the way up to the second-floor landing, and a few seconds later, she slammed her bedroom door.

Margaret sighed, her face crestfallen.

"She just needs a little time," I offered. I did wonder why Lizzy was still so mad at Margaret. I would have thought that after what Lizzy had been through, she'd feel comforted by seeing her sister, but she seemed angrier than ever.

"I don't know what to do with her." Margaret's eyes sought mine. She sipped her lemonade. "I never imagined Lizzy would ever meet someone like Edward Travis. Why was he even here?"

Oh gosh. She had no idea.

"We both work for Ambassador Films," I explained. "I'm a

costume designer. We are—*were*—working on a film together. He asked if he could have a party here at the farm."

"I see," she said, biting her lip. "Did you see them talking? At the party?"

I took in a deep breath, feeling extremely guilty at not having taken better care of my charge. "Yes, I did."

"How did he seem with her?"

I thought it a strange question. "Do you mean, was he acting inappropriate with her?"

"Um, yes."

"I didn't see anything inappropriate going on aside from . . ."

She furrowed her brow. "Aside from what?"

"Well, there was another man who was talking with Lizzy, and Mr. Travis intervened in their conversation. I almost got the sense he was being protective of her. And if that were the case, why would Lizzy harm him?"

"Right." Margaret chewed on a hangnail.

Guilt pressed in on my chest, making it cave in on itself. "I'm sorry I didn't keep a closer eye on her."

A tear streamed down her cheek. "Lizzy is a willful child. Always was. If I had been more . . . I don't know. It's my fault she's here, that she got into trouble."

"How can you say that?" Although I didn't believe her statement, I could relate to it. I, too, felt at fault for Lizzy's current predicament. She didn't answer, only shook her head, blinking back more tears. I sighed and reached for her hand. "You can't look back. The best way to help Lizzy is to move forward. Be there for her. Even if she doesn't seem to want your support, she does. You are her family. She'll come around."

Margaret sniffed and wiped at her cheek. "You are right, of course. I'll stand by Lizzy no matter what."

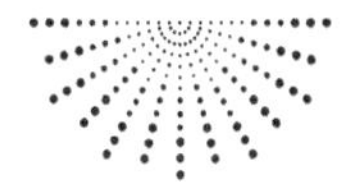

CHAPTER NINE

The following morning I didn't wake until 9:00 a.m. It was unheard of for me, and bound to mess up my entire day, as it always did on the rare occasion I overslept. I'd had trouble falling asleep, and staring at the clock at 3:30 a.m., I had finally dozed off to its ticking and the sound of Chet's soft snoring.

I had woken with a start, my heart and head pounding. With a shaking hand, I reached over to the glass of water on the night-stand and drained it. I then made my way to the medicine cabinet to take some aspirin. After washing it down and splashing cold water on my face, I closed the mirrored cabinet door, and my heart stopped. I was staring straight on into a face that was not my own. It was Sophia's. Her mouth was moving, but I couldn't hear what she was saying.

What is happening? This can't be real. Am I still asleep?

I closed my eyes, shutting out the image. The rush of blood pulsating through my ears was like a deafening roar, and my head spun. When I opened my eyes, there I was. I looked like hell. The curls of my blond hair, recently cut into a bob, stuck out at all angles. Dark-purple moons hung below my eyes, and my skin, typically my finest feature, looked sallow. Still shaking, I rested my weight on my hands as I pressed my palms against the edges of the sink until I could collect myself.

I took in a deep breath and then splashed more cold water on my face. I reached for a towel and pressed it against my eyes. *Am I going crazy?*

I firmly decided no and chocked it up to a lack of sleep. I couldn't remember the last time I'd slept through the night or even for more than two or three hours at a stretch before being awakened by disturbing dreams. I rubbed the sleep from my eyes.

Downstairs, the phone rang, and I pulled on my dressing gown—or rather, Sophia's dressing gown. I had worn it every morning since the day she'd died four years earlier. It was growing threadbare, but I didn't mind. It always brought me a sense of comfort.

Desperate for some coffee, I made my way to the bedroom door and opened it to find Ida standing there, her hand poised to knock. "Oh! Good morning," she said. "Telephone for you."

"Morning. Thank you, Ida."

I followed her downstairs and went to the hallway to the telephone niche where the receiver was lying on its side. "Hello, this is Grace Michelle."

It was Mr. Comb's secretary informing me the studio heads were calling a meeting, and I needed to be there by 11:15 a.m. I agreed and hung up the phone.

"Morning!" I greeted the children cheerily when I walked in the kitchen, hoping to lift the tension. I wondered if Lizzy had done her early-morning chores. She looked as if she'd just gotten out of bed, too. I wasn't about to chastise her if that were the case, but it would be best for her to get back to her regular routine as soon as possible.

They all murmured hello. Daniel got up from the table with his empty plate and took it to the sink. He poured himself more coffee and sipped it while standing there. His eyes were fastened to Lizzy, who sat staring at her plate of untouched food.

I caught Miss Meyers's eye, and she tilted her head toward the morning paper sitting on the counter. I went over and picked it up to read the headline, HOLLYWOOD DIRECTOR FOUND DEAD AT BURBANK RANCH, FOUL PLAY SUSPECTED.

Oh no. I read on. I was relieved to see that although the story mentioned there was also a young girl at the scene, Lizzy's name had been omitted.

"What's everyone so sad about?" Susie asked. "No one has talked since we came in from chores."

Apparently no one had filled her in thus far. I didn't know if that was a blessing or not.

"Let's get ready for school," Miss Meyers said, probably in an attempt to bypass her question.

Ida leaned toward Susie, her eyes on Lizzy, who scowled at her. Apparently, the two had resumed their difficult relationship. "A man was killed in the barn on Saturday night, and the police think Lizzy did it," Ida whispered loudly.

"Ida!" I folded the paper as if to shield Susie from the news, which was idealistic, I realized. Kids would talk.

Susie's face blanched, and her gaze searched the group, landing on Lizzy.

"You shut up!" Lizzy yelled at Ida.

Ida's brows pressed together, and she lifted her chin in defiance. "I didn't say you did it. I said the police *think* you did it. Why else would they have taken you to jail?"

Lizzy narrowed her eyes at Ida. "I *didn't* do it!"

"Okay, you two," I intervened. "We aren't sure what happened, and neither are the police. So until we know, I don't want any of you talking about it to anyone outside this house, understood? I don't believe Lizzy did this horrible thing, and I am going to support her through this. I expect you all to do the same."

"I believe you, Lizzy, " Daniel said. They were the first words he'd spoken since Detective Walton had been here. While he wasn't the talkative sort, he'd been even quieter than usual. I knew he was concerned about Lizzy.

Miss Meyers stood up and took her plate and coffee cup to the sink. Ida did the same. Lizzy sat holding her head in her hands, her palms pressing into her eye sockets. Susie got up from the table and wrapped her arms around Lizzy's shoulders. She hugged her for a moment and then took Miss Meyers's hand, and she and the others left for the schoolroom.

I sat down next to Lizzy. "I'm sorry you're going through this, Lizzy. I'm here to help. Really."

She put down her hands, leaving red splotches around her eyes. She sniffed loudly. "I didn't do it, Grace."

I rubbed her back. "Can you remember anything, anything at all, leading up to when I found you in the barn?"

She sighed and swiped at her tear-filled eyes. "I was standing in the living room by the double doors to the back porch talking to that Mr. Johnson. At first I thought he was rude, you know, how he bumped into Mr. Smith, but he was actually pretty nice. He gave me some champagne. I didn't really want to drink it, but I thought I would look—"

"What, Lizzy?"

"Foolish. Like a child." Her eyes flicked up at me, and then her gaze dropped to the table. "I know that sounds stupid."

"It's not stupid." I understood how she had felt. Sixteen was such a confusing age. She wasn't quite a woman, yet she wasn't a child, either—just a girl trying to find how she fit into the world.

She looked over at me and continued. "It was such a lovely party, and there were so many movie stars there, I wanted to fit in, so I drank the champagne. I'm sorry—I know you told me not to . . . I guess I was a little too giggly, so Mr. Johnson brought me a glass of water. There were so many people around—someone bumped into me, and I remember my arm hurting, almost like I'd been stung by a bee. The door to the back porch was open so maybe I *was* stung by a bee. I can't remember."

I recalled the bruise on her upper arm. I had assumed she'd gotten it from a tussle in the barn, but at her mentioning it felt like a beesting got me thinking. Perhaps she had been drugged. It would explain why I'd had so much trouble rousing her. But who would drug her? And why?

"Anyway, then Mr. Travis came over and told Mr. Johnson to stop socializing and get back to work. Said he wasn't paying him to stand around or something like that. They argued, and Mr. Johnson—James, I think that was his name—he left." Lizzy paused for a beat, clearly trying to remember what happened next. "Then Helen Clark came over and said she wanted to talk to Mr. Travis alone. She handed me her drink, and they went outside."

Come to think of it, it was strange that Mr. Johnson had been fraternizing with the guests. None of the other staff had been.

"After a few minutes, Mr. Travis came back and started talking to me again. He asked me what kinds of things I liked to do here at the farm," Lizzy went on. "I told him I liked the horses. He asked to see them so we went out to the barn. I wasn't feeling very well after all that champagne, and I thought the fresh air would make me feel better, but I just kept feeling more and more sick to my stomach. Everything is blurry after that. The next thing I remember is you and that other lady cleaning me up." She looked down at her palm, which was still bandaged. "I don't know how this happened."

If Lizzy couldn't remember anything after going into the barn, and I'd found her unconscious, how could she have stabbed someone? And with what? There had been no murder weapon found. Detective Walton had said something about a knife, but why would Lizzy be carrying a knife? Someone else had to have been in that barn with them and then took the murder weapon with them after killing Mr. Travis. But who?

"We will get to the bottom of this, Lizzy. I promise." I gently squeezed her forearm.

She nodded and wiped her eyes again.

"I have to go to the studio this morning for a meeting. How about after school you ride Goldie for me? She could use the exercise."

She turned to me with wide eyes. "Really? You'd let me ride her?"

I smiled, glad to see her excited about something. "I trust you. And maybe this evening, if you are up to it, you can help me with some drawings for the Sophia daywear line."

"Gosh, that would be swell."

"Okay. Off you go now," I said, feeling like I may have lifted her mood, even if just a little.

I ARRIVED at the studio at 11:00 a.m., about fifteen minutes before the meeting.

Once in the wardrobe room, I laid my handbag on the table and set to work organizing things in there. I collected my sketch pads, pencils, my favorite pincushion, and a couple of other items to take into my office, but I couldn't find my tape measure. It had been a gift from Lady Duff Gordon, and I was never without it at work. It was housed in a beautiful, etched, sterling-silver case. What had I done with it?

Worried about the time, I looked at my watch. The meeting would be starting any second. I'd have to come back to look for it later.

I walked into the conference room to find that I was the last to arrive. I looked at my watch again and then at the clock on the wall. My heart sank when I realized my watch was five minutes slow. Why hadn't I checked it? It was probably on account of all the commotion at the house.

"I am so sorry," I said, my cheeks burning with embarrassment.

"It's all right, Grace. We were just getting started. I was late myself," Mr. Steinberg said. He was an arresting figure, with jet-black hair and dark, deep-set eyes. He had the air of a great intellectual, but an intellectual who rarely smiled.

I scanned the people seated around the table. Mr. and Mrs. Steinberg and Mr. Combs, of course, then Helen Clark and her husband—though I couldn't fathom why he was there—and an actress named Milly Tankersley, who was in a supporting role. Bill Havers and Mark Clemmons, two actors I'd seen around the set, were there, as well as Nathan Brand, a screenwriter. To my surprise, Timothy O'Malley and Felicity sat at the far end of the table. Felicity crooked her finger at me. She'd apparently saved me a seat next to hers.

I sat down and raised my eyebrows at her, wondering what in the world she was doing there. She gave me a "you'll see" look and sipped her coffee.

"Well let's get started, then," Mr. Combs said and lit a cigarette. A small man with boyish, athletic good looks, he effused charm. His secretary sat in the corner with her notepad and a pencil in hand. "The death of Edward Travis is a loss to all of us," Mr. Combs continued, his brow set with a gravity appropriate for the situation.

I scanned the room, looking to see the expressions on other people's faces. Helen Clark sniffed loudly and reached into her handbag for a handkerchief. Her husband heaved a disgusted sigh, rolling his eyes. Mr. and Mrs. Steinberg looked fittingly doleful, while Bill Havers bit at a fingernail, nonplussed. Mark Clemmons and Milly Tankersley were whispering to each other, and Nathan Brand, who was notoriously broody, looked as he always did—broody.

"I want you to know that we are cooperating with the police in every way we can to help with the case," Mr. Combs said. "We've also decided the best way to deal with this tragic reality is to push forward with *The Queen of Whitehall*. We've invested a lot of time and money on this film, and as you may or may not know, Mr. Travis and Mr. Brand here co-wrote the screenplay. This film meant a lot to Mr. Travis, and we'd like to honor his memory by making it the finest film we can make. As they say, the show must go on."

I blinked. There hadn't even been a funeral yet, and the studio was going to go ahead with production of the film? I was certainly no stranger to show business, having been raised in the theater in New York, and I knew that it could be a shallow and often callous industry, but I was continually surprised by the lack of sensitivity that was often shown to the very people who made these works of art possible.

Mr. Steinberg spoke next. "Please join us in welcoming Timothy O'Malley as the replacement for Edward Travis. I know you all know one another, but I don't believe you've all worked together before. Bill Havers will be replacing Robert Smith as the lead, and Mark Clemmons has been brought on in a supporting role.

So they *had* fired Robert Smith. I wondered if it had been before or after the party. We all had seen it coming, but I had hoped he would get himself together and that they would give him another chance. I was happy for Timothy in that he would at last get a chance at this film, though I certainly didn't like the reason why.

Mr. Steinberg continued. "Florence is absent today for obvious reasons, but she has expressed a wish to continue on in the role of Dorothea. We have decided to shoot her scenes at a later date. She didn't want to delay the schedule, but we felt that given the circumstances, it would be better for everyone if she gave it some time."

"As for Miss Felicity Jones, here—" Mr. Combs gestured toward her "—she is a talented designer, and Mr. O'Malley has asked that she come aboard to offer some consulting advice on the set. Dick Perkins, our original set designer, did a marvelous job, but he took another assignment at United Artists at the news of Edward's death. The sets are complete but may need some adjustments depending on Mr. O'Malley's vision for the film. He and Miss Jones have had a long working relationship and make a great team. So, welcome."

We all offered a quiet round of applause.

"All right," Mr. Steinberg said. "Are there any questions?"

Helen Clark raised her hand. I hadn't really looked at her in earnest until then and was surprised at her appearance. Usually bubbling over with effusive charm and sensuality, she seemed withdrawn. She was wearing a lot of makeup, too, which I thought strange because her skin was like fine porcelain. On closer scrutiny, there was a faint dark spot on her right cheekbone. Could it be a bruise?

"Yes, Helen?" Mrs. Steinberg asked. It was the first she'd spoken during the meeting. She often let the men do the talking while she worked her magic behind the scenes.

"Has anyone heard when there will be a funeral?"

"We've not heard from Florence in that regard," said Mr. Combs. "But once we do, we will make sure to give people time off to attend, don't you worry. So go home, rest tonight, and be ready to get back to work tomorrow."

Charles Wilson, Helen's husband, cleared his throat. "Just keep your focus on the film, darling." He reached over and laid a hand on hers. She quickly slipped it out from under his touch and set it in her lap. Again, I wondered why he was here. I'd seen him on set from time to time but to have him here at the meeting was strange.

Since there were no further questions, Mr. Steinberg ended the meeting. Everyone got up and left, except me, Mrs. Steinberg, and Felicity. Mrs. Steinberg approached me. She was an attractive woman, though I would not call her pretty. She had an air of importance that made people take notice of her. Today she wore a lavender-and-white cuffed long-sleeved dress with a flattering turned-back collar and tiered skirt gathered with a belt at her hips. Her matching cloche hat sported a bow at her left ear and set off the deep ebony of her hair. Her red lips popped.

"Listen." She looked over her shoulder to make sure everyone had gone. "Helen is in a fragile state. She has not taken the death of Edward well at all, and as you can see, there is tension between her and her husband. And I can't be sure, but I think she may be back on dope."

I had assumed the same but didn't comment. "Why was her husband here at all?" I asked.

"He's decided to be her manager. I presume it's to keep a closer eye on her. It was no secret she and Edward were having an affair."

This was true. Florence had said as much when Officer Clayton had broken the news to her of Mr. Travis's death. In fact, the chemistry between Helen and Mr. Travis had been so palpable, it practically had taken on a life of its own. No wonder there was strife in Helen's marriage. But at the same time, something was off about her husband. And with that hidden bruise, I was a little worried about her safety. Was her husband prone to violence? Had he hit her? She had been crying at the party. Could Charles Wilson have followed Lizzy and Mr. Travis out to the barn? He certainly had a motive for killing the man. Helen Clark did, too, for that matter. According to Chet, love, jealousy, and money were the primary motivators for murder.

"I'm telling you this, Grace, because I'd like for you to support her in any way you can," Mrs. Steinberg continued. "Since you will be working intimately with her, you can help her to stay focused. You can be a sounding board, a friend. We women need to stick together." She turned to Felicity. "I'm glad Timothy has brought you aboard. Welcome."

Felicity gave her a warm smile. "Thank you. I'll do what I can to help Helen, as well."

"Excellent," Mrs. Steinberg said. "The girl has a bright future. As long as the men in her life, my husband and Mr. Combs included, stay out of her way and let her be the actress she's meant to be, that is."

With that, she left the room.

"Well," I said to Felicity, "how great is it that we get to work together?"

"Pretty great," she said. "Things are a little slow at the Travises' mansion, as you might expect, so this is a welcome diversion for me."

"How *are* things, you know, at the mansion?"

Felicity shook her head. "Grim. Florence has been drinking —heavily—and she isn't a kind drunk."

I sighed. "It's so sad. The way Mr. Travis died. Who could hate him so much they'd want to kill him?"

Felicity snorted. "A number of people."

Florence had said so, as well. I raised my eyebrows at her. "Who do you have in mind?"

"Well, Florence for one. They argued all the time about his affairs, though one could hardly blame her."

I hoped Mr. Travis hadn't planned to make Lizzy a conquest. Perhaps that is what Florence had feared, too? She'd seen him chatting with Lizzy at the party. Maybe she'd seen them go to the barn and had imagined the worst.

"I'm sure there were others," Felicity said. "Men like him make sure they are never alone and never without a beautiful woman on their arm. Must be some kind of insecurity."

"Like Joe Marciano?" I added. That's how I'd met Felicity. She, as well as my sister, had been in a relationship with the mob boss, and not a healthy one. I was glad she was finally rid of his cruelty and abusiveness, that she'd risen above the damage he'd created. I wondered if she would ever give her heart to someone else again.

She slapped my arm. "Don't remind me!"

"Sorry." Then I remembered what Lizzy had told me earlier about the argument Mr. Travis had with his employee at the party. "What do you know about the man, Mr. Johnson, who worked for Mr. Travis?"

Felicity shook her head. "Not much. He's a bit of a loner. I think he was an actor at one time. Not sure why he's not working in that capacity anymore."

"He was sure buzzing around Lizzy the night of the party. She told me he and Mr. Travis had words about it that night." Again, I wondered if Mr. Travis had been trying to protect her or lay claim to her.

Felicity crossed her arms over her chest. "Men. Ugh! Why can't they find someone their own age? That's disgusting."

"It is," I mused, no stranger to being propositioned by older —and younger—men.

"And what about Helen's husband?" Felicity placed her hands on her hips in indignation. "He's old enough to be her father. I'm sure he wasn't a fan of Mr. Travis."

"No," I agreed. "And then there's Robert Smith."

Felicity's brow furrowed. "What about him?"

"He might have blamed Mr. Travis for his getting fired. They had an altercation on the set a couple of days before the party. When Detective Walton was questioning Florence on the night of the murder, she'd said Mr. Smith had come to the mansion the day before, yelling and screaming at Mr. Travis."

Felicity's composure relaxed a bit. "Sounds like he did blame Edward for his getting fired. How's the kid holding up?"

"Lizzy? She's traumatized, as you can imagine." I shook my head, wishing I could come up with a way to provide more comfort for her. "She doesn't remember much after she and Mr.

Travis left the house to go to the barn. He wanted to see the horses."

"Mm-hmm. Maybe that's not all he wanted to see," she said.

Yes, that idea kept coming up. And with Mr. Travis's track record with extramarital affairs, it was only logical.

"Maybe he wanted to get Lizzy alone, but I'm not sure his reasons were so nefarious," I admitted. The idea that he was actually trying to protect Lizzy still sat at the forefront of my thoughts.

"Why do you say that?" Felicity asked.

I really couldn't explain it. "I don't know. Just a hunch?"

I shuddered. The image of Lizzy trying to defend herself against unwanted advances made my stomach turn. I refused to believe Lizzy could kill a person, even in self-defense.

"Well, I'm going to go find Timothy. See what he wants me to do," Felicity said.

"Okay. I need to go back to organizing the wardrobe room. Looks like we'll be working, first thing in the morning."

CHAPTER TEN

Felicity and I parted ways, and I headed back to the wardrobe room. I passed by the massive outdoor set of *The Queen of Whitehall*, our own little Camelot glistening in the California sun with its white castle, complete with moat and drawbridge. Set design was an amazing art—an eye for scale was paramount, and one also had to determine how the set would look on camera. Since the majority of the sets were already in place, Felicity's job would be easier, but I still didn't envy her the task. Luckily, she and Timothy worked extremely well together and had a similar aesthetic so there would be few if any clashes of opinion.

As I left the car park, I saw them together, assessing the structure of the castle, Timothy standing with his hands on his hips and Felicity pointing to something at the topmost turret. I tried not to gasp as Robert Smith and Lenora Lange emerged from within the castle. What were they doing there? Robert Smith had been fired.

They approached Timothy and Felicity. Miss Lange looked like a fairy snow queen, wearing a white ermine fur over a white dress that, in combination with her silvery white hair and striking blue eyes, gave her an ethereal look.

"You know I'm the only one for this role, Timothy," Mr. Smith said with a raised voice, marching fast toward them. Miss Lange hung back as if she couldn't keep up with him, or perhaps she didn't want to interfere with the conversation.

Unable to deny my curiosity, I walked toward her. As I approached, I cleared my throat, catching her attention. She gave me a nod in greeting but remained riveted to Robert Smith and Timothy.

"What are you doin' here, Robert?" Timothy asked.

"I misplaced something, either on set or in the dressing room and was looking for it. But I also wanted to talk to you. I need that role, O'Malley. Gotta pay the bills." He stood close to Timothy, so close that Timothy took a step back. Mr. Smith was usually a quiet, reserved man, and this aggressive side that presented itself lately was strange indeed.

"You're a fine actor, make no mistake," Timothy said. "But the studio has the last say, mate."

Mr. Smith placed his hands in his pockets. "But as the director, you do have some influence. It was that bastard Travis who wanted me gone, and now I'm gone. Surely, you could persuade them to bring me back."

Timothy shook his head, running his fingers across his chin. "When you don't show up for work, it costs the studio time and money. You need to get the drinking and drugs under control, my friend."

Drugs? I had heard through the Hollywood grapevine that Mr. Smith had become addicted to morphine after the war, but I never paid much attention to gossip, despite the fact that it was a second language in showbiz. Rumors abounded about everyone.

"I haven't had a drink since Saturday," he said. "I don't need the booze, man. It just helps me cope. I can't sleep without it." He didn't mention the drugs.

I was so engrossed in the conversation between him and Timothy, I didn't see Miss Lange come closer to me, and suddenly, she was at my elbow.

"You carry a burden," she said, giving me a half smile.

The hairs on my arms rose. The woman had such a cryptic way of speaking. "Oh?"

She nodded. "Those who have gone beyond can see all, my dear."

What was she talking about?

"Poor Robert," she said, her eyes misting over. "This job meant everything to him."

I was touched by her sympathy for the man. They surely were close, but in what capacity, I wasn't certain.

"He does seem upset," I agreed. "When did he get the news about being fired?"

She sighed. "Early this morning. The phone call from Mr. Combs got him out of bed, and Robert called me straightaway. He was in a terrible state."

So they didn't live together. And he hadn't been fired before the party. But had he known it was coming?

He doesn't seem any better now, I wanted to add. His eyes were wild, unfocused, as if he'd been drinking, even though he said he hadn't. I wondered how things had gone at the police station for him on the night of the party.

"He seemed in bad shape the night of the party, too," I said, trying to be crafty. "I saw him out in the field before I found Lizzy and Mr. Travis."

She gave me a sideways glance. "Yes. He drinks to forget the war," she said wistfully. "But the drinking only heightens his memories."

"Did the police detain him long?" I asked. I needed to know if they considered him a suspect. I couldn't imagine they didn't, given what I had told them, but knowing for sure would tell me a lot about what kind of reasonable doubt the police had when it came to Lizzy.

"Overnight. I was called midmorning to come get him." She spoke as if we were talking about him being picked up from a casting call, not from a night—or morning, after he'd sobered up —of interrogation.

"So they didn't think him a suspect?" The words slipped out before I could stop them.

She turned to face me full-on, her contemplative demeanor gone and in its place a scrutinizing look. "I have no idea what the police think, Miss Michelle. What do *you* think?"

I blinked back my astonishment at being put on the spot like that. The skin on the back of my neck tingled. I wasn't sure how to answer. The woman seemed to always put me off my guard.

"I-I don't know," I stammered.

She gave me a serene smile. "The girl will need your help. But to help her, you must rid yourself of the burden."

"Um, what?" I asked, still trying to get my feet under me again. I didn't really have time for these riddles. How had she so quickly turned the conversation?

"I feel a heaviness around you. They tell me it surrounds your family."

What on earth were we talking about here? I had no family left. It was also impossibly rude to bring up my family when she knew nothing whatsoever about them. *"They?"* I asked, unable to hid the irritation in my voice.

She gave me that endearing smile again, the lines around her eyes crinkling in a motherly way. "Joshua."

I shook my head, feeling as if I'd gone into one of my strange dreams. "Who?"

"Joshua. My collective of souls. I know, the name in the singular throws people off."

That's not all that throws people off.

I stared at her, again, not quite sure what to say. Was this woman mad?

"I'm sorry, I—" I wanted to tell her I had to go, but her penetrating gaze had my feet rooted to the ground.

"It is of no consequence," she said.

"Hey, buck! Get off!" Timothy's shouting drew our attention back to the two men and Felicity.

Mr. Smith had grabbed Timothy by the lapels of his gray Oxford sweater coat, his teeth bared in frustration. Felicity stood by helplessly, her eyes full of alarm.

"Robert!" Miss Lange scolded him as if chastising a dog. He quickly let go of Timothy's lapels and jammed his hands back in his pockets as if he didn't trust himself not to strangle the director. He had an aggressive side, indeed.

"I'm sorry," he said to Timothy, taking his hands out of his pockets and holding them up in apology. "I don't know what came over me."

Timothy straightened his coat but kept silent. He simply shook his head and walked away, leaving Mr. Smith holding his hand over his mouth, as if surprised by his own actions.

"Robert suffers so," she said, turning to me with a sigh. "The war, you know."

"Yes," I said, growing more impatient with her by the minute. "You mentioned that."

And, yes, I did know. Chet had his own demons when it came to the war, but since we'd moved to the ranch and he'd retired from investigating, he had settled a great deal. My heart went out to Mr. Smith, but at the same time, his behavior gave me pause.

"We must go," she said. "Remaining here will only agitate him further."

"Yes, I see. Well, goodbye." I hope I didn't sound too eager to be rid of her, but this woman unnerved me, especially her continued mentions of my family. The familiar fluttering in my stomach and heaviness in my chest returned as I thought about them. The truth was, I didn't remember much about my mother and father, which was strange because I had been twelve when they'd died. It's not as if I had been an infant. I had a few photos, too. My mother was girlish looking, like Sophia, with wide expressive eyes, high cheekbones, and charming dimples. The only real difference between her looks and Sophia's was their hair. Sophia had my father's dark hair while I had inherited my mother's golden locks.

Suddenly, the ground seemed to shift beneath my feet, and I faltered. I placed my fingers at my temples, taken by surprise at the sudden wave of dizziness.

"Hey, you okay?" Felicity came up to me, concern in her voice.

Embarrassed at how I must have looked, I quickly lowered my hands. "Oh yeah, fine. Just a little dizzy spell." I did not want to tell her about my conversation with Miss Lange. "Maybe you should ask Timothy that question, though," I said, nodding toward him. From the castle, he was watching Robert Smith and Lenora Lange walk away, shaking his head.

Felicity scoffed. "Yeah. I will. That Robert Smith is a real hothead."

I nodded. "Yeah," I said under my breath, my uneasy thoughts still with Miss Lange's cryptic words.

"Grace? You look like you just lost your best friend. What's going on?" She put a hand on my shoulder.

"Oh, it's nothing," I said, trying to reassure her.

Truth be told, I had lost not only my best friend in Sophia but those who had mattered most to me as a girl, the two people who had brought me into this world. What would it have been like if they hadn't died? Would Sophia still have become a Broadway star in the Ziegfeld Follies, an occupation that eventually led to her death? Would I have become a costume designer? I certainly wouldn't have met Chet. Had we not worked for Flo at the same time, our paths would never have crossed. The very thought made me sad.

"You sure?" Felicity asked.

"Yeah, I'm sure," I said, not sure at all. I was just about to escape back to wardrobe when I remembered what I might have done with my tape measure. I had used it to measure the width of the skirt on the Santa Maria, the nickname I had given one of Helen Clark's costumes. She had been having trouble managing the massive volume of the skirt while going through a doorway of the castle, and I'd been measuring it on set, trying to figure out how to scale it down.

"I need to check something on set," I told her.

"I'm going to catch up with Timothy. See you later." She waved and then jogged toward the director.

I walked under the imposing arch into the castle's courtyard and turned the corner to go to the area deemed "the banquet hall." Spying something metallic on top of the large banquet table, I headed over there. It was, indeed, the tape measure. I let out a sigh of relief and swiped it off the table. It would have been a shame to have lost such a precious memento of my time with such a world renowned designer.

On my way out to the courtyard, I felt something make contact with my shoe. Something small and cylindrical went skittering across the set and wedged itself under the base of one of the standing candelabras. I walked over to see what it was and reached down to pull it out. It seemed to be some kind of glass medicine vial, dark brown in color and about two inches high and half an inch in diameter. It was void of a label and sealed with a rubber stopper.

I remembered Timothy's comment to Mr. Smith about his drug use and the fact that the actor had been looking for something on set. Had this been what he'd left behind? Did he always carry around a glass medicine vial?

Holding the vial by the stopper, I twirled it in the light. It was empty.

Suddenly, what Lizzy had told me about the party flashed in my mind—that someone had bumped into her and then she'd had the sensation of being stung by a bee. I had thought then that she could have been drugged, but now . . . Could it have been Robert Smith who'd bumped into her? Had he drugged her? Did this even belong to him?

I slipped the vial into my dress pocket and hustled outside to see if Mr. Smith and Miss Lange were still there, but they were nowhere to be found.

CHAPTER ELEVEN

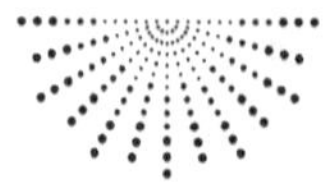

For the rest of the day, I spent the time off giving extra attention to the children, who were all understandably upset by what had happened at the ranch Saturday night, especially Lizzy. She never left my side as I worked in my studio, in the garden, or with the horses, although she didn't speak much. I tried to engage her in conversation, to get her to talk about what had happened and to talk through her feelings, but she remained quiet. I decided it best to let her process her emotions in her own way. Miss Meyers had taken Susie under her special care, and Ida wanted to spend time with Daniel and Ned outside doing the more strenuous ranch work.

I was still trying to process all that had happened, too. My nights were filled with lucid dreams of Mr. Travis, Lizzy, and of course, my mother and Sophia. I woke tired, confused, and feeling helpless. I wanted to know what Detective Walton and the police were doing in the investigation, who they were questioning, and what was being said. I was comforted by the fact that they hadn't come for Lizzy again, which meant they hadn't found any concrete evidence pointing to her guilt. I, on the other hand, resolved to find evidence pointing to her innocence. I wasn't going to take any chances.

The conversation at the dinner table that night was unusually light, except for the quiet discussion Chet was having with Joe about the horses. Chet had invited him over for dinner, which was not unusual as Joe lived alone and wasn't handy in the kitchen.

Lizzy hadn't eaten much and pushed the food around on her plate while Daniel shoveled food into his mouth at a rapid rate, then heaped seconds and thirds onto his plate. Ida ate slowly, watching Daniel's every move. Susie had pulled her chair close to Miss Meyers—so close, Miss Meyers had trouble lifting her right arm to eat. Poor Susie. I knew the events of the last few days had left her feeling scared and insecure.

"Slow down, Daniel," Rose scolded. "You'll give yourself a bellyache."

He stopped mid-chew, rolled his eyes at her, and continued.

"The cheek," she murmured under her breath.

Everyone was on edge and lost in their own thoughts, me included. My mind was focused on Robert Smith and the medicine vial, and how I might question him about it. I didn't know when I might see him again, nor where he lived or even his phone number. Perhaps it would be better to take the vial to the police, but even if it was Mr. Smith's how would it prove he drugged Lizzy? And, would Detective Walton even take me seriously? I needed to be certain. Yes, I would pursue this line of inquiry on my own. I'd find a way to reach Mr. Smith.

Ned, sitting next to me, seemed lost in thought, as well.

I set my fork down, only half of my food eaten. I didn't have much of an appetite, my concern for Lizzy and the other children overriding my need for sustenance. Perhaps it was overambitious of Chet and me to take on children with such troubled pasts. Were we really equipped to provide what they needed? To keep them out of trouble? Given the last few days, I was seriously beginning to doubt it.

When Sophia and I had been living on the streets of New York City, before Flo had found us one cold night outside his theater, I had dreamed of a life like this. Flo had done his best, but parenting hadn't come naturally to him. He had been so preoccupied with his starlets and his theater, he hadn't had time to address our emotional needs. I supposed when he and Sophia had had their affair, he'd thought he was providing love and support for her, but it had turned out all wrong. His dalliances with his other starlets was disturbing enough, given he was married to the lovely and talented Billie Burke, but those other starlets had not been raised as a daughter.

The affair hadn't lasted long. Flo had ended it. I knew he felt bad about it, and even deeply regretted it, but it had left Sophia confused, heartbroken, and angry. So angry, I had often thought it had contributed to her taking up with Jack Pickford and his destructive ways.

My thoughts were interrupted when I felt Ned's hand on top of mine. Surprised, I looked over at him. His eyes met mine, and I saw such tender concern in them that it made my heart stutter.

"You look a million miles away," he said quietly, his voice as smooth as butter.

Shocked at his forwardness, I pulled my hand from his and rested it in my lap. Thankfully, Chet had not seen the exchange, as he was still talking to Joe.

"Yes, I'm fine," I answered, smiling. I picked up my fork again and forced myself to take a bite of my mashed potatoes.

"Can I be excused?" Susie asked me in a loud whisper. She had eaten almost everything on her plate, which was good.

"Yes," I said. "Take your plate to the kitchen."

"I'll take it," said Rose. "I've got to see to the pies in the oven." She got up from the table.

"I need to excuse myself, as well," said Miss Meyers. "I need to get ready for the lessons tomorrow." She got up from the table and followed Rose into the kitchen, Susie on her heels.

Lizzy stopped moving the food around on her plate and set down her fork. "I'm not very hungry. I think I'm going to go to my room."

Daniel took the last swig of milk from his glass. "You want to go for a walk?" he asked her, his voice hopeful.

She shook her head. "No, I have some studying to do."

A look of disappointment swept his face, and he stood up and picked up his plate. Lizzy did the same.

"Daniel, don't forget you need to check the horses' water tonight," Chet reminded the boy.

"Yep." Still eating a piece of buttered bread, he slipped through the doorway to the kitchen.

Chet resumed his conversation with Joe, and I picked up my water glass and took a sip. I set it down, turning the base of it between my fingers, studying it. The detective had mentioned glass shards in the barn. Shards that were too small to cause a fatal injury, leading him to believe that the killer had used a knife or other sharp object. But then where had the shards come from? Our kitchen? The caterers? Or had it been glass from a liquor bottle? Had the killer used the glass to kill Mr. Travis and then broken it in an attempt to get rid of the evidence?

"Grace?" Ned's voice, soft and insistent, once more brought me back into the present. I turned to him, and he smiled at me, his eyes twinkling. "You've got that thousand-yard stare again."

"Oh," I said, wondering if he always scrutinized me so closely and suddenly feeling a bit vulnerable. I turned my attention back to the glass between my fingers. "What did you do with the hay that had the glass shards in it?" I asked him.

He swallowed a bit of food and wiped his mouth with his napkin. "I wanted to make sure there was no possibility of the horses getting any of it so I pitched a large portion of it into the back of the truck and then emptied it into a pile out behind the barn. I burned it, so the horses wouldn't eat it. Then I went back to the hay room and swept up the area, to get any remaining glass."

"Was there much waste? I mean, of the hay?" I asked, the practical side of me taking over for a moment. We'd already baled for the season, and we'd had a good cutting, but would we have enough to get us through to the next one?

"Yeah. Quite a bit, actually. But Chet said we couldn't take the risk."

"No. I suppose we couldn't. What did the shards look like?" I asked him. "Could you tell what they had come from?"

He shook his head. "The pieces were too small. Why do you ask?"

I shrugged. "Just curious. Wondering about the murder weapon." I stifled a yawn, suddenly exhausted from the stress of the day. I longed to soak in a bath and then get into bed and read. "Excuse me," I said, a little embarrassed. "I don't mean to be rude, but—"

"You do look tired." His dark eyes settled on mine "Here, let me." He stood, picked up his plate and mine, and took them into the kitchen.

"I'm exhausted," I said, interrupting Joe and Chet. "I'm headed upstairs, unless you need me for anything."

"You feeling all right?" Chet asked. It was the first time he'd looked at me in earnest all evening.

"Yes. Just tired." My brain felt mushy from the long day, but I couldn't stop thinking about Lizzy and the murder. I needed to take a mental break and try to relax.

His eyes lingered on me for a moment. I could tell he was trying to read my mood. "Okay. I'll be up later," he said.

Joe saluted me. "Good night, Grace."

I headed upstairs to our bedroom and immediately ran a hot bath. I soaked in the tub for a long time, trying to clear my mind of all the drama that had transpired over the last several days.

When the water started to get cold, I got out, toweled off, and put on my favorite silk, Crepe de Chine nightgown, and settled into bed with my latest read, *The Man in the Brown Suit* by Agatha Christie. I had purchased it because of the title, which was oddly serendipitous as I had referred to the man whom Sophia and I had encountered in that alleyway in New York all those years ago as the Man in the Brown Suit. I hadn't learned his name was Lefty until later. Although in my story, the man in the brown suit was far from a good guy. In fact, he was wasting away in prison for his association with Joe Marciano and his role in my sister's murder, a reality that gave me a degree of comfort.

As I read, it became harder to keep my eyes open. The book fell onto my chest, startling me awake. I don't know why I didn't put the book down and turn out the light to go to sleep. I needed it so much. My eyes drifted closed again, and my awareness settled on the blissful sensation of nothingness.

MOTHER STANDS OVER ME, screaming in rage, but her outburst isn't directed at me. It's directed at my father. He tries to calm her, but she will have nothing of it. My shoulders fall in on themselves as I retract, trying to make myself smaller, to protect myself from the rage on her face. I look past her to see Sophia crying, begging Mother to stop yelling. She covers her ears, shaking her head.

Somehow, I find myself in a corner of the room, clutching one of my dolls, but I am a grown woman. Mother grabs a knife from somewhere and raises it above her head. Then, the room is full of people, full of voices, all colliding with one another. Lenora Lange appears from nowhere, dressed all in white, backlit and glowing, her hair shimmering.

I sat up, breathing hard.

Chet stirred beside me. "Grace?"

When I didn't answer, he took hold of my hand. "What is it?"

I pulled my knees up, rested my elbows on them, and ran my hands through my hair. "Bad dream."

He propped himself on an arm. "Want to talk about it?" His voice was thick and groggy with sleep.

"No." I lay back down, my heart racing. He folded me into his arms, and I pressed myself into him as if I were trying to crawl inside him, to get outside of myself and somewhere safe. I finally let out a slow breath, comforted by his warmth and strength. We lay there for a while without speaking. I thought he would fall asleep again immediately, but I could tell he hadn't.

"Have I ever told you about my parents?" I whispered.

He didn't answer at first, but I could feel his breath in my ear.

"No. Not really," he said. "Only that they died in a train accident when you were young."

"Yes. I guess I haven't told you much because, the truth is, I don't really remember much. I remember things from the age of three or four until I was about ten, but not much after that."

"Like what kind of things?"

"Sitting on my dad's lap. Him reading to me. My mother's smile. Sophia looked just like her. I remember a picnic we all took one day. It was a sunny, beautiful day. We sat near a stream on the grass somewhere, under a tree. Sophia and I had been playing in the stream, and we were drenched. We lay in the sun to dry off. Mom and Dad were laughing. That's the last good memory I have of my family. All the others are—"

"Not good?"

I sighed. "No. I have memories of my mother being upset. Crying. Yelling. Sick. Or at least I thought she was sick. She wouldn't get out of bed for days. Dad was gone a lot, and when he was home, he always seemed preoccupied, like he was not really there. Mother was so hard on Sophia. She was only a year and a half older than me, but Mother put the onus on her to take care of me and keep the house. Sophia had such a burden to carry. I remember that with vivid clarity." I swallowed the growing lump in my throat, the one that made me want to stop sharing. "But then it all gets blurry. I remember snippets, but they're fractured. Sometimes I wonder if they are real memories or if I've made them up. Then the memories get clear after Flo found us and took us in. I remember almost everything after that."

Chet rubbed my arm. His hand was warm, rough from ranch work. "Maybe you can't remember because it was too painful. I don't remember parts of the war. I think the mind forgets to protect us."

I snuggled closer to him, reveling in his strong embrace. His breathing slowed and lengthened and then turned to soft snoring. I felt my muscles relax, my mind loosen, and soon I, too, drifted off to sleep.

CHAPTER TWELVE

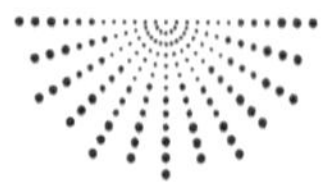

Tuesday morning I went to the studio early to view the dailies, the unedited footage of the Thursday before the party, with Timothy and some of the other crew members. Timothy was not at all happy with what he saw. Thank goodness it didn't have anything to do with the costuming, but mainly with the script. It wasn't playing out on the screen as he envisioned. He canceled filming for the day, and he and the writers set to work.

Felicity wasn't needed on set for the day, either, so was headed back to her cottage on the Travis estate to catch up on some work there. I still had some party items that had been left at my house, and we agreed to meet there later.

I had plenty of work to do but decided to take advantage of not being immediately needed and went to the office of the studio heads to speak to their secretary about getting Robert Smith's address to show him the medicine vial and ask if it was the item he'd left on set. Luckily, after telling the secretary I had something to return to Mr. Smith, she complied.

Mr. Smith lived in West Hollywood, and when I pulled up to his home, I found a quaint little Spanish Revival–style house with two identical tiled gables over large-paned windows and framing the front door. The curtains were pulled closed. The yard, though small, was well-kept. Two flower beds stuffed with bright-pink impatiens lined the front walk that led to the door.

I parked the car, got out, and made my way up the walk. I knocked on the door and waited. Hearing nothing from inside the house, I assumed he was either not at home or didn't want to answer the door. I was about to turn and leave when the door opened a crack.

"Mr. Smith?" I tried to peer inside.

He opened the door, looking as if he'd just stepped out of the bath. His hair was wet and dripping onto his shirt, which had not yet been tucked into his pants.

"Grace? What are you doing here?" he asked, blinking into the light. Behind him, the house was shrouded in darkness.

"I think I may have found something that belongs to you," I said, rummaging through my purse. At last, my fingers grasped the small medicine vial. "You said you'd left something on set, and I was wondering if this was it?" I held it up to him.

He squinted his eyes, and his brow furrowed in confusion. "What is it?"

I blinked up at him. "It's a medicine vial."

He opened his eyes wide, and his brows shot up. "Oh, I see," he said, his face hardening. "You, like the rest of them, think I'm on drugs. Well, I'm not. Yes, I drink. I drink a lot, but I got the morphine habit licked."

"Oh, I . . .I didn't mean to imply," I stammered, suddenly flustered. What had I hoped to gain by this inquiry? That he would say, *Oh, thank you so much. Yes, it's mine*, and reach for it? It had seemed so reasonable when I'd decided to ask him about it.

His mouth twitched in annoyance. "I think it's exactly what you meant to imply. For your information, I was looking for a writing pen—a very special writing pen given to me by Lenora. I misplaced it somewhere and thought perhaps I'd left it on set while going over my script. Did you happen to find *that*?"

I smiled at him, trying to soften his anger. "No. No, I'm sorry, I didn't."

"Why don't you ask Helen about that vial? I'm surprised you haven't noticed she's often stoned on the set. If she hadn't been sleeping with Travis, she would have been fired, too."

I had noticed strange behavior from Helen at the party . . . "Perhaps I will. I'm sorry if I offended you, Mr. Smith."

He scoffed and shook his head. "Is there anything else?"

I pressed my lips together, contemplating what to say next. Given his hostility, I wasn't sure I wanted to proceed, but I was there and I needed to help Lizzy.

"Mr. Smith, I'm sure you are aware that one of the girls who lives with me, Lizzy, was at the party on Saturday night. She was the one found with— Well, I found her with Mr. Travis's body. She has been accused of killing him, which I do not believe to be the case at all."

He heaved an irritated sigh and leaned his shoulder against the doorframe. "What does this have to do with me?"

I swallowed, trying to bolster my courage. "You see, when I went out to the barn to look for Lizzy, I saw you in the field."

He crossed his arms, and his eyes narrowed. "Yeah, what of it?"

I smiled again, feeling a little intimidated by his defensive posture. I'd witnessed the man fly into a rage with my own eyes. I needed to tread carefully. "Did you happen to see anyone other than Mr. Travis and Lizzy going to or from the barn when you were out there?"

He shook his head at me again. "So what are you now, a cop? I answered all those questions already. Now, I have to go."

With that, he slammed the door in my face.

I blinked, stepping backward, and exhaled a shaky breath. I quickly turned and headed back to my car. After I got inside, I shut the door and leaned my arms and head against the steering wheel, my heart pounding.

When I had settled myself, I placed the vial back into my handbag and replayed my conversation with Mr. Smith in my mind. He'd seemed genuinely baffled by the medicine vial so I was fairly sure it did not belong to him. Now, it seemed, I would have to make an inquiry of Helen Clark. It was too bad we had stopped filming until the script was revised to Timothy's satisfaction. I'm sure Helen had gone home by now, and I didn't know where she lived. What kind of excuse could I give Mr. Steinberg's secretary this time? I'd have to find another way.

I started up the car, Mr. Smith's words echoing in my head. He never answered my question of whether or not he'd seen anyone come or go from the barn, I realized. In fact, he'd gotten quite upset by the question. Did that portray a guilty conscience? Had my question hit a little too close to home? What *exactly* had he told the police?

By early afternoon, I was headed to Beverly Hills to return Mr. Travis's tableware from the party to Felicity. As I drove up to the Victorian mansion situated on Canon Road, my breath caught in my throat at its architectural beauty. A large circular driveway led up to the front door, and several cars were parked along its graceful curve. Felicity had told me to take the adjacent drive toward the back of the house that led to the cottage.

I drove past a large swimming pool and generous grounds of verdant grass and trees. The yard resembled a well-manicured park. In the near distance, I spotted the cottage. It looked like a miniature version of the main house, complete with its own circular drive flanked by flowering bushes. I pulled the car up to the front door just as Felicity was coming out to greet me. She wore cream-colored wide-legged trousers with a matching cream top, and a multicolored turban covered her hair.

"Hello," I said as I got out of the car.

Her smile broadened at my greeting.

"Beautiful place." With a sweep of my arm, I indicated the manicured acreage. It was a far cry from our dusty ranch.

"It'll do," she said with a laugh. "Come on in."

"Should we get the boxes?"

"In a minute. I'm having some coffee. Join me?"

I closed the car door. "I'm gasping for some.

We entered the cottage into a small foyer, brightly lit with natural light from the semicircle window above the front door. The foyer opened to a modestly sized living room with wood floors partially covered with a Persian rug in soft pinks, blues, and greens. Two tufted, watermelon-colored accent chairs sat on either side of a white, ornately carved fireplace.

"Come through to the kitchen," she said, leading the way. We walked across the living room to the adjacent kitchen. The room was a study in white, with lavender and champagne accents.

"Wow," I said, duly impressed. "Did you do this?"

Felicity nodded. "Yes. Mr. Travis said that while I'm staying here, I could decorate the cottage as I liked. Said it would only improve the value of the property."

"I can only imagine what you've done in the mansion."

She poured coffee into a dainty teacup, placed it on its saucer, and handed it to me. "Cream and sugar?"

"No. Black is fine. Smells wonderful." My mouth watered at the fragrant aroma dancing in my nostrils.

"The mansion's color palette is a bit darker, heavier—more masculine," she continued. "That's how Mr. Travis wanted it."

I took a sip of the nutty brew, fully appreciating its richness. I proceeded to tell her about my conversation with Mr. Smith and how I needed to speak with Helen Clark.

"So I still don't know much of anything," I said, disheartened. "I wish Lizzy could remember more about that night."

Felicity sighed. "Yes. She was pretty out of it when you brought her into the house."

I shook my head, crestfallen at Lizzy's predicament. "She's still not herself, as you can imagine."

We sat in silence for a moment. Each ruminating on poor Lizzy, I suspected.

"Well, I won't keep you," I said. "I know you must have a lot to do."

Felicity nodded. "Yes, the east wing is kind of torn apart. Florence asked me to continue with the work but not today. Apparently, the lawyer has called a meeting with the beneficiaries of Mr. Travis's estate. It seems there are quite a few, judging from all the people I've seen going into the mansion."

"That's why there were so many cars out front," I said. "How strange that he wants them all together. And so soon after his . . . well, his demise."

"I'll say." Felicity took her coffee cup in both hands. "Florence said this gathering was stipulated in the will by Mr. Travis. He must have had his reasons. I was invited, too, which is even odder."

My mouth flopped open. "Really? What do you think he left you? He must have updated his will quite recently, then. You haven't known him for very long." I briefly wondered if there had been more than friendship between the two. "You two weren't . . . ?"

Felicity looked at me aghast. "No! I swear it. He's not really my type anyway." She waved a hand in the air. "We were just friends. I can't think of what he would leave me— Wait!" She pursed her lips in thought. "There is a set of eighteenth-century Chinese vases in his study that I greatly admire, and I told him so. He seemed very pleased that I liked them so much. Said no one in his family appreciated them and that maybe he'd give them to me one day. I thought he was joking, but . . ."

I tapped my fingernail on the edge of the coffee cup. Why had he so recently updated his will? Was it just coincidence, or did he have some kind of premonition about his death?

"You know, come to think of it," I said, "maybe this type of gathering is not so unusual. Chet once told me about a murder case where the potential beneficiaries were gathered together shortly after the death. It was another high-profile murder case, and there was much contention among the family and other beneficiaries. The lawyers decided it best to have everyone hear the reading of the will together to dispel any disputes. Perhaps Mr. Travis knew there might be trouble in the event of his death?" Another thought came to me that quickened my pulse. "What do you think about me accompanying you to this meeting?"

Felicity raised an eyebrow at me. "You want to go?"

"Yes. It might shed some light on who may have killed Mr. Travis. What other opportunity would we have to see who might have a monetary motive to get Mr. Travis out of the way? Love, revenge, and *money* are the primary motives for murder. But it might look kind of funny for me to be there." I suddenly had my doubts about the plan.

Felicity set her coffee cup down and put her elbows on the table. She rested her chin on her clasped hands. "You'll be my guest—to offer emotional support."

I considered her thought and took a sip of my coffee. "I suppose that would be reasonable . . ."

"The worst anyone could do is ask you to leave," she said with a shrug.

"I suppose you're right. It's worth trying—for Lizzy." A pang of sadness stabbed at my heart. "I know she didn't kill him, but I think Detective Walton is convinced she did. I need to find out who might have done this terrible thing. It could be the only way to save her if the detective decides she's guilty and tries to make a case against her."

Felicity's brow furrowed, and she pressed her lips together. "Now, don't get upset, I'm just playing devil's advocate here, but how can you be so certain she didn't do it?"

I blinked at her. "She was unconscious when I found her."

Felicity gave me a sympathetic look and placed her hand on my forearm, which was resting on the table. "Honey, that doesn't mean she's innocent."

"But if she did it, what did she do with the murder weapon? How could she have done away with it or hid it if she was unconscious?"

Felicity shrugged. "I don't know. Maybe someone did it for her. Maybe another one of the kids? Maybe one of them came out to the barn, saw her there, saw the weapon, suspected she killed him, and got rid of the weapon to protect her?"

Daniel immediately came to mind. Maybe Detective Walton thought that, as well, and that's why he'd wanted to question him. Daniel did nothing to hide the fact he was sweet on Lizzy. A sinking feeling came over me, but then it suddenly vanished. A voice, like a whisper, sent a shudder through my core.

No, that's not what happened.

I marveled at the overwhelming certainty in my mind. Was the voice my intuition?

"I can't explain it, Felicity. It's just a feeling in my gut, but I know she didn't do it. I'd bet my life on it. I need to explore other possibilities."

She released my arm. "Don't you think the police are doing that?"

"I don't know, to be honest. I wish I did. But, *I* have to help her. It's the whole reason Chet and I decided to open up the ranch to the kids—to help them, support them, advocate for them if need be. So that's what I am doing. I have to try."

Felicity sighed and then smiled at me. "You're a good egg,

Grace. I should know that when you back someone, you really back them. I won't ever forget what you did for me."

I returned the smile, despite my confusion. "What I did for you?"

She nodded. "You helped me to believe in myself again. Those years with Marciano made me feel hopeless, helpless, worthless. You had nothing to gain from helping me, yet you did it, even when it meant putting yourself at risk."

I waved a hand in the air, embarrassed yet touched by her words. Truth be told, if it weren't for Felicity, I'm not sure I could have gotten out of the mobster's grasp myself. She had been instrumental in helping me with my plan to escape after he'd kidnapped me. Having invested heavily in one of Flo's shows, in which I had a starring role, he'd considered me his property. And when the show had failed, he'd wanted his money back. But Flo had been broke so Marciano had taken back his investment: me.

A heavy silence hung in the air, and then I met her gaze. "We did it together, Felicity. We make a great team."

She pressed her lips together in a smile, nodding. "That we do, my friend. All right. Let's go to that meeting. We'll have to hurry."

I clapped my hands together, delighted at her willingness to help me. But then I remembered the reason I'd come over in the first place. "What about the boxes in my car?"

"How many?"

"Four."

"Okay," she said. "We'll take two to the kitchen now and then come back for the other two later."

We went to my car to get the boxes. I'd placed one in the passenger seat, and the other three in the back seat. I handed one to Felicity and took another myself. Felicity then led me down a path that wound from her little cottage to the back of the mansion.

"The kitchen is back here. We can set the boxes there and then go on to the ballroom."

We walked down the winding path edged on either side by thick bougainvillea bushes with bright orange and pink blossoms. Eucalyptus trees soared overhead, providing shade and a wonderful, sweet aroma that floated on the air. We passed the large, crystal-clear swimming pool adorned with fountains at each corner, and finally we stopped at a Dutch door at the back of the mansion, which I presumed led to the kitchen. Balancing her box on a knee, Felicity opened it.

We entered a large, sunny kitchen, with gleaming white walls and black-and-white tiled floors. Huge windows to the west let in a flood of natural light. It was a chef's dream, this kitchen, with two massive tables in the center for food preparation, and a hanging rack with cast-iron and copper pans was suspended above one of the tables. There were four iceboxes, two gas oven ranges, and loads of cabinets for storage. We set the boxes on one of the tables and then made our way out of the kitchen, our heels clacking against the tiled floor.

I followed Felicity through another door into an enormous wood-floored hallway carpeted with expensive Persian rugs. Two open double doors stood before us at the end of the hall, and I knew from the grand piano at the back of the room that this was the ballroom. A murmur of voices wafted from that direction, as well.

We entered the room to find about twenty people milling about. There was a table set up against one wall, laden with light fare—pastries and cookies, and large urns of coffee or tea. Those who weren't standing or talking in small groups sat in the white, wooden folding chairs that faced a table at the front of the room. A gentleman sat at the table, going through some folders. I assumed this was the lawyer. I quickly took stock of the hopeful recipients.

Of those I recognized, I first spotted James Johnson, Mr.

Travis's hired man, standing alone near one of the windows. He was dressed in a dark suit, white shirt, and dark bow tie. He held his hands behind his back, surveying the room. A woman in a maid's uniform came up to him and they exchanged a few words and she went to the food table. Was Mr. Johnson a beneficiary or was he meant to be working? His actions didn't seem appropriate for the latter, but I still didn't understand what exactly he did for Mr. Travis.

Florence Thomas was standing with a couple of older women who all seemed to be clucking over her. She wore a beautiful tweed dress—Coco Chanel, if I was not mistaken. The acclaimed designer had made the headlines this year by taking fabrics usually used for men's sportswear in Europe and fashioning dresses for women. Very new. Very avant-garde. I was completely impressed.

I spotted Helen Clark at the opposite side of the room and couldn't believe my luck. I'd have to find a way to speak with her, but at the moment, she was talking with none other than Lenora Lange. Why on earth would Miss Lange be here? She had an arm around Helen, who dabbed at her eyes with a hand-kerchief. Her face was blotchy and her nose red. I wondered if she'd been in that state since the party. Her husband was absent, making me wonder if he knew she was there. He never seemed to let her out of his sight.

I recognized a few other faces, those I'd seen around Ambassador, but the majority of them were strangers to me. My eyes traveled back to Lenora Lange. "What is *she* doing here?" I asked Felicity, gesturing with a tilt of my head in her direction.

"She's here a lot," Felicity said. "She and Mr. Travis had become close."

My mouth dropped open. "Ah yes, come to think of it, she mentioned she knew Florence. Commented on how unhappy she was."

Felicity nodded. "She performed a few séances for Edward, I heard tell. A friend of mine attended one."

"You don't say?" I mused. "Why'd he have a séance?"

"I guess it was in regard to some young thing. Would you expect anything else from him? The man had more women than Henry VIII. That's all I know."

Looking around, there were a few that fit the bill—young, beautiful, all wearing the latest fashions. My eyes drifted to a woman at the back of the room near the piano. She had platinum-blond, bobbed hair and wore dark, round-framed sunglasses. She stood apart from the others. She wore an expensive-looking dark suit with a fox stole pinned around her shoulder and a wide-brimmed bucket hat. She didn't come any closer or speak to anyone, just stayed by the piano.

The man at the table, a wiry specimen with a shock of gray hair and a bushy beard framing his elongated face, banged a gavel against the tabletop. "Please take a seat," he said.

Everyone made their way to a chair. I exhaled a silent breath of relief that no one seemed alarmed or surprised by my being there. Felicity and I each took a seat in the back row. I noticed the woman at the piano stayed where she was, standing. She also hadn't removed her sunglasses. I looked toward the double doors on the other side of the room, at the entrance Felicity and I had used. Detective Walton was there, Officer Clayton with him. I guessed he was here to see who had to benefit from Mr. Travis's death, as well. In truth, I was glad to see him there. Perhaps he would be further questioning anyone who might be guilty of the murder.

I turned back around to face the front, and the man at the table stood up. "Good morning," he said. "I'm William Redmond, attorney for the estate of Edward Travis. Thank you for coming today. I will first start by saying that I am terribly sorry for your loss. This came as quite a shock to all of us. It is a terrible business, indeed.

"You are all here," he went on, "because you either have a claim to part of the estate or you may have inherited either assets or goods from Edward Travis. He has made some bequests, and I will get to those later, but first I want you all to know, the beneficiary of the bulk of Mr. Travis's estate has not been located."

"What?!" Florence Thomas stood up. "What do you mean, the beneficiary? *I'm* the beneficiary!"

"You can't be." A woman's voice came from the back of the room, and all heads turned to see a darked-haired woman coming through the doorway. She wore a full-length sable mink coat and wide-brimmed hat with dark feathers shooting out the back. She strode into the room.

"Who the hell are you?" Florence said.

"I'm Pearl Davis, Edward Travis's wife. Who the hell are you?"

I gasped. His wife? This was a strange turn of events.

Florence's eyes widened in rage. She stabbed at her chest with her index finger. "*I'm* his wife! Get out of my house!"

The lawyer raised his hands. "Ladies, please." He took off his spectacles and rested his fists upon the table. "Well, this certainly complicates things, but not in terms of the last will and testament. Mrs. Trav— Miss Davis, will you please take a seat? You too, Miss Thomas."

I pressed a hand to my mouth in surprise. So the lawyer apparently hadn't known about Pearl Davis, either.

A sob issued from the front of the room. Helen Clark held the handkerchief up to her face—no longer wiping away her tears but bawling into it. Miss Lange quietly shushed her, trying to comfort her. I exchanged a look with Felicity, who rolled her eyes. She had no patience for melodrama.

Miss Davis gracefully lowered herself into a chair, and Florence sat down in a huff. Exactly who was this woman? I'd never heard of her before. She certainly wasn't of the Hollywood set.

The lawyer, still standing, cleared his throat and continued. I wasn't sure if he hadn't taken his seat in order to yield command of the room to prevent further outbursts or if he'd simply forgotten to sit down again. "In recent days, Mr. Travis has made changes to his will, but the bequest to the main heir has been in place for many years now."

There were murmurings around the room.

"Well, who is it?" a male voice shouted out.

The lawyer raised a hand again. "The bulk of the estate, all holdings, properties and assets go to Elsa Mayfield, Mr. Travis's only child. As of yet, we have not been able to locate her, however. If anyone might have information as to her whereabouts, please see me after we conclude."

Gasps and murmurings filled the room.

"Well, what do you know?" Felicity whispered. She turned to me with raised eyebrows.

I was just as confused as everyone else. Where had this child come from? Obviously not Pearl Davis. From the look of shock and surprise on everyone's faces, apparently no one knew about these two other women in Mr. Travis's life.

"This is ridiculous!" Florence stood up again. "Edward has no children. Said he never wanted children. This makes no sense!"

The sound of someone lighting a match pulled my gaze away from Florence. Mr. Johnson, sitting at the far end of the first row, calmly lit a cigarette. I wondered again what he stood to gain from the will, if anything.

"Miss Thomas, please sit down." The lawyer made the request a bit more firmly this time. "The will further stipulates that if the child is not of age, her mother, Greta Mayfield, will stand in as executor until said child becomes of age. Is Greta Mayfield present?"

Again, no one answered. I glanced over at Miss Davis, who seemed nonplussed by the whole event. Either she had quite the poker face, didn't care, or knew this bit of information already. I turned to the back of the room, to the piano, and the woman who'd been standing there was gone. I wondered if she might be Greta Davis, but she hadn't stepped forward. That wouldn't make sense, though. Why would she come to the reading if she wasn't going to take what Mr. Travis left her? She was probably just another one of Mr. Travis's conquests, disappointed at not getting his riches.

I noticed, to my disappointment, that Detective Walton was gone, too. I would have thought he'd want to speak with Miss Davis at least. It made me doubt how hard he was working on this case.

Voices filled the air as people speculated on the private affairs of Edward Travis. The lawyer banged his gavel again. "If we might continue," he said. "I am not finished."

A hush fell over the room.

"Should the heir, Elsa Mayfield, be deceased, or in the event of her death, the bulk of the estate will go to Pearl Davis—well, that explains that—and the mansion to Florence Thomas."

"No!" Florence, again, could not contain herself, but this time she remained seated. "How could he have done this to me? I am his lawful wife!"

Ignoring her tearful outburst, the lawyer continued. "Should these said heirs not be able to accept these bequests for any reason, the estate, holdings, assets, and mansion will be put into a trust under the management of Mr. and Mrs. Alastair Travis, and Preston J. Travis, parents and brother of Edward Travis, respectively."

Florence stood up again. "I can't listen to this anymore." Her voice cracked with emotion, and she put the back of her hand to her mouth. She practically tripped over people as she scurried through the row. She ran out of the room, and Lenora Lange gracefully got up from her chair and followed her. As she passed the back row where Felicity and I were seated, she glanced my way, and our eyes locked. Goose pimples rose on my forearms, and tingles went down my spine.

The lawyer continued listing items and their recipients for the next five or ten minutes. Pearl Davis left before he finished, and since she no longer had claim to the house—at least for the moment—I couldn't help but wonder where she currently resided. For that matter, did Florence even have a right to remain at the mansion? I supposed she could until this daughter was found. Then she'd have to leave. And what about Felicity and the cottage?

Finally, the lawyer read the last bequest—the Chinese vases. They were to go to Felicity, who seemed quite touched and pleased about it. The will also confirmed she could remain in the guest house for as long as she wished, regardless of who ended up inheriting the mansion.

Before the meeting adjourned, Mr. Johnson strode out of the room.

Helen Clark stood up abruptly and fled from the room, also, sobbing. Nothing had been left to either one of them. Had this been an act of cruelty on Edward Travis's part? To insist they be there to learn they hadn't received anything?

"I'm going after Helen," I whispered.

Felicity's eyes went wide. "I'm going, too."

We hurried in the direction she'd gone. At the end of the long hallway, Helen turned the corner into a large foyer and out of the house. We broke into a jog. When we reached the foyer, she was already rushing through the front door. She walked up to a car parked at the foot of the steps and got into the back seat.

"Helen!" I yelled after her.

She slammed the door, and the car took off.

"Rats! We missed her." I watched the car pull around the arc of the drive and head toward the street.

Felicity, a little out of breath, placed her hands on her hips. "That we did. But if I know Timothy, he'll get that script

whipped into shape in a jiffy and we'll be back at work tomorrow. You can talk to her then."

I sighed. She was probably right. If not, I'd find a way to
speak with Helen.

My thoughts drifted back to the reading of the will. "I
wonder why this Greta Mayfield didn't show up," I said, turning
to Felicity.

"Sounds like she is missing, as well as the child," Felicity
speculated.

I took in a sharp breath. "Maybe someone knew about this
heir and her mother and—"

Felicity looked at me with large eyes. "Did away with
them?" she whispered, finishing my sentence.

"And what about his other wife? Pearl Davis? She could
have done it. Or as much as I hate to think it, Florence . . ."

Felicity shook her head. "Florence seemed genuinely
surprised. Either that or she's a really good actress, which—don't
tell her I said this—we both know she isn't."

"I can't believe Mr. Travis has two wives," I said, still reeling
at this new information.

"Who knew?" Felicity shook her head.

"It's been a strange day." I sighed. "I should get back to the
ranch. Let's get those other boxes out of my car." We left the
ballroom and went back down the hallway to the kitchen.

"I guess you just never know about people," Felicity mused,
her thoughts obviously still with the reading of the will. "Even
when you are living on his estate!"

"You made out pretty well," I said to her, referring to the
vases. "And you get to stay here until the roof of your rental is
fixed."

"Yes. I'm so grateful I can stay in the cottage for a while,
because it seems that not only am I out of a house but I'm out of
a job, except for the work at Ambassador, and to be honest, it's
not paying much. Who knows if this Miss Mayfield will want

me to continue with the remodeling project—if she's ever found."

"Right."

We passed the swimming pool to see Lenora Lange sitting in one of the lounge chairs lining the concrete-and-tile deck. When she saw us, she got up and glided toward us. She was wearing her customary white, this time a cotton and lace afternoon dress with an ivory-petal trim cloche and pearls.

"Miss Michelle, Miss Jones," she greeted us.

"Hello," I said, not really wanting to talk to her. She made me feel things I didn't like feeling.

"May I speak with you alone?" she asked me.

I stifled an impatient sigh. With raised eyebrows, Felicity gave me a look and went to my car.

"I fear a tragedy for someone in your circle." Miss Lange's light-blue gaze penetrated mine.

My eyebrows dipped down. "A tragedy? What do you mean?"

"I can't be certain, but Joshua has spoken to me, and they claim it will happen soon. Within the next forty-eight hours."

Joshua? Oh yes. Her collective of souls. I wasn't sure what to make of him, or them, or whatever. Yet, the news, whether or not she was to be believed, was unsettling. Or was it her obvious need to impart this information to me that made me feel that way?

"Who is this 'someone'?" I asked.

She sighed. "I don't know. Joshua does not always know. But you keep coming up in my conversations with them."

Irritation pricked at me. Why me? And why give me only part of the information? All this would do was cause anxiety. With Lizzy's needs, Daniel's surly attitude, Ida and Susie's trauma, and my lack of sleep and horrible nightmares when I did get a wink, additional anxiety was the last thing I needed. Why was this woman hounding me?

I crossed my arms. "What am I supposed to do with this information?"

She smiled. "Take heed."

Oh, for god's sake!

"Well, thank you, Miss Lange. I will bear that in mind."

She reached out and placed a hand on my forearm. It was ice cold, and the goose pimples returned.

Take heed. When? Against what? Or whom?

CHAPTER THIRTEEN

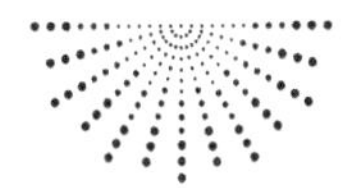

I returned to the ranch late in the afternoon, my mind awhirl with all this new information about Mr. Travis's wives—plural—and the mysterious Elsa and Greta Mayfield. They could be the whole key to his murder because they had the most to gain by Mr. Travis's death. Had someone killed them, too? Could one of them have followed him to the party? Had they been just waiting for their chance to get him alone somewhere that couldn't be traced back to them? Or perhaps they'd hired someone to follow him around. There were so many possibilities, it was overwhelming. And where to start?

As I motored up our long driveway along the alfalfa pasture sloping up to the hills, I was bothered by a whisp of hair that had fallen into my eyes. I looked into the rearview mirror to straighten it, and my eye caught two Model T's coming up behind me. I didn't recognize them.

When I pulled up to the house, Chet came out from the barn. I parked and got out of the car. "Hello, you," I said. He came over and planted a kiss on my cheek. "Who do you think this is?"

He shrugged. "Don't know." But our question was quickly answered.

Detective Walton, in his rumpled trench coat and battered fedora, got out of the passenger side of one of the cars, and Officer Clayton got out of the driver's side. Another officer got out of the other car. What did they want now? I hoped they weren't here to question the children again. This situation was pressingly stressful.

"Detective Walton," Chet said with a questioning tone in his voice. "What can we do for you?"

"We'd like to search the house, if you don't mind?"

Chet and I exchanged a glance.

"Of course," Chet said. "What are you hoping to find?"

"Murder weapon."

"Ah. Well, I'm not sure why it would be in the house. Don't you think the killer would have disposed of it or taken it with him?" Chet asked.

"Or hid it—in the house." Detective Walton smiled, but the smile didn't quite reach his eyes. "We'd also like to speak with Daniel Blaine again."

"Daniel?" I asked.

"He here?"

"I think he's out checking the fence lines," Chet said. "At least that is what he's supposed to be doing. Not sure when he'll be back, but I can go find him."

The detective smiled again. "I'd appreciate it. In the meantime, we'll check the house first."

My stomach turned. I wondered why they wanted to speak with Daniel again.

"Maybe you'll be back with him by the time we finish searching the house." The detective took off his hat, signaling to us he was headed inside. Taking the cue, we led him to the kitchen door. When we entered, Rose was there, cleaning things up and getting ready to prepare that evening's supper.

"What's all this?" she asked.

"Ma'am," Detective Walton greeted her.

"They'd like to search the house," Chet explained.

Rose placed her hands firmly on her hips. "But I'm trying to cook in here," she said impatiently.

"We need to cooperate, Mother," Chet said.

"You can continue, Mrs. Riker," the detective said. "If you don't mind Officer Faraday looking around downstairs."

Officer Faraday was another young officer, probably as old as Officer Clayton, but was shorter, stockier, and had full, rosy cheeks. He tipped his hat to Rose.

She heaved a great sigh. "As I live and breathe," she muttered under her breath.

We led Detective Walton and Officer Clayton through to the living room.

"Officer Clayton, let's head upstairs," the detective said.

I paced the living room while Chet went back outside to look for Daniel. My mouth felt as if I'd just swallowed sawdust so I decided to go into the kitchen to get a drink of water. Rose was stirring something on the stove, a scowl on her face while Officer Faraday rummaged through some cabinets.

"This is just a terrible business." Rose peered at me over the top rim of her spectacles. "I knew that girl was trouble."

I bit the inside of my lip so I wouldn't say something I'd regret. "We don't know that Lizzy did it, Rose." I went to the cupboard to retrieve a glass. Then I went to the sink to fill it.

She opened her mouth to say something when Ned came into the kitchen through the outside door, Chet on his heels. Officer Faraday stepped aside to let them in.

Ned looked from me to the officer and back to me. "Did you tell Lizzy she could ride Goldie today?" he asked. "She left all of Goldie's tack out."

"Yes, I gave her permission," I said.

"But Goldie has been in the field all day." Ned took off his hat and scratched his head. "And Chet's truck is gone. So is Daniel."

"One of them must have taken it." Chet's jaw flexed. "Without asking."

"Or both of them," Rose chimed in. "I told you—trouble."

I wanted to tell her to be quiet but refrained. "But why would either of them take the truck?" I wondered out loud.

Chet ushered me into the living room and gestured for Ned to follow us out of earshot of the officer. "They might have run away," Chet suggested. "Maybe Lizzy got scared."

My stomach tied itself into a knot, and I pressed a hand against it. Running away would be the absolute worst thing Lizzy could do in the situation. It would make her look guilty.

"Daniel might have gotten scared, too," Ned said. "He hasn't been himself since the party. I can't get two words out of him, and if I do, it's something churlish."

"No," I shook my head. "No! You can't really believe that they would run away." Then I remembered the police upstairs. This didn't look good. Not at all.

"Think we should say something to the police?" Ned asked.

Rose walked into the living room, wiping her hands on her apron. "Yes," she said.

"No. Not yet," I jumped in. "They're searching the house. Lizzy or Daniel might come back before they are done. We shouldn't assume anything just yet."

"She's right," Chet said. "Hopefully they will return soon."

I was glad Chet supported my suggestion, but I'd be lying to myself if I didn't admit I was worried about the prospect of them running away. Neither one of them would take the truck without asking; they knew it would get them into trouble.

"Well, I'm headed out to the fields to check those fences." Ned secured his cowboy hat back on his head and walked back into the kitchen. Rose followed him.

"What if they don't come back?" I whispered to Chet, my anxiety turning to dread.

He shook his head and released a breath. He gently took hold of my arms. "It's not good. Lizzy is the prime suspect in the murder case, and Daniel would be seen as an accomplice. They could be in really hot water."

"Maybe Joe took the truck," I added, hopeful. Chet had lent it to him on occasion, if he needed an extra set of wheels over at his ranch.

"I told him he could use it today, but, he's out at the arena working with the new horse. And even if he did take it, where are Lizzy and Daniel?" Chet let go of my arms.

Detective Walton and Officer Clayton came down the stairs. The detective was holding something in his hands. It looked like a white handkerchief.

"Find something?" Chet asked.

He approached us and held out his palm. "Recognize this?"

I blinked. My best pair of scissors, the ones I kept on my pattern-making table, were nestled in the handkerchief. They looked like they'd been in the dirt, and they were crusted over with something dark.

"Those are mine. What happened to them? Where did you find them?" I swallowed hard, my throat feeling dry.

"First bedroom on the right, under the chest of drawers."

"Susie's room," Chet said.

The knot in my stomach tightened. Could *my* scissors have actually been the murder weapon? Did Susie know something, and she was just too scared to tell us?

"We'll need to speak with her." Detective Walton folded the handkerchief over the scissors.

I looked directly into his eyes. "She's ten!" Why was he so determined to interrogate the children? Based on the little I knew, there were a string of people who had motive to kill Edward

Travis. Was the detective talking to all of them, too? He'd left the mansion before the lawyer had even finished reading the will. Why wouldn't he have stuck around and questioned people?

He raised his eyebrows at me. "Can you explain what the scissors were doing in her room under the dresser?"

I crossed my arms over my stomach in an attempt to quell the anxiety swirling around in it. "No, but—"

"Where is she?" he interrupted.

"She's probably with Miss Meyers in the schoolroom. She has chores there after school," Chet said.

Detective Walton tilted his head toward the door. "Officer Clayton, let's go. You can talk with this Miss Meyers."

"Susie is very fragile!" I nearly shouted at him. I felt Chet's hand on my shoulder, but I continued. I wanted them to proceed very carefully. I'd hate to have her upset. "She was abandoned when she was six and taken to an orphanage. She hadn't spoken in years. She only started speaking again when she came here almost a year ago."

"We'll be gentle with her," Detective Walton said.

Helplessly, I looked at Chet who gave me a reassuring nod.

"Well I'm coming with you." I left no room for objection. I wanted to be present when they questioned Susie, to show support and to give her reassurance. They may not have let me do that for Lizzy, but there was no way I was leaving this young girl to fend for herself. To my relief, the detective didn't attempt to stop me.

We walked across the yard toward the west end of the house. The schoolroom was kitty-corner from the back stairs leading to my studio. We entered the cheery space. Miss Meyers had done wonders with the old shed. Lace curtains hung on the windows on either side of Miss Meyers's desk, sitting on a brightly colored hook rug. Hanging on the wall behind her desk was a black chalkboard framed in dark wood, and on either side of the chalkboard stood tall bookshelves. A globe on a pedestal stood to the left of the desk, next to the small wood-burning stove, and an upright piano graced the wall on the right. Susie was busy printing tomorrow's lesson on the chalkboard. Her hand was slow and steady, and I could tell she was intently concentrated on her task. I hated to interrupt her.

Hearing us, Miss Meyers looked up from her papers and Susie turned from the chalkboard to face us.

Miss Meyers stood up. "How can I help you?" she asked in her most professional tone. She lowered her glasses, which were fastened to a chain around her neck, and let them fall to her chest.

I smiled at Susie. "These gentlemen would like to speak with Susie." I kept my voice calm.

Still, Susie's face went pale, and she looked at Miss Meyers for support.

"It's all right, Susie," she said.

Susie whispered something in Miss Meyers's ear.

"No. They aren't taking you anywhere."

Detective Walton must have sensed her apprehension and nodded for Officer Clayton to leave the room.

"Miss Meyers?" Officer Clayton directed his gaze toward her. "Do you mind stepping outside with me? I'd like to ask you some questions."

Miss Meyers looked at me with hesitation in her eyes but nodded and followed the officer out of the building.

The detective wedged his bulk into one of the student desks. If I hadn't been so wound up about this little interview, I might have found the sight hilariously amusing, but in my present state, I didn't.

"Do you want to sit down?" Detective Walton asked Susie.

She vigorously shook her head.

"That's fine," he said. "You can stand. But can you come over here to me?"

I was somewhat comforted at how the detective had stayed

true to his word at being gentle with Susie. It made me wonder if he'd had children of his own. Perhaps grandchildren? He certainly had not been so sweet with the other kids. The ache in my stomach lessened.

After a cursory glance at me, Susie stepped forward a few feet.

"Susie, how old are you?" he asked. I'd already told him, but this must have been a script he'd used for talking with children, an attempt to make them more comfortable. From the quiver of her chin, it was obvious it wasn't working with Susie.

"Ten and a half." She rolled her ankles outward, standing on the outside edges of her Mary Janes.

"Do you know what these are?" He held out the scissors, still nestled in the white handkerchief, and unwrapped them for her to see.

Susie nodded.

"Are they yours?"

She shook her head, sticking the tip of her index finger between her front teeth.

"Have you seen these scissors before?"

She looked up at me and took her finger out of her mouth. She pulled her lips between her teeth. No answer.

"We found them in your room," he continued. "Do you know how they got there?"

She shook her head.

"They're awfully dirty." He held them up to his face, as if giving them closer inspection. "Do you know how they got so dirty?"

She flipped her ankles back so the soles of her shoes rested solidly on the floor again. Her gaze met mine, and I smiled at her. She didn't smile back but stood frozen, rooted to the spot. I tried to still the fluttering of my heart. I could tell she was shutting down.

"Is there anything you can tell me about these scissors?" he pressed. "Anything at all?"

Her eyes glazed over, and she stared into space. I was just about to intervene and say something, when the detective worked his way out of the desk and stood up.

"Well?" he said.

"Detective—" I started.

He held a hand up in the air, silencing me. "Okay, Susie. If you think of anything, will you have Mrs. Riker or Miss Meyers call me?"

She finally blinked and gave an almost imperceptible nod.

"That's a good girl." He smiled at her, wrapped the scissors in the handkerchief, put them in his pocket, and headed out of the room. When we stepped outside, I met Miss Meyers's gaze. She didn't seem flustered in the least.

"Is that all, Officer?" she asked Officer Clayton.

"Yes. For now," he said, tipping his hat to her. She smiled at me and went back into the schoolroom.

"Let's see if Lizzy and Daniel are back," the detective said as he passed by Officer Clayton. The taller uniformed officer quickly fell in step with his superior.

Curious to see if either one of them had turned up, I followed them. We rounded the corner of the house, giving us a good view of the barn and the fields behind it. I breathed a sigh of relief as I saw Daniel and Lizzy talking with Chet and Joe, all of them standing next to the truck.

At the sight of the two officers, Lizzy crossed her arms over her chest in a gesture that said, *What now?* Daniel shoved his hands in his pockets and stared at the ground by his feet as if fascinated by it.

"You've returned," Detective Walton said.

"I gave them permission to take the truck," Joe said. "I had an errand for Daniel to run, and Lizzy wanted to tag along."

"And you are . . . ?" the detective asked.

Joe stepped forward. "Joe Manetti." He held out his hand.

The detective took it. "Detective Walton. You work here?"

Joe crossed his arms over his chest and widened his stance. "No, I live next door. I'm a horse trainer."

"Joe and I are working together to rehabilitate injured racehorses so he's here a lot," Chet explained.

The detective nodded. "Were you here the night of the party, too?"

Officer Clayton took a notepad and pencil from his pocket and held them poised in front of him, ready to take notes.

Joe rolled back and forth on the balls of his feet. "Yeah, but just to drop off Chet. He and I had just come back from Calabasas where we were checking out some horses."

"Bring any back with you?"

"No," Joe said. "Just went to have a look-see. But we're headed back down there to pick up one of them next week."

The detective hesitated a moment, then shifted his weight on to one leg and bent the other. He tucked his thumbs into the waist of his pants. "So did you go out to the barn on the night in question?"

Joe shook his head. "No. I went straight home."

"See anyone near the barn before you left?"

Joe shook his head again. "Nah."

Detective Walton, still scrutinizing Joe, scratched at his chin. "You said you let Daniel and Lizzy take the truck for an errand. What kind of errand?"

"I needed some things for the horses at the local feed store," Joe said.

"How long ago did they leave?" the detective asked.

"About three hours ago. Around noon."

The detective focused on Daniel, who was still staring at his shoes. "Seems like a long time to run just one errand. Is that the only place you went?" he asked.

Daniel didn't respond. The detective went up to him and

tapped him on the bottom of the chin. "I'm asking you a question," he said, his voice stern.

"Didn't hear you." Daniel's upper lip curled in defiance.

"I said, was the feed store the only place you went?"

Daniel still didn't answer.

"Daniel," Chet warned. "The detective asked you a question."

"Yeah. Yeah, that's the only place," he said with a sigh.

The detective tilted his head at Lizzy and gestured for her to come over to him. Her arms fell to her sides, and rolling her eyes, she did as he had bid her. He pulled out the handkerchief from his pocket and unfolded it, revealing the scissors. "Have either of you seen these before?"

"Nah." Daniel shook his head.

The detective turned to Lizzy.

"They look like Grace's scissors," she said. "But why are they so dirty?" Her eyes opened wide, and she gasped. "Is that the— Is that what was used to kill Mr. Travis?"

"So you have seen these?" The detective ignored her question.

"Yes. In Grace's studio. She keeps them on her pattern-making table."

"Ever use them before?"

She shrugged. "Sometimes." Then her jaw dropped slightly. "Wait, but I didn't—"

"Lizzy helps me with my patterns," I jumped in. "She also cuts fabric for me, so of course, she's seen the scissors." I didn't like the way this line of questioning was going. Just because she'd used the scissors before didn't mean anything when it came to Mr. Travis's death.

The detective held up a hand and gave me a pointed glare. "Mrs. Riker, please."

I bit my lip, duly chastised. So much for the compassionate man I'd seen in the schoolroom . . .

"Where did you last see these scissors?" he asked Lizzy.

"In the studio. Where they belong," she said, her mouth quivering. She looked at me with fear in her eyes. I wanted to reach out and hug her, but I knew Detective Walton would frown upon that and probably scold me again.

"You sure about that?" he pushed.

"Yes. I swear! I didn't kill him! I didn't!" Her eyes flashed in indignation, and she clenched her hands into fists at her sides. Daniel straightened up and stepped forward, as if to protect her.

The detective held her gaze for a moment longer, then placed the scissors back in the handkerchief and then his pocket. He turned his attention to Daniel.

Lizzy looked at me with desperation in her eyes. Unable to help myself, I went to her and wrapped an arm around her shoulder, trying to offer some comfort.

"Daniel, I forgot to ask you something the other day," the detective said, squaring his shoulders. He clasped his hands behind his back. "I see from your records that you were arrested for pickpocketing. Well, stealing, actually. That takes a great deal of stealth, does it not? You have a way of quietly making things disappear?" He raised his eyebrows.

Daniel's jaw tightened. "What are you saying?"

"Well you'd do almost anything for your friend Lizzy, right?" He unclasped his hands and gestured with one of them toward her. "Perhaps you followed Lizzy and Mr. Travis to the barn and did away with the murder weapon? Or if these scissors are the murder weapon, then maybe you wanted to make them disappear? Buy why in the little girl's room? I'd think you'd be a bit craftier than that. After all, criminal stealthiness runs in the family, right? Isn't your dad in prison?"

Daniel's nostrils flared, and his eyes narrowed at the detective. I wanted to reach out and prevent Daniel from doing anything stupid.

"Is this really necessary, Detective?" I asked instead. "Just because Daniel made some mistakes doesn't—"

"It's fine, Grace. I don't have to answer any of this." Daniel gave the detective a smug look. "I haven't been arrested."

The detective pressed his lips together and smiled. He then turned to me. "Well, okay. Sorry for the intrusion, Mrs. Riker, Chet. Thanks for your time." He turned on his heel, motioning for Officer Clayton to follow him. "Go get Faraday will you?" he asked him. Officer Clayton trotted toward the kitchen.

Lizzy turned to me, her eyes tearing over. "Why doesn't he believe me?" Her voice came out in a whine.

"That bull's just a damned bimbo," Daniel said.

"Watch your mouth, son," Joe admonished.

Daniel shook his head, his teeth clenched, and went back to the barn clearly upset. I couldn't blame him. Joe followed him, hopefully to give him some solace, but more than likely it was to give him more work. Joe believed work solved all life's ailments. Lizzy, stifling a sob, ran into the house.

"Why does that detective seemed determined to continually badger these kids?" I asked Chet. "They've all been through so much."

Chet took in a deep breath and let it out slowly. "It's unfortunate, but he has a job to do. They were all here the night of the party. He has to question everyone."

I sighed. He was right, of course. I only hoped the other party guests were under the same amount of diligent scrutiny.

CHAPTER FOURTEEN

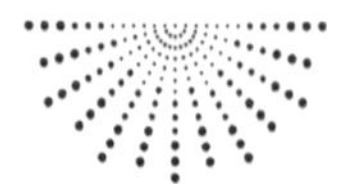

On Wednesday morning at about eight o'clock, I went out to my car to go to Margaret's to check in on her. She'd been so distraught at the news of Lizzy, not to mention the fact Lizzy didn't really want to talk with her, that I thought I should pay her a visit to see how she was faring before I had to be at the studio at ten o'clock.

I pushed the starter of the car, but the engine only whirred and sputtered. It had been a little temperamental lately, but today it was as dead as a doornail. I went to the barn to seek out Chet. He was in Goldie's stall.

"The car won't start," I said to him as he scooped Goldie's leavings into a wheelbarrow. He stopped and leaned on the handle of the rake.

"Well, I have to run a couple of errands in town, so I can drop you off at the studio and then pick you up later today," he offered.

"I'd like to go by Margaret's first. She was so upset the other day."

"Okay, sure." He came out of Goldie's stall with the wheelbarrow and closed the stall door. I smiled at him, grateful for his accommodating nature. It wasn't the ideal situation for either one of us—sometimes I worked late into the evening—but we would make do until we could take care of the car.

Forty minutes later, Chet pulled up to Margaret's little bungalow and parked in the driveway that led to a small garage.

"Should I wait for you here?" he asked.

I tilted my head toward the front door. "No, why don't you come in?"

We both got out of the car and made our way up the path to her front steps. When I knocked, the door creaked open.

"Margaret?" There was no answer. "Margaret? It's Grace and Chet. May we come in?"

When there was still no answer, I turned to Chet. "Why do you think the door is open?"

He shrugged. He pushed it open farther. "Margaret, we're coming in!"

We stepped inside. The living room was as neat and tidy as it had been before.

"She has a little studio on the sunporch at the back of the house," I said. "Maybe she's there and can't hear us."

I led Chet through the kitchen and out to the screened-in sunporch. Her easels looked as if they hadn't been touched that morning so I went through the screen door to the backyard. There was no sign of her. I stepped back into the sunporch. Chet was admiring some of her artwork lying on a table in the corner.

"She's talented," he said. "I don't know much about art, but these look like they are really good."

I sighed. "Well she's obviously not here. I guess we should go."

We walked back into the kitchen. There was a doorway at the opposite end of the kitchen, near the icebox, which seemed to lead down a little hallway. It looked as if there were two additional rooms.

"Margaret?" I tried one more time, starting across the kitchen.

"Let's go," Chet said.

I looked over my shoulder at him. "Let me just check down here."

When I turned back around and peered down the hall, my eye caught something on the floor in front of one of two additional doorframes. I gasped. Someone had fallen to the floor, their hand just sticking out into the hall.

"Margaret?" I called out. Then I shouted for Chet as I rushed down the hallway and looked inside the room to find Margaret prostrate on the floor. "Margaret! Margaret!" I gently shook her shoulder.

Chet came in and knelt down on the other side of her. He pressed his index and middle finger against her neck, looking for a pulse. Our eyes locked, and he frowned and shook his head.

I opened my eyes wide, not quite comprehending his meaning. "She's dead?"

"There's no pulse." He leaned down and lowered his cheek to her face. "And she's not breathing."

My heart slammed against my ribs as tears filled my eyes. "Dear god . . . What happened?"

Chet moved a lock of hair away from her neck with the tip of his finger. There was slight bruising across her throat—a straight line about a half an inch thick. My eyes traveled down to her legs. One of them was covered in a black stocking but the other was bare, and there was a bruise the size of an egg on her thigh. Discarded next to her was the other stocking.

"Chet, look." I pointed with a shaking finger.

He looked over at the stocking. "She was strangled—most likely with that." He craned his neck to see behind me. "What's that? On the floor?"

I turned around and saw something shiny. I reached over to pick it up.

"Don't touch it," Chet said. "We need to keep everything as it is."

I leaned my face down closer to it. It was an earring—a gold earring with a suspended blue stone. "That's strange," I said.

"What?

"This looks like one of Lizzy's earrings." I met Chet's gaze. "What is it doing here?" A sinking feeling hit the pit of my stomach. Had Lizzy and Daniel come over here when they'd taken Chet's truck? Had they— No. No, I refused to believe it. There had to be another explanation.

Chet shrugged. "Maybe they have matching pairs." He carefully moved the hair away from Margaret's ears. She wore a tiny pearl on each lobe.

"I doubt it," I said quietly, wishing I could believe it. "Lizzy told me they were once her grandmother's." Turning my gaze back to Margaret's lifeless body, I raised a shaking hand to my forehead. "Oh, this is horrible, Chet."

Chet stood up and stepped over her to get a closer look at the earring. "Do you think Lizzy gave them to her when she was at the ranch?"

I lowered my hand to my mouth, trying to keep my tears at bay. "Maybe." I swallowed, then asked, "How long do you think she's been like this?"

Chet looked down at Margaret again. "From the looks of her, she's been dead quite some time. And her skin is cold to the touch, too. We need to get the police over here. Does she have a telephone?"

I nodded. "Yes. In the living room, I think."

Chet left the room, and I studied Margaret's beautiful face, which had turned a ghastly shade of blue. Who could have done this to her? And why? Was it just some random killing? A date gone bad? A shudder ran down my spine. It had to be something like that, I reasoned.

Poor Lizzy. Her elder sister, her only family, dead. How would I tell her?

Suddenly, Lenora Lange's warning flashed in my mind. She'd said that something tragic would happen to someone in my circle—within forty-eight hours. I shook the thought away, and another memory stole its way into my mind.

I had been sitting in Flo's office at the theater when I'd learned that Sophia had died. My hands and feet had gone cold as ice, and an ache in the pit of my stomach had crawled up my throat, strangling me. I had felt like I was suffocating. I'd gasped for breath but couldn't pull the air into my lungs.

I grabbed hold of the doorframe now and tried to blink the memory away. When my head finally cleared, I took a deep breath. Holding a hand against my temple, I staggered out of the room and down the hall. I made it to the kitchen before I collapsed in one of the chairs. I could hear Chet talking in the other room and felt some comfort at his presence. I concentrated on breathing.

He stopped talking and then walked past the kitchen.

"Chet." My voice was weak and quiet.

He popped his head into the doorway and seeing the state of me, rushed over. He knelt down next to the chair. "You're white as a sheet." He took my hand. "And your hands are freezing. You're in shock." He took off his jacket and wrapped it around my shoulders. He went to the kitchen sink and took a glass from the cupboard, then filled it up and brought it over to me.

"Here. Drink this."

I sipped at the tepid liquid. He sat in the chair opposite me and took hold of my hand. "I wish you hadn't seen that."

I wished that, too, though, truth be told, the state of Mr. Travis's body was much more gruesome. But it didn't pack the same emotional punch as seeing Margaret for some reason.

"I should call the studio," I said, raising my other shaking hand to my temple. "Tell them I'm not coming in."

"Let me," Chet said, his voice soothing. "Are you okay if I go to the phone again?"

I nodded, and he let go of my hand. He went back to the living room, and I covered my face with my hands. Sophia's image pressed in on my thoughts. As much as I tried, I couldn't stop seeing her collapsed on the bathroom floor. She blinked up at me, and her mouth moved as if she was trying to say something, a white cloud floating from her throat. I yanked my hands away from my face, the vision vaporizing like mist. I pulled Chet's jacket tighter around my torso.

"I let the studio know you wouldn't be coming in. I told them you weren't feeling well. We shouldn't mention this to anyone until the police arrive." Chet pulled his chair close to mine. His nearness broke open the dam I'd been keeping my finger in, like the little Dutch boy and the leaking dike. I shuddered, waves of emotion rolling through me like a torrent.

"Hey, hey." He wrapped me in his arms, his chin resting on my head.

"She's all alone," I croaked.

"Margaret?"

"No. Lizzy. She's all alone. What's she going to do?"

"She has us. She has you." He stroked my hair, still holding me close.

I pulled away from him. "But she's facing a possible murder charge. What if she goes to prison? What if she . . . hangs? I can't. I can't let it happen. I have to prove she didn't kill him."

"It's going to be all right," Chet murmured. We sat there quietly for some time, waiting for the police. The tension in my body eased, and I began to relax in his embrace.

I wasn't sure how much time had passed, but a knock at the front door broke the silence. "Hello?" A male voice called out.

"In here," Chet said. He pulled away from me and his gaze met mine. Something in his eyes sent a sinking feeling to my stomach.

Detective Walton came into the kitchen, followed by Officer Clayton.

"The door on the right, down the hallway," Chet said.

We followed the two policemen and stood at the doorway while they examined the body.

"Looks like she was strangled," the officer said.

Detective Walton picked up the stocking. "Looks like." He studied Margaret's face, and with his fingers on her chin, moved her head one way and then the other. "She look familiar to you, Clayton?"

The officer nodded.

"You've seen her before?" Chet asked.

The detective frowned. "Maybe. Can't say for sure yet."

I looked over at Chet, confused. He looked equally confused. Did Margaret have a police record, too?

"I'll start to search the place." Officer Clayton stepped over the body and squeezed past us in the doorway.

"Did you two find anything else?" Detective Walton moved Margaret's clothing about, then looked up at Chet.

Chet pointed to the earring. "That might be something of interest. We think it belonged to Lizzy."

My heart sank at Chet's words. They gonged in my head like a betrayal. "But she wasn't here this morning," I said feebly, hoping to convince the detective.

"This woman wasn't killed this morning," said Detective Walton. "I'd say it was at least a day ago. Have you been aware of Lizzy's whereabouts?"

"She hasn't left the ranch," I said.

"She wasn't there when I arrived yesterday." The detective gave me a hard glare. "She and that Daniel fellow had taken the truck. Were gone longer than expected, am I right?"

I swallowed the walnut lodged in my throat at his insinuation that I didn't have any idea where my charges were or what they were doing. Did he really believe that? Guilt punched me in the gut. I had been busy with work since Lizzy had arrived, really, but I had always been apprised of the children's whereabouts, what they had been working on in school, how things were going with their chores and various projects. It had been an agreement between Chet, Rose, Miss Meyers, and me that my greatest contribution was the financial well-being of the kids and the ranch. And I always made time for the children when I could. So why did his statement make me feel like an utter failure?

"Well, yes, but—"

"You told me earlier that Lizzy and her sister were estranged, correct? Bad blood between them?"

My heart beat a staccato rhythm against my ribs. "I don't think I said that. It wasn't like that. Lizzy was just rebelling against—" I realized how awful my words sounded, how they painted a picture of Lizzy's possible guilt, and I wished I could take them back. She would never have killed Margaret, no matter their differences. They were two sisters alone in the world. Why would Lizzy kill her?

The detective turned his attention back to Margaret. "She was there"—he pointed at her—"at the reading of Travis's will. You know anything about that? Why she might have been there?" He looked up at me as if I had all the answers.

"She was? I didn't see her." Surely, I would have known if she had been there.

"She was there all right." Pushing his hands against his knees, he stood up with a grunt.

I shook my head, not understanding. She couldn't have been there.

"Sir?" Officer Clayton edged between Chet and me and entered the bedroom. In his hands he held a platinum-blond wig.

"Just as I suspected." Detective Walton took the wig, holding it up for me to see. "Now what had she been doing at the reading of Edward Travis's will?"

I stared at him openmouthed. I had absolutely no idea.

"Looks like we need to make another visit to your ranch. See if Lizzy can tell us anything—and find out how that earring got here." He directed the statement at Chet, who nodded in agreement.

My heart wilted.

WHEN WE ARRIVED at the ranch I went in search of Lizzy. She was just coming out of the schoolroom, books in hand. The children were often done with their lessons by noon and had the rest of the day for chores, projects, and homework.

"Lizzy, I need to speak with you. After you take your books upstairs, would you meet me in the living room please?"

"Sure," she said with a nonchalant shrug. I mustered a weak smile, my heart heavy with despair at what I had to tell her. I then took Miss Meyers aside and asked her to keep Susie after school. She could do her outdoor chores later.

Daniel and Ida were gathering their things, and I told them Chet needed them to start outdoor chores right away.

A few minutes later, Chet and I were in the living room breaking the terrible news to Lizzy.

A look of horror crossed her face. "That can't be. You're lying." Her eyes darted from Chet to me and back to Chet.

I took her hand. "I'm so sorry, Lizzy."

She ripped her hand away from me. "No. There's been some kind of mistake. She's not dead. She can't be dead!" Her voice came out shrill.

"I'm afraid it's true," Chet said, sitting down on the coffee table to face us.

"But I—"

I laid my hand on her knee. "Yes?"

There was a knock at the door. I took in a deep breath, knowing it was Detective Walton. He'd said he be out to the house directly after seeing to the body. I wish he could have given us more time with Lizzy. It seemed cruel to question her when she hadn't had time to even process that her sister was dead.

Chet opened the door and directed the detective to where we were sitting. He came around the sofa and took a seat in the chair adjacent to it.

"I'm sorry for your loss," he said to Lizzy. "I'd like to ask you a few questions."

"But why?" she asked.

He gave her a pointed look. "Your sister has been murdered."

Lizzy's eyes opened wide, and her mouth quivered. She grabbed my hand back. Hers was clammy and cold. Of course, she'd be in shock.

"Did your sister know Mr. Travis?" he asked, his voice calm, cool.

Lizzy looked over at me and then back to the detective. "Mr. Travis? I . . . I don't think so."

"Had you ever met Mr. Travis before? Before you came to live here at the ranch."

Her mouth trembled, and her eyes pooled with tears. "No. Like I told you before, I'd first met him when Grace took me to work with her a couple of days before the party."

"I see." Detective Walton paused and leaned back in the chair. "Did your sister have any boyfriends that you knew of?"

She shook her head, her cheeks waning of color. "Um . . . no."

"You're sure?" Detective Walton interlaced his fingers over his protruding belly.

"If she had boyfriends, I never saw them."

Another pause. This one annoyingly long. He took a deep breath. "Where were you on Tuesday afternoon, Lizzy?"

"Tuesday?" She looked at me, as if for further clarification.

"When you and Daniel left the ranch," the detective explained. "Where did you go?"

She squeezed my hand tighter. "We told you." Her voice came out calm and sure. "We ran an errand for Joe. Went to the feed store."

"And that's it? Nowhere else?"

"No." Her jaw tensed. "That's what I said."

Detective Walton reached into his pocket. He pulled his hand out and opened his palm to reveal the sapphire earring. "Recognize this?"

Lizzy stared at the earring, her brow knit in confusion. "Where'd you find that?"

"Do you recognize it?"

Her grip on my hand intensified again. "It looks like one of my earrings. It was my grandmother's."

With the index finger of his other hand, Detective Walton rolled the earring back and forth in his palm. "We found this at your sister's house." He lifted his gaze to meet hers. "Any idea how it got there?"

Her eyes widened in alarm. "N-no. I put them in my jewelry box."

"When was that? Before the party?" He held the earring up as if admiring it. I didn't like the way he was playing with her. It seemed unfair.

"Um, yes. Yes," she repeated with more certainty. "After I went riding."

He placed the earring back in his pocket. "Did you wear them to the party?"

Lizzy's eyes trailed his hand as if she wanted to take the earring back. "No. I borrowed a pair of Grace's earrings. To match the dress she loaned me."

Detective Walton raised his hands in question. "Did your sister have a similar pair of earrings?"

"No. What does this have to do with—"

He leaned forward in his chair and cut her off. "I'm going to ask you again. Did you and Daniel go anywhere else the day Mr. Manetti asked you to run an errand for him?"

Lizzy bit her lip. Her palm was drenched in sweat, but I didn't let go of it.

The door opened, and Officer Clayton came through, holding a stricken-looking Daniel by the arm. He shoved him onto the love seat. Daniel's face was red, and he looked on the verge of tears.

Detective Walton looked up at the officer with raised brows.

"Just as we thought, sir." Officer Clayton crossed his arms. "The feed store was not the only place they visited that day."

Detective Walton turned to Lizzy. She let go of my hand and ran her palms down her thighs, I supposed to dry them on her dress.

"Lizzy?" the detective pressed.

She burst into tears, holding her hands over her eyes. "Okay, okay!" She lowered her hands and lifted her tearstained face to the detective. "We went to my sister's house. But we didn't go in, I swear it." My heart stuttered at this revelation.

"Why did you go to your sister's?" the detective asked coolly.

"I wanted to talk to her." She sniffed loudly, and Chet handed her his handkerchief. She unfolded it and dabbed at her eyes.

Detective Walton's lips pressed into a firm line. "Did you speak with your sister?"

"No." She shook her head. "Like I said, we didn't go in. We just sat in the truck outside her house."

"Why didn't you go in?" The detective rested an elbow on one knee and palm on his other knee.

Lizzy lifted her shoulders up to her ears. "I don't know. I got cold feet, I guess."

"Why? What did you want to talk with her about?"

Lizzy held the handkerchief to her face and squeezed her

eyes shut. She let out a great sob. "I wanted to tell her I was sorry. Sorry for getting in trouble. Sorry for being so horrible to her. But—"

I grabbed her hand again. "So why didn't you?" I asked gently.

"Because I was afraid. She hated me!"

A sob caught in my throat. I hadn't known the two of them for very long, but I knew that nothing could be further from the truth. I was just about to say so when the detective cut me off.

"Did you hate her?" he asked Lizzy.

Her eyes flashed, and her jaw tensed. "No!"

"But there is still the matter of the earring. Which puts you at the scene of the crime."

"We never went inside!" Daniel shouted. Officer Clayton shot him a look, and Daniel flinched.

"Can you take me to this jewelry box, where you kept these earrings?" Detective Walton asked.

"Lizzy wiped her eyes again and blew her nose. Yes." She stood up and then led the detective upstairs. I followed close behind.

We entered her room, and Lizzy went to the jewelry box on her dresser and opened the lid. "I always keep them in the same spot." She lifted the top level out of the box and froze. She turned to us, her face draining of color. "It was there, I swear it."

Detective Walton walked over and peered into the box. He pulled out a single gold-and-sapphire earring and held it up, then placed it in his pocket. "Lizzy Moore, you are under arrest for the murder of Margaret Moore."

"Wait, what?" I stepped forward and grabbed a hold of the detective's arm, anger and fear blending until I was seeing red. "You can't! You have no proof!"

Detective Walton looked down at my hand gripping the sleeve of his coat and I quickly retracted it. "I have all the proof I need," he said, taking Lizzy by the arm. He led her out of the room. My heart thumping, I followed them, not understanding how this could be happening.

We all clattered down the stairs.

"Clayton," the detective pointed to Daniel. "We are taking them in."

Officer Clayton went over, grabbed Daniel by the arm, and pulled him to his feet.

"You're arresting me? What for?" Daniel's voice cracked.

"Just taking you in for more questioning, son," Detective Walton said. "But we are arresting your friend Lizzy, here."

"Chet, do something!" I pleaded.

He came over and wrapped an arm around my shoulder. "I'm afraid our hands are tied, Grace."

Detective Walton stopped before he took Lizzy out the door. "If you want to do something, I suggest getting this young lady a lawyer."

CHAPTER FIFTEEN

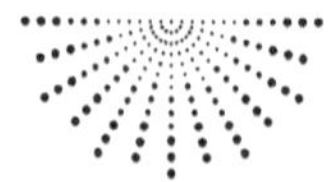

I took Chet's truck and followed them down to the station, determined to wait there until one or both of them were released. I paced the floor of the dingy lobby, the flickering overhead light causing an ache behind my eyes. The sounds of phones ringing and typewriters clacking added to my misery.

At about 6:00 p.m. an officer finally came out to greet me. "Mrs. Riker?" He was an older man, tall, thin, and near retirement age if I had to guess.

I wrung my hands together. "Yes. That's me."

"Detective Walton says to go on home. He's holding Miss Moore until bail can be set, and he's keeping Mr. Blaine until tomorrow at the earliest. The young man has chosen not to be cooperative. We will call you when we have further information."

"Oh dear." I practically wilted. Why did Daniel not see that he was making things worse?

"Do you know how soon bail will be set?" I asked, miserable for Lizzy.

The officer shook his head, and all I could do was go home.

When I arrived, everyone was at the dinner table. My bones ached, and the pain behind my eyes had only increased. My stomach swirled with anxiety.

Rose got up from the table and greeted me in the foyer. "I'll take your coat and hat. You go on in and get some supper."

Grateful, I handed her my things and went into the dining room. I did my best to put on a smile for Ida and Susie.

Chet looked up at me. "No luck?"

I shook my head.

"Where are Lizzy and Daniel?" Ida asked, putting down her fork.

I thought about making up a story to protect their feelings, but the situation had gone far beyond that. I sighed and gave them a weak smile. "They are at the police station. Hopefully, not for long."

The rosy glow in Ida's cheeks faded. "They're in big trouble, aren't they?"

I pressed my lips together. "We aren't sure what kind of trouble they are in just yet. Right now, the police still have some questions for them and are going to keep them overnight. But Chet and I are going to do everything we can for them in the morning." I looked to Chet. "Were you able to find a lawyer for Lizzy?"

He shook his head. "Not one we can afford. I'll keep trying, but by law, she will be assigned one by the court."

By dessert, my headache had crawled over the top of my skull and down the back of my neck. Despite my best efforts, I could manage nothing more than a bite of the pineapple upside-down cake Rose had baked that afternoon. As I sat with my elbow propped on the table and my fingertips at my temple, I felt a tap on my shoulder. Susie, who was sitting next to me, looked up at me with her big, hazel eyes.

"Are you sad, Miss Grace? Pineapple upside-down cake is your favorite."

I lowered my hand to my lap and forced a smile. "I'm just a little tired. And so full from that marvelous dinner." I glanced at Rose with thanks.

"It was really good, Mother," Chet said. I couldn't help but think he was trying to placate her. The stress of Lizzy's, and now Daniel's, situation had been difficult for everyone.

"Glad you enjoyed it." Rose gave Chet a nod and stood up, gathering her plate, utensils, and glass. "Ida, help me in the kitchen, would you?" She took her dishes into the kitchen.

Ida rolled her eyes and heaved a sigh.

"Hey," Chet warned her with a pointed look.

"Okay, okay," she said and gathered her things and Chet's. She went for Ned's, but he held her off. He was still enjoying his dessert.

The phone rang, sending a jolt of pain stabbing into my ears.

"I'll get it." Chet went into the hallway to answer it.

"How are you holding up, Grace?" Ned asked. "You look exhausted. Is there anything I can do for you?"

I shook my head. "No, Ned. Thank you. I'm fine. Well, I'll be fine once I can help Lizzy—and now maybe Daniel. I wish I'd never let Mr. Travis have that party here," I said with a sigh. "If I hadn't, we wouldn't be in this mess."

Ned reached across the table, but his hand didn't touch mine. "You've been really good for the kids. Don't doubt yourself. I know this is all very hard, but you've done nothing wrong."

I shook my head. "I'm not so sure about that."

He put down his fork. "You know, my mom raised me on her own. My dad lit out on us when I was just a boy. She worked three jobs just to keep a roof over my head. I was alone a lot growing up. I would have loved to have someone like you to take care of me."

I scoffed, feeling very unqualified at the moment. I played with my napkin in my lap.

"I'm serious," he said, breaking into a smile. "You are such a good influence on them. You're smart, full of life, loving. You are like a beautiful angel. The perfect woman."

The perfect woman? I looked up at him and heat ran up my neck and into my face. I was once more taken aback at his boldness.

I was rescued from having to respond when Chet walked back into the room. His face grim. "They have posted bail for Lizzy."

My heart lifted. So why did he look so serious? "Really? That's wonderful, isn't it?"

He sat down and his shoulders sagged. "It's twenty thousand dollars."

"What? That's a fortune." My chest went into spasms. "How will we ever raise that kind of money?"

"Geez." Ned shook his head.

I put my hands up to my cheeks. They were cold as ice, and my face was hot. My head pounded. "What are we going to do?" I asked Chet.

He looked over at Ned. "Ned, do you mind?"

Getting his meaning, Ned wiped his mouth with his napkin and, with a quick glance at me, grabbed his plate. "Of course. I need to go check the horses."

When he left the room, Chet came over and sat next to me, where Susie had been.

"Can we pay the bail?" I asked.

Chet shook his head. "I'm afraid not. We can't afford it."

Well, we certainly couldn't off my salary. "What about the money from the lease to Mr. Lambert? I thought you said you were putting that and our cut of the cantaloupe crop into savings. And you also put your share of the money from the Harper case into savings. If we sell something—"

"Grace." Chet took my hand. "We don't have nearly enough in our savings account. We've had to make repairs to the barn, the fencing. We have enough to get by on but not much extra. I'm so sorry."

Suddenly the small amount of dinner I had managed to get down felt like it was going to come back up, and the ache in my head made me feel like my brain was in a vise. Weak from pain and nausea, I pulled my hand away from him and slowly got up from the table, wishing I had never pursued a career in film and wishing I had never met Edward Travis.

THAT NIGHT, after a long soak in the tub, I crawled into bed aching with misery and worry—not to mention that my headache still had not subsided. I pulled open my bedside table drawer and reached for the aspirin. I popped two in my mouth and washed it down with a glass of water I'd brought up from the kitchen.

I was heartsick at the thought that I had failed Lizzy, who was now completely alone in the world. It was bad enough to have lost everyone in her life, but add to it that she was in a jail cell accused of murdering her sister? It was almost too much to bear.

It took me hours to drift off to sleep.

And then Lizzy was there.

She sits in a chair, blindfolded and gagged, her hands tied behind her back. A bright light shines on her face, and Detective Walton shouts accusations at her. Sophia and my mother stand behind her. Robert Smith and Lenora Lange are there, too, but they move in and out of the scene. Margaret holds a crying baby in her arms, trying to shush it. Sophia is again speaking to me. Suddenly, I am behind a group of boulders, looking down onto a body of water. Sophia is calling me toward her, but getting to her requires going over the boulders and through the water. My mother and Lenora Lange join in her efforts to get me to cross. I want to get to them so badly, but I keep slipping on the boulders, and I'm afraid I'll fall into the water to my death. I hold my hand out to Chet, who suddenly appeared, but when he reaches for it, he turns into Robert Smith and both his hands are covered in blood. He grabs onto mine, but I pull away from his grasp and tumble headfirst into the water.

I woke up gasping for air. I opened my eyes and breathed a sigh of relief to find myself lying in my bed, the room bathed in the gray of early morning, and the only sounds in the room were the whisper of the drapes as they fluttered against the opened window and the ticking of the clock on my nightstand. I looked over to see the time. It was 5:00 a.m. I sighed with frustration knowing I would never get back to sleep, and if I did, I'd only get forty-five to fifty minutes at most. I'd probably only gotten about four hours once again. I put my hand out to touch Chet for reassurance, but he wasn't there. He must have already gotten up.

I closed my eyes in an attempt to get a few more winks, and the image of Robert Smith passed through my mind again and again. I recalled his bloody hands in my dream. Realizing I would just replay the scenario in my mind for the next hour, I got out of bed. I pulled on Sophia's dressing gown and went to the bathroom to splash water on my face.

I stepped into my slippers and then opened the door to the hallway. All was still quiet in the house, and I was grateful for it. In an hour it would be bustling with activity and I would need to get ready for work, as much as I didn't want to go with Lizzy sitting in jail. It didn't seem right to have life go on as if nothing had happened when hers was in jeopardy. If she was found guilty of the crime, she would hang. Bile swirled in my stomach at the thought.

As I passed by the living room to go into the kitchen, I spied Chet on the sofa. He'd slept in his clothes—even his boots—and without a blanket. He must have stayed up late and then slept down here to keep from disturbing me. I smiled at his thoughtfulness. The room was chilly, and I grabbed the crocheted blanket from the back of the love seat and draped it over him.

I padded into the kitchen and boiled the water for coffee. I scooped some grounds into the Drip-o-Lator and waited. Once the water was ready, I set the Drip-o-Lator on the pot and poured in the water. In minutes, I had a fresh brew and inhaled deeply as I looked out the kitchen window at the fields. The sun had turned the sky a pale pink.

As I sipped, my gaze drifted over to the area where I'd found Robert Smith the night of the murder. My mind flashed to the dream and him reaching for me with those bloody hands. I shook my head to rid myself of the image, but it kept pressing into my thoughts. The sky was now a deep peach and the hills in the distance glowed, bathed in mauve. I left the window, went to the kitchen door, and stepped outside to get some air and immerse myself in the sunrise.

Taking in a deep breath of cool air, my head began to clear. I rolled my head in a circle to work out the kinks in my neck, which was still sore from the headache the night before.

The field where I'd seen Robert Smith drew my attention again. He was the only person I'd seen out here on the night of the party. I walked toward the fields, trying to relive the moment. I couldn't help but think he had something to do with the murder, even though I didn't want to believe it. He had been so angry at Mr. Travis, not to mention intoxicated.

I looked to the barn and estimated that it was about five hundred yards away. I stepped off the drive and walked out into the field. The dew unleashed the alfalfa's sweet aroma, and the tension in my shoulders began to melt. I never imagined I could be so contented living on a farm when I'd been born and raised in the city. But the hills, the grass, the sky, and the air, they sang to me, and I felt a rush of gratitude that I was able to share this with those who needed some stability in their lives. But it was quickly replaced by a pang of guilt at the notion that I hadn't been able to do that for Lizzy

I walked a bit farther into the field when my slippered foot hit something. I knelt down to see an empty bottle of Gibson's Rye—obviously Mr. Smith's. How had the police missed this? Maybe they'd only searched the barn? As I stood up, my gaze landed on something else about six feet away. It looked to be more glass, and I wondered how many bottles he'd taken out there. I had also seen him with a flask. I bent down to pick it up. A sharp prick pinched my index finger, and I pulled my hand back. A tiny pearl of blood beaded on my finger, and I stuck it in my mouth. I then pushed some of the alfalfa aside and stared in amazement. It was a broken, pink drinking glass. Like the ones we had in our kitchen. Perhaps like the shards in the barn?

More carefully this time, I reached for the rounded base of the glass and held it up. One side of the cylinder had completely broken away, leaving the other half almost whole, but jagged and coming to a fine point. It was coated in something dark. Something like blood.

I sucked in a breath. I'd found the murder weapon. And now I knew for certain who'd committed the crime.

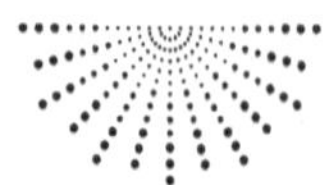

$\mathcal{I}$ ran back to the house and dashed into the living room. "Chet, wake up." I shook his foot at the end of the sofa. He attempted to roll over, and I pinched his toes.

"Ow!" He opened his eyes.

I pulled the blanket off of him. "I need to show you something. C'mon, get your shoes on."

"What time is it?" He reached up and swiped his hands down his face.

"It's early. Get up!" I picked his shoes up off the floor and held them out to him. Reluctantly, he took them and put them on.

I led him outside and jogged toward the area where I'd found the broken glass. Sensing he wasn't behind me, I turned to see him yawning and stretching. His hair stood up at various angles, and his shirttail hung partially out of his pants. I took in a deep breath, annoyed at his sluggishness. I moved on, and when I reached the spot waited for him.

"Look," I said when he got there. I picked up the glass and held it out for him to see. "Think you could kill a person with this?"

He took it from me and examined it. "Yeah, it's possible."

I reminded him of what I had seen before I went in the barn to look for Lizzy. "I think Robert Smith killed him. At the studio a couple days before the party, Mr. Travis humiliated him on the set in front of everyone. Then he saw to it that Mr. Smith was fired. I also witnessed Mr. Smith threaten Timothy O'Malley. He has a severe problem with alcohol and possibly drugs—although he said he'd quit the morphine, if he is to be believed—and he's shell-shocked from the war. He's mentally unstable."

Chet took in a deep breath and then let it out slowly. "Well he certainly had a motive. And yes, he could have used this to stab Travis. Can't be sure if that is blood, but if it is . . ."

"There was broken glass at the murder scene. Lizzy had a cut on her hand. She said Mr. Johnson gave her a glass of water before she went out to the barn. What if she had been trying to stop Mr. Smith, intervened on Mr. Travis's behalf and the glass broke in her hand, then Mr. Smith used it to stab Mr. Travis?"

"It's plausible."

"Yes! I think we need to get Detective Walton out here."

Chet ran a hand through his unruly hair. "Let's go in, and I'll call him." He reached out to touch my arm. "Hey, I'm really sorry we don't have the money to get Lizzy a lawyer or pay for her bail. I'm just sick about it."

I took his hand. "Me too. But who could have known something like this would happen? It's not your fault. It's mine. For having the party here. I never should have exposed the kids like that."

Chet wrapped an arm around me. "They need to learn how to handle themselves in social situations, Grace. It's part of growing up. I wish I'd had that kind of opportunity. But Mother felt she couldn't keep me, let alone raise me and teach me about things like how to behave at a party."

"I know. And I had Flo to teach me. But both Daniel and Lizzy were drinking at the party. We failed them."

Chet squeezed my shoulders. "They're teenagers, Grace.

They are going to see what they can get away with. Didn't you? I know I certainly did."

I shrugged. "Yes, I suppose so. But Lizzy is facing a *murder charge*."

"For her sister," he reminded me. "They haven't found substantial evidence to charge her for Travis's murder."

A sudden thought came to me. "The murders have to be linked. They both involve Lizzy."

Chet nodded. "That's why Detective Walton thinks Lizzy is guilty of both crimes." He looked at me like I wasn't quite getting it.

I pressed my lips together, thinking. "Why would Lizzy be involved at all?" I wondered aloud. "She's just an orphaned teenage girl."

"Maybe it has something to do with the robbery she was involved with. She didn't get a prison sentence, but we should find out if the man she'd been helping did and where he is now."

"Perhaps," I said, not entirely convinced. Murder and robbery were two very different crimes. "But they both could involve greedy, dangerous people . . . " I muttered to myself.

"What's that?" Chet asked.

I gasped as something clicked in my mind. "Chet, what if Lizzy is Elsa Mayfield, Mr. Travis's heir? Someone could be setting her up hoping to get her inheritance." Images of Mr. Travis's two wives flashed in front of my eyes.

"But then who is Margaret?" he asked. "Travis only had one child."

I bit a fingernail. "Maybe a stepsister? Maybe their mother remarried and Margaret is only her half-sister? We have to find out, Chet. How do we find out?"

Chet rubbed at the stubble on his chin. "I don't know. But believe me, darling, I'll find a way."

∼

I WAITED by the front room window in silence for I don't know how long, pondering my newfound theory and praying Detective Walton would show up soon, hopefully with Daniel in tow. They'd only been questioning him. It was about time he came home.

My breath hitched as I spotted the detective's Model T pulling up to the gate and coming down the drive. I called to Chet, and he met me by the front door. We hurried out onto the porch. When only he and Officer Clayton got out of the car, my heart sank.

"Where's Daniel?" I asked.

The detective took off his hat and held it to his chest. "We're still holding him. We believe he might have been persuaded by Lizzy to kill Miss Moore. He made it clear he'd do anything for her."

"What?" I nearly shrieked. Chet wrapped his arm around me.

"And we have reason to believe he might have killed Mr. Travis, too," the detective continued. "We have a witness who saw him go to the barn that night, shortly after Lizzy and Mr. Travis headed out there."

The air in my lungs froze. "What? Who? What witness?"

Detective Walton gave me a half smile. "You know I can't tell you that, Mrs. Riker." He looked over my shoulder. "May we come in?"

"This doesn't make any sense," I said under my breath. But, in actuality, the theory was plausible—probably more so than Lizzy being some long-lost heiress to a Hollywood fortune— which was more terrifying. Perhaps Daniel, worried—or even jealous—of Mr. Travis's attention to Lizzy caused him to follow them out to the barn. If Daniel thought he'd caught them in a compromising position, he may have retaliated. But still, murder was a tall order, especially for a boy like Daniel.

The detective took his hat off and held it between his hands. "Neither one of the kids is budging on their story. There's something they aren't telling us, and until we get more information, they are both staying put. I can't risk them going on the lam."

I clenched my jaw, knowing I wasn't going to persuade him otherwise. Instead, I turned to what I could do. "Detective Walton, you took my scissors as evidence the other day. Were you able to find out if they were the murder weapon?"

He let out an irritated groan. "We were, but it was determined that the substance on them was not blood."

I smiled with satisfaction. "Well, I found something this morning—something you and your officers missed." I couldn't keep the condescension out of my voice. "I believe it to be the murder weapon, and I think I know who most likely killed Mr. Travis."

"Oh?" he said, glancing at Chet.

"She's right," Chet said. "We'll show you."

When we reached the spot, Detective Walton picked up the empty rye bottle and handed it to Officer Clayton.

"There," I said, pointing to the broken glass. "This is where I saw Robert Smith right before I found Lizzy and Mr. Travis in the barn. Mr. Smith had motive, means, and opportunity. So you see, you have to consider him as a suspect."

The detective shot me a look. "Everyone's a suspect, Mrs. Riker. But I'm afraid Mr. Smith had an alibi."

That was impossible. "What? But he was out here alone. I saw him. No one was with him."

"Miss Lange claims they came out here together. She left him for about two minutes to go get her wrap from the car, and then she came back. There wasn't enough time for Mr. Smith to get to the barn, kill Travis, and then come back here."

"But don't you agree the broken glass could be the murder weapon?" Chet asked.

Detective Walton nodded. "Could be. And it if is, my guess is that Lizzy or Daniel killed Travis, and then Daniel disposed of the glass. He saw you, Mrs. Riker, heading to the barn so he skedaddled."

It was difficult to argue with his reasoning, but something inside me still could not believe either one of the kids had done this. Was I just fooling myself?

"If that is true, Detective, doesn't it stand to reason that it could have been self-defense?" I asked. Surely that would work in Lizzy's favor.

He held up both hands. "That's for the court to decide."

"So you are charging her?" Chet asked.

"Yep. Afraid so."

"For which crime?" I asked.

The detective's gaze met mine. "Both."

I closed my eyes, wanting to chase away this horrible reality. It couldn't be true, and if it was, how could we have been so blindsided by this girl?

It's not true, a voice rang out in my head. It was that same voice again.

I opened my eyes and turned to him, crossing my arms over my stomach. "What about Daniel?"

"Seems they were in collusion."

I shook my head, unwilling to believe it.

"Do you have any proof to that effect?" Chet asked.

"Circumstantial evidence. And that's enough for my part of the deal, you know that. The court will decide whether they are guilty or not."

My hopes wilted. From what he was saying, Detective Walton would have no reason to continue to search for the real murderer. He believed he'd found her—or him. The detective just needed to decide which one of them did it, and I imagined he would do so by continuing to interrogate them. I felt sick to my stomach at the thought. But with that thought came the determination to prove him wrong. I just needed to figure out how.

~

Later that morning I went to work with a heavy heart, my mind swirling with all kinds of horrifying thoughts. To make matters worse, I arrived late to the set. Timothy was none too pleased because there was another problem with Helen's costume, the Santa Maria, and Martha, the lead seamstress, and Hilda needed my input on how to fix it. Helen was still having trouble moving in the dress, and we needed to come up with a solution that gave her more freedom but also stayed true to the time period.

"This is taking too much time, Grace," Timothy said to me after I'd been briefed by the seamstresses. "It should have been taken care of the first time."

Felicity was with him and gave me a sympathetic smile.

"I'm sorry," I said. "We will have the problem rectified by this afternoon." Secretly, I was actually a little pleased at this turn of events. It would give me the perfect opportunity to speak with Helen.

"It needs to be rectified *now*, but this afternoon will have to suffice. I'll give you till one o'clock. I can't have my production schedule compromised more than it already has been." He tamped out his cigarette. "Everyone, we'll meet back here at one o'clock *sharp*. Please be ready to shoot—*all* of you." He gave me a sideways glance and then stalked off. Felicity stayed behind.

"Hilda." I crooked a finger at her. "Help Miss Clark get undressed. With a nod, Hilda led Helen off the set.

I turned to Martha. "Hilda and I can take care of this. Would you mind double-checking the other costumes for any potential problems? We can't have any more issues."

"Of course," she said, and followed the other two. I exhaled a deep breath.

"How are you holding up?" Felicity asked me. "You look tired."

I shook my head. "I'm obviously not holding up very well."

"Are you sleeping?" She picked a stray piece of thread off my sweater.

"No. I can't even remember when I had a full night's sleep."

She nodded sympathetically. "Still having those dreams? About Sophia?"

"Yes. And my mother has been making a star appearance, as well—all on top of what happened to Mr. Travis and Margaret."

Felicity crossed her arms and then rested her chin on her fist. She cocked her head at me.

"Do you feel like Sophia is trying to tell you something?"

I wrinkled my brow. "If you had asked me that a week ago, I would have said you were crazy. But—" I thought about the voice that had come to me a few times since the murder of Mr. Travis. "Yes. Maybe."

"Hmm . . . Have you thought about having a psychic reading?"

"Do you mean like a séance?" I never imagined Felicity would put stock in something like that. She was always so practical and pragmatic.

"No. A reading. Lenora Lange has been hanging around the mansion at Florence's behest. She's trying to contact Edward from the beyond. Actually, Florence just had a séance the other night. She invited me to come."

I scoffed. "You're kidding. Did the ghost of Mr. Travis show up?"

"No." She gave me a demure smile. "But Joe did."

I raised my brows. "Joe? You mean as in Joe Marciano?"

Felicity pressed her lips together and nodded.

"Do you really believe it was him?" A tingling sensation ran down my arms. This was too strange to be true.

"Not at first, but, later, Lenora approached me and suggested

I do a private reading. She said it would be easier for the spirit to come through and communicate with me."

"And?" Perspiration dampened my palms. Had anyone but Felicity told me something like this, I wouldn't have believed them, but Felicity was a no-nonsense type of person. For her to be saying this was incredible.

"He showed up again during my private reading. Lenora mentioned things Joe had said and had done to me that no one else knew about. It was uncanny. She even mentioned the day he died—gave some pretty accurate details. And she mentioned you."

"Me? Why me?" I ran my sweaty hands down the skirt of my dress. Their coolness penetrated the fabric and radiated onto my upper thighs.

"You were there when he died," she stated matter-of-factly.

True. I had been. My mouth went dry, and my scalp prickled. I shook off a shiver. I wanted to protest, to tell her this was absurd, but I found it difficult to do so.

Felicity placed a hand on my shoulder. "You okay?" She must have seen the color drain from my face because then she said, "Sugar, you don't look very well. Do you want to sit down?"

Unable to speak, I shook my head, tears starting to surface.

"My goodness but you are under a lot of pressure, aren't you?" she said, more as a statement than a question.

At her words, emotion welled up inside. She only knew the half of it. My lip quivered, and I placed a hand over my mouth to hide my distress, but my eyes pooled with tears.

"Come sit down," Felicity said softly. She put an arm around my shoulders.

I sniffed loudly and shook my head. "No. I can't. I have to get Helen's costume fixed. You heard Timothy."

"Just for a few minutes." Her voice was like honey, smooth and soothing, and I felt lulled into obeying her.

We made our way to some chairs at the back of the room, and I sat down with a sigh. Looking into my friend's startling blue eyes, everything I'd been holding in tumbled out. I told her about Margaret and how Lenora had said something tragic would happen within forty-eight hours. How Lizzy had been taken in again, and this time under arrest for the murder of her sister. And about Daniel and how Detective Walton was convinced he was in on both crimes.

"You still think Lizzy is innocent? And Daniel?" she asked, her voice dubious.

"Yes. Maybe I'm crazy, but yes." I looked down at my hands clenched together in my lap. Something compelled me to believe they were innocent.

Felicity took in a deep breath. "Listen. You've got a lot to contend with here, Grace. You need to rest or you are just going to crumble."

I chuckled, wiping away a tear. "Going to? It's already happening."

Felicity took hold of my hands, which were still cold and clammy. "Let me set up a reading. Maybe we can put some of these unresolved issues with Sophia and your mother to rest at least, and that will ease your mind a little. I got some resolution with Joe through the readings. With each one I feel lighter, like a weight has been lifted. And I'm sleeping better than I have in years. Better than when I used to take laudanum, if you can imagine."

I sighed again, and holding back tears, I nodded, desperate for some kind of relief. "Okay. I don't suppose it could hurt."

I WENT BACK to wardrobe and vowed I would dismiss the conversation I'd just had with Felicity from my thoughts. If I didn't, I would never be able to concentrate on my work. The

Santa Maria was in desperate need of some alteration, and I needed to get information from Helen Clark.

"Ouch!" Helen yelled at Hilda. She stood in front of a three-way mirror on top of the eighteen-inch platform while Hilda worked at the cinched-in stomacher of the dress. "That is the second time you've stuck me with a pin!"

I was surprised at the outburst. Although a little ditzy and "off with the fairies" much of the time, Helen was mostly sensitive and always polite with the crew. And today, she seemed completely sober.

"I'm sorry, Miss Clark," Hilda said, still pinching the bodice of the dress together.

"Let go of me!" She stepped down off the platform. "Grace, will you please come over here?"

"On my way, Helen. What seems to be the problem?"

"This dress is impossible." She flopped her hands down on either side of the dress, looking like a frustrated four-year-old whose princess gown was too uncomfortable for her. "And *she* —" she pointed at the seamstress "—is so clumsy, I'm sure I'll have a dozen holes poked into me by the time she's finished."

I gave Hilda a sympathetic look. "Why don't you go get things ready for another makeup and wardrobe test for Miss Clark. We may have to talk with Mr. O'Malley about moving some of her scene shoots around until we get this dress figured out. And also get my sketchbook and pencils, will you? I have a feeling we may have to start from scratch on this one."

Helen stepped back up onto the platform and looked at herself in the mirror. She issued a theatrical sigh. "This bodice seems to hit me in all the wrong places."

I scrutinized the dress with a studious eye and had to agree with her. "What if I lowered the waist a little?" I suggested. "It seems too high."

She put her hands on her hips and swiveled on the platform.

"Perhaps that would work but then look at the bust. I'll be coming out of it."

"I'll just replace the stomacher. Don't worry. We won't have you creating a scandal on the screen."

I caught her eye in the mirror, and she scowled at me. "No. Only off-screen, apparently."

My fingers flew to my mouth. There had been much talk of her affair with Mr. Travis on the set and in the papers. "Oh, Helen, I didn't mean—"

"It's all right." She stepped down from the pedestal. "I knew what you meant. I just—" She dropped into the club chair next to the platform and pressed her forehead into the palm of her hand, shaking her head. "I don't know what I'm going to do without him."

I stood there silently, allowing her time to say more if she wished. I also was trying to figure out how to couch my questions. She looked up at me with her large, sorrowful eyes, and they filled with tears. I reached for my handbag and pulled out a handkerchief.

I handed it to her, and she dabbed at her eyes. "I know what people say about me. That I was just another amusement for Edward. But I wasn't. It was different between us."

"Of course it was," I said the words just to appease her, even though I tended to agree with the rest of our gossipy little movie colony. Mr. Travis was notorious for his affairs.

"He said this picture was going to be a wild success, and after he proved it to everyone, he was going to divorce Florence and marry me. I've been speaking to a lawyer about divorcing Charles. He doesn't know it, of course, but Edward wanted me to get the process started."

I wondered if Mr. Travis had truly spoken to a lawyer about divorcing Florence or if he'd just been trying to placate Helen—to get the most out of her performance. I've heard of directors doing worse to manipulate their actors' emotions to get the results they wanted. And it seemed he hadn't been successful in divorcing his other wife, Pearl Davis, if he truly was still married to her.

"And what about Florence?" I asked.

She screwed up her face. "He wanted to keep her happy so she wouldn't sabotage his film. She's that vindictive. I only wish —" She pressed the handkerchief to her face and cried into it in earnest.

I sat down on the other club chair next to her and placed my hand on her arm, distressed to see her so upset.

"I only wish we had made up before—" She blew her nose. "Before the party."

So, they had been arguing before that night. "What happened between you two?"

She shook her head as if trying to rid herself of a memory. "We had a horrible fight. We hadn't spoken—except on set—for a week. Sure, we'd had our arguments, but this time— Oh, I feel so stupid now. Of course women would fling themselves at him."

I furrowed my brow, not following her line of thought.

"Charles wanted to take me to the Monterey Room at the Rosslyn Hotel to listen to some jazz," she explained, "and, well, Edward was there, dancing cheek to cheek with some floozy. She couldn't be more than sixteen if she was a day."

Just like Lizzy, I mused.

"I couldn't believe it," she continued. "He said *I* was his special girl! So what was he doing with her?"

I shrugged. A few things came to mind, but I refrained from mentioning them. It seemed she needed to unburden herself so I listened. "So what did you do?"

"I stormed up to them, and then I slapped him." She squeezed her eyes shut and shook her head. "Charles was furious. First that I'd made such a scene, and second because I foolishly as much as admitted that I was having an affair with Edward. I was just so . . . so . . . I was so hurt. It was a stupid thing to do, and I paid for it in more ways than one." Her voice cracked.

I remembered seeing makeup covering a bruise under her eye. Had Charles been so infuriated that he'd hit her?

"Helen—"

She gave me a teary smile. "Yes?"

"Helen, if you don't mind my asking, if your husband knew you were having an affair with Mr. Travis, why did you agree to come to his party and bring your husband?" The thought had crossed my mind that Charles had gone in order to get Mr. Travis alone somehow and kill him. Or had Helen seen him speaking with Lizzy and flown into another jealous rage?

Helen took in a deep breath and let it out slowly. "Charles had heard that Mr. Chaplin and Mr. Fairbanks would be at the party. He wanted to talk with them about the possibility of me working for United Artists. He wanted me away from Edward and Ambassador."

"I see."

She wiped her nose again and folded the handkerchief over on itself several times, then clenched it in her fist. Her crying had calmed to occasional gulps of air. She looked exhausted.

"Helen"—I kept my voice quiet—"did you, or perhaps your husband, go out to the barn that night?"

She looked up at me with confusion on her face. "No. Why do you—" Her eyes opened wide, searching mine. "You don't think I had something to do with Edward's murder, do you? I didn't kill him, I swear it! I told that police detective as much when he came round the house to talk to Charles and me."

I figured this was as good a time as any. "Helen, as you know, the girl who is living with me has been arrested for Mr. Travis's murder."

She nodded and sniffed into the handkerchief.

I tried to gauge the expression on her face, looking for anger, but I didn't see it. Only a sad vacancy. Still, I pressed onward. "I don't believe she did it. She says you might have bumped into her at the party. Then later, you came up to her and Mr. Travis to speak with him. Were you angry at him for talking to Lizzy? Were you jealous?"

She blew a puff of air through her lips. "Of her? No. He wasn't flirting with her. Believe me, I knew when Edward was flirting. He had this way he looked at women he was interested in, you know? He wasn't looking at her that way. I was angry because he was avoiding me."

I pulled my top lip between my teeth, not sure what to make of this or if I even believed her. "I have something to show you."

Her brows pulled together in confusion. "Okay," she said uncertainly, and sniffed.

I went over to my purse, which was lying on the desk. I opened it, pulled out the vial and sat down next to her again. "Is this yours?"

She blinked at me, shaking her head, her eyes flicking from mine to the vial. "No . . . No. Why would you ask?"

"I found it on set. I thought maybe—"

She held up her hand in protest. "I know you've read the gossip sheets. Yes, I use laudanum on occasion, but never at work."

Fair enough.

"Did you use it on the night of the party? Did you bring it with you?"

She sighed, getting impatient with me. "Yes, I took some before we left the house. Things had been tense with me and Edward, and I knew it would be uncomfortable seeing him at the party. But I didn't bring it with me." She leaned close to me and looked me straight in the eyes. "I didn't kill Edward. I loved him."

I stared back at her, and she didn't flinch. Either she was an excellent liar or she really didn't do it. "What about your husband?"

He vehemently shook her head. "No. No! Charles was with me all night. Wouldn't let me out of his sight. He may be a controlling bastard, but he's not a murderer!"

I pressed my lips together, couching what I was going to say next. I decided to come right out with it. "But he is prone to violence."

She blinked at me and then lowered her gaze. She tilted her head to the left. "He has been prone to violence, but it's only because he loves me so much. He can't bear to lose me."

"Do you love Charles?" I was having trouble understanding this strange love triangle.

Her expression belied her inner turmoil. "I . . . I . . . I wouldn't be where I am today without Charles. My life was horrible before him. He saved me from a dreadful existence. My father was gone, and my mother was . . . well, she drank. She didn't love me. I was working in a hotel as a hat-check girl, and he discovered me there. Got me into pictures. I didn't mean to fall in love with Edward, but—"

"But you did," I finished for her.

She nodded and pressed the handkerchief to her eyes.

"Did you know about Pearl Davis?" I asked.

She took in a weary breath. "Yes. But I only found out about her by accident."

"What do you mean?"

"She came to town about two weeks ago. She lives on the East Coast somewhere. Anyway, Edward and I had booked a room at the Roosevelt for a weekend getaway. We were having dinner in the restaurant, and she showed up at our table. At first I thought she was just another smitten actress trying to get Edward's attention, but then she said, 'I'm here to discuss our divorce.' I was so shocked I choked on my Chateaubriand. I mean, really choked. The waiter came over and slapped me on the back a few times. It was quite embarrassing." She shook her head as if reliving the discomfort. "Anyway, she left during all the commotion."

"Did you see her after that?" I asked.

"No. Not until the reading of the will."

"How did Mr. Travis react to Miss Davis showing up at the hotel? Did you talk to him about it later?"

She folded and unfolded the handkerchief in her hands. "Of course I did. I was furious with him. Here he was, married to Florence, and then I find out he was married to someone else, as well? How could we marry if I divorced Charles? I wasn't about to be his third wife like some concubine in a harem."

I reached out and stilled her hands. While I couldn't condone her behavior of carrying on with another woman's husband, I certainly understood the devastated feeling of betrayal. "Did Mr. Travis mention why he and Miss Davis hadn't divorced?"

Helen blew her nose into the handkerchief. "He said they couldn't come to terms on the financial aspect of the agreement. She comes from a wealthy family and had property all up and down the East Coast. As her husband, Edward felt entitled to at least half of it, but she didn't agree. She was able to secure a really tough lawyer, someone who had been a family friend for years. So Edward wouldn't agree to the divorce until she met his demands." Another fresh batch of tears fell from her eyes, bathing Helen's cheeks.

"Oh dear." She wiped her eyes again. "I am just blathering on. I didn't mean to dump all this on you. I'm sorry."

"It's quite all right." I patted her knee. "You're distressed, and sometimes unburdening yourself is just what you need. But we really should get back to the matter of this costume."

"Yes, of course." She stood and stepped up to the platform again. I set to work, my mind swirling with the information she'd just given me.

Pearl Davis had come to town to discuss divorce. Had she finally agreed to his terms, or had she come up with a scheme to avoid them? If things didn't go as she planned, killing him might solve all her problems, but only if she didn't know about his heir. She hadn't been at the party, but what if she'd hired someone to do the deed? I had to find out more. A visit to Pearl Davis at the Roosevelt was definitely in order.

CHAPTER SEVENTEEN

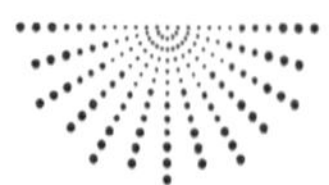

We finally got the dress figured out, but because we were so late getting started, Timothy wanted to push through the evening. It was about 10:30 p.m. when we wrapped for the day. My trip to the Roosevelt would have to wait until tomorrow.

When I got home that night, I was dead on my feet. I entered the house and heard rattling around in the kitchen. Opening the door, I found Miss Meyers there, brewing some tea.

"Oh, hello," I said. "Everything all right?" Early to bed and early to rise, it was unusual to see Miss Meyers about at this time of night.

"Yes, I think so. Susie's come down with a head cold. Thought I would make her some chamomile with honey. Hopefully it will settle her a bit."

"Oh no. Do you think it's serious?" My stomach seized with a flash of panic.

"I don't think so. She's just a little agitated."

"It's been a rather trying several days." I set my purse and my coat on one of the kitchen chairs.

"Want some tea?" she asked.

"That sounds lovely."

She poured me a cup and then one for Susie. "Shall we take it to her together?" Miss Meyers blew on Susie's tea. "She's been asking for you. I think it would give her some comfort to see you."

I pushed my lip out in sympathy for the girl, feeling terrible at not giving her any attention over the last several days. "Poor dear. Of course."

We climbed the stairs and entered her room. It was bathed in a soft glow of light. Miss Meyers had put a scarf over the lampshade on Susie's night table. Susie rolled over when she heard us and sat up. Miss Meyers set her tea on the table, and I sat on the bed next to Susie.

"I hear you don't feel well." I gently pushed her hair out of her eyes. Her skin was warm to the touch, and her cheeks were pink with fever.

"I have a stuffy nose and my throat hurts." She looked up at me with big hazel eyes.

"I'm so sorry, dear."

"Why weren't you home for dinner?" she whined.

"I had some work to do. But I'm home now. Should we let Miss Meyers go to bed?"

Susie nodded, and I turned to Miss Meyers, who smiled and left the room. I set my teacup and saucer on the table and handed Susie hers. "Here. Drink some of this. The honey will make your throat better."

I held the cup to her lips, and she drank. "It tastes good. It's warm in my tummy."

"Good. When did you start to feel poorly?" I let her hold the cup and reached for mine again.

Her gaze dropped to her teacup. "Well, my throat started to hurt yesterday, but I've been feeling bad for a while."

"You have?" I asked with alarm. She hadn't mentioned anything.

"Well, not sick or anything, but bad about something else." She handed me her cup, and I set it back down on the saucer.

"Do you want to talk about it?"

She nodded. "Yeah, but I'm afraid you'll be mad at me and you'll make me go away." She wouldn't meet my eyes, and a tear rolled down her cheek.

I swallowed the lump forming in my throat. "Oh, sweetie. I promise you, no matter what you tell me, I won't make you go away."

She sniffed, and then her gaze met mine. "It's about your scissors."

I raised my eyebrows in surprise and waited for her to continue.

"I wanted to cut out some clothes for my paper dolls, and I couldn't find my scissors. I remembered that you cut out patterns in your studio so I took yours."

"I see."

"Then Daniel said it was time for me to go give the horses their oats so I put the scissors in the pocket of my jumper. When I leaned over the molasses to scoop it out and put it into the oats, the scissors fell in. I got them before they fell all the way in, but when I pulled them out, they fell in the dirt. I tried to clean them, but they were just so sticky, and I—" Her voice broke.

"Aw, honey. It's okay." I pulled her to me and wrapped my arms around her.

"I'm really sorry," she blubbered into my shoulder. "When that man came to ask about the scissors, I thought I would be in trouble and then he would take me away like he took Lizzy away. And now Daniel is gone, too. I thought we would all have to go away."

I held her close for a few minutes and let her cry. This was such a mess, and really, at the moment, I couldn't see my way out of it. I wanted to cry, too, but I needed to be strong for Susie, for all of them.

"Listen to me." I gently relaxed my hold on her and lifted her chin with my finger until her eyes met mine. "We are going to stick together, you understand? Chet, Miss Meyers, Rose, and I have all made a promise to take care of you kids, and we are going to do everything in our power to do so."

The corners of her lips lifted in a smile. "I won't have to leave?"

"No." I used all the conviction I could find in my voice. "You will not have to leave. Cross my heart." I drew a cross on my chest with my finger.

"What about Lizzy and Daniel?" she asked.

Of course she was worried for them. They were stability for her. I wasn't quite sure what to say, though, given the situation was out of my control at the moment.

"No matter what happens with Lizzy and Daniel, we will not turn our backs on them. So you need to help us."

She batted her eyes at me and wrinkled her brow. "How can I help?"

"Well, you just be a good girl, do your schoolwork and help with the chores—like you always do—and you think good thoughts for Lizzy and Daniel. That would help them the most."

"Can I pray for them?"

"Of course." I smiled at her. "Do you want to pray for them now?"

She smiled back, revealing a gap where she'd lost a tooth recently. She put her hands together and closed her eyes tight. "Dear God, please take care of Lizzy and Daniel and help them come home to us soon. Amen." She beamed up at me.

"Amen," I said, hoping with all my might that if there was a God, he—or she, or it—would answer this little girl's prayer.

ANOTHER DREAM WOKE me at 3:00 a.m. and I couldn't get back
to sleep. It was different than the ones I'd had before, though. I
had been standing in an art gallery, looking at paintings, and as
I slowly passed by them, I came across a small portrait of my
mother and father. My mother was painted with both her own
physical qualities and Sophia's. She held a baby in her arms,
but it wasn't me. It was Sophia. Strange as that was, what I'd
found so fascinating as I was looking at it was the frame. It was
gold and ornate, stylized with a terrace with columns, vases, a
profusion of flowers and plants, and a swallow flying in
the sky.

I lay there in the dark, staring at the ceiling, the image of the
frame dancing in my mind. Chet's soft snores soothed me. I
hadn't left Susie's room until she'd fallen asleep. Completely
exhausted, I had taken off my clothes, put on my nightgown, and
gone to bed without even washing my face. I had fallen asleep
instantly, which was a blessing, but then after the dream, I'd only
lightly dozed until the gray of early morning filled the room.

I got out of bed and went downstairs to make coffee. My plan
was to take my coffee and the newspaper into the sunroom and
watch the sunrise. If I wasn't going to get any sleep, I was going
to do anything I could to find some peace in my day, if only for a
few moments.

My limbs dragged with fatigue, and my thoughts were fractured and disjointed as I padded into the kitchen and made
coffee. I made it extra strong. I absolutely *had* to be to the studio
on time today or Timothy would have my head. Once the coffee
had brewed, I poured some into one of the Hall China coffee
mugs—the largest cups in our cupboard—and stepped outside to
walk down the lane to the ranch entrance gates to get the paper.
The summer breeze was soft, but there was still a bit of a chill in
the air from overnight. Casually strolling down the road, I could
hear Joe and Ned in the barn feeding the horses, and birds
singing in the trees. I took in a deep breath and relished the

heady smell of alfalfa floating on the breeze and tuned in to the sounds of the ranch waking up.

As I reached the gate, Jimmy, the paper boy, had just ridden up on his bike and tossed the string-wrapped paper over the gate. It landed at my feet.

"Morning, Mrs. Riker!" he hollered as he turned in an arc and sped back down the road.

I bent down to get it but stopped when I read one of the headlines: PEARL DAVIS, WIFE OF BIGAMIST DIRECTOR EDWARD TRAVIS, FOUND DEAD IN HOTEL ROOM.

I picked up the paper and stared at it in disbelief. How horrible! I placed a hand on my chest, my mind reeling. The story claimed she had committed suicide, as an empty bottle of Secobarbital was found on the night table next to her. *Suicide?* But she was second in line to inherit Travis's estate, and for all we knew, she might have thought she was first in line before the reading of the will. Why would she kill herself?

I wish I'd been able to speak with her, but now . . .

I hurried back into the house just as Chet was coming down the stairs. I handed him the paper. "Second story on the right."

He read it and then looked up at me. "What a shame."

I took the paper back from him. "I know. But why would she commit suicide? With Edward Travis dead, she stood to gain from his estate. It wouldn't make sense for her to kill herself."

"She would have inherited only if Mr. Travis's heir isn't found," Chet reminded me.

"Right. But so far, she hasn't turned up. Pearl Davis committing suicide makes no sense. Do you think the police will investigate the possibility of foul play?"

Chet lifted a shoulder. "I don't know, but I'd assume so since she was married to Travis."

I followed him into the kitchen where he poured himself a cup of coffee. We sat down at the kitchen table.

I took another sip of my coffee and leaned my elbows on the

table, my mug between them. The pungent aroma wafted into my nostrils, clearing my head. "Chet, these deaths are connected. I know it."

He added some sugar to his cup of coffee and stirred it slowly. His eyes were puffy from sleep. "But how is Margaret's death connected to Travis and Miss Davis?"

"Detective Walton said Margaret was at the reading of the will," I reminded him. "They even found the blond wig in her house."

Chet held his coffee cup up to his lips. Steam swirled beneath his nose. "She could have just been curious. Snuck in. Like you. Maybe she was there for the same reason you were. To see who would gain by killing Travis in an attempt to exonerate her sister."

"But then, why wear the wig?"

"Maybe she wanted a new hairdo for the day?"

I sighed. "Really, Chet?"

"Sorry," he said, his gaze resting on mine. "That was insensitive. In your conversations with Margaret, did she ever mention an association with Travis?"

"No—other than the fact that Lizzy was a suspect for his murder."

"And did Lizzy ever mention knowing him?"

"No. She met him on the lot at Ambassador with me the week of the party but that was all." I set my cup down. "I wish I knew more about Margaret. And about Pearl Davis. "

He took a swig of his coffee, his eyes narrowed. I could almost see the wheels turning in

his head. "Do you remember the name of Travis's estate lawyer?" he asked.

"Oooh." I scrunched up my face, trying to remember. "Yes, I think it was Redford. No, Willford? No, wait, Redmond. William Redmond!"

Chet nodded, going pensive on me. "I'm going to pay him a

visit. See if I can find out anything more about this mysterious heir."

"But why would he talk to you?" I asked.

He gave me a smile. "I'm a private investigator working on behalf of Lizzy Moore, and I have questions about Mr. Travis's heir—what he might know about her, why she might want to frame my client for murder."

I tucked my chin and pulled back in surprise. "But you're retired."

Chet shrugged and took another sip of his coffee. "My license hasn't expired yet." He placed his hand over mine. "And I want to do my bit to help Lizzy," he said, his eyes tender with concern.

How could I possibly say no to that?

And in the meantime, I would try to find out more about Margaret.

TIMOTHY HAD SAID shooting wouldn't start until ten o'clock that morning. It was only 7:30 a.m. by the time I got ready for the day, so it gave me plenty of time to begin my investigation in earnest. Margaret had worked at the Art Students League, which seemed like a good place to start.

After joining Rose, Miss Meyers, and the children for a quick breakfast, I went to the phone and asked the operator to connect me with the Art Students League. A man answered. I told him I was interested in taking some courses and wanted to come see their school. I hated lying, but I thought it would be indelicate to bring up Margaret over the phone. He told me they were located on the third floor of the Lyceum Theater and gave me the address.

Since it was still early, I was able to find a parking spot out in front of the four-story, Romanesque revival–style building, complete with narrow turret. The poster in the window indicated that *Secrets*, starring Norma Talmadge, was playing. I hadn't seen the film yet but was curious to see the work of costume designer Clare West. I'd seen her work in D.W. Griffith's *The Birth of a Nation* and was duly impressed. But that would have to wait for another day.

I entered the building and found my way to the third floor. I spotted the Art Students League sign on the double doors to the right and walked into a large studio. Several easels surrounded a large dais furnished with a fainting couch. I imagined a scantily clad model reclined there having her portrait done.

An older man came out from behind a wall carrying a wooden painter's box. He was tall and thin, with salt-and-pepper hair, piercing blue eyes, and a gray goatee. He wore an eye monocle.

"Hello. I'm Grace Michelle. I called earlier?"

"Ah yes. You are interested in taking some classes." He set the box down and came over to shake my hand.

"Well, sir, not exactly," I admitted, feeling a slight twinge of guilt. "I'm actually here to talk to you about Margaret Moore."

He released my hand and removed his eye monocle. He tucked it into the pocket of his jacket. "Such a pity. Are you a relation?"

"No. I'm a, well, a friend. A new friend. I know she didn't have much family—"

"Aside from the sister who is accused of her murder," he said, raising his eyebrows at me. "Despicable."

I swallowed the knee-jerk reaction that was about to come out of my mouth. Instead, I cleared my throat. "I thought I would put together a little obituary for her—for the paper. I was wondering if you could tell me about her job here." The guilt of lying clawed at me again, but I didn't know how else to get the information I needed from this man.

"Oh. Well . . ." He scratched at his goatee. "She did some

administrative work, registered new students, and did some light bookkeeping. I paid her, of course, but she also took classes in lieu of a full salary."

"Did you advertise for her position? How did she find out about you? It was my understanding she came to you from Lake Tahoe."

"Yes, yes, she did. And no, we didn't advertise the position. In fact, we hadn't even considered using a secretary. We are on a rather tight budget here, but one of our benefactors made a large donation with the stipulation that we hire Margaret. But she wasn't to know about the arrangement."

My pulse quickened at this new information. Someone went to great lengths to get Margaret to Los Angeles . . . How cryptic.

"Oh my, that is generous indeed," I said. "For both you and for her."

He shook his head and chuckled. "I was dubious to say the least. But we really couldn't afford to turn down the offer. Once Margaret arrived and we saw what a talented artist she was, I quickly changed my opinion on the subject. She was a stand-up secretary, as well."

"Well, if she wasn't to know, how did she learn about the position?" I asked.

This benefactor asked a friend to visit her boarding house in Lake Tahoe and claim he was one of our members. He stayed the weekend, saw some of her work, and made the offer."

My eyes widened at the new lead. "Do you know who this friend was?"

"No."

"Who was this benefactor?"

He chuckled again. It was a deep-throated and pleasant sound. "I'm afraid it was anonymous. I don't know, but I am eternally grateful."

"I see. How terribly puzzling," I said, hoping I didn't sound too disappointed. But I wanted—no, I *needed*—more. "Do you know if she had any friends here? You know, any one she was particularly close to?"

He stroked his goatee with his thumb and forefinger. "Hmm. Well, she was quite friendly with Barnaby Maxwell." He pulled out his monocle and pocket watch. "He should be here in a few minutes if you'd like to wait. We will be starting class shortly, but you could probably speak with him for a moment."

I smiled at him. "Yes. I think I will. Thank you."

He clapped his palms together. "If you'll excuse me, I need to get prepared for class. Make yourself at home." He then wandered back to where he'd come from.

I strolled quietly through the room, studying the easels. They were painting a portrait of a woman wearing a Grecian gown seated on the fainting couch and holding a lyre, with a man standing behind her looking over her shoulder. Several of them were in the classical style while others interpreted the scene with the newly popular Abstract Modernism.

"Hello?" A dead ringer for Cary Grant walked into the room. "Are you the new artist's model? Please say yes." He stood back and appraised me from head to toe. "You are lovely." He made a beeline for me with an outstretched hand. When he grasped mine, he laid a wet, rather sloppy kiss on my knuckles.

I pulled away and refrained from wiping the back of my hand on my dress. "No. I'm a friend of Margaret Moore's. Are you Mr. Maxwell?"

He let out a chuckle. "Hardly. That man's got more talent in his little finger than I can ever hope to have. George Perry, at your service." He bowed with a flourish, then sobered. "Yeah. Tough luck about Margaret. She was a nice kid. She had her fair share of talent, too."

"Yes, I know. I was lucky enough to see some of her work."

Another man entered the room. He took off his coat and hat and hung them on the coat rack at the door. He was small and narrow shouldered, and had a disheveled look about him.

Mr. Perry held his arm aloft. "Barnaby! Just the man. This lovely creature was looking for you."

Mr. Maxwell appraised me with intelligent, dark eyes.

"I'm Grace Michelle, a friend of Miss Moore's. I was wondering if I could speak with you for a few moments?"

He gave a slight nod.

"I'll set up for you, sport." George Perry slapped him on the shoulder.

I decided to continue the charade about the obituary and told him I was writing something for the paper. He pressed his lips together, and his jaw twitched, clearly trying to hold back his emotions.

"I'm sorry, I don't mean to upset you," I said.

He shook his head. "It's just such a shame. She was the whole package, you know. Smart, beautiful, talented." He diverted his gaze to the floor. I wondered if theirs had been a romantic relationship but didn't quite know how to ask. I decided to stick to my obituary script and took a small pad of paper and a pencil from my purse.

"I wonder, did she ever talk about any distant family? Cousins? Friends?" I asked.

He shook his head. "Just her sister. Not friends. Like me, she was quite a loner. I think that's why we got on so well." He crossed his arms over his chest and settled his stance.

I scribbled something on the pad. "Did she ever talk about her time in Lake Tahoe?"

He nodded. "Yeah, sure. She owned a boarding house."

"Yes, I knew about that. She sold it, if I recall?"

He pressed his lips together again. "Got to be too much work for her. She wanted to focus on her art. Said some guy who was visiting up there saw her work and told her about us. He recommended her to the old man, and he offered her the job."

So, the "old man" had been telling the truth. Not that I had doubted him. It was simply good to have someone corroborate his story.

"Do you know how long she lived in Lake Tahoe? Was she from there originally?" I continued.

"No." He shook his head. "She moved to Tahoe from New York City. Said she didn't want to leave New York but had a bad breakup and wanted to start over, so she came to California."

I tapped my pencil on the pad of paper. Neither Margaret nor Lizzy had made any mention of New York City or a bad breakup. "Do you think this old flame caught up with her? Do you think he could have, well . . ."

He shrugged. "I know her sister is accused of killing her, but I don't buy it. They were pretty close."

I smiled at him, glad he didn't feel Lizzy was responsible either.

"To answer your question," he continued, "I believe this ex-boyfriend could have killed her, yes. But he wasn't the problem so much as his brother. I guess the guy was a criminal, served some time in the Big House. Margaret said he threatened her—came after her once."

I raised my eyebrows. "Oh my. Did she say why?"

He shook his head. "She started to once, I think, when we were at her house painting. We'd had a bit too much wine, and when she'd realized what she'd said, she clammed up. Never mentioned it again, and I didn't ask. Figured it was too painful for her."

"Yes, I imagine so." The wheels in my head were spinning. How had this person threatened her and why? Could he have followed her here to Los Angeles? Found out where she was living? Strangled her? But it wouldn't explain the earring, why he'd want to frame Lizzy.

A group of people filed into the room all at once and started to hang their coats and hats. I took it as my cue. "Well, thank you, Mr. Maxwell. I won't keep you any longer. If you should happen to think of anything else—for the obituary—would you please contact me?" I handed him one of my calling cards.

He took it, looked it over, and then tucked it into the pocket of his trousers. "Yeah, sure."

I thanked him again and took my leave.

It wasn't much to go on, but it was a lot more information than I'd had before.

CHAPTER EIGHTEEN

My mind was buzzing with all the new information I'd gathered from Margaret's place of employment as I drove to the studio. Who was this ex-boyfriend, and who was his brother? When Detective Walton had asked Lizzy about Margaret's boyfriends, she had claimed not to know of any. But according to Mr. Maxwell, there had been at least one.

I was still pondering this as I sat on set watching a scene with Helen Clark and Bill Havers, the replacement for Robert Smith, unfold. It was a scene in which the queen is in the bedchamber with her lover and she finds out he is the king's brother when the king interrupts them. Helen's performance was so mesmerizing to watch, it pulled me away from my thoughts. Her range of emotion and facial expressions were astounding. Suddenly, she looked away from the camera and over my shoulder.

"Cut!" Timothy yelled. "What are you doing, Helen? You should be looking into the camera."

I swiveled my head to see Florence Thomas standing there, looking fresh and beautiful in a caramel-colored silk dress with apron front and lace collar. Scalloped lace ran down the front and across the hem. It beautifully set off her auburn hair, which was pulled back in a neat chignon.

James Johnson, Mr. Travis's hired man, accompanied her. He carried her wrap, which was a fox stole complete with tiny white points on its head and beady black eyes. Mr. Johnson looked as if he were carrying the thing like a treasured pet.

"Florence!" Timothy rushed over to greet her. He looked particularly charming today with his white shirtsleeves rolled up and his unruly hair flopping in his eyes. He planted a kiss on each of her perfectly alabaster cheeks. "Good to see you, lass. How are you keeping?"

She raised her chin with a determined air. "Well, all things considered. I'd like to come back to work."

"That's smashing, love. But are you certain?" He looked at her earnestly.

Florence gave a theatrical sigh. "Yes. I believe work will keep my mind off things."

"But are you *sure*? There hasn't been a funeral yet, has there?" Timothy asked, looking around the room as if he had been the only one who hadn't been told. I, too, would have thought Florence would want the closure of a funeral before coming back to work.

She pressed her fingers to her trembling mouth.

Mr. Johnson cleared his throat. "We had a private service yesterday," he said. "Florence wanted to keep it secret, didn't want the press involved."

Well, that *did* make sense.

"Yes." Florence looked over at Mr. Johnson adoringly, giving me pause. Just how close were those two?

It did seem odd to me, though, that she wouldn't want a regular funeral, despite the press. It was customary to give others closure, as well, and their own venue and space in which to grieve. I'm sure there were many people who had wanted to pay their respects, myself included. Perhaps Florence merely didn't want Helen Clark—or any other paramour of her husband—to show up at the funeral to diminish her shine as the grieving widow.

I realized the callousness of that thought and tried to dismiss it from my mind. I got up from my chair and wandered over to them.

Then I remembered what the executor of Mr. Travis's will said would happen to his estate if no heir was found. "Didn't Mr. Travis have family? Parents? A brother?" I asked.

Florence regarded me coolly and ignored my questions.

"They live in England. The parents are too ill to travel," Mr. Johnson chimed in sharply.

"Oh, I see." Perhaps the brother stayed behind to care for them? I cast a glance in Florence's direction. She abruptly turned her head as if she didn't want to have anything to do with me. I assumed this was on account of the fact that I had harbored her husband's supposed killer. I inwardly scoffed. In my estimation, Florence, as the cuckolded wife, had a pretty good motive for wanting her husband dead herself.

"Well." Timothy clapped his hands together. "We don't have you on the schedule for shooting, my dear," he said to Florence. "We weren't sure when you'd return, but I think we can make some adjustments."

Florence smiled at him. "You'll have to make further adjustments. I won't be on set with *her.*" She lifted her chin in Helen Clark's direction.

Helen heard the exchange, and with hands pressed against the stomacher of her costume, she muttered something under her breath.

"But, Florence, you have a number of scenes together," Timothy protested.

She raised an eyebrow at him. "So I guess you'll have to fire her."

I stifled a gasp. Helen had the lead in the movie, and she was marvelous in the role.

"Come on, now, lass." Timothy circled his arm around her waist, turning up his charm. "You know I can't do that."

Florence sniffed. "Well, it's her or me. How do you think your movie will be received if you fire Edward Travis's bereaved widow? The press will eat you alive."

Well played, I thought. Timothy needed this movie to be a success considering the fact that no other studio would hire him at the moment because he had cast Felicity, a colored woman, as the lead in his last film. Incredulous as it was, it was true.

My gaze traveled to James Johnson. He returned the look with an uncertain smile. There was something in his eyes that conflicted with the smile, but I couldn't quite put my finger on it. Was it sadness? He had the air of a sensitive being, someone who was not entirely comfortable in his own skin.

"You can't ask me to do that, Florence," Timothy insisted.

"Yes, I can, sweetie," she said, running a finger down his cheek. "And one more thing. I will need James to replace Mark Clemmons in the male supporting role." She took Mr. Johnson's arm and pressed herself against him.

"This bloke?" He pointed at Mr. Johnson. "Can he even act?"

Mr. Johnson smiled at Timothy in that same uncertain way. "I graduated from the London Academy of Music and Dramatic Art. My forte is music, but I took my fair share of acting classes there."

The name rang a bell. Hadn't Edward Travis graduated from LAMDA, as well? Was that where the two had met? And what exactly had been the nature of their relationship? He and Florence seemed awfully cozy. Too cozy. But at the party, Mr. Smith had alluded to the idea that Mr. Johnson was homosexual.

Florence looked at the director expectantly. "Will you speak to the Steinbergs and Mr. Combs or shall I?"

During the exchange, Felicity had wandered onto the set. She wore a pair of cream wide-legged trousers and a bright-red top. She was checking the curtains hanging from the castle windows. I didn't see Helen any longer, though. She must have snuck away.

Timothy placed his hands on his hips, apparently speechless, which was a rare thing indeed.

"I'll check in with you tomorrow, dear." Florence took her fox stole from Mr. Johnson and wrapped it around her shoulders. "We can go over the new schedule and any adjustments that need to be made for James here. Oh, and—" she turned her full attention to me and narrowed her eyes "—we'll need to make some alterations to my costumes. I've lost some weight due to my grief. James will need to be fitted, too, of course. Come, James. I'm suddenly feeling a little tired."

Throwing the fox head dramatically over her shoulder, she and Mr. Johnson left the set.

"Bollocks!" Timothy said, running his hand across the stubble on his chin.

"What's going on?" Felicity asked.

I gave her the rundown.

"And that Johnson fellow is a sap, i'nt he?" Timothy said. He looked over at the set. "Now where in the hell did Helen go?" He took off to find her, surely to smooth things over.

"What a mess," Felicity said, watching him go.

"You're not kidding," I agreed. "Have Florence and Mr. Johnson always carried on like that? Like best friends, like, well, lovers?" Perhaps Mr. Smith had been wrong about him.

Felicity snorted. "Yeah, but I try to mind my own business."

"What did Mr. Travis think?" I wondered out loud.

Felicity placed her hands in her dress pockets. "From what I could tell, he didn't care. But if he did, he didn't do anything about it."

So maybe they *were* just friends.

"Felicity!" Timothy called to her from across the set. "I need a word."

"Guess I'd better go," she said. "Oh, I almost forgot. Remember how I said you might benefit from a reading with Lenora Lange? Well, I've set one up for you. Can you come to the mansion after shooting tomorrow evening?"

I had completely forgotten about Felicity's suggestion I consult with the medium about my unresolved issues with Sophia and my mother. "Um, sure, I guess. If we *are* shooting tomorrow." Would there be more delays as Timothy worked out the issues between Helen and Florence? "I'll have to check with Chet and the kids to see if I'm needed at the ranch first, though."

"Ah, speak of the devil." Felicity nodded over my shoulder.

Chet walked toward me with purpose, wrapped his arms around me, and spun me in a circle. I squeaked in surprise. It wasn't like Chet to visit me at work, and it certainly wasn't like him to behave so demonstratively in public. He was usually so reserved and stoic. He set me down but didn't let go of me.

"Looks like someone's happy to see you." Felicity winked at me. "I'll leave you two alone."

"What are you doing here?" I asked.

"Remember how I said I was going to pay a visit to Travis's estate lawyer?" He released my waist and put his hands on his hips, smiling at me.

"Yes. It went well I take it?" I was still surprised at his enthusiasm.

"Turns out he's a pretty small operation. Just him, a secretary, and an errand boy. He and Travis met before Travis was worth anything. Anyway, they are in over their heads with finding this mystery heir and keeping up with their other clients."

I frowned, confused. "Well that doesn't sound good."

"But it is," he said. "Since we are both looking for Travis's heir, he's offered to hire me."

"You're kidding," I said, still not quite believing this turn of events.

Chet shook his head. "No, I'm not, Grace. This way, I'll have more clout to investigate. And I'll get paid. Although, not a lot. But I'll be helping you, Lizzy, and Daniel. For me, that's enough."

I smiled up at him. "You really are the cat's pajamas, Chet Riker."

"Oh, and there is something else. I did some nosing around at the police station after I left the lawyer's office. Detective Walton is less than five weeks away from retirement, but because he botched his last couple of cases, the Chief is threatening to fire him if he doesn't make good on the Travis case—and fast. If he's fired, he won't get his pension."

I sucked in a breath, indignation coursing through me. "That's why he's so eager to charge Lizzy and Daniel with the murders of both Margaret and Mr. Travis. He's got a bird in the hand—well, two birds!"

"Exactly," Chet agreed. "Unfortunately, until he has evidence to prove otherwise, he's got enough to go on."

I slammed my fists onto my hips. "Well we'll just have to find that evidence, then."

CHAPTER NINETEEN

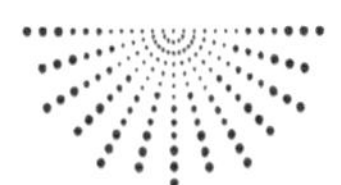

$\mathcal{E}$arly the following morning I received a phone call from Timothy. He was halting production until he could get the situation with Florence and Helen figured out. Neither of the parties were being cooperative. In fact, they were acting like temperamental, narcissistic movie stars. No surprise there. I wasn't sure we were ever going to get this picture made. Timothy said the studio bosses wanted both actresses in the film and told him he needed to work it out between them. I didn't envy his dilemma.

When I asked him about Mr. Johnson, he simply replied, "Don't ask," so I didn't know the status of his being in the film.

Felicity also called to make sure I'd heard from Timothy, and added that since filming was halted for the time being, she could arrange to have Miss Lange do my reading earlier than planned, at 4:00 p.m. as she was going to be at the mansion anyway to do another reading with Florence. I wondered if she'd gotten any results in her attempts to communicate with her late husband.

I met Chet in the kitchen for breakfast. He had mentioned he would be getting up even earlier than usual to take care of things in the barn and confer with Joe on the new horse before starting his investigation into Mr. Travis's mystery heir.

After pouring our coffee, Rose brought Chet his preferred breakfast of bacon, eggs, and potatoes. I opted for some of Rose's freshly baked toasted bread with butter and jam.

The comfort-inducing aromas filled the kitchen, fortifying me with a sense of hope. "I think I'll go to the jail today to see Lizzy and Daniel. They must be feeling so forlorn." I bit off a corner of my slice of bread. "Rose, would you mind preparing a couple of baskets of food for them?"

She didn't answer but gave me a nod. I took another bite and turned to Chet, who was tucking in to his breakfast.

"How do you propose we start to find this person?" I asked, eager to get on with the mission at hand.

Chet waited until he swallowed his food before answering. "I'd like to start at the mansion, but I'm not sure Miss Thomas will allow it. I'm sure she doesn't want Travis's heir found. At least I wouldn't if I were her."

"Right. Well, Felicity can probably get you in. She's still working at the mansion. Actually, I am going over there at four o'clock this afternoon. Why don't you come with me?"

"Sure. What are you going there for?" Chet popped the last of his bacon in his mouth.

"Um . . ." I hesitated. I didn't want to tell him why I was really going. I wasn't sure how I even felt about it, so I wasn't ready to share it with him just yet. "Felicity wanted to get my opinion on some upholstery fabrics."

"All right. I'll go down to the city records office today and see if I can find anything more there. Redmond's secretary got a start on it but didn't make much progress. Meet you back here at three?"

"Perfect." I raised my coffee cup to my lips and reveled in the aroma tickling my nose.

He got up from the table, kissed me on the cheek, and took a piece of toast with him out the door. I sat in silence eating the rest of my toast and sipping my coffee as Rose bustled around in the kitchen preparing baskets for Lizzy and Daniel.

I didn't have much energy due to the fact that I barely had slept again. I'd have to have another cup of coffee if I wanted to get anything accomplished during the day.

When I had gone to bed last night, I had lain there staring into the darkness, unable to turn off my thoughts. Truth be told, I hadn't relished the idea of falling asleep only to be awakened by more disturbing dreams. I hoped Felicity was right and I could get some kind of relief from Miss Lange. If not, at this rate, I'd have to visit my doctor to get a sleeping medication. The prospect filled me with dread. My sister had been hopelessly addicted to sleeping pills and hadn't been able to function without them. She had barely functioned *with* them in the end. But I had to find a way to sleep or it would kill me—literally.

THE VISITORS' room at the city jail was a sparse chamber and smelled of mildew. Only a table and two chairs at the opposite ends of the table. A dirty glass window cast dim, yellow light into the room. There was a door by which the visitors entered, and another door for the inmates. I was told I could see Lizzy for a few minutes *only*, but I couldn't see Daniel at all that day. I'd have to come back again. My heart deflated.

When Lizzy was brought into the visiting area, I was aghast. She had a black eye, and her right cheek was red and swollen. "My god, what happened?" I asked, a lump forming in my throat.

Lizzy looked at me, despondence in her eyes. "There are three other women in the cell with me—there are only a few cells back there—and I made the mistake of sitting on someone else's cot."

"Heavens! Was something done about this?"

She shrugged, her eyes filling with tears. "Someone paid for her bail, so she's gone."

My heart was breaking in two. "Oh, sweetheart. I'm so sorry."

Her face crumpled, and she shook her head in dismay. "Grace, I want to go home. It's filthy here. The only time I get any peace at all is when they let us sit in the yard for an hour or so each day."

I gritted my teeth, angry at the appalling conditions. "Have they assigned you a lawyer yet?"

She nodded. "I've been told I have one, but I've yet to see him. I take it you can't afford the bail? I know it's a lot of money . . ."

My anger quickly dissipated to guilt and sorrow, making my whole chest hurt. "We are doing everything we can to get you out of here. We are trying to find proof that you are innocent of these crimes," was all I managed to say.

After a thorough check, the guard permitted her to take my basket of food. I imagined she would be under pressure to share it with her cell mates, but perhaps it would soften them toward her a little.

"What about Daniel? What's going to happen to him? He looks awful, Grace. I saw him from a distance in the yard. I'm worried about him."

I smiled at her tender concern for him. "We're helping him, too, Lizzy. Try not to worry."

When we parted, I longed to rail against the guard, telling him it wasn't fair that she was here, or Daniel. I wanted to grab hold of Lizzy and flee, but I knew neither scenario would benefit her or even work.

After I left, I ran a few errands in town before going home for lunch. I spent the hour visiting with Susie and Ida, who were both anxious to hear about Lizzy and Daniel. I tried to keep my voice cheerful as I explained that Lizzy seemed well but that I had not been able to visit Daniel. I sent them off to do their homework and chores feeling like a hypocrite at not revealing my own worry and anxiety, but why bring them down, too? They were just children, and as their guardian, it was my job to protect them.

As he had promised, Chet met me at home at 3:00 p.m., and we headed over to the mansion. The afternoon had a lazy feel to it with the warmth of the sun radiating through the open car window, and the cool marine breeze swirled around the loose waves of my hair. Despite my worries, I fought off sleepiness.

"Did you have any luck with the city records?" I asked as we drove down the lane.

"I found nothing pertaining to an Elsa Mayfield or a Greta Mayfield."

A wave of disappointment coursed through me. "Obviously they're not from here, then. Mr. Travis is from England. Perhaps they are there, as well?"

Chet let out a whistle. "I hope not. That's going to make them a lot harder to find."

"I wonder if Pearl Davis knew them. She didn't seem surprised to hear about them at the reading of the will. Maybe they live in New York?"

"Could be," he said. "Let's hope we can find them here in California, though."

I had called ahead telling Felicity that I was bringing Chet. I explained to her he'd been hired by the lawyer on behalf of the estate to find the Mayfield women. She suggested we park in front of the mansion, and she would meet us there.

We rang the bell, and she greeted us at the door.

"Is Miss Thomas about?" Chet asked. "I'd like to ask her a few questions."

"No," Felicity said. "She and James just left."

"Probably just as well," he said. "It will give me a chance to look around without putting her nose out of joint."

We walked into the expansive entry. The grand foyer had black-and-white-checkered flooring, much like the kitchen, with a double wooden staircase lined with black railings that soared to the second-floor landing. The white walls on the lower floor were adorned with black furniture, and a large, glittering crystal chandelier cast elegant rainbows across the walls.

"Wow!" Chet said. "Did you do all this Felicity?"

She closed the door behind us. "No. This is one part of the house Mr. Travis wanted to leave the same. Beautiful, isn't it?"

"Yes. So where do you suppose Mr. Travis keeps his files?" Chet was through with idle chitchat and wanted to get down to business and quickly.

"That would be in his study. I'll show you." Felicity led us up one of the staircases to the second-floor landing. From there, we took a left turn and walked down a wide hallway furnished with plush and expensive-looking rugs. At the end of the hallway, she opened a door to the right, and we entered a very masculine room with a heavy, paneled wooden desk. A window behind the desk provided enough light to balance the darkness of the furnishings. The room smelled faintly of cigar smoke or pipe smoke, I couldn't be sure which. It was as if Mr. Travis had just been sitting in his office moments before we arrived.

A glass-doored barrister's bookcase lined one wall, and a heavy walnut credenza furnished with picture frames lined another. One of the frames caught my eye, and I walked over to it. The photo was of a young Florence Thomas on a beautiful thoroughbred, but what really captured my attention was the frame. It was gold, depicting a charming garden scene with a Greek-style colonnade with a vine growing up the side of it. Above the scene was a bird in flight—a swallow.

My breath caught. I'd seen this before. It had been in one of my dreams. Marveling at it, I picked it up and turned it over in my hands.

"Great photo of Florence, isn't it?" Felicity asked.

"Yes," I said absently. How could this have been in my dream? I had never seen it before in my life.

Chet sat down in the leather chair behind the desk and started to go through the drawers. The deep sound of a bell rang from downstairs.

"Is that the doorbell?" I asked.

"Ah, yes. That will be Lenora."

"Oh. Of course." I sat the frame back down on the credenza. "I'd like to say hello to her."

Felicity looked at me incredulously. I shook my head at her and tilted my head toward Chet, who was so absorbed in his task he wasn't even paying attention to us.

Oh, she mouthed at me. "We'll be in the drawing room downstairs, Chet," Felicity then said aloud.

He nodded, and Felicity led me out of the study. I was so caught up with the image of the photo frame in my mind, I followed her like a zombie, down the stairs and to the front door. She opened it, and there stood Lenora Lange, dressed in her customary silver and white. Felicity ushered her into the house.

Miss Lange greeted me with an outstretched hand, and when I took it, we locked eyes.

"You've seen something," she said. An icy chill radiated from her palm into mine. I didn't know how to respond, for I wasn't sure what was even happening. Could it be the photo frame or was she speaking of something else? She truly was the strangest creature I'd ever encountered.

Felicity led us to the parlor. It, like many of the other rooms in the manse, was gorgeous, steeped in European luxury. Felicity had really outdone herself. The room was beautifully decorated with pale-yellow walls, white trim, and intricately carved white moldings along the edges of the ceiling.

"Can I bring you something to drink?" she asked. "Tea perhaps?"

"None for me." I was nervous about this whole thing. Miss Lange's mere presence unsettled me, let alone anything that came out of her mouth.

"I'm fine, as well." Miss Lange settled herself in one of the French mahogany parlor chairs upholstered in a lush, green brocade fabric. I opted for the matching love seat opposite her. We were separated by a gold-footed tea table. I waited for Felicity to take a seat, but she remained standing.

"I will leave you two alone." She turned to go.

"Wait. Won't you stay?" I was feeling particularly vulnerable at the moment and wanted the emotional support of my friend.

"It is best if she goes." Miss Lange rested her hands on the arms of the chair. "We do not want any interference from souls connected to her. They could overpower the souls connected to you, and then you will not get a clear reading."

I swallowed. "Oh. I see."

Felicity gave me a reassuring smile. "I'll be in the great room getting some measurements." And then she left.

"Shall we begin?" Miss Lange asked once we were alone.

I nodded. Despite the sudden cold sensation that had still not left my right palm at Miss Lange's touch—and that had trans-ferred itself to my left, as well— perspiration bloomed on both palms, and I clasped them together.

"Yes, yes, I understand." Her eyes shifted to her right, and she nodded at something in the corner of the room.

"Excuse me?" I was confused by this random statement that had no context in regard to my gesture to proceed.

"Oh, I'm sorry, dear. There are just so many souls present, and they are all clamoring for my attention. It can be a bit over-whelming." She smiled graciously, her pale-blue eyes sparkling and fixing on mine.

"Oh. And are these souls connected to me?" I asked.

"Not all of them. It's Joshua, my collective. They say there is someone waiting to speak with you." Miss Lange closed her eyes and lowered her head. A sweep of different emotions crossed her face, and her hands alternated between gripping the arms of the chair and relaxing. "Yes, yes, I see her. An older woman is coming through," she said. She raised her head but kept her eyes closed. "I get the sense she might be a grandmotherly type. She's in a shop of some kind, a haberdashery or a dress shop. She's wearing a beautiful dress—finely made with rich fabric. It's something from the early Victorian era. She's telling me she made it." Miss Lange opened her eyes and looked at me. "Does that sound familiar to you?"

I shook my head. "No."

"She's telling me she's your grandmother. Did your grandmother sew?"

I shrugged. "I don't know. I never knew my grandparents on either side. My father's parents passed away when he was a young man, and my mother never spoke of her parents."

Miss Lange looked down at the floor and cocked her head as if listening. "She says she is connected to someone whose name begins with the letter *B*. I'm getting *B-E* . . ."

My heart leaped. "My mother's name was Belinda."

"She says this woman didn't mean to harm you. She was— She was—"

My hands tingled. This wasn't making sense to me.

"Your grandmother is saying this woman was out of her mind."

I shook my head, not understanding.

"What?" Miss Lange cocked her head again, and I knew she wasn't questioning me but questioning this woman, or Joshua, from the beyond. Suddenly, her eyes met mine. "She's saying something about a knife."

I sucked in a breath. Could it be the knife I'd seen in my dreams?

Miss Lange closed her eyes again. "Wait. Let her through," she said. "I see her now. She's beautiful, with a girlish face. She's crying. No, sobbing." She grabbed her chest, and her face contorted with pain. "She keeps saying she's sorry, over and over."

"Who? Sorry for what?" I scooted to the edge of the love seat, my hands squeezing together.

Miss Lange's face contorted as myriad emotions skimmed across it once again. With her head bowed, she said, "She's gone. She's faded into the collective."

I sat in silence watching her for what seemed an interminable about of time. I wanted to say something, but Miss Lange had her eyes closed. She raised her head again, emotions flitting across her face like a movie reel. She almost looked inhuman. My mouth went dry, and a spike of adrenaline shot through me. I looked away from her, wanting to leave, but I felt glued to the cushion.

"Gracie," she said finally. Her voice was not her own. It was higher pitched.

The blood drained from my face at the use of my nickname. I stared at the woman, whose eyes were still closed. Was she all right?

"Gracie," she said again.

Could this really be Sophia coming through?

"Yes?" I whispered.

She lifted her head and opened her eyes, leaning her weight upon one of the armrests. With her other hand, she pushed her hair off her forehead, just as Sophia used to do. Then she giggled like Sophia used to—before life had become too heavy for her.

"Sophia?" I peered into Miss Lange's face.

She batted her eyes in a girlish way. Then her face took on another expression. Her eyebrows rose, and her lips protruded into a frown. "Mommy, don't. Mommy, I'm scared. Leave her alone. Leave Gracie alone."

What was she talking about? Had my mother been trying to hurt me? Is that what Miss Lange had been trying to say earlier?

I studied her expression, which had now become more relaxed but still serious. "What you seek is beyond the garden," she whispered.

"Garden? What garden?" I shook my head in confusion.

Miss Lange convulsed, her eyes rolling back into her head, her neck snapping backward as is she'd been hit in the face. She righted herself and blinked several times. "They're gone," she said with a shudder. "Only Joshua remains."

I gaped at her, unable to process what had just happened. Some of it had rung true, but the rest I couldn't make sense of.

"Oh, there you are!" The sound of Chet's voice pulled me away from Miss Lange's gaze. "Hello, Miss Lange."

She gave him a nod in greeting and then pressed her fingers to her temples.

"Are you all right?" I asked.

She squeezed her eyes shut as if in pain. "Yes. Yes. Just fatigued. It's not unusual after a reading."

Chet tilted his head toward the door. "I think I may have found something."

I stood up from the love seat. "Will you excuse us?"

"Of course, dear." She set her elbow on the arm of the chair and cradled her head in her palm.

"Thank you . . . for the reading," I said quietly so as not to further disturb her.

"You're welcome." She released her head to wave her hand. "Please let me know if I can be of any more assistance."

I smiled shakily at her, still unnerved at the experience.

I followed Chet out of the room, down the hallway, and into the foyer. "What is it? What have you found?" I asked, wanting to focus on the tangible. Just then, Felicity entered the foyer, probably on her way to the parlor, and came over to us.

Chet scratched his temple. "I'm not sure it means anything,

but I found the deed to a property in Reno, Nevada."

I pulled my chin back in confusion. "Reno? What significance does that have?"

"Maybe none. But what if this Elsa and Greta Mayfield live there? Maybe he lived there with them for a time. Had he ever mentioned having a home there?"

I frowned. "Not to me. Felicity?"

She shrugged. "No. Never."

Chet squeezed his bottom lip between his thumb and forefinger. "I'm going to go up there."

I blinked at him. "You're going to Reno?"

"Yeah. See if I can find them there. It's a long shot, but I have a hunch. I combed through those files. This was the only thing I found." Chet looked to Felicity. "Does Travis have a safe?"

"Yes. There is a safe in his study. I found it when I redecorated in there. It's behind a panel in the wall. But obviously I don't have the combination. Florence doesn't, either. It was always a bone of contention between them. She wanted to have it in case—" She looked at me and then at Chet. "In case something happened to him."

Chet placed his hands on his hips. "Well if it comes down to it, we may have to see about getting some kind of search warrant to get into the safe. But I'm going to follow this lead first." He held up the deed.

As important as this trip was, I hated for Chet to leave with Lizzy and Daniel in jail. What if we needed him for something? In addition to all my other responsibilities, plus trying to redeem Lizzy, I would have to work with Ned and Joe to keep things running smoothly at the ranch *and* go back to work if Timothy was able to start production again. A pang of anxiety took hold of my chest, its sharp claws sinking into my heart. I wished I felt as strong as everyone thought I was, but after the strange reading with Miss Lange, my nerves felt more frayed than ever.

CHAPTER TWENTY

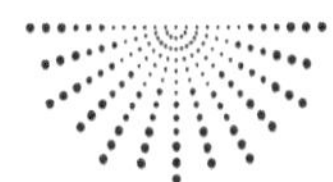

*C*het left for Reno shortly after dinner. He wanted to do most of the five-hundred-mile drive at night to avoid the desert heat. I hated to think of him tired and driving all night, but I had to put my worrying about him to rest. I had so many other things to worry about at the moment.

By the time I'd gotten Susie into bed and had said goodnight to Ida, it was late. I went back downstairs to do some reading. I thought it would help take my mind off things. I needed to find a way to relax and recharge. Besides, I still hadn't finished *The Man in the Brown Suit*. I had intended to read it every night when I went to bed, but every night I'd reasoned that I'd been too tired to do so. The result had been a lot of tossing and turning, and then dozing only to be awakened by nightmares. Perhaps if I read it downstairs and not it bed, it would give me the desired effect of drowsiness.

Rose and Miss Meyers had retired to their rooms, and I was thankful for the quiet. Remembering that Chet had stashed a couple of bottles of red wine in the dining room sideboard, I pulled one out and poured myself a glass. Hopefully the wine would help, too.

I walked into the darkened living room and turned on the lamp on the side table next to the sofa. Feeling completely decadent, I settled on the sofa with the novel. I kicked off my shoes and tucked my feet under me. I sipped my wine, opened the book, and started reading. When I had drained the glass, I still didn't feel sleepy, so I got up to pour some more. When I came back, I picked up the book again. I had just gotten to the part when Colonel Race was telling Anna the story of the diamond theft by the son of South African gold magnate John Eardsley when my mother entered the scene . . .

She is wearing only a nightgown. Her hair is disheveled, and the look on her face fills me with terror. Sophia is in the background, crying, begging her to leave me alone. Suddenly, we are off the ship and in our family home. I observe the scene as if I am watching it on the screen in a movie house. I see myself cowering in the corner of my parents' bedroom. I can't be more than eleven or twelve years old. My mother is raging at me, but I can't hear what she's saying, only Sophia's pleading.

I watch in horror as the scene unfolds. My mother clutches a knife dripping with blood. She heads toward me with it held high above her head. I scream, but no noise comes from my mouth. She's just about to plunge the knife into me when my father grabs her by the hand. Suddenly, the sleeve of his shirt is torn and soaked with blood. I scream again and then start to cry.

"Grace! Grace!" Someone shook my arm.

I opened my eyes to see Rose's face inches from mine. She was kneeling in front of me. Still completely shaken and sobbing, I threw my arms around her neck.

"It's okay, Grace. You were having a nightmare." She stroked my hair, and with my eyes squeezed shut to block out the horrible scene I'd just witnessed, I took comfort in this unexpected tenderness from her.

"I'm sorry," I gasped, suddenly embarrassed.

She sat down on the sofa beside me. "Don't apologize, dear. That must have been a doozy of a nightmare."

I took in a deep breath and then shuddered, the tears still streaming down my face.

"Want to talk about it?"

"I . . . I . . . ." I wasn't sure I could utter the words.

"Okay," she said softly. "Just sit here, then, and catch your breath."

I shook my head. "No. No, I'm sorry. I—"

She took hold of my hand and patted it. I felt my shoulders relax a little. Truth be told, I was glad she was here. I didn't want to be alone.

"I think I've remembered something," I said. "Something too horrifying to believe." The memories started to flood in. The arguments between my parents. My mother lying in bed. My father pleading with her to get help. Her going into a rage at him. The memory then shifted. She ran into the kitchen where I was eating some cookies with Sophia. Frightened by her madness, I stood from the table too fast and knocked over a glass. It fell to the floor and shattered. She grabbed the knife and screamed at me that I was a stupid girl, that I had broken her best glass, one of the set her mother had given her. Terrified, I fled from the kitchen and ran into their bedroom. I heard my father growl in pain and then suddenly my mother was standing over me with a bloody knife.

"My mother stabbed my father in the arm, and then tried to kill me . . . when I was a child."

"Oh my goodness," she said, her hand flying to her mouth.

"I must have suppressed the memory. But today, Miss Lange —she's a spiritualist—she gave me a reading, and some of it came back. It must have unlocked the memory." I looked into her eyes. "That's why my parents left. My father was taking her to a sanitorium, but—" my eyes filled with tears again "—they were killed in a train accident."

She pulled me into her warm arms again, and I cried into her shoulder, the anguish so great it threatened to push all the air out of my body. Years of pent-up denial washed over me, breaking like a dam. My own mother, in her deranged madness, had tried to kill me—had been actually going to kill me.

Sophia and I had never spoken of it. Perhaps she knew I had erased the memory from my mind and was glad of it. Perhaps she had suppressed it, too. Or in her compassion, maybe she never brought it up. She had always protected me from everything, even the truth. Because the truth was too horrible to give voice to sometimes.

Rose pulled away from me and patted my knee. "Let me fix you some tea," she said.

I shook my head, completely drained from the dream. "No. I just want to go to bed. I think I'm okay now," I said, not really sure if that was true but I felt bad at keeping her up when she had to wake so early in the morning to prepare breakfast. I put my hand over hers where it was still resting on my knee. "Thank you, Rose. Thank you for listening."

She smiled at me and stood up, all business again. "You go get some rest now. If you need me, you know where to find me." She walked away, leaving me to my thoughts.

I stood up and made my way to the stairs. I thought back to the dream that had unlocked a truth so vile I'd shoved it away to some dark place in my mind. But had it been the dream that had unlocked the truth or had it been Lenora Lange with her reading? Was that what Sophia had been trying to tell me? But what about the woman Miss Lange thought might be my grandmother? She was trying to tell me that my mother hadn't meant to hurt me, that her mind had been sick, and in its confusion had overridden her instinct to protect rather than harm her child.

And hadn't Miss Lange inferred that my grandmother had been a seamstress? And possibly owned a dress shop? Maybe that was where I'd gotten my passion for sewing all those years ago.

When Sophia and I lived on the streets, she would somehow find fabrics and I would make doll clothes to sell. It didn't bring in much, but during those hard years, it had given me something to be proud of, a way to help Sophia and myself any way I could. The act of creation also had made me feel free, even though the two of us had been prisoners of our poverty.

My thoughts shifted again to what had been revealed during the reading. Hadn't there been something about a garden? Finding what I was seeking beyond the garden?

My mind clouded over with fuzziness or fatigue, and I couldn't string my thoughts together in a way that made sense anymore. But one thing was clear: despite being so intimidated by the idea of a reading previously, I now wanted to do another.

I'D MANAGED to get a few hours of sleep. It wasn't enough, but at least I hadn't had any more disturbing dreams. In fact, I didn't recall having dreamed at all. I dragged myself out of bed and drew a bath, hoping it would refresh me.

I lingered in the tub until the water started to feel cool. I forced myself out, toweled off, and proceeded to get dressed. I usually didn't wear much makeup, save for some mascara and lipstick, but today I had to call out the reinforcements of Max Factor and used some foundation under my eyes to disguise the purple moons. The effect was satisfactory, but my lids were heavy and my skin was pale. I quickly dabbed on some rouge. I looked like a porcelain doll with painted cheeks. I grabbed a tissue, then wiped off the smudges of pink. A little remained, giving me somewhat of a glow. Resigned to looking ten years older, I gave up. I ran a brush through my hair, pinned my bob away from my face, and called it good.

Downstairs, I was relieved to find that I had missed the children, as well as Miss Meyers and Ned, for breakfast. Rose was cleaning up.

I entered the kitchen and poured myself some orange juice.

"I saved you a plate. Did you get some sleep?" she asked. I smiled and held my hand out, palm down and turned my wrist from side to side, indicating it was only so-so.

"I'm not really hungry." The thought of food made my stomach curdle.

"You won't be of help to anyone if you keep eating like a bird."

I couldn't argue with that, so I didn't. I took my glass of orange juice to the table. "I'm going to go see Lizzy and Daniel again," I said. "I hope they let me see Daniel this time."

Rose stood at the sink, washing dishes. "I'll prepare some baskets," she said.

She stopped what she was doing and leaned her hands against the sink. "I know I'm not the warmest person in the world. In truth, I don't have much use for people. Never have." She dried her hands on her apron, walked over to the counter next to the stove, and then brought me a plate of scrambled eggs and bacon. She set it down, and I stared at it, not sure I'd be able to force down a bite.

"Thank you." I picked up my fork but only held it over the food.

"I've not been a good mother to Chet, I know, but I do consider you a daughter of sorts, and I want you to know I care about you."

I looked up at her, stunned. "Thank you, Rose. I care about you, too."

"I know you do, girl. Now eat your breakfast." She gave me a wink and went back to doing the dishes.

Touched by her words, I forced myself to eat everything on my plate. Though still tired from lack of sleep, I did feel my energy restored by the nourishment as I pondered the horrible dream I'd had last night and the experience with Lenora Lange yesterday, including the message about the garden.

What you seek is beyond the garden.

What exactly was I seeking? Proof of Lizzy's innocence. Proof of Daniel's innocence. The truth. The murder weapon.

The garden! Maybe there was something there that could prove that Lizzy and Daniel were innocent.

I drank the rest of my coffee and hustled out to the garden, which was situated beyond the schoolroom. It was a modest size, about fifteen feet by twelve feet, with neat rows of green beans, lettuce, squash, and a variety of other things the kids and I had planted earlier that spring. I searched each row, looking under the plants and vines, but found nothing. I walked the perimeter of the garden and beyond. Nothing.

Frustrated, I gave up and headed back to the house to get my things to go to the jail.

I walked back into the house to hear the phone ringing. I hurried to the telephone niche in the hallway and picked up the receiver. "Hello?"

"Hi, darling." It was Chet.

"It's so good to hear your voice," I said, my own voice wavering. He'd been gone less than twenty-four hours, but given what had transpired last night, I wanted him home as soon as possible.

"Grace, I have some news. I've tracked down the house in Reno." His voice was exuberant. "Apparently, the deed I found in Travis's office was a copy. He sold the place to the current resident, a Mr. Maddox. I told him I was working for the estate, and he said he had found a box in the garage that must have belonged to Travis and gave it to me. Guess what I found in the box?"

I shook my head. "I don't know. Tell me."

"Receipts from 1912 for repairs to a house in Lake Tahoe, which is about thirty-five miles from here—substantial repairs."

My breath caught in my throat. "Lake Tahoe? Did he have a house in Lake Tahoe as well? But that's where Margaret and Lizzy lived before they moved here. I wonder if they knew Mr. Travis or if it is just a coincidence."

"Not sure. But Walton did say that Margaret showed up at the reading of the will, right?"

"Yes."

"It *could* be a coincidence, but it feels a little too convenient to me. I'm going to see what I can find out. How are things there?"

I hesitated, wanting to tell him about my dream last night but figured it was a conversation best to be had in person. Besides, I was still trying to make sense of it. "Fine. They're fine. I'm going to the jail to visit Lizzy and see if they will allow me to see Daniel this time."

"You sound tired." There was concern in his voice. "Trouble sleeping again?"

"I'm fine. Really. Let me know what you find out."

"Will do. Goodbye, darling."

The click at the other end let me know he'd hung up. I placed the receiver back on its cradle, thinking about what Chet had discovered. Lake Tahoe was not a big town. Surely Margaret and Lizzy had crossed paths with Mr. Travis if he had owned a house there. But why lie about it?

CHAPTER TWENTY-ONE

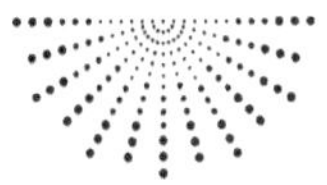

The guard at the jail assured me I could speak with Daniel after I spoke with Lizzy, for which I was grateful. At least I would be able to see both of them today. I handed the officer the basket meant for Lizzy. He said that after examination, he would see to it that she received it.

I tapped my fingers on the table until the door for the inmates opened. Lizzy came in, escorted by an officer, and walked over to me. She sat down while he stood guard.

"Hello, dear." I mustered a smile for her. She half-heartedly returned the gesture. Her mass of loose curls was an unkempt mess, and her skin was pale, accentuating the sprinkle of freckles across her nose. Her eyes looked glassy, like she hadn't had much sleep, and were rimmed with red. Dark circles under her eyes gave her a haunted appearance. "How are you?"

She shrugged. "I want to go home to the ranch."

"I know. I want you there, too. So does Goldie. I haven't had much time to ride her." I tried to lighten the mood to no avail.

I decided to change course. I was pretty sure Lizzy didn't want to talk about how wonderful things were on the outside. All she could deal with was her own pain. "Has Detective Walton asked you any more questions?"

"They sent the lawyer to speak with me," she said.

Finally. I breathed out a sigh of relief and offered her a warm smile. "That's good, then."

Lizzy's mouth tightened, and her eyes narrowed. "No. It's not. It means I'm done for."

I reached my hand out onto the table. "No, it doesn't," I said, trying to use a soothing voice. The poor girl had all but given up hope, it seemed.

"He's awful," she said, her eyes shifting away from mine.

"The lawyer? In what way?" I asked, a little alarmed.

"He's old and smells of whiskey."

She looked so forlorn I wanted to hug her. Suddenly, her eyes filled with tears and she buried her face in her hands. I felt helpless watching her in such agony.

"Lizzy, I'm still trying to find out what happened on the night of the party and also what happened to your sister. Nothing has changed. I still believe you. So does Chet."

With her face still in her hands, she shook her head, hopelessness wafting off her in waves.

"I want to ask you a question." I scooted closer to the table. She peered at me over her fingertips. "Did your sister ever mention knowing or meeting Mr. Travis?"

She lowered her hands. "No."

"You're sure?"

"How would she know him? She wasn't in the movies."

"Right," I muttered. "Do the names Greta and Elsa Mayfield mean anything to you?"

She shook her head.

"Did you maybe meet them in Lake Tahoe? Maybe they were guests at the boarding house or perhaps your neighbors?"

"I don't know the names," she said, impatience in her voice.

She crossed her arms and then scratched at the inside of her fore-arm. My eyes traveled to the heart-shaped birthmark.

"I wonder if Margaret knew them." I was thinking out loud. At the mention of Margaret's name, Lizzy's face contorted with emotion, and she again burst into tears.

"Oh no. I'm sorry if I upset you. You must be missing your sister—"

"She wasn't my sister," she interrupted. Her teary, red-rimmed eyes met mine.

I blinked. "What do you mean she wasn't your sister?"

"She wasn't my sister. She was . . . She was my mother." Her voice broke, and she let out a sob.

I stared at her, stunned.

She collected herself and then sniffled, wiping her nose on the back of her hand. "I didn't know it— Well, I didn't know it until a few months before we left Lake Tahoe."

My mind reeling, I managed to close my gaping mouth. "How did you find this out?"

She crossed her arms over her chest. "I found a piece of paper —a hospital record. When I was seven, I had croup and went to the hospital for a few days. Anyway, under the title of 'mother' she put her name. There was nothing under the title of 'father.' When I asked her about it, she didn't say anything at first, but I kept at her. Finally, she said it was probably time I heard the truth anyway."

I sat back in the chair, amazed at what I was hearing. "And?"

She looked at me as if I were a simpleton. "She said he was dead."

"Oh, Lizzy. I'm so sorry." I leaned forward and reached my hand out across the table again, and the guard cleared his throat. I quickly retracted it.

"She also said we couldn't let anyone know that she was my mother." Lizzy's face hardened.

"But why?"

"She said it was for my protection. That my father had been involved with some bad people and those people had killed him. She was scared they would come after us, and if everyone thought we were sisters, we'd be safer. That's why we moved from New York to Lake Tahoe. But I didn't believe her." She crossed her arms over her chest. "I think she just wanted me to stop asking questions."

My brow furrowed. "Why didn't you believe her?"

"Because she was a liar! She'd lied to me my whole life!"

I reached my hand across the table again, and this time, the guard didn't do anything so I let it rest there. "But, Lizzy, don't you believe she was trying to protect you?"

She slammed her hand down on the table, prompting the officer to step forward. "No! I think she made it up. She was ashamed of me. She didn't want to claim me as her child."

My heart wrenched. "Is that why you started to act out? Because you thought she was ashamed of you?"

She nodded as her face crumpled again. She squeezed her eyes shut and took in a deep, gasping breath. "I was so confused, so mad at her. But now I'm sorry. I'm so, so sorry. I still loved her." Her eyes widened. "And I didn't kill her, I swear it! I was mad at her but not mad enough to kill her. Why would I kill my own mother?"

"Oh, Lizzy." I choked back a sob and swallowed the walnut-sized lump that had formed in my throat, my own recent experience concerning my mother tearing my heart open again like a gaping wound.

"I went to the house that day to talk to her. To apologize." She ran her hands over her cheeks, wiping away her tears. "But I got scared and Daniel was worried about getting back to the farm. We'd been gone so long."

"Did you tell the lawyer this?"

"Yes, but I don't think he believed me. He said he would look into it."

The guard walked over to us. "It's time."

I looked up at him and implored him with my eyes. "Please. Can't she stay for just a few more minutes?" I hated for her to have to go back to her cell in such a state.

"Let's go, Miss Moore." He took her by the elbow, forcing her to stand up. With sad eyes, she gave me one last look and let him lead her out of the room.

MY VISIT with Daniel was no more uplifting than my visit with Lizzy. Already prone to sullenness, his demeanor was, dare I say, morose. He was so downcast, and his eyes had a vacancy to them that alarmed me. I tried my best to lift his spirits.

"I promise you, I will prove you didn't do this. You will be out of here in no time."

He hadn't yet met my gaze but stared down at the table. "I'm never going to get out of here unless it's in a pine box."

"Don't say that, Daniel." Like with Lizzy, I wished I could reach out and touch him, give him some kind of physical comfort.

He shook his head. "I never should have told them that I had gone to the barn that night."

I was surprised at this declaration. "You did?"

He nodded.

I leaned forward in my chair. "Who did you tell?"

"Detective Walton and the lawyer."

I nodded. "And what exactly did you tell them?"

His raised his gaze to meet mine, his cheeks pink with emotion. "I was sick of seeing Lizzy flirting with all those men, so I went into the kitchen to talk to Mrs. R. and ask her if I could have another plate of food. While I was at the table eating, I saw Lizzy head out to the barn with that Travis guy. I was worried she might be getting herself into trouble, but I was pretty steamed about the whole thing so I decided to go upstairs to my room. But then I got to worrying about her again," he admitted. "I went to your studio and then down the stairs, and hoofed it over to the barn. By the time I got there, Mr. Travis was dead and Lizzy was muttering something—like she was out of her head. I saw the broken glass lying next to Mr. Travis with the blood all over it. I was scared for Lizzy, that she'd be accused of his death, so I took the glass and threw it into the field."

"Oh, Daniel." My voice deflated.

"I was going to go back to the barn to get Lizzy, but then I saw you walking out there with Ned. I got scared so went back into the house. Anyway, because of that, Detective Walton charged me with withholding evidence and being an accessory to the crime."

I shook my head, worry clawing into my chest. I was still more dedicated than ever to helping these children, but I was feeling adrift as to how it would be possible.

"Was there anything else?" I asked.

"Yeah. But it wasn't because I was trying to hide anything. It was because I forgot."

"What was that?"

"That waiter guy? The one who was also talking to Lizzy."

Mr. Johnson.

"When I came downstairs from your studio, I saw him heading toward the back of the house, like kind of by the schoolroom. I thought it was strange because why would he be out there . . ."

He had a point. The partygoers who were outside were either on the back porch, in the side yard in front of the kitchen, or—as in Miss Lange's and Mr. Smith's case—out near the field. Mr. Johnson could have killed Mr. Travis. Maybe he and Florence had been working together, thinking Florence would get the entire inheritance if her husband was out of the way.

"Did he see you?"

He shrugged. "I dunno. It was pretty dark."

"And you told the detective this?"

"Yeah."

"And what did he say?"

He shook his head. "Nothing."

I didn't have much hope for this revelation because it didn't put Mr. Johnson at the scene of the crime, or anywhere near it, but it *was* odd that he was out by the schoolroom away from everyone else.

"Was there anything you didn't tell Detective Walton about the visit to Miss Moore's house?" I braced myself for the worst.

"No. We didn't go in. I swear it. Lizzy said she changed her mind, that she would talk to her sister later."

I sighed, relieved their stories matched. "I believe you, Daniel. Don't give up hope."

He gave me a half-hearted smile.

"I brought over a basket of food. Did you enjoy the last one? I'm sorry I couldn't see you that day. They wouldn't let me."

He scoffed. "Never got to taste anything. The guys in my cell took it all."

I worried my bottom lip, my heart breaking for both Lizzy and Daniel. They were just children, really. My insides churned at the thought of them being taken advantage of in this horrid place.

My pity for him was quickly replaced with anger. "Well, something has to be done about that."

He leaned forward and looked over his shoulder, shaking his head. "Don't say anything about it. Please, Grace. It will make things worse for me in here."

"But—" I pleaded.

"Please!" His voice cracked. "I'm begging you."

I gritted my teeth. "Okay. But it's not right." I had half a mind to say something anyway, but I had to trust him.

The guard at the door stepped forward, signaling that our time was up.

Daniel stood. "Well, I gotta go. Thanks for coming by."

"Of course," I said, forcing a small smile. "I'll be back as soon as I can."

He nodded and turned to go, despondent.

"Daniel," I called after him. "Chin up." The words felt insignificant and hollow, but he gave me a tight-lipped smile as the guard took him by the elbow.

As I left the visitation room, I spotted Detective Walton at the end of the hall talking to a uniformed officer. Then he began to walk away so I picked up my pace.

"Detective Walton," I said loudly and in a way that demanded he see me. I broke into a jog.

He turned, and when he saw me, he took his fedora off with a sigh of irritation. "Can I help you, Mrs. Riker?"

I tightened my hold on the basket handle. "I've just been to see both Lizzy and Daniel."

"You've been busy."

I wasn't sure but I thought I detected a smirk on his face.

I narrowed my eyes at him. "Is it true that you've charged Daniel with accessory to murder in the case of Mr. Travis?"

"Yes, and hiding evidence, given that he admitted to disposing of the murder weapon."

"So it's been determined that the broken glass was without a doubt the murder weapon?" I asked.

"Yes." He puffed up his chest. "The coroner has confirmed it. There were bits of glass in Mr. Travis's wound."

"And you are still determined that Lizzy killed him?" I couldn't keep the anger out of my voice. My nerves were on edge and my emotions right at the surface, threatening to spill over like lava bubbling up from a volcano, ready to erupt.

"There has been no evidence to prove otherwise. She was the last to see him alive, she was in close proximity to the body, there was no witness, and she had blood on her hands. Literally." Another smirk.

I had to admit, it was hard to argue the point. And what evidence did I have that she didn't do it? I was just going with my gut, and I couldn't ignore it. Still, I pressed on. "But what motive would she have for killing her own mother? She said she went over to apologize, to make amends."

Detective Walton put his hat back on his head, signaling to me that he was done with this conversation. "Things get out of hand sometimes. Let's call it a crime of passion."

I hated the way he was so cavalierly confident in his conclusions. It made my blood boil.

"But Daniel told me he saw Mr. Johnson outside that night, at the back of the house. He could have committed the crime." I realized I sounded defensive, but . . . well, I was defensive.

The detective held his hands up in the air. "Johnson said he wasn't outside, other than earlier in the evening when he was helping to carry items into the house for the party. So either he or Daniel is lying."

I wanted to scream at him, he was so arrogant. I took a breath and said as steadily as I could, "I believe Mr. Johnson and Florence Thomas are having an affair."

He raised his eyebrows at me. "And?" The look of condescension on his face left me flustered.

"Well, what if they colluded to kill Mr. Travis to get Florence her inheritance?" I lifted my chin.

He heaved a great sigh, obviously growing more and more impatient. "Can you say with certainty that they are having an affair?"

I blinked several times, knowing I would never be able to prove this. "Well, no, but you could—"

The detective thrust his hand toward my face, stopping me in my tracks. "Are you trying to tell me how to do my job, Mrs. Riker?" His jaw twitched, and I knew I had pushed him too far.

"No, but—"

"Then don't." His voice carried a weight to it that sounded like a threat.

I swallowed but didn't want to back down. "You've been known to make mistakes, am I right, Detective?" I shot back. "You've botched criminal cases before? And this time, you need things wrapped up as soon as possible, correct?" My hands were shaking as I spoke. I was treading on dangerous ground, but his pompousness was completely infuriating.

His eyes narrowed at me, and his mouth tightened. "Look, Mrs. Riker, I don't owe you any explanation here. The matter of Lizzy's and Daniel's arrests have been settled. It's now in the hands of the courts. The DA has set Lizzy's trial for a week from today."

His words deflated my anger like a pin popping a balloon and replaced them with despair. I had to find evidence that Lizzy did not commit these crimes, and I had to find it fast.

CHAPTER TWENTY-TWO

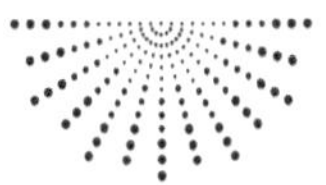

I arrived home at 2:30 p.m. and walked into the house to find Rose writing something on a pad of paper by the telephone.

"There you are," she said. "I was getting ready to go out to the garden and didn't want to miss you, so I was writing you a note. The studio called." She handed me the piece of paper. "Said they are having a meeting at three o'clock and you are expected to be there."

"Oh no!" I gasped. "When did they call?"

"About an hour ago."

"Rats!" I said, exasperated. I needed to freshen up and change my clothes. "Thank you, Rose. Any more word from Chet?"

"No." She pointed to the basket. "Daniel didn't want it?"

"It's not that." I handed it to her. "His cell mates stole the one I'd given him before. He thinks it best we don't bring him any more food."

I read Rose's note again with the time of the meeting, just to make sure I'd heard her right. I thought it odd to call a meeting so late in the day, but it must be important. Perhaps we would resume production yet again. If so, that meant Florence's demands had most likely been met somehow. I hoped they hadn't decided to fire Helen Clark because, in my estimation, her performance carried the film. Not that the others weren't talented, but she was outstanding. And were they really going to replace Marc Clemmons with Mr. Johnson?

If Edward Travis had wanted him in the picture, wouldn't he have been in it already? Especially given his impressive dossier? Mr. Travis must have had his reasons not to hire him. Perhaps it was because Mr. Johnson had been a bit too chummy with his wife? Although, Mr. Travis did not strike me as the jealous type. He was prone to affairs himself.

I looked at my watch, and my heart went into spasms. I would have to choose between freshening up and changing clothes. The dress I had opted to wear to the jail was one I wore around the house, not one I wore to work. Yes, changing clothes was the best call.

I dashed upstairs, set my coat and purse on the bed, and then decided on one of my favorite suits. It was a double-breasted, navy, gaberdine number. The skirt had roomy pockets that were optimal for buttons or basting tape or whatever I might need on set. And since I didn't know the purpose of this meeting, I thought it best to be prepared. I opened my wardrobe to find the skirt but not the jacket. What had I done with it?

Then I remembered I had placed it on one of the dress forms in my studio the last time I had worn it.

Grabbing my purse, I walked to that end of the house, and sure enough, there it was. I took it off the form, shoved my hands through the sleeves, and left my studio through the outside door. I made my way down the staircase, and when I reached the landing halfway down, something on the wooden planks caught my attention. It was a leather-covered button. It wasn't one that I recognized, but I had dozens of buttons in my studio so it very well could have been mine. What was it doing on the stairs? I picked it up and put it in my pocket. I would check later to see if I had a match.

Once at the studio, I ran up the stairs to the business offices and hurried to the conference room. I entered to find everyone in the meeting getting up from their chairs. All heads swiveled to see me standing in the doorway.

"You're late," Mr. Steinberg said through clenched teeth.

"I'm so sorry," I said, gasping for breath.

"I'll see you in my office in ten minutes," he said.

I gulped and nodded. I caught the eye of Mrs. Steinberg, who simply raised her brows at me as she headed out of the room. Following her was Florence Thomas, whose face looked like a thunder cloud; Mr. Johnson, who appeared equally displeased; and Timothy O'Malley, who gave me a tight-lipped smile. Helen Clark seemed mildly annoyed, as did her husband. A man I didn't recognize nodded to me in greeting. Only Felicity gave me a smile.

"What happened?" she asked. "Why are you late?"

I shook my head. "I went to the jail to see Lizzy and Daniel. I had no idea there was a meeting until I got home at two thirty."

"You look exhausted."

I sighed. This picture was my big chance, and showing up late for a meeting—or missing it, rather—wouldn't do at all, especially since this film was teetering in the balance already. I hoped Mr. Steinberg wasn't going to fire me. "Yeah, that pretty much sums it up."

"How's it going with the kids?" Felicity asked, concern in her eyes.

I shook my head, not wanting to go into it or my infuriating conversation with the detective. "Don't ask. So what did I miss?"

Felicity leaned closer to me and lowered her voice. "Basically, it was a dressing down by Mr. Steinberg. Florence and Helen were adamant they wouldn't work together, and he reminded them of their iron-clad contracts and made it clear that he would make the decisions as to who was in the film or not. Timothy made a concession and said he was going to rearrange the shooting schedule so they would not have to be together on set."

I furrowed my brow. "But what about the scenes they have together?"

"The cinematographer said he can shoot them separately and make it look like they were together."

"Nice trick." At least that had been settled. "And Mr. Johnson? Is he in the film now?"

Felicity scoffed. "Not a chance. He and Florence were apoplectic about it. Florence created a bit of a scene, but Mr. Steinberg put her in her place. And how!" She laughed.

I nodded. "I didn't think they'd hire him. Has he even been in a film before?"

Felicity shrugged. "Don't think so. Hey." She touched my arm. "I'm worried about you, Grace."

I waved my hand in the air. "Don't be. I'm fine. I'll get it together."

Felicity put her hands on her hips, emphasizing her tiny waist. "I think as far as Mr. Steinberg is concerned, you'd better."

I looked at my watch. "Right. Don't want to be late again."

"Chet still out of town?"

"Yes."

"Why don't you come over for dinner? I'll make my famous Chicken á la King."

It would be nice to have the company, and quite honestly, I needed a bit of time for myself. Miss Meyers and Rose often went to their rooms after dinner, and Susie and Ida usually did homework.

"Sounds great."

"We can leave from here, if you don't have to go home first. I might even break out some booze and we can have a cocktail."

I led the way out the door, and together we walked down the stairs toward the business offices. Felicity gave me a quick peck on the cheek and left. I took in a deep breath, collecting myself, and headed down the hallway toward Mr. Steinberg's office. I walked into the reception area where his secretary was seated behind a desk. She was a birdlike woman with a long nose and sharp cheekbones.

She peered at me over her spectacles. "Mr. and Mrs. Steinberg are waiting for you in his office."

"Thank you." I walked past her to the double doors on her right, my heart in my throat. I knocked.

"Come!" came from behind the door, so I opened it.

Mr. Steinberg was seated at his desk going over some papers, and Mrs. Steinberg was standing next to him, leaning over his shoulder.

"Sit, Miss Michelle." He indicated the chair opposite his desk.

I obeyed and placed my hands in my lap. They were moist with perspiration.

"Have you seen the dailies lately?" he asked.

"Not since we stopped filming, no. I haven't seen the latest ones."

"You need to see them. Helen's dresses just aren't working. They look flat on the screen." He placed his hands in a steeple formation on his desk. "You really need to make some adjustments."

I clenched my hands together. "Yes, sir. No problem." But what kind of adjustments? I wanted to ask but didn't. I would have to put my creative thinking cap on and figure it out.

His face went grim. "We took a chance on you, Miss Michelle."

My eyes traveled to Mrs. Steinberg, who looked at me with what I could only determine was disappointment.

Mr. Steinberg continued, much to my chagrin, his voice

stern, like a father scolding a child. "There aren't many women who are lead designers in this business. You have a unique opportunity here. We resume shooting tomorrow. I don't want to have to have this discussion again. Understand?"

"Yes," I said.

He unfolded his hands and pointed a finger at me. "And tardiness will not be tolerated. Time is money."

Pressing my lips together, I nodded. "It won't happen again. I apologize. I'll pay closer attention to the dailies."

"No apology necessary." Mrs. Steinberg finally spoke, her voice calm and soothing. "Just do your job, Grace."

I thanked them and left. Once outside, I leaned against the wall of the building and tilted my head back against it. My eyes burned with fatigue, and my stomach rumbled with latent nerves. I took in a deep breath and was suddenly, blissfully aware of the warmth of the sun on my face. It radiated through me, melting the tension from the muscles in my forehead, around my mouth, and down my shoulders. I would never tire of the balm of the California sun. I longed to go to the beach and lie on the warm sand. Chet and I did that a lot when we had moved to Los Angeles, but work and the responsibilities of the kids and the ranch had robbed us of that kind of carefree time.

I pushed myself away from the wall and walked toward the set in search of Felicity. As I neared it, I spotted Mr. Johnson leaning up against a car talking with Marsha Christopher, a particularly sharklike gossip columnist. She had her notebook poised in front of her and was furiously writing on it, occasionally looking up at Mr. Johnson. Given his and Florence's disappointment at him not being cast in the film, I hoped he wasn't divulging something vicious or salacious about the picture.

As I walked past, he stopped talking. He raised his chin in greeting and gave me a slippery smile, as if he'd just rudely propositioned me. I felt his eyes on me as I walked out of earshot, and a chill snaked down my spine. What exactly did Florence see in that man?

I STOOD in Felicity's cute little French Provincial kitchen cutting up the mushrooms for the Chicken á la King while she sauteed the chicken breasts in a pan over the stove.

We were both on our second lime rickey. It was not unheard of for me to have a drink now and then—and by drink, I meant one, with the exception of the other night when I'd had two glasses of wine. However, given the stress of the last two weeks, I'd opted to have a second. I sipped this one much more slowly as I told Felicity what Lizzy and Daniel had shared with me on my last visit to the jail.

"So her trial is late next week. Haven't heard about Daniel's yet." I set the knife down and handed her the bowl of sliced mushrooms. She dumped them into another pan simmering with melted butter. I took my drink to the kitchen table and sat down while she kept an eye on the stove and continued to prepare the creamy mushroom sauce.

"That doesn't give us much time to find the real killer, but I have to be honest, Grace. It doesn't look good for her. Or for Daniel. Especially since in the case of Mr. Travis, Lizzy claims not to remember anything."

"But indulge me here, Felicity. Assuming she's not lying, which I don't believe she is, why wouldn't she be able to remember? Could she have had that much to drink? I only saw her with two different glasses in her hand. That doesn't mean she had more somewhere along the line, of course," I added. Then I remembered how difficult it had been to wake her and my earlier consideration that she'd been drugged.

I told Felicity about my theory, and the medicine vial I had found on the set. I'd also explained what happened when I'd gone to Robert Smith's house to ask him about it.

"It didn't go well," I added, remembering his outrage.

"What did Helen Clark say when you talked to her?" she asked.

"She admitted to using drugs."

Felicity raised a brow. "Did she admit the vial was hers?"

"No." I thought back to the conversation. "But she didn't say it *wasn't* hers, either. You know, Lizzy said that Helen handed her a drink. I suppose she could have put something in it, either for herself or for Lizzy. But she said she wasn't jealous of Mr. Travis talking to Lizzy and that she would never kill Mr. Travis because she loved him. She seemed sincere."

Felicity gave me a dubious smile. "What was it you said about love, money, and revenge being the prime motives for murder? The woman is an actress, after all."

I pinched my brows together. "You think she was lying?"

Felicity took the chicken off the stove and set the pan in the oven to keep the chicken warm while she worked on the mushroom sauce. "Somebody is."

"Who else could it belong to?" I wondered out loud.

"Oh, honey." She waved a hand in the air. "This is show business. Drugs come with the territory, you know that. It could belong to anyone." Felicity rested her hip against the edge of the stove. "But, to your point, yes, Lizzy could have been drugged. Depending on the drug, it could cause memory loss when mixed with alcohol."

"Exactly!" I said, setting my drink down.

She gave me a crooked smile. "You remember how we subdued the boys who were guarding you at the hotel when Marciano took you captive?"

The memory dawned in my mind. "You gave them laudanum."

"Lots of it," Felicity added. "I used to slip it to Joe when he was getting out of hand or out of control, remember?"

I did. She'd used it on him when he came after me, planning to do unspeakable things. He was rendered completely helpless and didn't remember anything of the incident later.

I picked up my glass and sipped the cool liquid, the tang of the lime waking up the back of my mouth. "But if Lizzy was drugged, how can we prove it?"

"I'm not sure that we can. Maybe Lenora can help?" She raised a shoulder.

I took another sip of my drink. "I'm not sure how. Apparently, she only speaks to the dead." Then my eyes widened. "You mean maybe Mr. Travis could tell her if Lizzy was drugged and by whom?"

"You never know." Felicity placed an oven mitt–covered hand on her hip. "Hey, you didn't tell me how it went with Lenora the other day. Did you have any luck?"

"Yes, but I'm not sure what to think of it," I said honestly. I told her about Miss Lange channeling a woman who might have been my grandmother. I shuddered at the reminder of what my dreams had revealed that night—that my mother tried to kill me. I tried to shake the thought away. I didn't want to talk about it. With anyone.

"Well did Sophia come through, too?" Felicity asked.

"I'm not exactly sure. Although, it was pretty eerie. Miss Lange took on the mannerisms of Sophia, and she referred to me as 'Gracie,' which no one else but my sister called me. Miss Lange said something else also that gave me pause. She said that what I sought was beyond the garden."

"Hmm." Felicity tapped a finger on her chin. "Do you have a garden?"

I nodded. "I went out there the next morning, but nothing spoke to me."

"Strange. Well, speaking of gardens, would you go out to the back of *my* house to the garden? I need you to get some lettuce and vegetables for the salad, and some carrots for the á la King. I'll set the table."

"Sure." I stood up. "Point me in the right direction. Maybe I'll find something enlightening," I said, half joking.

She handed me a basket, and I followed her out her front door. She led me down a tree-lined path to an open expanse of lawn. A lovely vegetable garden with perfectly neat rows lay before us.

"Did you plant all this?" I asked, marveling. Rose would be green with envy.

"No." She laughed. "The groundskeeper did. He's also a master gardener."

"I'll say." I admired the beautiful array of colorful vegetables.

"I'll leave you to it, then."

I walked over to the tomatoes, their vines suspended by a net hanging from a wooden arbor. They were fat, red, and juicy looking. I plucked off two of them and put them in the basket. Some lush heads of lettuce caught my eye, and I made my way over to them. A squirrel darted out from beneath some of the lettuce leaves, making me jump, and I watched him scamper toward a wooden shed on the other side of the garden. It was old, the wood gray from sun and weather and the glass of the windows cloudy.

A wave of dizziness washed over me, and I knelt to put my hand on the ground to steady myself. I set the basket down.

What you seek is beyond the garden. I heard Sophia's voice in my head, and my heart skipped a beat. I looked up at the shed. It was indeed *beyond* the garden. Had this been what Sophia had been trying to tell me?

When the dizziness passed, I slowly stood up again. I walked past the garden and over to the shed. The door hung slightly ajar, and the corner of it had sunk into the grass. It took some effort, but I pulled it open far enough for me to slip through.

Light filtered through the clouded windows, shining on the dust motes floating in the air. As my eyes adjusted to the dimness, I noticed the neatness of the place. A table under the windows held various tools, pots, and gardening items. Underneath the table were shelves with pruning shears, more pots, and other sundry things. Opposite the table were additional shelves that held boxes and crates.

One of the crates jutted out from the rest, throwing off the perfect symmetry of the rows. The impulse to straighten it overwhelmed me, and I shoved it back into place. My eyes roamed over the contents of the crates. Some of them contained glass jars and bottles, others picture frames and candles, and still others with household items and books. There was even one box filled with old files. I pulled out one of the crates of books and perused the neatly stacked spines. I smiled when I saw some of Agatha Christie's titles and pulled out her first published novel, *The Mysterious Affair at Styles*. I hadn't read it yet, but it was on my list of books to read. I opened it to read the jacket cover when something fell out of it. It was a piece of paper.

I knelt down and picked it up, surprised to feel the thickness of it. Someone had scrawled something across it in ink. It read, *Central Park, 1910*. I turned it over. It was a photograph of a man, a woman, and a young child, a girl, probably around the age of two. I moved closer to the window to see it better. The trio was standing near a picnic blanket with various items on it. The man was holding the child, and the woman looked adoringly up at both of them. The little girl had her arm outstretched, pointing at something.

Then I saw it—something unusual on the inside of the girl's arm. I peered closer and my breath caught in my throat. It was a mark in the shape of a heart. I looked more intently at the man, whose blond waves hinted at a young Edward Travis. My eyes traveled to the woman, and I gasped.

It was Margaret Moore.

"Grace?" Felicity's voice came from outside the shed. "Grace, where are you?"

Holding the photograph, I left the shed.

Felicity was standing at the garden. "There you are. What were you doing in the outbuilding?"

I walked toward her, holding out the picture. She took it from me and examined it, then looked up at me with a furrowed brow. "Wow. You found this in there?"

"Yes, there are loads of boxes and crates. This fell out of a book."

She looked at it again. "This must be the mysterious heir and her mother."

I nodded. "Elsa and Greta Mayfield."

Felicity shook her head. "Yeah. So?"

"Look at the little girl's arm."

She studied the photograph, and her mouth dropped open. A zing of excitement coursed through my body like electricity. She looked up at me. "Lizzy."

"Yes. I knew it!" I cried.

She raised her fingers to cover her opened mouth. "Oh god. Do you think she knew Edward Travis was her father?"

"She told me her father was dead. Or at least that's what Margaret—or Greta—told her. So, no, I don't think she knows. But it explains why Margaret was at the reading of the will—in disguise and lurking at the back of the room."

"She knew she was a beneficiary," Felicity said, nodding with understanding.

"But the lawyer hadn't been able to find her," I added. "She must have known the stipulations of the will—that Edward wanted the beneficiaries gathered. Maybe she kept an eye on the mansion to see when they would meet." I mused. "I wish I had been able to talk with her about this. Do you think she knew that her daughter would inherit virtually everything?" I studied the photo again. "They look so happy. I wonder what happened between them. And why did Margaret feel the need to change their names?"

Felicity shrugged. "People break up for a variety of reasons. During the reading of the will, the lawyer never referred to Greta as Travis's wife. Only Florence and— What was her name?"

"Pearl Davis." I tapped the photo against my chin. "Who recently committed suicide. Or so the authorities say. . . So we have Edward Travis murdered, Margaret Moore aka Greta Mayfield murdered, and Pearl Davis also dead in a somewhat suspicious fashion.

"Who else stood to inherit, other than Pearl Davis, if Elsa wasn't found?"

"I think it was Florence—but she was only getting the house, not the fortune—Edward's parents, and his brother. But they didn't show up to the reading of the will. Mr. Johnson alluded to the fact that the parents were too ill to travel. Do you know if the brother has been here at the mansion?"

She shook her head. "No. It's been pretty quiet here."

"So who would have motive to kill these people?"

I caught Felicity's gaze, and she gave me a look of pity. "Think about it, Grace."

My stomach curdled. "You're thinking Lizzy did it." I shook my head. "But if she knew she was the heir, why would she kill him?"

"Maybe she wanted to speed up the process. Travis was only in his early forties. He could have lived to be in his seventies, even eighties."

I shook my head. "But if she knew she was the heir and wanted to kill her father, why would she be passed out at the scene of the crime?"

Felicity pressed her lips together. "She could have staged it, to make herself look innocent. And she could have had help. Someone who would dispose of the murder weapon for her. Like Daniel."

I considered her reasoning. "So you think she lied about Margaret telling her that her father was dead? That she also lied when I asked her if the names Greta and Elsa Mayfield meant anything to her? That she's lied about everything? But why wouldn't she come right out and say her name was Elsa Mayfield if she knew she stood to inherit?" My voice came out sounding shrill and defensive, but didn't Felicity remember the state Lizzy had been in that night? That couldn't have been an act.

Felicity's gaze softened. "Because she knew it would make her look guilty."

I didn't want to accept this argument. "But if she was the murderer and she was found not guilty, what then?"

"She changes her appearance—I don't know, dyes her hair, gains or loses some weight—and comes out as Elsa Mayfield before the six-month period is up."

I stared at her in stunned silence. What a devious mind she had. Although, I shouldn't have been surprised after learning how she'd dealt with Marciano all those years.

Had I been such a fool? Had Lizzy been playing me all along, hoping upon hope that I would find her a scapegoat?

Felicity came closer and laid an arm across my shoulders. "Grace, I'm not saying this is what I believe. But when it comes out she is the heir to Mr. Travis's vast fortune, it's not going to look good for her."

"Who says anyone needs to know about this right now?" I had no intention of telling anyone. "I just need more time to figure this out. You won't say anything, will you?"

Felicity raised her hands. "I'm not going to say anything, but these things have a way of coming out, especially in such a high-profile case."

I shook my head. "No. If she had planned this murder, there

are so many other ways she could have gone about it. Why would she put herself at the scene of the crime? I mean, would you do that? And if you were going to have help, why not pay someone else to do it? No, it has to be someone else. I just have to figure out who."

CHAPTER TWENTY-THREE

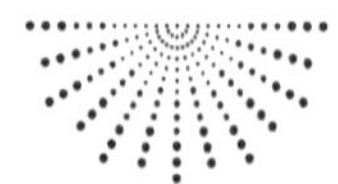

$\mathcal{I}$ walked into the house later that night to find it quiet, for which I was grateful. I needed to think about what I'd just discovered.

I made my way into the kitchen to put the teakettle on. As I waited for the water to boil, I rummaged around the refrigerator in the hope of finding an errant piece of pie, but alas, the troops had devoured Rose's latest delectable creation as they usually did.

When the teakettle whistled, I quickly took it off the burner, afraid I would wake someone. I grabbed the tea tin from the shelf above the stove and scooped some chamomile into the tea strainer and poured the water over the tea leaves and blossoms. With my cup in hand, I then went into the living room to settle myself on the sofa. I kept the lights off, not wanting any distractions.

The question remained: had Lizzy told me everything when she'd told me that Margaret was her mother? Did she know Mr. Travis was her father? Or maybe he wasn't her father. Just because they were in the photo together didn't mean that he had fathered the child, although it certainly looked that way. If only I could find actual proof.

I remembered what I'd learned from Barnaby Maxwell at the Art Students League. He'd mentioned a ne'er-do-well brother of one of Margaret's boyfriends. Could that boyfriend have been Edward Travis? It was well-known he'd gotten his start in show business in New York City as a stage actor so it stood to reason that he and Margaret could've met while there.

Loud ringing startled me, and I spilled the scalding hot tea on my leg. After setting my cup down on the coffee table, I ran to get the phone.

"Hello, darling," Chet said on the other end of the line. "Did I wake you?"

I smiled, glad to hear his voice. "No. I actually just got in."

"Work?"

"No. I went to Felicity's for dinner." I started to tell him about what I'd learned that day when he said something at the same time.

"You go ahead," he offered.

I stated what Lizzy had shared with me, how Margaret was actually her mother and her father was dead. "But I think I may know who her father is—or was." Then I told him about the photograph I'd found on Mr. Travis's property. "What if Lizzy is really Elsa Mayfield? Margaret left New York City because of a past boyfriend whose brother threatened her. Mr. Travis's lawyer said that if Elsa Mayfield and all the other beneficiaries could not inherit, the estate would go to Mr. Travis's parents and his brother, so clearly he has a brother." I paused. Chet was quiet on the other end of the line. I continued my thought. "So maybe she changed their names when they moved to Lake Tahoe."

Chet took a deep breath. "It's possible. Him being Lizzy's father would explain why Margaret was at the reading of the will —but, the lawyer obviously didn't know who she was."

"Right. So, somehow she found out about the gathering of beneficiaries," I added.

"But the photo isn't proof that Lizzy was Travis's daughter. He and Margaret could have met after she was born."

"Agreed ," I said. "But, it does prove that Mr. Travis and Margaret knew each other.

"I found something else that links them," Chet said. "Do you remember me telling you I'd found receipts for repairs to a house in Lake Tahoe?"

"Yes," I answered.

"I went to that house, and I spoke with the owner. I asked him if he knew Edward Travis."

I waited patiently for him to continue, but he hesitated. "And, did he?" I asked.

"No. But, when I asked him who he'd purchased the house from he said it was none other than Margaret Moore."

"Oh, my goodness!" I said. "That was *her* boarding house. The one she inherited from Mrs. Hillson."

"Right. After hearing that, I went through the box again, and I found something really interesting." He paused once more. My heart was racing.

"What? What was it?" I could barely contain my excitement.

"It was a contract between Edward Travis and Mrs. Hillson stipulating that he would help her make needed repairs to her house and pay her—an exorbitant sum by the way—if she left the house to Margaret Moore upon her passing."

I gasped, suddenly feeling not-so-sleepy anymore. "I wonder if Margaret knew about this?" I shook my head. There were so many questions I wished I could ask her. "Well, this is further proof that Edward Travis and Margaret Moore had some kind of relationship. Either in the past, and/or even more recently. But why didn't Margaret say anything about this relationship when Mr. Travis died? When Lizzy was accused of killing him?"

Chet clucked his tongue. "But the more pressing question is, why was she murdered?"

MY ALARM CLOCK went off at 5:30 a.m., but I was already awake. I had been awake since 3:00 a.m. It seemed I was in a never-ending pattern of two to four hours of sleep per night, complete with haunting nightmares. This time, my parents had retreated into the background of my dream. Was it because I had confronted the horrifying memory of my mother? It had finally come into the light so maybe it had less power over me.

Yet, my dreams were still plagued by Sophia trying to impart some kind of message to me. This time she was standing in a white, lattice gazebo in a beautiful flower garden pointing to a flock of birds. Her last cryptic message through Lenora Lange about a garden and then what I'd actually found "beyond the garden" seemed to be more than sheer coincidence. Or perhaps I was merely going mad. I wondered if I should see a doctor, but with Lizzy facing trial next week, I didn't have time for such things. If I could just ease the nagging sense that Detective Walton did not have all the answers, or that he hadn't even fully explored them, I might be able to rest. But some force was driving me onward.

My conversation with Chet last night had left me feeling as if there were still a number of stones unturned at Margaret's house. There had to be something the police had missed in regard to the connection between Mr. Travis and Margaret—and now Lizzy.

Giving up all hope of further sleep, I went to the bathroom to brush my teeth and my hair, determined to go to Margaret's before heading to work. I just hoped I would be able to get into the house. When I looked into the mirror, I was startled at my appearance. Whereas before I had looked merely tired, the woman staring back at me had aged by several years. I dabbed on some makeup to disguise the dark moons under my eyes with little consequence. I skipped the mascara, reasoning that to use it would only draw attention to those hollow windows into my tortured soul. I put on some lipstick and decided that would just have to be good enough.

After a quick cup of coffee, I was out the door.

I arrived at Margaret's house just as the paper boy rode by on his bike. I got out of the car and made my way to the front porch, where several newspapers were strewn about. The door was locked, as I had suspected. Gathering up the newspapers, I walked around the back of the house to try the door to the screened-in porch, prepared to crawl in a window if need be. But when I got to the back door, I immediately noticed that the handle to the door had been broken off.

I pushed on the door, and it creaked open. I walked in to find everything in disarray. Furniture had been moved, cushions upturned, tubes of paint had fallen to the floor. I moved into the living room to find it much the same. Rugs had been folded over, chairs moved, and sofa cushions stood at odd angles on the couch. I passed by the kitchen to see cupboards open, as well. Then I peered into the other room Margaret had used as an office. Papers were everywhere, files were strewn across the floor, and her desk drawers had been left open.

The police wouldn't have been this careless, would they? Someone else must have been here looking for something.

I walked in and sat down in her desk chair. I set my handbag and gloves on the corner of the desk, trying to determine what the police could have missed—or what they hadn't thought important. I picked up the loose-leaf papers on the desk one by one. There were receipts, ledgers, sketches, and notes. If there had been any kind of significant correspondence, I imagined the police, or whomever else had been in here, would have taken it.

I gathered the papers and stacked them in a pile on the desk, then picked up a pencil box and set the scattered pencils back inside. I skimmed notebooks, but finding only sketches and artist's notes within them, I set them on the bookshelves along with novels and books on art.

There was a door at the back of the room, which I assumed was some kind of storage area or closet. I opened it to find coats, clothing, hats, and shoes. If she had been anything like me, her wardrobe would have required more than one closet so it made sense for this to be her "overflow" unit. Amazingly, this space had been left intact. I rifled through the coat pockets and found only a lipstick tube and a handkerchief. My eyes settled on the suit she'd been wearing at the reading of the will. I inspected the fabric. It was not of the finest quality but not the worst, either. The sewing had been fairly uniform.

I closed the closet door and turned to face the room with a sigh. "This was a bad idea," I said aloud. "What was I thinking? Of course the police would go over everything with a fine-tooth comb."

I supposed I'd just needed to see it for myself. Had they really left things such a mess, though? I couldn't shake the idea that someone else was looking for the same proof I was.

I returned to the desk and picked up my gloves and hat. As I passed by her bedroom on my way out, I stopped. It was in the same condition as the living room and office, with her bedclothes rumpled and piled into a ball at the foot of the bed. A corner of the mattress had been pulled away from the bedframe, as well. I walked in and surveyed the mess more closely. I opened the closet door and found more of her wardrobe neatly hung on hangers, but her hatboxes had been opened and lay in a pile on the floor. I picked up a crimson felt cloche with a charming bow on the side. I tossed it back into a box and surveyed the room again, looking for some kind of clue.

My eyes were drawn to a painting hanging next to the door. It looked like one of Margaret's, if the style were any indication. On the wall at the corner of the painting, though, were marks, as if the frame had scratched the wall. But how would that have happened?

Unless it repeatedly had been taken on and off the wall . . .

I walked over to it and lifted it from its hanger. The painting concealed a panel in the wall, approximately twenty-four inches by twenty-four inches, that was hinged on one side and closed with a metal hook and eye.

Curious, I opened it. Inside lay a baby bonnet, some old wooden toys, and a wooden box with a rusted metal clasp. I pulled it out and wiped the dust off the top before taking it over to the bed and sitting down. I opened it to find papers, a sterling-silver rattle, and a roll of cash secured with a blue ribbon.

One by one, I took the items out and laid them on the bed, and then I started to go through the papers. Some of them were old photographs, one of which showed a cheery-looking picnic with smiling women in dresses that had been popular at the turn of the century and men in shirtsleeves playing croquet. I shuffled through several similar photos and stacked them on the bed. At the bottom of the box was an envelope with the words *New York City Hall of Records* stamped across the front. I opened it up and pulled out a neatly folded piece of paper. As soon as I unfolded it, my hand flew to my mouth.

It was the birth certificate of Elsa Mae Mayfield. Her parents were listed as Greta Mayfield and Edward Travis.

Stunned at this piece of evidence, I looked through more of the papers and found a letter written to the State of New York. As I read, my heart raced, the sound pulsating through my ears. It was a copy of a petition to change the names of Greta Lynn Mayfield and her three-year-old daughter, Elsa Mae Mayfield, to Margaret Moore and Elizabeth Moore respectively.

My hands shaking, I folded the papers and tucked them back into the box, unsure of what to do with this new evidence. This unequivocally proved that Lizzy was the daughter of Edward Travis and Margaret Moore. But it might also be the final nail in her coffin.

CHAPTER TWENTY-FOUR

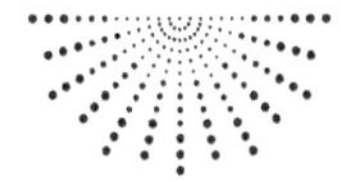

Still rattled from my find, I showed up for work thirty minutes late. So much for my resolve never to arrive late again. I placed the box I'd taken from Margaret's house under the driver's seat of my car for safekeeping and hurried inside.

To my chagrin, I walked into my office to see Timothy standing in front of a dress form adorned with one of Florence's costumes, studying it. Florence and Mr. Johnson were also there. She was cooling her heels at my desk, smoking a cigarette while he was perusing the multitude of costumes on the rack. He pulled off one of the men's suits and held it up to himself in the mirror.

"Glad you could join us, lass." Timothy scowled at me. "We can't do anything until you make some alterations to this dress. I don't need to remind you we are already behind schedule."

I set my things down on the desk. "I'm so sorry. I was, um . . . I was detained at the ranch," I lied. I didn't like to lie, but how could I explain that I was late because I had been snooping around a dead woman's house?

Florence stood up. "I'm not sure this dress is in keeping with Dorothea's character."

Before I could offer her an ashtray, she dropped her cigarette to the floor and stomped on it with her delicate T-strap Mary Jane. I flinched, hoping the burning ember hadn't left a mark on the wood floor. "This dress says demure, shy. It lends her no . . . confidence. Really, Grace, I'm surprised you would think it was appropriate."

"It doesn't show up well on camera," Timothy added. "It's too heavy."

"All you see is the dress, not me," she added.

I bit my lip. "I see." I went up to the dress form and turned it to face me. "Well, perhaps we could change out this velvet bodice with something lighter, like silk. And we could use a lighter color than the indigo. Perhaps sky blue. It will show up as white on film, but it won't be too brash. We would keep the skirt the same."

"Florence?" Timothy turned to her for her opinion, which slightly annoyed me. Yes, women often knew what looked best on them, but it was the job of the designer to decide what worked best on film, not the actors.

She casually examined her fingernails. "I suppose that will work."

"How long will it take to fix this?" Timothy asked.

"I think I have some fabric that will work for the bodice. Give me two hours?"

He looked at his watch. "So now we're two hours and thirty minutes behind schedule today."

I gave him an apologetic look, knowing that to say much more would only land me in further trouble.

Just then, Hilda came into my office carrying the Santa Maria. She looked up in surprise to see us all there. I quickly explained the situation and had her go to the wardrobe room to find the fabric.

"We'll also need to fit Mr. Johnson," Timothy added. "He will be playing the role of the guard. Billings was admitted to the hospital last night with acute appendicitis. His wife said she wasn't sure when he would be able to return, and the lads upstairs said they'd put him on another project."

"I see."

"The bosses want to get this film made toot suite, which I seem to be failing at already," Timothy continued. "You'll have to alter Billings's costume, lass. We don't have time for you to start from scratch."

I studied Mr. Johnson with a sinking feeling in my stomach. He was a good four inches taller than Mr. Billings and half his girth.

"How soon will you need it?" I asked, hoping it wasn't this week.

Timothy looked at me with raised eyebrows. "Yesterday, love."

I gave him a tight-lipped smile. "Of course. I'll get right on it."

"I'll leave you to it, then." He saluted as he left my office.

Florence settled herself in one of the club chairs. "The dress is also too big for me now. I've lost some weight—you know, with everything that's been happening lately." She reached for her handbag on the desk, and in doing so, she knocked mine off the corner of it. It dropped to the ground and popped open, spilling its contents.

"Oh dear," she said but made no effort to clean up the mess.

"I've got it." I knelt down and started to pick up the numerous items. The medicine vial I had found on set rolled away from my grasp.

"I say—" Mr. Johnson bent down to pick it up "—is this yours?" He held it out to me.

"No, it isn't. I found it on the interior castle set."

He reached down and patted his coat pockets absently, as if looking for something he was afraid he'd lost.

"Do you know who it belongs to?" I asked.

He shook his head. "No. Why would I?"

I wasn't quite sure what to say. He seemed interested in it for some reason. "Oh. Well, I didn't—"

Hilda came back into the room with the fabric I had asked for, thankfully interrupting us. I placed the vial back in my purse along with the other contents and placed it on the chair behind my desk. I set Hilda to work dismantling the dress and cutting the fabric to form while I asked Florence to go behind the screen and undress down to her slip. Mr. Johnson made no effort to leave.

"Mr. Johnson, would you . . . ?" I indicated toward the door.

"Oh, Grace," Florence said from behind the screen. "Don't be such a prude. Jimmy is fine where he is."

Jimmy? Just how intimate were these two? And for how long?

"Very well," was all I said aloud, though. "Mr. Johnson, I'll take your measurements in the meantime. We will see what we can do to fit you into a costume we already have. You would be swimming in Mr. Billings's costume, and it'd be far too short." I went to my desk drawer and pulled out my tape measure, a pad of paper, and a pencil.

"Shall I undress down to my slip?" he asked with a grin, an obvious attempt to be funny.

I avoided his gaze. "No, you're fine."

He stepped up to me and stood unnecessarily close. Instinctively, I took a step back, then took a measurement of his head and wrote it down on the pad. Florence came out from behind the screen, sat down in one of the club chairs again, and lit another cigarette.

"So how long did you work for Mr. Travis?" I asked Mr. Johnson as I measured his neck and then took up my pad and pencil.

"Oh," he said casually, "Edward and I go way back."

I wondered how far back. "Oh yes. You are from England, like he is. So did you go to grade-school together?"

"No. Not until we were at the London Academy of Music and Dramatic Art. Edward went to the finest primary and grammar schools, and was set up to enter university. I was not afforded that luxury."

"Edward was spoiled rotten," Florence chimed in. "His parents are filthy rich."

"Some people have all the luck." Mr. Johnson gave me that unsettling grin again. "But look where that got him."

I glanced over at Florence, who was taking a drag of her cigarette. She let the smoke linger in her mouth, her lips slightly opened in a cryptic smile, giving her the appearance of a dragon who'd just burned her prey to a crisp.

WE HAD to wrap up filming early because it had grown too dark to continue, as the scenes we were shooting were outdoor scenes. By early, I meant 7:30 p.m., which was late enough for me. I was so tired I felt as if I was walking in a dream, disconnected from reality and having trouble forming my words.

I was headed back to my office in the wardrobe room when Felicity came running up behind me. "Hey, I haven't had a chance to talk to you all day. How are you doing?"

I sighed. "I am dead on my feet."

"Any word from Chet about finding the mysterious heir?"

"Oh my goodness! I haven't told you yet." I lowered my voice to a whisper. "I found proof that Edward was Lizzy's father."

Her eyes popped open wide. "You're kidding?"

"Not in the least. Come to my office and I'll tell you all about it."

"I can't stay," she said with a frown. "Miss Lange is having a séance tonight in her suite at the Hollywood Hotel. Why don't you come with me and you can tell me about it on the way over?"

We reached the wardrobe room and then went into my office. I tossed my pad and pencil on the desk and ran a hand through my hair, rolling my head from side to side to release the kinks in my shoulders. "I don't know, Felicity. I think I need to go home. I feel like my head is going to explode."

"Still having nightmares?" she asked.

I nodded.

"Then do you really think you'll sleep?"

I gave a her a defeated smile. "No."

"I think you need to give Miss Lange another chance. You obviously still have some unresolved feelings and memories."

"Yes, that's true." I still didn't want to talk about what Miss Lange's last session had provoked in me, but sadness swept through me like a cold wind as I recalled the horrifying visions I'd had about my mother coming at me with a knife. "But I'm not sure I want to relive the past. Maybe I want to remain in the dark about it."

"No, you don't, Grace. It is driving you crazy. And I think you still have some unfinished business with your sister."

"Well, she did lead me to the photo 'beyond the garden.'" I made quotation marks in the air with my fingers.

She lifted a shoulder in a half shrug. "Maybe Sophia has more information for you."

I lifted my brows, considering the possibility. "Let me ring Rose at home first and make sure she and the children don't need me for anything."

I picked up the phone on my desk and called the house. Rose said that Ida and Susie were upstairs doing homework, and she was about to retire for the night. It seemed I could accompany Felicity after all, though I wasn't sure if that was a good or bad thing.

I hung up the phone. "All's well at the ranch."

"Okay, that settles it. Grab your coat and hat. We're going to a séance."

Too tired to argue, I relented.

"Good," she said. "Now tell me all about this proof."

WE PULLED up to the Hollywood Hotel in Felicity's Packard Roadster. I had been to the hotel several times for parties and dances but was continually impressed with the architecture. It was sort of the classic Mission style meets Victorian—an odd combination but somehow it worked with its grab bag of arches, balconies, turrets, cupola, and broad veranda that served as a gathering place year-round.

As we passed through the lobby, we almost ran headlong into Hollywood's most popular leading man, Rudy Valentino, as he was hustling to catch the open door.

"Ah scusatemi, signoras!" he said as he whisked by.

Felicity's chin dropped, and she looked at me with wide eyes. "Was that . . . ?"

"Yes, I believe so," I said. Not that Mr. Valentino could be mistaken for anyone else. I gave Felicity an amused grin as she stared after him. I hadn't pegged her as someone who would be so beguiled by a movie star . She always seemed so above that kind of goggling adoration. But it was Valentino, after all.

Seated in two of the lobby's lounge chairs were his wife, costume and set designer Natacha Rambova, and her friend and mentor, the actress Alla Nazimova. They nodded their heads in greeting, and we made our way to the front desk to inquire as to the whereabouts of Miss Lange's suite.

In a matter of minutes we were knocking at her door. I was not surprised to see Robert Smith answer it. My surprise came at the realization that he looked to be completely sober.

"Welcome, ladies." He waved his arm toward the room, inviting us in. "Grace, I'm glad you could join us."

"Hello, Mr. Smith," I said, surprised by his warm greeting, all traces of his former hostility toward me gone. "You look well."

I only hoped I looked half as well as he did, but I knew I did not, given my frazzled nerves and lack of sleep. I really didn't need to be here and longed for my bed, if only to get horizontal as I knew that slumber would be beyond my reach.

"Come in," he went on, his voice somber.

We entered the suite to see two people already there. There was another knock on the door, and we stepped aside so Mr. Smith could open it again. Mr. Valentino and Miss Rambova entered the room.

Felicity raised her eyebrows at me and clutched my arm. "What are they doing here?" she asked in a raspy whisper.

Mr. Smith made the introductions. "Rudy and Natacha are also interested in spiritualism and have attended many of Lenora's séances. Please, come have a seat."

He led us to a round table with eight chairs circling it. The largest, an ornately carved chair painted in gold, was backed up against the fireplace. I assumed this was for Miss Lange. A sizable, well-coifed and elegantly dressed woman was already seated to the right of the ornate chair. Her pudgy fingers were adorned with a multitude of rings. She gave us a kindly nod as we sat down.

"I am Eugenie Delacroix," she said in a heavy French accent, holding out a bejeweled hand. Both Felicity and I shook her hand and introduced ourselves.

Madame Delacroix swept a hand toward an equally elegantly dressed man standing near one of the windows smoking a cigarette. "And this is Pierre, my son."

He raised a chin in greeting, a less than enthusiastic expression on his face.

"The *sceptique*," she added dryly.

I stifled a yawn, wishing I'd never let Felicity talk me into this. Miss Rambova and Mr. Valentino took their seats to the right of Madame Delacroix, leaving a space for her son. Felicity scurried to the chair next to Mr. Valentino's, and I was seated between her and Mr. Smith's empty chair. He had retreated to another room of the suite, I assumed to retrieve Miss Lange. I no sooner finished the thought than out she came, in a flowing white gown with ostrich plumes lining the long, bell-shaped sleeves and boatneck collar. She glided to her chair without a word.

"I am going to turn out the lights," Mr. Smith said. "Once I do, please hold hands and center yourself. Lenora requests there be no talking during the séance, unless you are addressed, and we must remain as still as possible to allow the spirit or spirits to enter through the portal. It is important to note that we do not always know who might come through, but they will make their presence known when they do."

I glanced over at Felicity, who shrugged.

Mr. Smith closed the heavy curtains adorning the windows and lit a candle near one of them. He then proceeded to turn out the lights. Pierre Delacroix languidly took a final drag of his cigarette and then pressed the butt of it into an ashtray. He made his way over to the chair next to his mother and sat down with a sigh.

Mr. Smith took his place next to me and blew out the candle, leaving us in complete darkness. I blinked, hoping my eyes would adjust quickly. The utter blackness was disorienting, and my head began to swirl. I squeezed Felicity's hand, and she squeezed mine back. I was grateful for the reassurance.

"Please hold hands," Miss Lange repeated, her voice soothing and rich.

We all sat in silence for several minutes, the only noise in the room the ticking of the clock on the mantel. I closed my eyes, and my shoulders lowered a fraction. Wrapped in a cocoon of darkness and silence, I felt the kinks in my muscles relax and untie themselves. My breathing lengthened, and I drifted into a pleasant state of obscurity.

A loud rapping on the wall sent my heart into spasms. Felicity squeaked.

"Who's there?" Lenora asked.

More silence, save for the pounding in my chest.

"Please, make yourself known," Lenora encouraged.

"Mama?" A high-pitched girl's voice said. "Mama?"

I opened one eye. Lenora was speaking in the little girl's voice. I squeezed my eye shut again, afraid I would somehow break the spell.

"Yes, darling." It was Madame Delacroix. "I'm here." Her voice wavered with emotion.

"Papa is here, too," the little voice said. I wasn't sure if it was my own nerves, but I felt a humming vibration in the room.

"Alexandre?" the French woman asked, her voice full of hope.

"*Sacré bleu,*" her son muttered, obviously annoyed.

There was more loud rapping on the wall. I jumped, and Felicity squeezed my hand.

"Oh, my dear Alexandre!" Madame Delacroix rattled off something in French. We waited to hear more, but silence filled the room once again.

My heart was beating so hard I wondered if anyone else could hear it.

Suddenly, a deep, male voice answered in French. Then a perky young woman's voice came through. "Hiya," it said.

I opened an eye again. Miss Lange, her eyes closed, was leaning forward.

"Who is there?" she asked. "Can you give us your name?"

Nothing.

"What was that? Can you repeat it? Was that an *M*? Rap once if there is an *M* in your name."

There was a single rap on the wall. I closed my eye again and pressed my lips together, waiting. I could hear Felicity's breath coming fast and shallow next to me.

"What is your message? Say again?" Miss Lange asked. "Swallow? Swallow what?"

More silence, more waiting.

"Beneath the swallows," the young woman's high-pitched voice spoke again.

"C'est absurd," Pierre hissed, more loudly this time, and slapped his hand on the table.

The sound of someone gasping filled the room. Mr. Smith released my hand, and I could feel him moving his hands erratically over the table. The sound of a match being struck was followed by a soft glow as he lit the candle on the table. I scanned the faces and took in a sharp breath when I looked over at Miss Lange slumped in her chair.

"Lenora!" Mr. Smith shook her.

"Someone get the lights," Miss Rambova demanded.

Mr. Valentino jumped up from his chair and turned on the lights. Miss Lange opened her eyes and blinked, righting herself in the chair. She hung her head and rested her forehead on her fingertips.

"What have you done, man?" Mr. Smith said to Pierre. "It's dangerous for the medium if she is interrupted that way. It leaves her between two worlds."

"Pierre!" Madame Delacroix slapped his arm.

"This is nonsense." He stood up. "*Maman,* we are leaving."

"But—"

"I said, we are leaving!"

Miss Lange raised her head. Her eyes were unfocused and glassy, and her skin was as white as her dress. "He wants you to forgive him." Her words were directed at Pierre, whose jaw flexed with anger.

"*Maman,*" he said impatiently and took his mother by the

elbow, forcing her to stand. He then proceeded to drag her from the room.

The rest of us sat there, looking helplessly at one another. Mr. Valentino pulled a cigarette case out of his coat pocket and opened it up, offering one to his wife and then one to me and Felicity. We both declined. He lit Miss Rambova's and then his own, and leaned forward on his elbows studying Miss Lange. "Are you all right, *signora?*"

"Yes," she said. The color had come back into her cheeks. "But I'm very tired. If you'll excuse me . . ."

With Mr. Smith's aid, she stood up and rested her fingertips on the table, as if orienting herself or trying to keep herself from falling over. He took her by the arm and led her away from the table. Before she reached the doorway leading to the other room, she stopped and fixed me with a stare. "The message about the swallows was for you."

CHAPTER TWENTY-FIVE

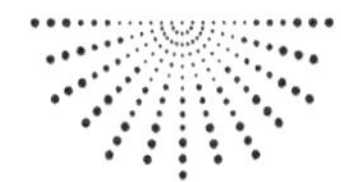

ose met me at the door when I arrived home. It was late, nearly 11:00 p.m., and when I saw the look on her face, I was prepared to get a scolding. But on further inspection, it wasn't anger she was projecting. It was anxiety.

"It's Lizzy." She took my coat and my handbag for me. "The jail called. She's been taken to the infirmary."

Pinpricks of adrenaline made my hands tingle. "What happened?"

"Said she's refused to eat. She's in quite a state."

"Oh god. She's supposed to stand trial in just one week." I went to take my coat and handbag back from her. "I'm going down there."

Rose held firm to my things. "It's far too late, my dear. You'll likely not be able to see her in the morning, either." She drew them slowly away from me and pulled me into the house. "I asked if she could have visitors, and they said not until she is in a more stable condition. They said maybe tomorrow afternoon."

I closed my eyes and put my hands over my face. If only we

could have afforded the bail money, she wouldn't be in such a state.

Rose led me to the sofa, and shakily, I sat down. "You look a fright, Grace. You really need to get some rest. You should go to bed," she clucked.

"I know, I know," I whispered. "I just can't seem to get any sleep these days."

"You stay here and let me bring you a plate of food. Have you had anything to eat today?"

I shook my head. I was moved by her concern for me. "No. I was late this morning, and I never did catch up."

She nodded. "I'll be back in a moment."

I sank onto the cushions and rested my head against the back of the sofa, grateful for Rose's maternal ministrations. My nerves were fraying and at risk of snapping at any moment, and I needed some tender loving care. I missed Chet. He was scheduled to return tomorrow, and it would be nice to be relieved of some of this burden.

Rose came back into the living room with a bowlful of rabbit stew and a plate of freshly baked bread slathered in home-churned butter. My stomach groaned in anticipation. She set the bowl and plate down, and promised to return with a glass of milk. I grimaced. I was not much of a milk drinker, and she knew this.

"It will help you sleep," she said, reading my mind. Or was it in my expression? Either way, I couldn't argue with her logic.

When she returned with the milk, she sat down on one of the wingback chairs adjacent to the sofa and watched me eat. "It's a pity the girl has no other family," she said absently. "Someone who could help us with the bail money. We could bring her back here and get her fighting fit for her trial."

I stopped mid-chew. Lizzy *did* have family. She just didn't know it.

"Rose, you are a genius!"

She blinked at me, and her brows turned down in an expression indicating I had finally lost my mind.

I told her what I had discovered at Margaret's house. "Don't you see? Mr. Travis's parents are her grandparents. Surely they would want to help their granddaughter." And if I reached out to them, maybe I could find something out about Travis's brother, discover if he was the one Margaret was so afraid of."

Rose gave me a dubious look. "But the girl's mother went to great lengths to conceal their identities. I don't know if you should meddle, Grace." She held the glass of milk out toward me.

I took it and forced down a mouthful. "I understand what you are saying. But, I'm running out of options, Rose. And time. Lizzy is giving up—falling apart, and she stands trial in a matter of days. I'll send them a telegram in the morning," I said with finality.

She gave a resigned sigh. "But, how? You don't know where to reach them."

"I could ask the estate lawyer." My mind began to race with the possibilities. If I could get them to wire the bail money, we could get Lizzy home and prepare her for the ordeal ahead. We'd have a little less than a week, but it was better than nothing.

"I can see your mind is made up so I won't say anymore on the subject. But tread cautiously, dear. It usually doesn't pay to interfere in others' family business. It can lead to disaster."

I knew she spoke the truth, but desperate times and all. "I have to try. Lizzy needs all the help she can get, and we are responsible for her, Rose."

Rose clicked her tongue and then pointed to the rest of my uneaten stew with a motherly sternness. Obediently, I took a few more bites, my appetite and energy returning with a vengeance. I took a piece of the bread and dipped it in the stew. The creaminess of the butter mixed with the savory broth was heaven.

Rose pulled something out from her pocket and held it in her palm. It was a white tablet. "Here's a sleeping pill. I don't take them often, but it does the trick."

I stared at the pill. I had considered calling the doctor to get a prescription for myself but had refrained. I shook my head. "I don't know." I'd never taken one before and had been a firsthand witness to Sophia's slow decline into addiction. "I'll be fine."

Rose leaned forward, pushing the pill closer to me. "You look like the walking dead, my girl. You need to get some sleep."

With some food in my stomach, my limbs suddenly felt weighted down, but my mind was still spinning. I looked at my watch. It was nearly 11:30 p.m. The thought of tossing and turning for the next few hours only to drift off into fractured sleep made my pulse quicken with anxiety. I took the pill from her outstretched palm.

She gave me a nod of approval. "Now wash that down with some milk, and then go wash your face. I wouldn't advise a bath tonight." With that, she took my empty plate, bowl, and glass into the kitchen.

I did as was told and made my way upstairs to my bedroom, then stripped off my clothes without even bothering to hang them up in the wardrobe. I slipped into my peach silk and ivory lace nightdress. I wrapped myself in Sophia's dressing gown and padded into the bathroom.

Rose had been correct. I did look a fright.

I slathered some cold cream over my face and gently removed it with a wash cloth. As I gently wiped away the makeup and this very long day, a wooziness overtook me, and I had to steady myself against the sink. I quickly brushed my teeth and staggered over to the bed, climbed under the covers, and sank into a blissful oblivion.

$\sim$

THE NEXT MORNING I took my coffee in the sunroom. I had fallen asleep the night before in sheer exhaustion and had managed to sleep the entire night, but somehow, I woke feeling weighted down, as if a pall had settled over me and was threatening to smother me. I had hoped that the infusion of sunlight in the cheery room would help to alleviate the sense of despair.

I hadn't dreamed of my mother but woke to memories of her and the realization that, as innocent children, Sophia and I had witnessed her slow decline into madness. Other memories came flooding back, too, particularly memories of my father—or rather, of his absence. It was so clear now. He rarely had been home. I remember him tucking me in to bed on occasion or me sitting on his knee while he read to me from the newspaper. But I didn't have many memories of us as a family. No meals together, no birthday parties, no holiday celebrations. Only a void of parental affection. Abandonment. Neglect.

After our parents had died, Sophia and I had lived in the house for a while until the bank reclaimed it. One of the neighbors, Mrs. Collingsworth, had written to the authorities telling them we were underage and alone. She had come over one day to let us know we would be taken to a home, an orphanage, and that one day, we might have new parents. For some reason this idea sent so much fear into Sophia that she told me we were packing our bags and leaving the house forever.

I closed my eyes remembering that day. We had left early, at dawn. The sky had been pink, painting the city in hues of gray and lavender. Shopkeepers had been opening their stores, and the milkman had been carrying his wire crates of milk from one doorstep to the other while the horse that pulled his wagon hung his head in a half sleep. Sophia had said storm clouds were gathering so we had to find shelter quickly. She had sounded so sure of herself, I blindly followed along. As we walked down the street, I had looked up to the sky sandwiched between the buildings and watched a flock of birds fly overhead. Their wings curved downward, tapering to a fine point and giving them the look of a crossbow.

"Come on, Grace." Sophia had pulled me along impatiently, but I had stopped, mesmerized by the birds.

One of the shopkeepers, who was sweeping the front stoop of his store saw us standing there. "Swallows," he said. "Beautiful birds."

I opened my eyes.

Beneath the swallows.

Isn't that what Miss Lange had said last night? And that the message was for me? How strange that I had just recalled that particular memory from my childhood. Perhaps the seed had been planted at the séance. Much like the message from the reading about the garden. But was that really possible?

Then something else occurred to me. I had seen the image of a swallow recently. In the golden photo frame in Mr. Travis's office. The scene depicted a swallow flying over . . . *a garden.*

I shook my head to clear it. In my exhaustion, my thoughts were running away with me. I had more pressing things to do, like sending a telegram to Edward Travis's parents.

Perhaps, I could get their information from Felicity instead of going to the lawyer. Surely Mr. Travis had it somewhere.

Resolved as to my next move, I finished my coffee feeling much better. I was just about to get up from my chair to refresh my cup when Rose appeared in the doorway.

"I thought you might want to see this." She held out the paper, and I went to her to retrieve it.

The headline read, Suicide or Homicide? The Mysterious Death of Pearl Davis, Wife of Late Hollywood Director, Edward Travis.

I scanned the story. While authorities previously had thought Miss Davis had committed suicide, it seemed a postmortem revealed bruising and puncture wounds, like those from a needle, in her buttocks. The coroner could no longer consider this purely suicide, and the police were now investigating the possibility of murder.

My heart started to race. Lizzy had felt a sting in her arm the night Mr. Travis was murdered. She'd had a small bruise there, too. Come to think of it, I remembered seeing a bruise on Margaret's thigh, as well.

"Oh my goodness," I said, staring at the words.

"The plot thickens." Rose looked at me over her spectacles.

"I knew it wasn't suicide! The murders *are* related!" Exhilaration coursed through my veins as I became more and more confident in my theory.

Rose tilted her head at me quizzically, and I explained.

When Rose still seemed uncertain of my excitement, I said, "Don't you see? Lizzy was already in jail when Pearl Davis died. Someone is trying to frame her!"

Rose took the paper back. "It says here they are still investigating. This isn't proof of either homicide or suicide."

I took her by the shoulders. "It's coming together, Rose. I can just feel it."

She frowned. "Don't get ahead of yourself, dear. How did you sleep? Did the sleeping pill help?"

"Yes. Thank you." I leaned over and kissed her on the forehead. "Have to run. I've got a lot to do today."

Before I went upstairs to get dressed, I hurried to the telephone to call Felicity. By the sound of her voice, I could tell I had woken her up, but I prattled on with my request for her to see about finding an address for the elder Mr. and Mrs. Travis and bringing it with her to work. Groggily, she agreed and then said goodbye.

"Wait!" I said, hoping I'd caught her in time.

"What now?"

"Bring the picture frame with you—the one from Mr. Travis's study with the photo of Florence on horseback."

"Why?" she asked, impatience in her voice.

"Just do it, please. I have a hunch."

FELICITY and I didn't have a chance to talk until Timothy had everyone break for lunch at around 1:00 p.m. Unfortunately, he was only giving everyone about thirty minutes to eat. He was on a mission to make up for lost time. He claimed the studio bosses were on a rampage, but I knew it was more likely he was worried about his reputation. Delivering in a timely, cost-effective manner was paramount for him.

Timothy had arranged for a local diner to bring in soup and sandwiches, and I had only been able to take a few bites of my turkey and rye before Helen tore the lace on the skirt of the Santa Maria while in the bathroom. That dress would be the death of me. And given the lack of time, we would have to fix it while she was wearing it. I sent Martha, the head seamstress to the wardrobe room to fetch more lace, and I set to work removing what had been ripped with the embroidery scissors I wore on a chain around my neck for just such purposes.

Felicity stood nearby, munching on her tuna salad sandwich.

"Did you find that thing you were looking for?" I asked her, intentionally being vague. I struggled with some of the threads holding the lace in place. One of the assistants was spoon-feeding Helen her soup while I worked on the skirt of the dress. A rush job would have to do. If I could just get the new lace tacked on, the camera would be none the wiser.

Felicity winked at me. "Sure did. And I also brought the other item you requested. I left both of them in your office."

Martha came back with the lace and measured a length of it for me.

"I'd love to sit down," Helen said. "I've been on my feet since early this morning."

"I'm sorry, dear," I told her. "I really can't do this with you sitting down."

I took pins out of the pincushion at my wrist one by one and set the lace in place.

She issued a theatrical sigh, and then I felt her body stiffen. "Oh god. What are *they* doing here? They aren't scheduled to shoot until tomorrow."

Timothy got up from his chair and handed his half-eaten sandwich to a bewildered assistant director who took it between his fingers with a pinched look of disgust.

"Florence." Timothy greeted her with a kiss on each cheek. "What are you doing here, love?"

"I've come to see the dailies. I'd like to assess them from yesterday, to see how I am coming across on camera."

"Like Attila the Hun," Helen murmured under her breath. "And *he* has about as much presence on the screen as a gnat." She lifted her chin toward Mr. Johnson. "Such an odious man."

"That's a strong term," Felicity said.

"But so deserving." Helen shifted back and forth on her feet. "So different from Edward. He couldn't even hold a candle to him, as an actor, as a director, as a human being. I don't know how Edward tolerated him—or why. But I suppose he had to."

I stopped mid-stitch. "He had to?"

"Oh." Helen pressed her hand to her mouth. "Nothing."

"Why would Mr. Travis *have* to tolerate Mr. Johnson?" I asked, the wheels in my head turning. Had he been blackmailing Mr. Travis?

"Well, he— I really shouldn't say, but . . ." She leaned her head closer to me and whispered, "I overheard them arguing once. Edward was upset at him, told him to straighten up or he'd be out on his ear, and—"

"Okay, you lot. Let's get back to work." Timothy clapped his hands to get everyone's attention. "You done over there, lass?" he asked me.

"Two seconds." I made the needle fly and tacked on the lace as fast as I could. Standing so close to it, it looked a mess, but the camera would not be able to pick up the uneven stitching. I looped the needle through the thread to make a knot and clipped the remaining thread with my scissors. "Off you go," I said to Helen.

She took in a deep breath, closed her eyes, and pressed her hands against her ribs, centering herself for the shoot. I left instructions for Martha to take over for me and told her to watch the dress like a hawk in case the lace came away from the garment. I tilted my head in the direction of the wardrobe room and motioned for Felicity to follow me.

As she had promised, Felicity had left a little black address book and the picture frame on my desk.

"The lawyer said the father's name was Alastair Travis, right?" I asked, recalling what he'd said at the will reading.

Felicity nodded "Yes."

I flipped opened the booklet, looked under *T*, and quickly found the name Alastair Travis along with an address. "This is excellent. I'm going to send him a telegram right away."

Felicity picked up the framed photo and studied it. "What about shooting? Won't you be needed on set?"

I worried my lower lip, thinking. "Yes, but Martha can handle it. This is too important, Felicity. I need to get word to Alastair Travis as soon as possible—for Lizzy's sake."

"But what if he was the reason Margaret changed their names?"

I hadn't thought about that. But did it matter now? The stakes were too high not to take the risk. Lizzy would likely be sentenced to death if we couldn't get her out of this.

"I have to take the chance. Besides, I have a feeling. It's all I have to go on, but this is too important for Lizzy. And maybe Mr. Travis will spring for a good lawyer—a *really* good lawyer."

I jotted down the address and handed her back the address

book. I then took the gold frame from her. My eyes went directly to the swallows flying above the garden scene, then drifted down to the photo of Florence on the horse. The message from Miss Lange—or was it Sophia?—was *beneath the swallows.* But what was I looking for? I scrutinized it so hard the photo blurred and my eyes watered, but I couldn't see anything resembling a clue.

I turned the frame over and studied the velvet backing, the little hinges, and the clasp that allowed one to open the back and insert photos. I pushed the clasp with the tip of my finger and opened the back. I flipped the frame over so the photo and glass fell into the palm of my hand. I set the glass on the desk and turned over the photo, surprised to see a second photo resting beneath the first. It was a picture of a well-dressed man and woman, both sitting in chairs angled toward each other, with two boys standing between them. The taller of the boys stood next to the man, and the smaller, seemingly younger boy was beside the woman. I turned the photo over and read the inscription: *Alastair and Edward Travis, Jane and Preston James Johnson Travis, 1887.*

I nearly dropped the photo on the floor. *Preston J. Travis.* One of the beneficiaries to Mr. Travis's estate. I showed the inscription to Felicity.

She looked up at me and her eyes met mine. "They're brothers?"

"Apparently so." I turned the photo over again and studied the faces. The older boy looked to be about ten years old, and the younger boy seemed to be seven or eight. Even though their faces were immature, there was no denying who they were—and who had motive for committing the murders. All of them.

CHAPTER TWENTY-SIX

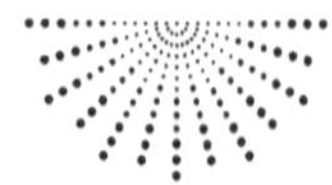

Determined to get my telegram off to Mr. Travis's parents, I left the studio for about twenty minutes to do so. In the message I made a quick introduction of myself as their granddaughter's guardian, then articulated that she was in trouble and I needed to speak with them as soon as possible. I included my address and phone number, hoping I would get a call. If I heard nothing back, I would assume they either didn't know of her existence or didn't care. Long-distance telephone calls were a huge expense, but given the urgency of my request, I hoped they would forgo a letter and the two to three weeks it would take to arrive.

When I returned to the set, Florence and Mr. Johnson had left. I thought about the photograph and again wondered why I'd had no inkling that Mr. Johnson and Mr. Travis were related. Did anyone else know? Was this common knowledge and I was just so far out of the Hollywood social loop that I alone was in the dark? But Felicity didn't know either, and she had worked very closely with Mr. Travis redecorating the mansion and had been in Mr. Johnson's presence on a daily basis. Did Florence know? Surely, she must have. And what about Helen? Was that what she was referring to when she had slipped earlier and said Mr. Travis had *had* to put up with Mr. Johnson?

The rest of the afternoon and early evening had zipped by as Timothy and the actors worked through one excruciatingly difficult scene. Now they were working on another, this time the scene in which the king dies. I watched Helen with fascination. Again, the emotion she portrayed in her performance was so raw and so real it was mesmerizing. I envied her gift to show her vulnerability in a way that was so tragically beautiful. It made my helplessness to face the tragedies of my own life all the more apparent to me.

"Cut!" Timothy's booming voice startled me out of my thoughts. "That's a wrap, people."

I looked at my watch. It was 8:00 p.m. Helen sank into the chair on set and covered her face with her hands, obviously drained from remaining in character, drenched in the emotions of fear, anger, and grief throughout the day. I wanted to ask her about Mr. Johnson but didn't have the heart to do it. If I was honest with myself, I was worn out physically and emotionally, too, and I longed to go home and crawl into bed, even if I didn't get any sleep.

I decided to leave her alone for the time being. I would talk to her tomorrow.

I arrived home shortly after 9:00 p.m., and once again, the house was quiet. I walked into the darkened living room, kicked off my shoes, and made my way into the kitchen. I opened the icebox to find Rose had left me a piece of shepherd's pie. I fired up the oven to warm it and then sat down at the kitchen table. The evening paper had been left there with a note from Rose. It read, *Page 3, Column 2.*

I opened the paper to page three. There was another story about Pearl Davis. Apparently, according to this story, the coroner claimed Miss Davis had died from an overdose of insulin, a medicine used to treat diabetes, but her medical records indicated she did not suffer from the disease. As a result, the coroner determined she had indeed been murdered.

I set the paper down, my mind swirling with the information, but I was too tired to make everything fit together. I got up and put my plate of food in the oven and set the egg timer for ten minutes. I had just settled back in my chair when I heard someone come through the front door.

Startled, I grabbed Rose's rolling pin on the counter and slowly pushed open the kitchen door that led into the living room. In the dark, I saw a figure moving around and then a lamp switched on.

"Chet! Oh, my gosh, you scared me." I placed a hand over my racing heart and lowered the rolling pin. I rushed over to him, and throwing my arms around him, I gave him a passionate, lingering kiss. His coat was cool to the touch, and he smelled of damp, night air and cigar smoke. His arms went around me, and he returned the kiss with the same ardor, his whiskers rough against my skin.

Finally, we broke apart.

"Wow. I should leave town more often if that's the reception I'll get when I get back." He smiled down at me, his light-gray eyes dancing.

"Well, if that's the case, I take it back. I hate it when you're gone. But boy, do I have so much to tell you. Do you have any more information from your inquiries in Lake Tahoe?"

He shook his head. "No. I kept looking but hit a dead end. Margaret liked to keep to herself. No one really knew much about her, and I couldn't find anything more in the records office."

I grinned up at him. "Not to worry, dear. I've found the proof we need."

I told him about the birth certificate and the petition to change their names I'd found at Margaret's house.

"This is wonderful," he said, smiling. "My gosh, you did it."

"Yes, but I want to keep it secret for a while. At least until I find proof that Lizzy did not kill Margaret or Mr. Travis. It would cast doubt on her innocence."

He pressed his lips together. "But, Grace, the police need to know about this. You are withholding information in regard to the case. They could arrest you for that, just like Daniel."

"I know, but I'm finding out more about Mr. Travis by the day." I told him about what I'd discovered about Mr. Johnson.

"Don't you see? That gives Mr. Johnson motive for killing Mr. Travis—and for killing Margaret and Pearl Davis. She died of an overdose of insulin, by the way." I pointed to the paper. "Oh! And the medicine vial!"

Chet shook his head, not understanding. I told him how I'd found it at work and had thought it belonged to either Robert Smith or Helen Clark.

"But when it rolled out of my purse yesterday, Mr. Johnson seemed to take particular interest in it. I wonder if it belongs to him? For all we know, he may have tried to kill Lizzy, too, but failed. It would make sense if he knew she was really Elsa." I paused to let it sink in. "I keep thinking about why she was unconscious in the barn, why she couldn't remember the incident. She would have had to drink an enormous amount of alcohol for it to have affected her like that, and I only saw her have a couple of drinks."

"You think he drugged her with insulin?" Chet asked.

"It's possible. The article in the paper mentioned a puncture wound and bruising on Pearl Davis's buttocks. Lizzy had a bruise on her arm, and she said she'd felt like she'd been stung by a bee at the party, around the same time she was talking to Mr. Travis and James Johnson. And remember when we found Margaret? She had that bruise on her thigh!"

Chet smiled at me. "I think you are definitely onto some-thing, Grace. Nice work. Let's call the police station first thing in the morning. *This* is something Detective Walton definitely needs to hear."

SOPHIA IS STANDING over me watching me sleep. She's dressed in one of the costumes I helped Lady Duff Gordon design for her. The headpiece I created is set askew on her head, and her eye makeup and lipstick is smeared. She's drunk and bleary-eyed, and looks like she's been crying. She clutches something in her hand, a glass vial marked XXX Poison. I try to reach for it but can't move. I try to tell her not to drink it, but the words won't come out of my mouth.

My heart races as she lifts it to her lips. Then she's gone and I am alone, sitting on the stage of the New Amsterdam Theater, reading the headline, SOPHIA MICHELLE DIES OF ACCIDENTAL OVERDOSE IN HOTEL ROOM. I look up at Flo, who was dancing with a showgirl on the stage. He is holding her tight and looking deep into her eyes.

"But, that's not what had happened to Sophia," I tell him. "Not exactly. She was poisoned—on purpose."

He keeps dancing as if I'm not even there. The girl in his arms looks over at me and kicks something on the floor toward me. It's a small medicine vial. I pick it up and try to read the label, but the words are distorted and misshapen.

A phone rings. Flo stops dancing and goes over to a phone set on a table on the stage. He picks up the receiver to answer it, but the phone keeps ringing, and ringing, and ringing.

I opened my eyes to find myself in my bedroom. The ringing was still happening. I looked over at Chet, who lay there peacefully, breathing the deep breath of sleep.

The phone!

I jumped out of bed and grabbed my dressing gown on the bedpost. Running down the stairs, I slipped my hands through the sleeves and tied it securely around my waist. Finally, I reached the phone.

"Hello?" I whispered breathlessly.

There was a woman's voice on the other end. "Miss Michelle, this is exchange seven-six. I have an overseas call for you."

"Yes, yes. I'll take it." I blinked in the dark, wondering what time it was. Rose came out into the hallway, and I put my hand over the mouthpiece. "It's okay, Rose. Go back to bed."

Without a word, she shuffled back toward her wing of the house.

"Hello?" a man's voice said on the other end. "Is this Miss Michelle?"

"Yes. Mr. Travis?"

"I'm sorry to ring you at this hour. It must be— Well, it must be the middle of the night there. But I was concerned about your telegram."

I smiled into the receiver. "It's no problem, Mr. Travis. I'm happy you called. First, I want to extend my condolences in regard to your son Edward. He was a fine man, and it's been my pleasure to work with him."

There was a brief silence on the other end.

"Thank you, my dear," he said after a beat. "You worked with him? Are you an actress?"

"No, I'm a clothing and costume designer."

"Ah. I see. A profession of some utility. I never understood Edward's passion for the theater or the movies. I had always hoped he would choose a more useful pursuit, but alas, he did not."

I wasn't quite sure what to say in response to that declaration so I didn't say anything.

He cleared his throat. "I must say, I was astounded to receive your telegram. You mentioned some trouble with my grand-daughter and that you are her guardian? Is Elsa all right?"

So he did know about her. I hadn't mentioned her by name in the telegram. Just as his granddaughter.

"Yes . . . well, no," I stammered helplessly, then pulled myself together and told him how she had come to be with us, as well as all about her current predicament.

"I see." He paused. I could hear his breathing through the phone. "Poor girl. I haven't seen her since she was a small child."

"Mr. Travis, I know that Lizzy—I mean, Elsa—did not kill your son. I firmly believe she had no idea he was her father, and if she—I hate to even think it—if she did kill him, it must have been an accident of some kind. As for her mother, Margaret—I mean, Greta—I just don't believe Lizzy—Elsa—would kill her, either. They had been at odds, yes, but she had set out to apologize for her behavior. Please, Mr. Travis—"

"Slow down, my dear," he cut in. "I am an old man and cannot keep up."

I took a deep breath and willed myself to calm down. There was just so much to say, so much to ask. "Could you answer some questions for me?" I asked softly.

"I will try."

I took another deep breath and let it out. "How well did you know Greta and Elsa?"

"Not well. Edward and Greta brought the child here on holiday shortly after she was born. She was the most beautiful infant I'd ever seen in my life. And it was the happiest I'd ever seen Edward, before or since. Greta was charming. We were saddened to hear the relationship did not last. I don't think Edward was ever the same after she left him."

"Do you know what happened between them?"

There was another silence on the other end of the phone. I heard the crackle of something on his end, and then he exhaled. I imagined him smoking a pipe.

"Edward was married to Pearl, though it wasn't the happiest

of relationships. I found her to be demanding and demeaning. He'd promised Greta he would divorce Pearl and marry her, but I am afraid that never happened. I understand they were still married when Edward died."

I wondered if he knew about Florence Thomas. I decided it best not to bring her up.

"Mr. Travis, I've only recently found out Greta's and Elsa's true names. Do you have any idea why they might have gone by Margaret and Lizzy Moore?"

More crackling and another exhale.

"Mr. Travis?"

"It was on account of my stepson." The register of his voice lowered.

My heart quickened. "Do you mean Preston J. Travis?"

"Yes. You know about him?"

"I've only met him recently," I said, my throat going dry. "I know him as James Johnson, though, and I had no idea he and Mr. Tra—Edward were brothers."

"I'm sure you didn't. Few, if any, in America knew. It was by design."

I waited for further explanation. "I don't understand."

Another exhale. "My wife was a widow when I met her, and I was a widower. Preston was four years old, Edward six. Preston was a difficult child. While Edward was always outgoing and gregarious, Preston was withdrawn and sullen. It wasn't until years later that we found out how disturbed he truly was. I won't bore you with his life story, but suffice it to say, the child needed to be institutionalized, but my wife wouldn't have it. We had a horrible time with him. While Edward flourished in school and with his peers, Preston got into more and more trouble and showed absolutely no remorse for his actions. He would leave us for days. The only person he would listen to was Edward. Somehow Edward saw through Preston's failings as a human being. But after Edward left home for America, Preston became involved with a gang in London. Terrible lot. He ended up in prison."

"Oh. I'm so sorry. But how . . . ?"

"The barrister I hired for him persuaded him to testify against the members of this gang in exchange for early release. In an effort to protect his stepbrother, Edward encouraged him to begin going by his middle name and father's surname and join him in America. Said Preston could work for him if he kept his identity secret. This was roughly around the time Greta left Edward. But Edward pursued her relentlessly, had Preston keep tabs on her. I believe this is why she changed their names. She didn't want to be found."

I thought about this for a moment. The agreement between Mr. Travis and Mrs. Hillson came to mind. So perhaps Mr. Travis had always known where she was, took care of her in spite of her wanting nothing to do with him.

"Oh dear." The elder Mr. Travis broke my train of thought. "I must let you get back to bed. I do apologize again for calling at such and ungodly hour."

"Oh, but wait," I said. "There's more. Lizzy—Elsa—isn't well, sir, and her trial is quickly approaching. I cannot afford the bail the court has posted, and I would like for her to come home, with me, to recover and to give her comfort while she stands trial. You are all she has, really, in a manner of speaking."

There was silence on the other end and then the sound of tapping. I assumed he was tamping out the tobacco from his pipe. I held my breath, waiting for his reply.

"How much is the bail?"

I swallowed nervously. "Twenty thousand dollars."

More silence. "Very well. I'll wire it tomorrow."

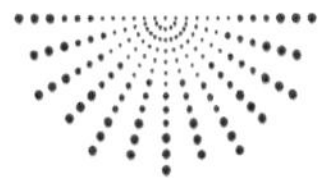

CHAPTER TWENTY-SEVEN

Flooded with relief that Lizzy, or Elsa, would soon be safe at home with us, I went back upstairs and crawled into bed quietly so as not to disturb Chet. I lay back on the pillow and closed my eyes in an attempt to fall back asleep, but my thoughts were awhirl. I opened my eyes and stared at the ceiling, replaying the conversation with Alastair Travis in my mind.

The information about James Johnson had been enlightening. When he'd came to America, he'd dropped Preston and Travis from his name to protect himself, obviously, but maybe to protect Edward, as well. A murderous criminal gang was looking for him, after all. Perhaps Edward had insisted upon this to protect Greta and Elsa, too?

I closed my eyes again and tried to organize my thoughts, but they were jumbled. They passed through and around my brain like a dust devil. The dreams I'd been having intertwined with the facts and the odd occurrences as a result of the reading with Lenora Lange, and then later at the séance. Some messages I'd absorbed from the living, and others had come from the dead.

Hints, clues, and brick walls. Family secrets, mental and emotional denial.

Suddenly, my mind settled on an image of Sophia. It was the last image I'd seen of her in my dream. She'd been holding out the bottle labeled *Poison*. But that hadn't been what killed her in reality. She'd been poisoned with arsenic, murdered. The vial I'd found on set and then later rolled across my salon floor popped into my mind.

Edward Travis was dead, clearly murdered. Margaret was dead, clearly murdered. Pearl Davis was dead, her death now determined a murder. And Lizzy was in jail. All three of these women were connected to Edward Travis, and all three stood to inherit, and now James Johnson. The only people now standing in the way of James Johnson getting everything were his own parents and—

Dear god! Florence!

I threw off the covers and scurried to my closet, rummaging in the dark to find some dungarees and a sweater. I jammed my feet into some flats, putting them on the wrong feet. Once I righted them, I dashed down the stairs, swiped my handbag and car keys off the hall table, and headed outside to my car.

I drove as fast as it would go, my mind focused on keeping the car from veering too far to the left or right. Thankfully, the streets were empty.

Thirty minutes later, I swung the car onto the circular drive of the mansion. I got out and ran to the front door. As I had figured, it was locked. I ran around the side of the house, past the swimming pool and headed for the kitchen door. It, too, was locked.

"Felicity," I said. "She'll have a key."

I ran to her little bungalow and banged on her front door. I got no response so I banged again. Finally, she opened it. Her hair was wrapped in a silk kerchief, and she pulled her dressing gown closed around her waist.

"Grace? What in the heck are you doin' here, sugar?" Her voice was groggy with sleep.

"I need a key to the mansion."

"What? What are you talking about, girl?"

"Now, Felicity! Give me the key to the kitchen door."

She stared at me dumbly.

I shook her by the shoulders. "The kitchen door! Now! Trust me!"

She left me standing at the door, and in a few seconds, she returned with a key. I snatched it from her hand. "Go call the police. Florence is in danger."

"But Grace—"

"Do it!"

Clutching the key in my palm, I raced back to the mansion. My hands were shaking so hard, I had trouble fitting the key into the lock but was eventually successful.

Once inside the kitchen, I grabbed a brass candlestick, fled to the foyer, and dashed up the staircase to my right. When I reached the landing I looked left and then right, trying to remember the layout of the upper floor. I had only been in Mr. Travis's study up there—no other rooms. Taking a guess, I tiptoed down the hallway to the first closed door on the right. Opening it gently, I stuck my head in. The drapes were open and the gray of early morning lit the room. It was a bedroom, but the bed was neatly made. I tried the door across the hall. Dim light illuminated this room, as well, and I took in a breath, worried someone had heard me. But the room was empty, and again, the bed was made. A small lamp on the nightstand bathed the room in a soft glow. I was about to close the door when something metal on the nightstand caught my eye.

Squinting into the dimness, I made my way over to it. It was a metal box about the size of my palm. There was nothing remarkable about it, but for some inexplicable reason, I was drawn to it. It was secured with a clasp on one side and had two tiny metal hinges on the other. I set the candlestick down and picked up the box. I flipped open the clasp and pried it open. Inside, nestled in hollows of red velvet, were two dark-brown medicine vials with rubber stoppers, set on either side of another longer hollow, and this one was empty. A hot prickling burned under my skin, and perspiration bloomed from my palms.

All the messages, real or imagined, all the dreams, waking or in slumber, all of my visions and memories led to this. The answer.

I picked up one of the bottles and turned it under the light. In large letters, the label read *Ampoul I'Letin*, and in smaller letters underneath, in parenthesis, *Insulin, Lilly.*

Insulin. I knew it!

I scanned the room, and my gaze landed on a coat that was thrown over a chair. I went to it and inspected it, reaching into the pockets, which were empty. I was about to set it down again when I noticed the cuff of one of the sleeves. A button was missing. I looked at the other sleeve. The button on it was a perfect match to the one I'd found on the staircase outside my studio.

A prickling heat coursed through me. I set the jacket down and flipped the kit closed. I was just about to set it back down on the nightstand when I sensed someone behind me. I turned to see James Johnson standing in the doorway. He was completely dressed, but his shirt tail hung out from his pants and dirt smeared his cheek. I grabbed the candlestick.

"Miss Michelle. What are you doing here?" His voice was amazingly calm—almost as if he had been expecting me. He closed the door behind him.

I swallowed hard, my mouth suddenly dry as dust. I held the candlestick in front of me. "Where is Florence?" I asked.

He smiled and took a step toward me. I backed into the bed.

"I don't know." He shrugged. "She never returned from the studio."

Never returned? They had left the studio together. "What have you done with her? Where is she?"

He held his hands in the air. "We aren't attached at the hip, dear girl. Well, at least not anymore." He slowly took off his tie and held it between his hands. I felt the blood drain from my head. "To what do I owe this unexpected pleasure? And so early in the morning? Were you dreaming of me? Are you tired of that old windbag of a husband?"

I took in a shaky breath. "Why do you have this?" I asked, holding up the metal box with my free hand.

"I have diabetes. Was diagnosed two years ago." He lifted a shoulder and took another step. "I'll ask you again. What are you doing in my room?"

"Is that how you killed Pearl Davis? Did you give her an injection of insulin?"

He let out a low chuckle. "And here I thought you were just another vapid blonde who liked clothing. But you surprise me, Miss Michelle."

He took another step closer. My heart was hammering in my chest. I suddenly remembered I'd told Felicity to call the police. If I could just remain calm and keep him away from me, they might get there before— A shudder escaped down my back.

"It's really not that complicated." I tried to keep my voice steady. "Almost everyone who stood to gain from Edward's will is dead. Except you, Florence—if you haven't killed her already — and your parents. Are they next?"

"And Elsa," he added, an evil grin splitting his face in two. "But I'm curious, Miss Michelle—Grace. May I call you Grace? Seems appropriate considering how intimate we are soon to become." He twisted the tie between his hands.

I clenched my teeth, my stomach roiling.

"How exactly did you figure out who I am?" he asked.

I raised my chin in defiance. "I found a photograph. And I spoke with your father, Alastair."

His eyes opened wide, and he moved closer. His jaw flexed, the sides of his nose twitching in anger. I could see the veins in his neck protruding. "He's *not* my father. He was *never* my father—only the ogre who shared my mother's bed. I was never good enough for him. Never as good as his cherished one, the golden boy." He flung his arm in the air, and I flinched.

I quickly composed myself again. "You mean Edward?"

"Of course I mean Edward," he sneered. "Who else?"

I swayed as a wave of dizziness overtook me. I realized I'd been holding my breath. I took in a gulp of air. "So your motivation for killing him was more than just the money. You hated him—even though he was pretty good to you, considering your past."

He let out a laugh. "Good to me? If you call demanding perpetual servitude being *good* to me, then you're not as smart as I thought."

"But, you didn't kill him with the broken glass, did you? At least, not at first. You followed him and Lizzy out to the barn, but then what happened? Did you intend to kill them both?"

He moved toward the desk, and I braced myself for the worst, expecting him to come after me, but he simply pulled the chair out from under the desk, placed it up against the door, and sat down. He crossed his right leg over his left. I wanted to shout at him that the police would be there at any moment, but I was worried he'd kill me and then escape before they arrived.

"What are you doing?" I asked, confused by his sitting down.

He shrugged again. "I was tired of standing. Besides, I need to rest before I take care of you." He pulled a syringe from his pants pocket and held it in front of his face. "Nope. Not enough left for the both of us. Florence didn't quite need the full dose."

I swallowed. So he had killed her, too.

He settled into the chair and smiled at me. A sickening chill washed over my body. "Now, where were we?" he went on. "I'm quite enjoying this. It feels good to unburden my soul."

Where are the police?!

I cleared my throat, mustering up my courage. "I asked if you had planned to kill both Lizzy and Edward. You obviously knew who Lizzy really was."

"Elsa. Yes, I knew. Had for quite a while. But it takes time, you know, to figure out how to commit the perfect crime."

I willed my legs to stop shaking, and I tried to steady my breathing. If only I could keep him talking until the police arrived. I cocked my head, feigning interest when, really, I just wanted to hit him over the head with the candlestick and run. But he was between me and the door.

"So imagine my surprise and delight when I found sweet Elsa at the party," he continued. "At your house! It seemed the stars had aligned for me. She really is a delightful girl. I quite enjoyed talking with her. And oh, how she loves those horses. Wouldn't shut up about them. But then Edward had to go and spoil our conversation. He told me to fetch him another drink and to get 'Lizzy' a glass of water. When I did, off they went to the barn."

"And you followed them."

He smiled. "I did."

"And?" I wanted to know how he'd managed to subdue both of them.

"It was nothing ingenious. Florence actually helped. She didn't realize it, of course. She followed them, too. Told Edward she wanted to speak with him. He told Elsa to go on, he'd join her in the barn in a minute. He and Florence got in another one of their famous arguments. You know, his philandering with young starlets, her jealousy. Ridiculous. Meanwhile, I slipped into the barn after the girl, and—"

"When did you jab her in the arm with the needle?" I interrupted. "Inject her with the insulin? Was it in the house?" I raised my chin, showing him I wasn't afraid of him, but my insides were telling me otherwise.

He sighed. "Yes. It takes a little while for the insulin to take full effect."

I closed my eyes, wishing Detective Walton had listened to Lizzy. She probably wouldn't be sitting in a jail cell awaiting trial right now if he had. I opened my eyes and looked James dead in the eye. "And what about your brother?" I asked. "Did you wait until you were in the barn before you gave him a dose?"

"Yes. I didn't really have an opportunity before then." He looked pensive, as if he were reliving how he could have done it better. "I simply stabbed him in leg with the rest of the insulin, and while he was distracted, I broke the glass Lizzy had brought to the barn and finished him off. It was perfect."

"You made it look as if Lizzy had killed him."

He nodded and stood up. "Yes. And that brainless detective was more than pleased to arrest Lizzy for the crime. It worked out perfectly. The state would take care of her for me. She would either hang or spend the rest of her life in prison and never be allowed to inherit." He held out his hand. "Now pass me the insulin kit."

Like hell.

Beads of perspiration dotted his forehead, and his lips had turned a sickly shade of white.

I needed to keep him talking. "So that gave you the perfect opportunity to frame her for Margaret's death, too. You went upstairs, found her room, and took the earring."

"The kit," he said between clenched teeth. He blinked rapidly and shook his head.

It suddenly dawned on me. He needed a dose of the insulin, and I had the vial. I had some leverage here. "Where is Florence?" I pressed again. "Tell me and I'll give this to you."

His mouth twitched, and he clenched his jaw. "I suppose it doesn't matter what I tell you," he said, his voice ominously low. "You'll be dead soon anyhow. Let's just say she met her unfortunate death at the train tracks. Silly girl was so distraught, she got drunk and, well, toppled onto the tracks." He grinned.

My body shook with rage. He was so calculating, so cold. "You mean you drugged her with insulin and put her on the tracks. You're despicable."

He held out his hand for the metal box. It was shaking, and his face had grown pale, giving him the look of a ghost. "Now give me the box."

I shook my head no. And then, like angels from heaven, sirens wailed in the distance.

James Johnson lunged at me, but I was able to dodge him. I ran for the door, but he grabbed me around the waist, and I struggled against him. I tried elbowing him in the ribs, but he was too close. He threw me to the ground and then straddled me on his knees. I flailed, trying to scratch his face, but he caught one of my wrists and twisted. While I howled in pain, he tied my wrists together with his necktie and then pinned them behind my head and wrapped the ends of the tie around my neck, rendering me completely helpless. I thrashed about, but somehow he managed to drag me closer to the nightstand. He grabbed hold of the kit, flipped it open, and took out one of the vials. He stuck the needle into the rubber stopper.

"You'll never make it in time," I said. "Don't you think the police will figure it out? If you kill me, they'll know it was you who murdered everyone. You can't frame Lizzy for me or for Florence, just like you couldn't frame her for Miss Davis's death. You've killed too many. Don't you see, you're the only one left!"

He pulled the needle out of the rubber stopper and held it in front of my face. "Shut up," he growled. He was about to plunge the needle into my arm when we heard a commotion coming up the stairs.

"If you kill me—"

"I said shut up!" he snapped.

The sound of doors banging open made him hesitate, and

with all my might, I thrust my body to the left, causing him to lose his balance.

"In here!" I screamed.

He got to his feet and ran to the window. He threw it open and disappeared onto the roof, just as two uniformed police officers burst through the door.

"He went out the window!"

One of the officers climbed onto the sill and followed him out. "Get downstairs and tell the others to come round the back!" he shouted to the other officer who ran from the room.

A gunshot sounded outside.

"Grace!" Felicity appeared in the doorway and ran to me. "Grace, are you all right?"

She helped me sit up and started working at releasing me from the knots. "He confessed to everything, Felicity. James Johnson. He killed them all."

"I can't find Florence," she told me.

"He's left her on the train tracks somewhere." I struggled to help Felicity loosen the tie from around my wrists. "Quick, we have to tell the police. God, I hope she isn't dead."

She released my wrists and threw the tie on the floor. "Here, let me help you up." She stood behind me and, placing her arms under my armpits, hauled me to my feet. Once I was standing, the blood drained from my head. My fingers tingled with renewed sensation, but my knees went week.

And then there was nothing.

CHAPTER TWENTY-EIGHT

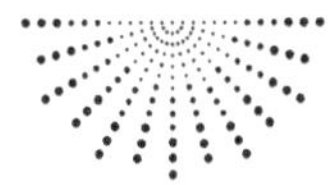

*B*right light penetrated my eyelids, and the soft sound of footsteps brought me back to consciousness. A warm hand took hold of my wrist and held it up. I opened my eyes.

A man wearing a white coat stood over me, looking at a pocket watch. He flipped it shut and turned his gaze to me.

"Miss Michelle. Welcome back," he said, his fatherly face breaking into a smile. His pale eyes crinkled in the corners behind round-framed spectacles.

"What happened?" I asked, groggy and disoriented. I raised my head and looked around. I was in a hospital bed in a bright room. How did I end up here?

"You had quite a bit of excitement." He released my wrist. Then it all came back. James Johnson. "Your heroic efforts are to be commended, but you've put your health in jeopardy. You are suffering from nervous exhaustion."

I laid my head back on the pillow and closed my eyes. The mere effort of raising it left me feeling wrung out.

Snippets of my encounter with James Johnson flickered

through my mind like clips from a film reel. He'd killed everyone, except Lizzy and—

I opened my eyes again. "Florence Thomas," I said, looking
up at the doctor. "Did she die?"

He shook his head. "No. Thanks to you, the police got to her
just in time. She's recovering from the insulin poisoning. I've
sent her home."

Home? I shook my head. But she'd been poisoned. "She's
gone home already? I would have thought—"

"You've been here for two days, my dear." His mouth turned
down, and he picked up a clipboard next to the bed and wrote
some notes on it.

A nurse came over to him, and he gave her a nod. She left,
and he continued jotting his notes. I closed my eyes again, the
light in the room almost too much to bear. More footsteps
approached the bed, and someone grasped my hand.

I opened my eyes. "Chet!" My heart flooded with joy at the
vision of his handsome face.

"Hello, you." His eyes were rimmed with moisture. My
breath caught in my throat to see him so emotional. I squeezed
his hand, and he bent down and kissed my forehead. "You are
quite the heroine, my love."

I managed a smile. And then Lizzy and Daniel suddenly
popped into my mind. My heart went into spasms. "The kids?"

"Home, safe and sound. Johnson was apprehended and
charged with the murders, and Lizzy and Daniel were released
right after his arrest."

I let out a sigh of relief, but then concern took hold of me
again. "How are they?"

Chet gave a tilt of his head and pressed his lips together.
"They're managing. Keeping busy. They're going to be all right,
Grace. They just need some time."

The doctor came back over and stood next to Chet. "And you
need some rest."

"Yes," Chet agreed.

As much as I wanted to protest, a weariness filled my body and my mind. I took a deep breath, closed my eyes again, and comforted myself in the knowledge that Lizzy and Daniel were safe.

A WEEK LATER, Felicity and I leaned against the fence railing of the eastern field. The afternoon sun penetrated through my blouse onto my back, wrapping me in its warmth. The air was soft and cool, and carried with it the refreshing scent of alfalfa and Bermuda grass from the east, as well as the pleasant aroma of the Spanish broom growing along the fence line to the south. Lizzy and Goldie were in the distance, galloping through the fields and soaring over fences.

"I bet you'll be glad to get your horse back," Felicity said with a chuckle.

I laughed. "I don't mind. Lizzy is really good with Goldie. And I'll have all the time in the world with her."

She turned her head to look at me. "How are you feeling?"

"Fine." I smiled. "Great, in fact."

I spent almost a full week in the hospital recovering from the ordeal and the weeks leading up to it. The doctor said I didn't need any further treatment as long as I promised to get plenty of fresh air and rest for the next few weeks. He let me go with a prescription of sleeping pills, which I never took, and a suggestion that I take some time off work. That had been an easy order to fulfill as the studio had shut down production of *The Queen of Whitehall* permanently as the making of it had been tainted with enough scandal to last years.

Lucky for Timothy, Felicity, and me, we were put on a new film at Ambassador that was currently undergoing screen tests. The brilliant Helen Clark had already been cast, as had her leading man—and lover—Chase Chandler. She was currently in the process of divorcing her husband.

"When does Lizzy leave?" Felicity asked.

"Next week."

The elder Mr. Travis had extended an invitation to Lizzy—or as he knew her, Elsa—to come for an extended stay with him and his wife in England. Chet contacted the judge who had sentenced Lizzy to come live with us, and he agreed to rescind his previous order.

Felicity picked up a strand of grass. "Is she excited or nervous?"

"A little bit of both, I think. She has no recollection of her grandparents but said she wanted the chance to get to know them. I can't blame her. I would have loved to have some family to retreat to after Sophia died."

"And the Travis estate?"

The breeze picked up, and I settled a stray lock of hair over my ear. "The lawyer will remain the trustee until Lizzy comes of age."

"What will she do with the mansion?"

"She wants to sell it, and Florence wants to buy it."

Like Lizzy, Florence Thomas had very little recollection of what had happened the night she and James had left the studio. She had come to visit me in the hospital, large bouquet and profuse gratitude in hand for saving her life. She had also presented me with a generous check for the sake of the children and the horses, just as Mr. Travis had promised he would.

"I figured as much." Felicity turned the stalk of grass between her teeth. "Florence wants to keep me on as decorator, but we are starting from scratch. She wants the mansion to be a reflection of her, not Edward. I think she's reinventing herself."

Probably not a bad idea, I thought with a chuckle. "I heard she was offered a contract at Paramount."

Felicity laughed. "I wonder if they know what they are getting into."

The sound of an engine starting interrupted our conversation. Daniel had turned on the hay baler, which was situated at the far end of the field, and he and Chet were loading it up with pitchforks full of alfalfa grass.

"With all this farm work, he's going to be as strapping as Chet before you know it." Felicity pointed her chin toward them.

"Yes. I worry about him, though. He's still struggling. He's such an angry young man. And with good reason, given his background with his father and then being falsely accused of murder. He had a rough time of it in jail, too. But Chet has really taken him under his wing, and has given him more responsibility on the farm."

"Well, with you and Chet helping him, I'm sure he'll be fine. In time." Felicity jumped down from the fence and then leaned her back against it, resting her arms on the railings.

"Yes," I said. If there was one thing I've learned from my troubles of the past, it was that time had the ability to heal all wounds.

We stood there in silence for a few moments, each of us lost in our thoughts.

"Miss Lange is doing another séance next week." Felicity flicked my arm with a strand of grass. "You interested?"

I placed my hand over my eyes to shield them from the sun as I watched Lizzy and Goldie sail over another fence. "No. I'm still dreaming about my mother and Sophia, but now they are pleasant dreams. I think whatever messages my sister had for me had been received. She helped me face the truth about our mother. It was hard to reconcile, but I know my mother loved me. She was sick and not in her right mind. In a strange way, it's been very healing to confront the darkness in my past."

Felicity nodded. "Not to mention she helped you with the murders."

"Yes. Sophia has always taken care of me." I jumped down from the fence, my backside having gone numb. "I expect she always will."

Felicity wrapped her arm around my shoulder and squeezed. "You were lucky to have each other. And I'm lucky to have you as a friend, sugar."

I tilted my head to rest against hers. "Friends are the only family I have left, and I'm grateful for you, too."

Down the lane, a motorbike pulled up to the gate. The rider hopped off, opened the gate, and continued on foot toward the house, a large bag slung over his shoulder.

"I wonder who that is," I said.

I climbed over the fence and walked toward him. He was a teenage boy in a Western Union telegram uniform.

"Are you Miss Michelle?" he asked.

"Yes." I looked over at Felicity, who shrugged.

"Got a telegram for you, ma'am." He held out a clipboard. "Sign here."

I signed my name, and then he handed me an envelope. "Have a nice day, ma'am." He tipped his cap to me, turned, and walked back down the lane.

I ripped open the envelope and read. I blinked several times at the words, my brain unable to comprehend what I was seeing. I read the words again, the black type making no logical sense. Slowly, I lowered my arms, the telegram and envelope in each one of my hands.

"What is it, honey?" Felicity asked. "You look like you've seen a ghost."

I turned to her feeling like I had. "It's from someone who says he's my father. He's alive."

~

I HOPE this book has brought you some entertainment and enjoyment! I am so grateful and honored that you have chosen to spend some time with me.

If you are so inclined, I would appreciate your spending just one more moment and writing a review. It doesn't need to be long, just a few honest words about your reading experience.

You can leave your review on Amazon, Bookbub, Goodreads or all three!

A priceless heirloom worth its weight in lives. Can she crack the case before she becomes a killer's trophy?

[Scan to buy book 3 of the series, *Grace Among Thieves!]*

I'D LOVE to connect with with you. Sign up for my mailing list via my website to participate in special giveaways, and receive news and information about my events and upcoming releases at https://www.KariBovee.com. And, when you sign up you will receive a FREE book! *Shoot like a Girl* is the prequel novella to my Annie Oakley Mystery Series.

ABOUT THE AUTHOR

When she's not on a horse, or walking along the beautiful cottonwood-laden acequias of Corrales, New Mexico; or basking on white sand beaches under the Big Island Hawaiian sun, Kari Bovee is escaping into the past—scheming murder and mayhem for her characters both real and imagined, and helping them to find order in the chaos of her action-packed novels.

An award-winning author, Bovée was honored with the 2019 NM/AZ Book Awards Hillerman Award for Southwestern Fiction for her novel *Girl with a Gun.* The novel also received First Place in the 2019 NM/AZ Book Awards in the Mystery/Crime category, and won First in Category in the International Chanticleer Murder & Mayhem Awards. It was also a finalist in the 2019 Next Generation Indie Awards. Her novel *Grace in the Wings* won First in Category for the 2019 International Chanticleer Chatelaine Awards. *Peccadillo at the Palace* won Grand Prize in the 2019 Goethe Awards, and was a finalist in the 2019 Best Book Awards Historical Fiction category.

Kari would love to connect with with you on a more personal level. Subscribe to her mailing list to participate in special give-aways, and to receive news and information about events and upcoming releases at https://www.KariBovee.com.

ACKNOWLEDGMENTS

To all of my readers and my awesome street team, you have my eternal gratitude. Your continued support and encouragement are what makes this endeavor worth all the effort!

To Danielle Poiesz of Double Vision Editorial, it has been wonderful working with you on this and other projects, and I hope we can continue to work together into the future.

Special thanks to my husband Kevin, who reads everything I write. I so appreciate your feedback, love, support, and wisdom. To Jessica, Hunter, Sumiko, Michael and Brita, thank you for always cheering me on and making me laugh. You bring light into my world.

And to my mom, for all your love and support. Thank you.